THE VERDICT ON EACH MAN DEAD

DAVID WHELLAMS

A PETER CAMMON MYSTERY

ECW Press

Published by ECW Press
665 Gerrard Street East
Toronto, Ontario M4M 1Y2
416-694-3348 / info@ecwpress.com

This is a work of fiction. Names, characters, places,
and incidents either are the product of the author's
imagination or are used fictitiously, and any
resemblance to actual persons, living or dead, business
establishments, events, or locales is entirely coincidental.

LIBRARY AND ARCHIVES CANADA
CATALOGUING IN PUBLICATION

Whellams, David, 1948–, author
The verdict on each man dead /
written by David Whellams.

Issued in print and electronic formats.
ISBN 978-1-77041-295-8 (bound)
978-1-77041-044-2 (pbk)
978-1-77090-811-6 (pdf)
978-1-77090-812-3 (epub)

I. Title.

PS8645.H45V47 2015   C813'.6   C2015-902789-6
C2015-902790-X

Cover design: Tania Craan
Cover images: abstract yellow wash © Roman Sigaev/
Shutterstock and © maxim ibragimov/Shutterstock;
man's silhouette © Naufal MQ/Shutterstock
Author photo by Jennifer Barnes JB Photography

The publication of *The Verdict on Each Man Dead* has been generously supported by the Canada Council
for the Arts which last year invested $157 million to bring the arts to Canadians throughout the country, and
by the Ontario Arts Council (OAC), an agency of the Government of Ontario, which last year funded 1,793
individual artists and 1,076 organizations in 232 communities across Ontario, for a total of $52.1 million. We
also acknowledge the financial support of the Government of Canada through the Canada Book Fund for our
publishing activities, and the contribution of the Government of Ontario through the Ontario Book Publishing
Tax Credit and the Ontario Media Development Corporation.

PRINTED AND BOUND IN CANADA   PRINTING: FRIESENS   5   4   3   2   1

for the Tuesday night Triv Team

PROLOGUE

The very green lawns of the cemetery fought for traction against the surrounding desert. This was a municipal cemetery, open to all, but Peter Cammon wasn't surprised to find that the Mormon zone dominated, larger than the Catholic, Lutheran, and Everyone Else sections combined. A strange oasis, he mused, under siege from the Utah desert but also thriving — like the church itself, its manicured lawns holding back the scrub and sand.

The mourners fell silent. His mind wandered as he waited for the tributes to begin. On his left, the lawn fell off to a silted trench. Did this qualify as an "arroyo"? A "dry wash"? He could imagine a flash flood carrying away all this scenery in an instant . . .

His reverie was refocused by the arrival of the coffin up the path to the grave. It passed, carried by six elders of the church. Peter stood with the throng, respectful, unmoving, black-suited, and bare-headed in the blazing, testing sun, and was surprised to find himself awash in bloody-minded, vengeful feelings. This flood of anger was useless, should be suppressed, he knew. None of the other mourners projected anything but sadness, except perhaps that detective at the front of the crowd, Mohlman, who had chauffeured them to the cemetery. He looked angry and still dazed from the night of the killing.

By any measure, Peter's professional link to Henry Pastern was a tenuous one, confined to a single investigation known in Peter's household as the "Carpenter Affair" (Peter's entire family had been drawn into it; one of the reasons Joan, his wife, had insisted on coming to the funeral was her own sense of connection to Henry as a fellow participant in the case). The detectives first met on a sweltering afternoon at the J. Edgar Hoover Building in Washington. Peter, who had a friendly history with the FBI, had travelled to America on the trail of a mysterious and deadly woman, Alice Nahri, and was seeking the FBI's help. Alice was thought to have murdered a Scotland Yard colleague of Peter's, John Carpenter, in Montreal by knocking him out and drowning him in a canal. She then fled south in a stolen car, which was discovered parked on the grounds of a yacht club on the Anacostia River in D.C. A body had been found in that same river.

Peter remembered Henry's sweating, shaved head as the young career agent, chattering away, conducted him out to Quantico to meet with the FBI medical examiner who had performed the autopsy on the sodden corpse. Both the veteran Scotland Yard chief inspector and the novice special agent had felt the seductive force of the strange woman, and they struck an odd alliance in their pursuit. For his part, Henry regarded Peter as Sherlock Holmes. He already knew Peter by reputation; Peter had helped the bureau with the Unabomber manhunt back in the nineties, doggedly visiting many of the sites where Kaczynski's bombs had detonated, and coming up with a profile of the Unabomber that proved remarkably accurate in the end. Peter Cammon's efforts earned him a mention in the case study materials used by FBI trainees at the Quantico school.

Henry's star-struck awe of Peter only increased as the old detective and the medical examiner quickly deduced that the woman from the river was not Alice Nahri but a prostitute Alice had killed during her flight. Henry stayed on the pursuit while Peter returned to England to wait for the murderess to reveal herself.

Weeks later Alice surfaced in a shabby hotel in Buffalo, New York. Police from the state, municipal, and federal levels laid siege to the hotel, and Henry was given a major role in coordinating the team as it moved in to arrest the young woman. Peter flew to Buffalo for the takedown.

It did not go well.

Alice escaped.

Henry wasn't officially blamed for the fiasco, but after Buffalo his career in the Bureau quickly declined, it seemed to Peter. Henry wanted to keep in touch, and although Peter preferred not to become anyone's mentor, he consented to periodic contact. Most of this was email traffic, but once in a while Henry called the Leicestershire cottage for professional advice. Joan had warm talks with him a couple of times. She took to the young Utahan, whose background was so different from her own, and appreciated his stories of American life, including his proud talk of his young wife, Theresa. Joan, who had never been to North America, developed an urge to see the American West. Peter's goodwill was largely based on sympathy for Henry after his bad luck in Buffalo. In his own career, Peter had been blessed with only good fortune, having solved almost all his cases.

When the call came from Detective Mohlman, there was no hesitation on the part of Peter and Joan. They flew at once to Salt Lake City for the funeral.

At the urging of his daughter-in-law, Maddy, Peter had done some quick research on Mormon funerals. Joan told her atheist husband that the preparation would help him understand the ceremony they were about to experience. In fact, she had noted his bubbling anger and was trying to calm him down. What she meant was, this crime had been solved, the villain identified and dealt with, and for once Peter should leave his suspicious chief inspector's mindset at home in England. He wasn't consulting on an active case, she hectored. But Peter seldom denied his professional instincts and he was tempted to delve further into the record of the murder investigation. (Joan never quite understood this point: she thought his tropism towards evil and death was resistible. It wasn't.) As he browsed online, his eye was caught by references to Blood Atonement.

The Church of Jesus Christ of Latter-day Saints has worked hard to abandon most of its unsavoury nineteenth-century practices, polygamy being the best-known; but, Peter soon remarked, the reason for the long struggle over doctrine within the church is that many harsh beliefs have had a visceral grip on the Mormon membership. Peter knew that it was dangerous to presume insight into anyone's theology, but his experience policing violence over fifty years allowed him to grasp the continuing resonance of Blood Atonement. It was all about murder, something Peter knew too well. At the height of his theocratic rule, Mormon patriarch Brigham Young pronounced this new dogma to his followers. Some murders are so vile, he stated, that the sacrifice by Jesus Christ of his own life cannot atone for them, and more blood must be sacrificed. Peter was taken aback by the angry underpinnings of the doctrine. Earlier, Joseph Smith, fountainhead of the LDS, had asserted: "Shoot him or cut off his head, spill his blood on the ground, and let the smoke thereof ascend up to God."

As Peter called up this quote in his mind, the casket stopped and he drew back, abashed. He chided himself: the concept of Blood Atonement was out of date. And today, the body almost in the ground, there was no more retribution to be achieved. Joan had it right. The killer was dead. His ashes had ascended to God for judgement. Literally. Or perhaps fallen to Hell for further torment.

So why was Peter still attracted by vengeance?

As he wallowed in his thoughts, the church elders got on with their rituals. The slow procession bisected the crowd. An elderly man trailed the casket. Church officials followed in monochromatic anonymity, but then, as they reached the podium, three of the oldest men moved forward and one opened a book of scripture. From his research, Peter realized that they were of the Quorum of the Twelve, a key governing body within the LDS church. The deceased had been accorded a high honour.

The shortest elder of the three, uncomfortable in his black funeral suit, welcomed the mourners. "Heavenly Father, we understand that death is part of your plan, but sometimes death is hard to understand . . ."

This was standard stuff at any funeral, but Peter's interest was piqued by the man himself. He realized that Tyler? — Tynan, that was it — had been Henry and Theresa's close friend. Detective Mohlman had mentioned him in the car. He was their neighbour, too, Peter recalled. Tynan continued in the language of the church, though his rhythm was conversational, occasionally ironic. He was like a toned-down Dudley Moore at age seventy-five. Peter reprimanded himself for this irreverent thought.

"He has reconciled you in His fleshly body through death, in order to present you before Him holy and blameless and beyond reproach."

Peter drifted in and out of the speech.

He could see to the bottom of the steep trench on his left. A movement caught his eye. A large bird scampered impossibly up one side, then darted down into the pit and, again, near vertically back. The heat was getting to Peter. The lovely bird, a roadrunner, reminded him of those snowboard artists performing the half pipe at the Olympics. He watched it disappear.

Joan stood quietly next to Peter as the grave was consecrated and the deceased pronounced Temple Worthy. She sighed; she had hoped to stay on a day or two to see the Great Salt Lake, but now her urge to be a tourist seemed frivolous. The flight had disoriented her. It felt as if they had flown directly to this strange cemetery from Heathrow, but of course they had landed at Salt Lake City International Airport, via O'Hare and transferred to a hotel in Ogden, a mile from Parkland Cemetery. She had wondered at the sign that read "Welcome to the Junction City." The junction of rivers? Trade routes? Destiny? Peter and Joan would be flying back home tomorrow at the latest. They would attend the luncheon organized by the women of the church's Relief Society and be on their way.

Peter's feelings of guilt returned. He was bored in retirement. He had occupied much of the last year organizing the papers of his late father and recently deceased brother, but he doubted that he would finish the project. It felt hollow now. He was full of regret for not helping Henry a lot more.

There was nothing more to do about the Hollis Street murders. But then why did he feel that the tragedy was unresolved? The killer was dead, yet Peter wanted vengeance. Blood Atonement. It was irrational. The heat was addling his deductive mind.

Peter's religion was Shakespeare. Mark Antony in *Julius Caesar* had intoned: "Woe to the hands that shed this costly blood!" That was the way Peter felt.

He looked around. Apparently angels were a popular motif among the Mormons. Carved angels hovered everywhere in the oasis-like cemetery. They gave him no comfort.

He knew that the police had wrapped up the case, just as this ceremony had confirmed the end of a life. In the green island of gravestones and angels, the funeral was ending. But Peter's deepest, if unfocused, instincts as a chief inspector of New Scotland Yard told him there was more to this saga of evil.

PART 1

HENRY

A good man is a good man,
whether in this church or out of it.
Brigham Young

EIGHT WEEKS EARLIER

CHAPTER 1

Corrine on the 9-1-1 desk judged the complainant, Miss Maude Hampson, to be crazy, and conveyed this conclusion, in milder language, to the assigned responder, a rookie named Jackson. There is no 10-Code in the West Valley City Police Department manual for "something very upsetting going on across the street," and so she reframed it in her hand-off to the young patrolman. "Dispatch. Officer Jackson, can you respond to an old lady, reports 'suspicious activity' in house opposite? Unspecified. Confused."

"Any report of weapons?" Jackson replied. A spate of shootings had hit the Valley in the last month.

"No. As said, woman was vague. She seemed a little . . . pixilated." Corrine dictated Maude's full name and her address: 4 Hollis.

It was mid-afternoon when Officer Jackson arrived on Hollis Street. West Valley, an adjunct to Salt Lake City, isn't all that big, but he had never been here, never noticed the street. Jackson liked to think he was an observant man. The first feature that struck him as odd was the pair of thick, incomplete stone pillars that flanked the entrance to the street, as if Hollis were a rich gated community — without the gate. The houses, mostly bungalows, formed a short, unimpressive row down to a cul-de-sac. He slowed and examined the Hampson residence, which was the first place on his right. The suspect house, Number 3, stood across the way, a mirror match of Maude Hampson's.

All appeared quiet. But it was a sign of Jackson's misgivings, almost foreboding, that he looked around and wondered, "What happened to houses 1 and 2?"

The sun beat down on his cruiser. Jackson got out and eyeballed Number 3. He hoped to earn a detective's shield one day, and he tried to think like a detective now, taking a long moment to look up and down Hollis Street. There wasn't a soul outside. What did the street want to tell him? Most properties were well maintained, the paint jobs recent, lawns cut. The exception was Number 5, which felt not only vacant but abandoned; the side lawn between it and Number 3 had gone to seed.

Jackson glanced at the stone pillars and the first pair of odd-numbered bungalows. A fastidious neighbour had done the mowing from the outer avenue all the way to Number 3, then stopped. These were property owners who helped one another, he reasoned. But there was no one to ask about this, and he returned to his patrolman's drill.

Musing on neutron bombs, Jackson rang the bell at Number 4. Maude must have been hovering by the door, for after only ten seconds, she began to fumble with the two heavy locks; then, quiet. He sensed her moving away. Maybe only ghosts lived on Hollis Street, he thought. He pushed open the door. Fifteen feet away, at the end of a dank corridor, stood a wizened figure leaning on a cane.

"Don't be afraid," he called. But Maude wasn't afraid; she was irritated. She darted looks into her living room. "My stories are about to start."

I'll never make detective at this rate, young Jackson told himself. He came fully inside and closed the door. One of the locks was a Yale deadbolt, gleaming brass, recently installed. Turning back, he confronted empty space. Maude had vanished into the ghost world.

He entered the living room to find the woman plunked down on her horsehair sofa, a channel changer in one hand pointed into space, as if she were guiding a model airplane or a personal drone. She clicked back and forth between two soap operas. Jackson sized up the décor as that of a paranoid recluse: permanent Christmas figurines, bird plates and a bird clock, kerosene lamp chimneys with electric bulbs inserted, Toby jugs, and a Hummel collection. Maude herself, draped in layers of shawls and beads, matched the furnishings. Her cane was a carved wood shillelagh, and Jackson wondered if the Home Shopping Network sold those things, too.

"I had to phone because my stories start at three. I need to concentrate on my programs." Her thumb remained poised over the remote, and she never looked at Jackson.

Maude was a watcher. That could be useful, Jackson thought. "What did you see that worried you, Miss Hampson? Was there someone breaking in across the way?"

Maude adopted a patronizing tone that Jackson hated. "No, Officer, there wasn't any activity near the house. In fact, it was the lack of it that struck me. Gabriella always walks Puffles at first light. Again in the late morning. Mr. Watson comes home for lunch most days. Didn't today."

"Let me be clear. You called in at 12:55 p.m. Was that because you saw nothing or because you saw *something*?"

She turned his way. Jackson later said that this was the moment he saw a spark in her eye that went beyond idle meddling or gossip. "I saw Puffles in the window."

Jackson ground it out. "Okay, Miss Hampson, what kind of dog is Puffles?"

"Miniature poodle. Losing his hair, though."

Jackson stared across the road at the front window of Number 3. "A miniature poodle wouldn't be able to see over the windowsill."

"He was hopping up and down. Wanted to get out and pee, I'm sure. Bouncing into view."

"Like a jack-in-the-box?"

"Oh, do African-Americans grow up with that game, too?"

Officer Jackson could have swallowed his badge. There weren't a lot of black cops in Utah, and he was used to the occasional obliquely racist comment from older white residents. He fought to keep his anger under control. Utah was what it was. The fact that the Mormon church had taken its time jettisoning its racial exclusions did not fuel resentment in him, for Utah was home, and both Jackson and his wife, Wanda, were Provo-born. *Utah society is evolving*, he mantra'ed. What mildly pissed him off was that Maude Hampson didn't appear to be a Mormon herself.

"What colour?" Jackson snapped.

Maude recoiled at the warning in his tone, then forced a sickly smile. "Oh, you mean the dog. Puffles is white."

Officer Jackson ambled across Hollis Street, which the hot sun had beaten into inertness. He had choices to make. He had no authority to enter an empty house, and nothing struck him as exceptional about Number 3, certainly nothing to justify an emergency break-in. The façade was well tended; the owners had painted the shutters within the past year and installed a quality aluminum door recently; the solid wooden door behind it was an attractive pale green, matching the shutters. Jackson walked up the concrete steps, opened the metal door and knocked.

"Mr. Watson? Mrs. Watson?"

No answer. He rapped again, called their names a second and a third time. From the top of the steps, he leaned over the iron railing towards the living room window but could see almost nothing of the interior. He knocked again.

As Officer Jackson backed down the steps, preparing to circle the silent house, a movement caught his eye. He saw a flash of white. He moved to the lawn foursquare in front of the living room window. There! — the top of the poodle's head. It jumped again. Its skull showed pinkish under scruffy curls, and its eyes were manic and rheumy. It trampolined a half inch higher each time. Jackson stared, fixed in place. The dog saw Jackson and found fresh energy. This time it bounced full-body above the living room windowsill.

Puffles had a soaking red beard.

CHAPTER 2

Corrine took the call-in from Jackson, which he made from his cell phone to shield his report from the geeks out there with police scanners. He summarized his actions: entering 3 Hollis Street by forcing the front door, he at once saw the scarlet lake in the living room and tasted the cannabis stench floating above the blood spoor. He gathered up the hysterical poodle and shut him in the powder room.

"I've got a 10-66 and likely a 939 Delta," Jackson reported. Corrine considered telling him to keep to English, since he was on a fairly secure mobile line. A 10-66 denoted a "major crime alert," and 939 told her that drugs were involved; "Delta" indicated a possible fatality. None of this made sense, but cumulatively the codes convinced her of the urgency of the call-in.

"What do you need out there, Officer?" She sensed his near-panic.

Jackson would have preferred that Corrine, a veteran on the desk, sort out that particular question, but now she had thrown the decision back onto him. He sucked it up. He surprised himself: he knew what to do.

"I don't need backup units per se," he said. "For now, I'd prefer a team from Homicide. There's about two quarts of blood pooling on the hardwood."

It was Corrine's turn to feel uncomfortable. Jackson's statement was oddly genteel ("per se"?) and threw her off. She told him to stand by and looked for the duty officer, Sergeant Blaine, but he had gone out back to catch a smoke. She hastened to the squad room of the precinct. The men lounging there ignored her, so she brayed, "Got a possible fatality! Assist officer on the scene but no immediate threat. But a possible 939 large."

At that moment, there were ten patrolmen but only two detectives in the big room, Phil Mohlman and his junior partner, Henry Pastern. All the men looked up now. A 10-66 in itself wouldn't have diverted them from their coffee break; a lot of cops first at the scene will exaggerate the "major crime" they find. But a combination of a 10-66 with a drug bust pricked their interest. It had been a slow morning, and the officers sensed a chance of excitement. Maybe a dead body somewhere in all this.

Henry Pastern at his beat-up desk failed to recognize the 939 code and reached to fetch the cheat sheet from his drawer. But something, instinct or a spark of electricity running through the air, made him stop and check with Phil across the room.

Phil was smiling, and Henry understood telepathically that his partner already had a thorough read on the call-in. Phil had noted Corrine's failure to wait for the duty man, Blaine, who had final authority over the dispatch of assistance. It must be serious. As Homicide detectives, Phil and Henry could expect a violent case to flow down to their level within a day, but a 939 signalled drug trafficking and the case could as easily be snatched away by the West Valley Narcotics Unit. Phil had also noted Corrine's waffling on the question of a dead body: maybe the investigating officer had found an ounce or two of blood, or maybe a corpse beckoned. Phil wasn't going to wait for the death certificate. He grinned at Henry and pressed the plunger on an imaginary syringe. Henry grasped that if they moved fast, they could scoop the case. The uniforms in the room saw the gesture; their hopes of latching on to the investigation, with the chance of scoring a drug bust collar, were now pre-empted. Henry closed his desk drawer.

Phil, who hailed from Boston and loved to play the Easterner card, as usual went too far and called out to the uniforms as he and Pastern left the room: "Don't get enough homicides in cowboy country. At least someone out there's making the effort."

Phil insisted on taking the wheel. He seemed to know where they were heading and he drove fast, though was not, Henry saw, in a frenzy to get there.

"Hollis is a dead end over in Forest Vale."

"A cul-de-sac?" Henry said.

"Yeah, but builders out here don't use the term; it implies a trap, going nowhere. Jesus, they think it's fancy French. Christ, these cow-pokes!"

Henry could have argued that "dead end" wasn't an alluring term either, but, as subordinate man on the team, he avoided being contentious. He didn't know if Phil's double blasphemy was a shot at him. Henry was lapsed Latter-day Saints.

"Oh, I know the area," he said. "Forest Vale. Theresa and I looked there when we scouted the market last year. For about five minutes."

Mohlman shot him a skeptical look. He had been in the Pasterns' new house out in the desert, and it couldn't have been more of a contrast to what he remembered of this second-, maybe third-rank neighbourhood.

There was nothing sylvan about Forest Vale, and no valley was in evidence, unless you counted the broader Salt Lake Valley in which it squatted. Phil turned onto Hollis, and Henry, like Jackson, noted the unfinished stone pillars. The crime scene at Number 3 was the first house on the left, although Officer Jackson's cruiser sat across the way, in front of Number 4. Henry was surprised that no one had emerged from the other houses to gawk or confront the police presence.

They sized up the real estate in the afternoon glare. Number 3 sat peculiarly distant from the wider avenue off which they had just turned. The stone posts served no purpose, Henry judged; they merely used up half a lot each and ceded the other halves to 3 and 4, expunging Numbers 1 and 2 from the blueprints. Henry looked down the row. All the houses on either side of Hollis were bungalows until the street widened to a circle, where four two-storeys crowned the dead end. The neighbourhood stood deaf and mute.

Jackson, nervous and apparently fixed in place in the vestibule of the Watson home, opened the aluminum door. Phil barged inside, followed by Henry.

They were almost at once at the living room. A taupe area rug bore a nasty red stain in its exact middle. On the polished maple floor beyond, a bigger pond of blood was refusing to dry; from there, crimson paw prints travelled up the hallway and out of sight.

"Where's the dog, Jackson?" Mohlman said.

"I locked it in the can," Jackson replied.

The forensics boys won't be pleased, Henry thought, but he supposed there were worse places to store a mutt with a panicky bladder and Jackson Pollock tendencies.

He scanned the room, charting the mix of vile smells. The blood scent rose in a metallic fog in the unventilated centre of the room, but the acridness was complicated by the sweetness of marijuana coming from the rear of the dining area. Two plump green trash bags lay on the floor under the back window, only one of them twist-tied. Jasmine perfume fought for his attention.

"Any more grass in the kitchen?" Mohlman barked.

"No, sir," Jackson said. "I went upstairs to check for . . . bodies. None there — bodies, blood, or bags."

Mohlman glanced over to check that Jackson wasn't being alliteratively sarcastic.

Henry examined the staircase for the first time. This wasn't a strict bungalow; there was a half floor above them. The house presented other contradictions. A repository for drugs but not actually a grow op. A killing ground but not Gabriella or Tom Watson's final resting place.

"There's no basement," Phil added.

"None of these places have basements," Henry said. "A lot of homes in the West skip the cellar, opting instead for big garages and man-cave storage sheds out back."

Phil shook his head. "In Boston, a basement is somewhere to keep your victims in."

The living/dining room stretched from the front of Number 3 to the back. Phil put on a pair of thin cloth gloves and circled through the hallway, avoiding the blood spill, to the trash bags by the back window. In Henry's view, it was already time to call in the forensics techies. The living room wasn't getting any fresher. The pool was turning gummy and rank, and someone was going to step in it. The poodle in the bathroom hadn't made a sound, but who knew, it might be chewing through the fixtures.

Phil opened the twist tie on the second bag and smelled deeply of the weed inside. The rich curl of marijuana hit Henry's nostrils.

"Whew! The real thing," Phil said. We need to check for drug processing paraphernalia. Our family — the family name again, Jackson . . ."

"Tom and Gabriella Watson," Henry replied, and Jackson nodded.

Mohlman brooked no disagreement as he summed up. "The Watsons are dealers, but small-time. This is quality weed, but it wasn't processed in this house." He stared at the blood and reflected, "So far as I know, no grow facilities have ever been busted before in Forest Vale."

Jackson had been listening deferentially, but now he jumped in. "Do you think they're trying to retain a credible possession argument? That amount of uncrushed marijuana, the courts might be persuaded it isn't trafficking." Jackson was on a roll. Mohlman nodded for him to continue. "I checked, sir. There isn't a school, community facility, or shopping centre within a thousand feet of here." What might be a trafficking misdemeanour automatically turned into a felony if the grass were sold near a place frequented by kids.

"Why didn't the killers just throw the trash bags in the trunk?" Phil said. "This is top grade."

"Perhaps the killers didn't arrive by vehicle," Jackson said, knowing the second he spoke that this sounded bizarre. The stench was making all three men light-headed.

"I think they were specialists," Henry offered, earning confused looks. "You know, an execution squad."

But Henry had to admit that the presence of the two bags made no sense. It was too much for personal consumption, too little for a grow op or distribution hub. Apparently, however, its mere existence was enough to kill for.

They stared at the mess until the odour became oppressive. "Let's caucus by the front door, gentlemen," Phil said.

They crowded into the entryway. Jackson was pleased that the detectives weren't cutting him out of the investigation.

"Officer Jackson, time to call in the cavalry. At least one backup pair of uniforms and a full forensics team. You're speaking for me. Tell them there's a small amount of weed. *Small.* If the Drug Squad wants a piece of this they can pay us a visit, but we defend Homicide's control. That blood on the floor isn't a shaving cut."

Jackson nodded. Henry said nothing. Phil continued his instructions, alternating between the two younger men. "Jackson, you and I will be occupied for the next two or three hours with the crime scene, but then I want you to help me with the door-to-door. I'll work this side, the odd numbers. I want to *command* this street. If that's not enough, Jackson, I suggest your smart move is to complete your report to your supervisor by tomorrow morning, copy on my desk. Henry, you start interviewing the south side, the evens. Go back to Miss Hampson at Number 4, see if what she tells you remains consistent with her 9-1-1 call and her first statement. By the way, Jackson, don't touch *anything* in this house. And Henry, if you see Boog DeKlerk or his Drug Squad boys, text me fast."

Outside, Jackson trotted to his vehicle to contact the precinct. Still none of the residents had come out to the street. Phil and Henry came down the concrete front steps and walked to the centre of Hollis, where Henry turned and took in Numbers 3 and 5 as a pair — the latter obviously vacant, maybe derelict. As Jackson had, Henry remarked on the contrast between the two bungalows. He pivoted and caught Jackson as he was picking up his transmitter.

"Jackson! Hold off."

The young patrolman stepped back out of his cruiser and gave him a questioning look. Unlike Mohlman, Henry Pastern was a little-known quantity among rank and file; Jackson had never worked with him.

Henry murmured, "Wait five minutes."

While Henry turned again to stare at the houses, his partner and Jackson waited by the curb. "Notice anything, Phil?"

"Like what?"

"The bungalows are similar but they don't match." The lawn at 5 was a bad haircut; ragweed and yarrow grew around the foundation on the west side. Weather-leached plastic toys spilled across the patchy grass between the ungainly bungalow and the Watsons'. Henry looked to the end of Hollis. Every house enjoyed a sightline on every other house. Why hadn't they mobilized against the owner of the dump at Number 5?

"Can we take a look at next door? Just for a minute." Mohlman shrugged, and the three men traipsed across to the no man's land between the Watsons and their absentee neighbour.

"Phil, you think this street is condo'd?"

"Nah. What, less than twenty houses? Awfully small for a condo. Your guess?"

"I agree. Freehold. But everyone works together on the common elements." The signs of house-pride were evident along the street, but not so much around Number 5. Phil and Officer Jackson stood back as Henry evaluated the second unit. The Watsons' neat green lawn ended sharply at the property line, replaced by yellow weeds and sandy soil all the way to the wall next door. Ragged shrubs clustered around the neighbour's crawl space. A fifty-foot extension cord drooped from a scrawny dogwood, part of someone's effort to hang lights for a long-gone Christmas.

The trio retreated to the centre of Hollis. The sun straight above them made the avenue feel even emptier. "Jesus, it's Stepford Wives quiet," Phil Mohlman stated. "Call it in, Jackson. No sirens."

And then Henry, taking in the slum that was Number 5 Hollis Street, understood. The electrical cord hanging from the dogwood wasn't for holiday bulbs. Tom Watson employed it to connect his pretty little bungalow to the slum next door. And that was why the east side of the Watson lawn was scruffier than the rest: to conceal the extension cord when it was in use.

"Wait one more minute, Officer," Henry called.

Phil regarded Henry's shaved skull, shiny with sweat. "You in a Zen trance, partner, or heatstroke?"

Henry marched over to the shrubbery that obscured the crawl space. Kneeling down and parting the bushes, he spied the end of the cord running through a hole in the lattice screening. A lifeline — a death line? — between the properties?

"Phil, what do you get when you put two bungalows together?"

"One decent-size house?"

"Correct. You get a main floor that serves for a basement."

CHAPTER 3

The detectives wasted ten minutes debating the legal niceties of entering Number 5 without a warrant. A cord and a pipe feeding into a crawl space didn't justify forcible entry. They could knock on the front door, but no one would answer, and it would take hours to find the owner.

"Could be some poor son of a gun alive in there," Henry suggested.

"Don't curse like that, you're a Mormon." The tired gag showed Phil's jitters. The sun and the smells of the killing ground addled both of them fleetingly. Phil said, his voice hard, "We're cops. We rescue people."

To which Henry responded, "Sometimes the dead must be rescued, too. We need to get inside."

"Let's work it through," Phil stated. "The houses are connected like with an umbilical cord. Can we argue they're one unit?"

"Doubtful, but we could consider them one active crime scene. Doesn't that trump the privacy of both owners?"

Finally, they agreed that the still-wet puddle in the Watson house made this a "crime in progress." It was thin, but Phil said he'd had enough of the Salt Lake City heat.

After telling Officer Jackson the plan, they went around and jimmied the back door. More blood and cannabis hit them, even stronger than next door. Henry, pistol drawn, led the way through the kitchen to the living room. He had seen grow ops before and wasn't surprised that Watson had stripped the walls out to the frame — the ceilings, too. The grow trays were gone, but the pungency of marijuana was embedded in the joists. The house cruelly mocked the Watsons' neat bungalow, to which it was tethered by the electrical cord.

Two long trestle tables remained in the centre of the room. A headless female body lay on one of them.

"Are you assuming what I'm assuming?" Phil said from behind Henry.

Neither had any doubt, but Henry said what had to be said. "It's Mrs. Watson," he intoned.

Phil moved around him and leaned over the woman. He bumped his head on a steel cone-shaped grow lamp that hung directly over the corpse, as if surgery had just been completed. Gabriella's blood and cerebrospinal fluid, except what she had left behind in her own living room, had spouted from her neck onto the wood floor in an almighty mess. The killer had hacked off her head, and not in a single guillotine slice.

Phil assumed control, and Henry watched his cool assessment of the crime scene.

"Here's all the reasons we need to keep Narcotics out. Homicide trumps weed."

"I'm surprised no one smelled the grass from the sidewalk," Henry said.

"I'm wondering if anyone ever goes outside on this mean little street," Phil answered.

Henry noted the heavy curtains on the front and back windows. He glanced into the kitchen and saw the painted-over windows above the sink. Gone were the days of tinfoil taped over the glass. "How do you figure it, Phil?"

Phil scanned the living and dining rooms. "Cold-blooded. It appears no one panicked . . . I guess."

"Except Mrs. Watson here," said Henry, whistling in the graveyard.

Gabriella Watson wore tan slacks and a floral top, now soaked monochrome crimson. Henry marvelled at his own hardness as he leaned over her to examine the wounds up close. He saw that the knife blow to her heart would have been fatal in itself. Sexual abuse apparently wasn't involved.

"Phil, here's the way I see it. The killers took their time — and that's important to note. A crew showed up at Number 3, stabbed Mrs. Watson, and left her on the rug while they entered *this* house. Let's call this the Second House from now on. They cleaned out the grow trays and the product, except for the last two bags, then went back for her body. Like some demented back-and-forth ritual. It must have taken them, what, two, three, four hours?"

"Yeah," muttered Phil as he scanned the corners of the room, "but why bother cleaning out anything? Stick around for several hours, risk being caught loading the grass in the driveway. Hell, I don't know . . ."

They made eye contact, both grasping the essence of the crime. They were in tune, a team. Phil said it first. "It was a warning. The drug gang who did this were sending a warning to Tom Watson, and to all small-timers. Cleaned out his operation to make a point. Killed his spouse, took the time to schlep her body next door, severed the head."

Henry nodded. "Tom Watson came home to Number 3, then rushed over here and found his dead wife and his hollowed-out little factory. They were waiting."

But the script sounded threadbare to Henry even as he said it. The killers had taken huge risks. For one thing, the hit squad, burning several hours to truck out the marijuana plants, had run the real chance of Maude Hampson and others seeing them. Also, why slaughter Gabriella in one house then move her next door?

21

"Maybe Tom Watson did it solo," Phil ruminated. "Fights with his wife, stabs her, hides the body here . . ."

"Or, leaves the body next door while he cleans out his stash in here," Henry tried. He didn't believe his own words.

Mohlman tiptoed around the trestle table to examine the neck trauma. "What the hell is that?"

Beneath the table in the blood pond sat a wooden box, ten inches wide, about sixteen long. Phil crouched down and eyed the polished surface. It was lovingly crafted. Henry stayed at the far end so that he wouldn't defile the spatters on the floor, but he knelt and scanned the box from a couple of feet away. "Look, Phil, there are screw holes in the lid, but no screws."

They had the same thought: the box was just big enough to hold a head.

Phil was closer. He reached across the thickening vileness and lifted the wooden cover. Two zinc-coated metal tubes lay inside, their ends plugged and soldered, and hooked to a timer. The detectives recognized the wiring of a pipe bomb.

"What's the clock set for?" Henry said.

"Sweet Jesus, I can't tell," Phil rasped. Henry pulled him out of the way before he could vomit into the mess.

Leaning in, Henry said, "It appears to be set for 4:30. That's forty minutes from now."

Officer Jackson entered the living room. He too seemed ready to puke his lunch. "I found her head under the sink."

Phil got up and dashed to the kitchen with Jackson, while Henry stayed by the trestle table an extra moment to be sure about the digital clock trigger.

"Get the hell out," he called to Mohlman and Jackson. "Save the head."

Phil handled the call himself from the concrete steps outside, streaming his commands to Corrine in a firm voice. "I want the

Bomb Squad *first*. Two squad cars. Then an ambulance, and tell them I have a headless body. In that order. The ambulance can leave its siren off."

"Because the victim is dead?" Corrine said.

"Because there's a bomb inside and the Bomb Squad has to disarm the device before the attendants can enter. Because I don't want to alarm the residents more than I have to. Because, because, because. Jesus, Corrine, I'm standing here with a head in a bag."

Corrine's efficient tone was her apology. "The disposal team are on their way, Detective. Patrol cars dispatched."

"And, Corrine, I need Emergency Services and the Animal Rescue wagon," Phil said.

Henry took the phone. "Corrine, tell the bomb guys that the device is an ordinary-looking pipe bomb but it's set to detonate at 4:30. That's less than forty minutes from now."

When the first cruisers screeched up to Number 5, Phil was still standing on the stoop with Mrs. Watson's head fermenting in the plastic trash bag in the last of her cerebrospinal fluid. Quiet though it was now, Henry recognized the potential for a circus on Hollis Street.

To Jackson and Henry beside him, Phil hissed, "Keep the uniforms back, Henry. Jackson, you bar the door until the Bomb Squad arrives. But I want space left in the driveway for the Emerge people. This head isn't getting any fresher."

The simultaneous arrival of the red Emergency Services van, the ambulance, and the Animal Rescue SUV immediately threatened to swamp them. Henry came down the steps and worked to control the crowd as the talk of bombs and beheadings cranked up the building horde of uniforms. Phil descended too, and the throng parted as they realized what was in the bag. With Henry's help, the Emergency Services driver found space at the end of the Watsons' drive and, unfazed, took Gabriella's head from Phil and retreated into his van to store it in his refrigerator. At one point Henry glanced back up the steps, where Jackson stood alone with his hand on the butt of his service pistol.

The heat was getting to everyone. There was nothing more to do until the bomb technicians arrived. Uneasy expectation became the mood of the crowd.

Henry and Phil moved to the curb to talk. "So, Henry, we're good? Start your interviews, if you want. I'll handle this nonsense, but come back and tell me if you spot Boog DeKlerk on the street. See what the neighbours know about the Watsons' habits. Jackson and I will start on this side and we'll connect up somewhere down thataway."

"We'll meet at the dead end," Henry said, and grinned nervously. He was happy to be heading out on his own. He had been on the West Valley force less than two years, and this was an opportunity. He would try to finish his segment by nightfall and move on to the odd numbers, knowing that his partner wouldn't get far down his half of the interview list before tomorrow.

Henry waited for the Bomb Squad before heading to Maude Hampson's. The appearance of the two composed and methodical technicians dispelled much of the tension in the crowd. At Quantico, it was called, with respect, the "nervous profession," but Henry admired the insouciance these experts always showed.

They were out of the house in ten minutes, one carrying the wood box in both hands like a mini Ark of the Covenant; clearly, it had been rendered harmless. The second technician came over to Henry at the curb. "It was a dumb pipe bomb. From what you told us, Detective, we went in figuring two possibilities. I mean, who sets a bomb to go off at 4:30 in the afternoon? We thought maybe he made a mistake and intended to set the timer for 4:30 *a.m.* but set it for p.m. Saw that once in El Paso. But really it was the flaw in the design that fouled the plan. He carved a piece of the trigger mechanism out of some kind of plastic and it warped in the heat. It would never have gone off." He paused for effect. "But I am glad we got to it before 4:30 rolled around."

CHAPTER 4

In his impatient mood, Henry was prepared to strangle Maude Hampson if she failed to explain how the Hollis residents had missed seeing, hearing, and smelling the grow op that had flourished in plain sight in their tiny neighbourhood.

She answered the front door before he could knock but then, as she had with Jackson, turned and tottered down the hall. Her disclaimer trailed behind. "I never noticed comings and goings, no suspicious characters."

She disappeared through the living room arch. Henry strode after, giving her no time to grasp the TV remote. "Did you know her well?"

She picked up the remote anyway. "I liked Gabriella Watson very much, watched her walking Puffles. I'd say hello the rare times I went out."

"Leave it on mute, please. What was *he* like?" Henry asked.

"Sociable enough."

"What's that mean?"

"They were joiners, participated."

"For example?"

"They both attended the annual barbecue. Brought steaks for

themselves, salads and banana loaf for everyone. I'm concerned about the dog."

"And what's Tom Watson do for a living?" Henry guessed the trades.

"He's in construction."

"How do you know that?"

"Or electrician. Yes, that's it. Sign on his truck. No, Officer, I don't remember the company he works for. And no, I didn't see him leave for work this morning." Henry anticipated Maude's next line. "He was always such a quiet man, Officer."

Sure, thought Henry. If people next door are always so quiet, why do so many noise complaints get called in? He had a long row to hoe this afternoon, and he had to get his first interviews in before the community had a chance to compare notes on the Watsons.

"I have to visit the other residents, Miss Hampson. Do you know the folks next to you along this side of Hollis?"

Maude paused, as if the question weren't straightforward. "I knew them, at least . . ."

"Why are you hesitating?"

"Because the house next to me is vacant now. They moved out months ago. But I think it's sold. The next one's vacant, too."

"You mean to say, the houses at Numbers 6 and 8 on your side are both empty, along with 5 directly across the street?"

Maude had drifted along the well-worn path to her front curtains. "Not at the moment. There's all kinds of folks pouring into Number 5 as we speak."

Henry cut the interview short and went outside to find Phil. The traffic jam made it dangerous to cross the road. The ambulance, back door ajar, had been given pride of place in the Watsons' driveway, and Henry guessed it would be an hour or more before the forensics crew would allow Gabriella's body to be removed. An unmarked SUV stood away from the crowd, down by the stone gates, and a woman in coveralls was carrying Puffles (whose bloody beard would end up being snipped for serology testing) in a blanket towards the vehicle. At least someone was being decisive, he thought.

Phil was standing where Henry had left him in the street, remonstrating with a large, barrel-bellied man. This was Bill "Boog" DeKlerk, head of the West Valley Narcotics Unit, a veteran detective disliked by most cops on the force. Boog hated Mormons and therefore was biased against Henry Pastern. Henry contemplated his next move. If DeKlerk learned that two more houses stood empty on the street, he would immediately call Chief Grady to argue that these vacant homes likely meant another grow op or two and that the Drug Squad should take over the investigation.

Several residents had finally come out onto the sidewalk way down at the end of Hollis, where the two-storeys began. In the forefront, a balding man of sixty seemed about to charge down the street.

Henry possessed a good temperament for the swirl of chaos. He watched the turmoil across the road and was suddenly content to be a detective. For the first time since returning to SLC from Washington, he felt it distinctly: professionalism. Policemen and -women were fanning out, controlling the scene, and he was part of it.

He pivoted and walked back to Maude's doorway, and rapped. She answered, looking annoyed, television voices wafting from her living room.

"Yes, Detective?"

"Miss Hampson, is there some kind of street organization in place, a neighbourhood improvement committee or the like?"

"Oh, not now. Hasn't met in a year."

"If it did meet, is there someone who would logically be in charge?"

"Oh, yes. That would inevitably be Jerry Proffet at Number 11." Maude clearly disliked Jerry. *Does she like anyone other than Puffles and the late Mrs. Watson?*

"Does he happen to be bald?"

"Yes, that's him. Goodbye."

This time Henry walked straight down the path and across the street to Phil and DeKlerk, turning only once to verify that 6 was entirely dark. The South African, as he was known around HQ, ignored Henry's approach. Phil was trying out a conciliatory strategy. "Bill, I'll make you a deal. The body is mine, but once we get the forensics, you can investigate the grow op. Let's just leave the tech team to do its work. They're helping both of us."

"Whatever it takes to get us out of this broiler oven," DeKlerk said.

One of DeKlerk's people came over and ruined the truce. "Lieutenant, don't 6 and 8 look empty to you?"

Everyone turned and scrutinized the pair of bungalows. Henry decided not to mention that he had seen a SOLD sign propped up against the side wall of Number 6.

"How long have they been empty?" DeKlerk demanded.

"Just guessing," Henry said, "but months at least. Not sure about 6. I'm told it's been bought, but the new owner hasn't moved in."

"That changes everything," DeKlerk puffed, still ignoring Henry.

Phil Mohlman grimaced, not keen on a fiefdom battle with the Drug Squad boss yet resistant to even minor concessions. "It changes nothing. No reason to imagine there's grass in there."

"We need to get into them," DeKlerk said. "If Number 5 was gutted by Watson to create a grow op, these sites may be active, too."

"Possibly," Henry murmured.

Phil frowned at him, but then he got Henry's game. Boog DeKlerk was mesmerized by the vacant houses. Let him concentrate on additional imaginary grow ops while Homicide took on the real case, namely the murder. Divide, divert, conquer, tie him up with paperwork, that should be their strategy. Phil couldn't resist needling his rival. "Okay with me, Boog, but you need warrants."

"It's urgent we do the search. It all flows from Mrs. Watson's death."

"You know that won't wash legally. Enter without a warrant, and everything that flows from it is tainted."

Boog clearly understood the point, but Henry couldn't resist hammering on the law. "Phil's right. It would be fruit of the poison tree."

"Screw the tree, college boy." But Boog's bluster didn't require further response, and his outrage petered out. The heat appeared to defeat him and he mopped his forehead. Henry wondered if he had a heart condition.

"We'll meet at six at the Rose. I'll figure something out by then," said Boog. He glared at Henry as he departed.

The big man headed for the two crime scene bungalows, where he hesitated, as if wondering if his bulk would fit inside with the crush of cops.

Henry led Phil a few yards in the other direction and whispered, "Phil, you see that guy hovering down the end of the street?"

"Bald, ex-military?"

"That's the one. Jerry Proffet. The old lady told me he's the former president of the street committee. I'm thinking he might be carrying a list of the residents. 'Cause right now, I can't tell who lives where."

They started up the row. Phil and Henry had the same feeling, that at any moment a scything blade might greet them at the door of any given house on Hollis Street. Was the vicious killer of Mrs. Watson one of the residents, fresh from his first beheading and primed for another?

They eyed Mr. Proffet, who was walking down the block to meet them. He brandished a sheet of paper that resembled a map. "Good guess, partner," Phil hissed.

Proffet was of medium height, fit for a guy of sixty, and firm in his gaze, with a touch of the politician. Henry was judging hastily, but he had encountered this kind of blustery aplomb in tinhorn community leaders before, including a few Mormon elders. As they approached the point where the street began to arc around the cul-de-sac, Henry confirmed that Proffet lived at Number 11; "The Proffets" was etched on a wood sign in the centre of the lawn. It amazed Henry that the man wore a zipped windbreaker in this weather, yet he did not appear to sweat.

Before Phil or Henry could speak, the bald man reached out a dry hand. Phil shook it perfunctorily. "I'm Jerry Proffet, past president of HASA, the Hollis Avenue Street Association."

"We're Detectives Mohlman and Pastern," Phil said matching Proffet's officious tone. "Could you explain what you mean by '*past* president,' Mr. Proffet?"

"We don't actually have a president currently. I suppose I'm de facto head, until we elect a new executive."

Henry inserted himself. "You said Hollis 'Avenue' Association. I thought it was Hollis Street."

"It is but we thought 'HASA' flowed better."

Henry stared at him. Who cared how the acronym flowed? Proffet was fussy and pretentious and Henry took a dislike to him.

"Could we talk inside, sir?" Phil said, as if in confidence, and Jerry Proffet brightened. He led the way — happy to help, elected or not. Henry noted the neatness of the Proffets' front path, which was flanked by geometric flower beds outlined in little painted rocks.

"You military?" Phil asked just before they entered the house.

"Warrant officer, Signals, U.S. Marines, retired," Proffet reported.

The house wasn't air-conditioned, it hadn't ever been, and an enveloping hothouse was the consequence. It occurred to Henry that marijuana plants would thrive here. Proffet ushered them into his living room, where the dampness oozed up tropically from the rugs and the sofa; two leather La-Z-Boy rockers seemed to Henry to be perspiring. Dozens of figurines, some of them identical to those on Maude Hampson's mantel, manned the perimeter of the room. Mrs. Proffet was nowhere in sight. *Is her head on her body?*

"Excuse the heat, officers. I have a condition where I'm super-sensitive to cold. But I did not get a *medical* discharge, I left with full honours."

A tall fan stood in one corner, but the breeze barely reached the detectives. Phil nonetheless took his time.

"Whatcha got there, Mr. Proffet?"

The ex-soldier handed over his diagram of Hollis Street, each house labelled with the owner's name; 5, 6, and 8 were marked "vacant."

"This is very helpful," Phil said. "Do you know all the home-owners personally?"

"All of them." Without pause, Mr. Proffet demanded tactlessly, "What's happened at the Watsons'?"

Henry moved back a step and relished Phil Mohlman's textbook interrogation of Jerry Proffet. It was evident that Jerry craved inside facts that he might dangle over his less-informed neighbours, and Phil threw him a bone. "Mrs. Watson was found dead in the vacant building next door." Before Proffet could jump in, he added, "The empty house. What do you know about Number 5?"

"It's been vacant for about two years. The previous owner, Robertson, just walked away one day. Casualty of the housing collapse. The George W. Bush recession hit SLC as hard as anywhere else, and . . ."

Henry, steaming in the shag-carpet jungle (his bald head dripped sweat; Jerry's stayed dry), decided that he despised Proffet. Maybe it was the bureaucratic self-importance. Henry was tempted to roll Gabriella's severed head into the conversation, but instead he performed his tag team role.

"What's this street like, Mr. Proffet?" Henry said. "We notice two or three of the sixteen houses are vacant."

"Fourteen. There's no Number 1 or 2. And the property at Number 6 was sold recently. Hollis is a good street."

"What can you tell us about Tom Watson?" Phil said.

"Tom Watson kept an eye on the old Robertson place. But you say Gabriella was found in Unit 5, not their own house?"

Phil said, "What do you mean 'kept an eye on'?"

"Tom volunteered to make sure no one broke into the house. Said he'd try to do some basic grooming around the property. He also volunteered to contact the city to force the mortgage holder to do the maintenance."

"I'll bet," said Henry. "Didn't do a very thorough job, did he?"

Proffet bridled. "Most of us are pretty house-proud. We put a lot of effort into our homes." Seeing that he was going nowhere with the detectives, he turned polite. "Won't you sit down, gentlemen?"

They reluctantly took the La-Z-Boys. "Let me get this straight," said Phil. "Watson tended the lawns at his own place, Maude Hampson's, Number 5, and also the undeveloped half lots at the mouth of the street. Right?"

"Tom was always willing to help." Proffet realized it was an error to defend Tom Watson and fell silent.

"Yet no one noticed him going in and out of Number 5?" Phil pressed. "He must've gone in there every day!"

"The executive designated . . ."

"While he was manicuring the lawns, he probably drove his John Deere mower right into the living room to harvest his crop," Phil persisted.

"The executive planned to contact the mortgage company to complain about the house left unattended," Proffet stated.

Henry fired his own rhetorical arrow. "I thought Tom Watson was minding the place."

"Kind of."

"By any chance, did Watson actually write that letter of complaint about the vacant house next to him?" Henry continued.

Proffet nodded. "Well, I guess he sent it."

Both detectives were dripping sweat. Phil levered himself out of the La-Z-Boy. "The street association was defunct. The executive collapsed, didn't I hear you say?"

Proffet pulled back like a hedgehog under attack. "Not exactly. I continued to serve my street as de facto chairman. I've always been there for everyone, even when no longer eligible to run for president."

Phil was in a mood, Henry could tell. Perhaps the recliner had aggravated his back problem. "Explain the executive structure again, Mr. Proffet."

"Presidents serve a one-year stint. You can only be re-elected for one more term, then must skip a year before running again. But you can be on the executive in another capacity."

"Little restrictive, isn't it? With only fourteen residents."

"Spouses can serve. That broadens the pool of candidates."

The extravagant rules bespoke condo politics, Henry thought, even though Hollis was entirely freehold.

Phil pressed. "So was Tom Watson on the executive?"

"From time to time. Never president. Gabriella ran the Beautification Committee. Tom volunteered for particular assignments." Henry sensed the man was about to say *missions*.

Henry tag-teamed. "You said earlier that this is a 'good street.' What did you mean by that, sir?"

"Everybody gets along. Most participate in the annual barbecue. No trouble."

The detectives' silence showed their disbelief. Jerry Proffet understood that the interview was in decline, and he rushed to make his case. "Every owner is hard-working, everyone has steady income, and Hollis is a very stable avenue."

"No shit," Phil said, adding a Boston inflection. "This is just a first contact, Mr. Proffet," he stated, moving to the door. "We'll be getting back to you, as early as this evening, if that's okay."

"Yeah, of course. Whatever I can do to assist. This is a good street."

Out on the front path, Phil could restrain himself no longer. "Term limits!" he cried. He looked along the street at the tumult before the Second House, then looked at the sky. "The heat just went up from *bake* to *fry*."

"I'll get moving," Henry said.

Phil Mohlman grunted. "Tell you what, if some resident on the evens leads you to someone on my side of the street, go ahead. Follow the leads. If we don't hook up here, let's meet at the Rose at six."

Both detectives had grasped that Proffet was holding a lot back. Neither was worried yet. When an investigation isn't generating momentum, a detective will fall back on protocol and start to plod through the steps. The next step was to wade through the Hollisites, one by one, and circle back to Jerry Proffet.

Henry was happy as he split off from Phil and strode up to Number 10.

CHAPTER 5

He had time for two or three interviews on the even-numbered flank of Hollis: 10, 12, and try for 14. Then he would join DeKlerk and Phil Mohlman at the Black Rose.

Two Drug Squad cops were creeping around the vacant bungalows at Numbers 6 and 8, peering in windows like peeping Toms with *Patriot Act* permits. DeKlerk would need two warrants to penetrate the buildings. Henry doubted that either was ever a grow house in any case. Tom Watson was small-time, neither ruthless nor foolhardy enough to attempt a major expansion along his own street. Henry and Phil were confident they could hold the drug boys at bay while they amassed evidence from all the Hollis residents. "We'll make early progress on all fronts," he promised himself as he bounded up to the door at Number 10 and stabbed at the buzzer.

Carleton Davis shattered Henry's complacency. He must have been seventy, grizzled and shabby. Slightly crazed, he played the pirate, standing back from the landing in a defiant pose, legs apart like the captain of a ship, not an ounce of welcome in his face. The eye patch on his left socket bolstered the performance.

"Better get out of the sun, Detective. Your bald pate is red as a chicken's ass."

Is every Hollis resident going to be hostile? "I wasn't aware that a chicken's ass was red."

Davis's cheeks were lined and sagging and his voice raspy, yet his gaze remained sharp. He stepped farther back into an air-conditioned hallway. "Come in if you have to."

Henry stepped inside. "How did you know I was a detective?"

"That train of vehicles over there doesn't mean tent show preachers have come to town, does it?"

"Mr. Proffet down the way gave us a list of residents," Henry said.

"Proffet. He's a cold bastard."

"Is that a joke, Mr. Davis?"

"It's a double entendre," Davis said. "He claims to be military. I, on the other hand, was really in Vietnam. Who's dead?"

What the devil is he talking about? That's not a double entendre. "Mrs. Watson."

"Shot?"

"Stabbed, it appears."

"Beheaded?" Davis's demeanour didn't change when he spoke the word.

"What makes you ask that, sir?"

"I was a military policeman in Danang. Policing is policing. You got Drug Unit folks over there. Emergency cube vans and an ambulance. One black plastic body bag carried from the house. Lots of special lamps. I know a marijuana operation when I see one . . . I was guessing about the decapitation."

"Oh, really?" Henry said. "I've never had a witness guess a decapitation."

"The husband didn't do it."

"Why do you conclude that? Guessing again?" *Nobody likes a smartass,* Henry thought but did not say.

"He was running the grow op, right? The big drug cartels took him out."

Henry knew the technique of tossing out salacious theories in order to open up a witness. Davis was playing it back at him. The fact that the old pirate's guesses were largely right so far didn't make Henry warm up to Carleton Davis. "We haven't found him — yet."

"Buckets of blood?"

"Why don't you believe the husband killed her?"

"Because Tom Watson is a mild-mannered guy. Not the most sociable dude but not the volatile, violent kind. Notice anything about the grow op site?"

"Such as?"

"These are damned bungalows! How many plants can you fit in one of these units? No basement, tiny attic."

Henry had cooled off now and, repelled by the man, determined to leave as fast as possible. "You mean, Watson thought small-time?"

Davis leaned in. "Detective, not only that, but I invite you to think through the *other* side of the equation. Whoever attacked the Watsons was hot, bothered, and bloody about very small-scale competition. Ask yourself why. It must have been a drug gang. They believe in zero tolerance." Davis grinned at his bad joke.

"Did people on the street suspect he was growing marijuana? Did *you*?"

Davis heaved an exaggerated shrug. "No. I don't bother with neighbours or their dogs."

Henry had tried to hook Davis with false intimacy. Now it was time to harden his approach. "That's exactly what you and the other residents on the street do, Davis, you mind each other's business. Did Tom Watson participate in the street association?"

"Not much. I myself dropped out of the committee a while ago."

"Why?"

"Too much autocracy. Nice word for fascism. Ordering people around, suggesting we all paint our front doors the same colour."

"What colour was that?"

"Can't recall."

"Did you participate in the barbecues, Mr. Davis?"

"Sure. I make a mean Texas chili. Detective, have you noticed something strange about our street executive?"

"I've only met one of them. What?"

"Why does a pissant street like this need such an elaborate association? Think about what I say, Detective. A cut-rate marijuana business produces a massacre. A small side street has an oversize mini-government. What's out of whack?"

Henry had a creepy feeling that the residents of Hollis were already closing ranks, like muskox at the approach of wolves. He decided to provoke Davis. "Are any of your neighbours LDS?"

Davis looked baffled, then livid. *Good.* "Uh, not unless Devereau at Number 13 is. Why? Oh, I get it. You think Mormons would have handled this problem more civilized, like. Well, you polygamist, one thing gets the wagons circled is Mormons laying siege all around us. We have our own unwritten rules on Hollis Street. No Mormon owners, nope."

What's out of whack is you, you thug. Henry marvelled at his own anger.

"You ever suspect Tom Watson of trafficking drugs?"

"You call what he does trafficking?"

"You seem to know the scale of the threat he posed to the cartels, or didn't pose."

Davis smirked. "Not hard to understand a mom-and-pop murder, am I right?"

"No, you're wrong, Mr. Davis. Murder makes it a big deal."

Henry left Davis ranting about magic underwear and secret teachings. Henry had heard it all a thousand times. Hollis was an uptight street, and Henry was becoming a connoisseur of its overreaction.

Henry went out into the heat. He ignored the murder site and loped to Number 12, his shaved dome rivered with sweat.

The feeling was growing in Henry that there was something off-kilter about these homeowners. They were defensive, quick with theories, but blinkered, as if a collective failure to see — to smell

— bags of weed flowing out of the death house was a trivial lapse. They spooked him.

He tried the buzzer at 12 and was greeted by the widow Anderssen in her nurse's uniform. She was about to leave for the swing shift at Pioneer Valley Hospital, and no, he couldn't come in. She had been at work during the crucial time period, seen nothing. She worked the night shift yesterday, got home at 5 a.m., and missed everything. She barely knew the Watsons. When Henry asked did the executive of HASA do a good job, she shrugged. "At least Jerry Proffet put in that pinyon tree across the way. Keeps it watered."

The owner of Number 14, Jakob Wazinski, was in his backyard firing up his barbecue when Henry came around the side of the house. Here was the first of the two-storey homes and the final residence on Henry's roster; Mohlman and Jackson would do the rest, although he hadn't seen either of them on the sidewalk.

About sixty and wrapped in a chef's apron, his weapon of choice a spatula, the emperor of Number 14 did not seem surprised by Henry's arrival, though he leered at his suit and tie. Almost bald himself, Wazinski smiled at Henry's shaved pate, as if they now had something in common. Wazinski adhered to the Hollis Street pattern, keeping one step ahead of every question by offering his opinions unbidden.

"I suppose you're here about Mrs. Watson. I'm Jake Wooski. Officially Wazinski. Don't call me Wazinski."

He grated on Henry. The smile was too broad and the patter too Three Stooges. Henry, the heat getting to him, said, "Only if I have to arrest you."

Jake got the joke right off and slapped the flaming barbecue with his spatula, sending sparks onto the parched patio. "Husband did it. Want a beer?"

"No, thanks."

"You a Mormon, then?"

"Yeah, but I still wouldn't drink that light beer."

"Hah! Be glad to answer all your questions if you can guess what kind of beer — real beer — I got in that cooler."

"Heineken."

"Jesus. How'd you guess?"

"Just a good judge of character, Jake."

The heat was pickling Henry's egg-domed brain. *How is it that everyone knows about the crime?* He looked down the line of thirsting backyards and caught one of DeKlerk's men poking around Number 8. *Ah, well, Hollisites, your sins will emerge, I have no doubt.* He needed an ally on the street, and Wazinski would serve for now. The man seemed harmless. Henry took a lawn chair in the shade of the house and accepted an orange juice.

"So what makes you think the husband did it, sir?"

Wooski took a walk around the inferno zone and waved his utensil like a laser pointer.

"The street lamp."

"How so?"

"The bulb in front of Number 5 is burnt out. Wait until sundown, then you'll see."

"But Number 5 has been vacant for months, and fixing the light would have been at the private owner's discretion," Henry said.

Wooski shook his head. "Watson made sure it stayed dark. That's an example of his cleverness. Concealed his comings and goings."

Wooski's theory wasn't wrong, it just wasn't enough, and Henry prepared to press, but then: "When the wife is murdered, don't the police start with the husband?" a female voice said.

Henry turned to greet Mrs. Wooski, who for some reason was carrying her own spatula. Paulette stood five-foot-nothing. She was cheerfully brazen and coxcombed with rooster-red hair. Her idea of sunblock was pancake makeup to cover her leatherized skin. *Maybe she puts it on with the spatula.* The Utah sun had carved runoff furrows into her cheeks.

"Dear, Detective Pastern. Detective, Paulette."

"Glad to meetcha. We always wondered about the Watsons . . ."

"Yes, we did," Jake said.

Henry worked to keep the discussion on track. "I hear that Mr. Watson was on the executive committee at one time. That sounds like he tried to fit in."

Paulette leaned close. "He was on, what was it, Jake, the Street Improvement Subcommittee? She was on the Plantings and Grooming Subcommittee."

"Not sure. Those committees changed names more often than a Nazi in Argentina."

"Was Tom Watson ever president or vice-president or treasurer?"

Jake thought over the question. "No. The most important thing he was ever assigned was contacting the city about the mess at the empty properties at 5 and 8. She had her hands full with the plantings on the street. See how scorched it gets. She was good. No one volunteered their water feed to keep the plants irrigated, but she strong-armed the owners into opening their taps, so to speak."

"Weren't you on the street committee yourself, Jake?" Henry said.

"I quit. Couldn't stand Jerry Proffet."

"You had a fight?" Henry said.

"Nah, not about the vacant houses particularly. What we had in common caused the rift, you might say. He was a sunshine soldier. I *fought* in Vietnam. Me and Davis at Number 10 were on the front line."

Henry had the feeling that not every resident wanted to talk, but those that did felt compelled to diss Jerry Proffet.

Jake finished his Heineken, opened another. He grew philosophical. "After ten years, something happens. Lethargy sets in, a community becomes apathetic somehow. The centre cannot hold."

Henry was startled to hear Yeats quoted. Over the next ten minutes, he annotated Jerry Proffet's house chart with the number of years each owner had lived on Hollis Street according to Jake. The majority had resided here the full ten years since Forest Vale broke ground in 2002. The owners maintained standards, but the rules put in place by Jerry Proffet eventually proved abrasive, providing the touchstone for each neighbour's disillusionment with the community's prospects. Wooski and Davis dropped out of the committee. Widow Anderssen ignored the committee. Maude Hampson was content to spy and scold.

Henry took his leave and returned to the street. The heat refused to relent. He could have begun working on Mohlman's list — Henry felt he was collecting Monopoly deeds — but instead he strolled towards the pinyon tree that Nurse Anderssen had mentioned. It stood out in the open space between Jerry Proffet's house and the place next door (labelled "Henneker" on Proffet's chart). Proffet had planted it on the municipal right-of-way to mask the electrical relay box that served the street.

Henry glanced west and noted that most of the police vehicles were still parked in front of the grow house. He saw Officer Jackson coming down the sidewalk and met him halfway.

"They anywhere close to finishing?" Henry asked. Jackson looked exhausted.

"*They* are, for the day. I pulled another shift, till midnight."

"Anything I should know?"

They began walking together back towards the pinyon tree.

"No breakthroughs," Jackson said. "They're rushing the analysis, but that's gotta be Mrs. Watson's blood in the residence. She was stabbed there, then carried to the grow house, where the killer cut off her head."

"Obviously the husband hasn't showed up," Henry stated.

"He's either dead himself or took the warning and hightailed it."

They paused at the tree. Henry was surprised to see that the mulched ground around it was wet. Jerry Proffet had found time for his pet tree even in the presence of murder.

"You don't think the husband did it, sir?" Officer Jackson continued.

"I doubt it," Henry said. "I'm getting the picture from the neighbours of an affectionate, if dull, couple. Husband and wife had an arrangement, it appears to me. She got a stable life in a respectable neighbourhood, walked her dog. She could be sociable with the neighbours. He promised to keep the marijuana operation low-key and quiet. I can't see him executing his spouse like that. Would he chop off her head under any circumstances?"

Jackson, who smelled of marijuana, completed the morbid logic. "And if he did it, would he have dragged her body all the way next door, severed her head, *and* posed her on the table?"

"Too grisly," Henry agreed.

He looked at the tree, sad and defiant like a Hollis Street resident. Tom Watson didn't kill his wife. It was all too crazy, and there was something . . . *perverse* about putting the head in the garbage.

After a pause, Officer Jackson said, "Detective Mohlman says Tom Watson didn't show up for work today. If he comes back home tonight, I'll be waiting."

Henry looked at the young patrolman. He was starting to like him. Yet he didn't confide in Jackson that he was on his way to do battle with Boog DeKlerk.

CHAPTER 6

The Black Rose Restaurant was the former Rocco's Bar. The name change had become necessary two years before, as the owners struggled to adapt to the liberalization of Utah's byzantine liquor rules. They called the Rose a "restaurant" so that they could legally serve a full range of alcoholic drinks, including "heavy" beer — brew containing more than 3.2 percent alcohol by volume. This was important to Boog DeKlerk, who favoured Guinness, which even in its American version contained over four percent. Henry, who didn't drink, found it all too confusing and kept quiet, but this didn't stop DeKlerk from holding forth on "Mormon bluestocking laws" whenever he encountered Henry.

Henry arrived at the Rose to find Phil already in the regular booth with DeKlerk. They were on their second round. An untouched plate of deep-fried zucchini and garlic sauce sat at the edge of the table. The big man looked up from his Guinness. "You're late."

Mohlman said, "He's not bloody late."

"Yeah, you're late, preppy. We settled everything."

"Nothing's settled," Phil said.

Henry sat beside his partner. The waitress came over and asked if the food was okay. That was another complication. Utah liquor rules for this kind of establishment required the patron to order food with his drink. No one knew why the law was this way. *Sometimes you just can't win with the Mormon thing*, Henry thought. The regulations compelled DeKlerk to choose something from the menu even when he wasn't hungry. He had put on weight, for which, absurdly, he blamed Henry. Henry ordered a tall Coke and DeKlerk glared at him.

"No eats, Pastern? Going home for a leisurely dinner with the wife in your desert spa?"

DeKlerk wasn't married, and Henry had once suggested to Phil that Boog was married to the night shift. "Not true, Henry. Boog is married to his pension plan. He hopes to retire to a place in the desert in the next year, and that's why he envies you your new house. He also suffers from the delusion that the Utah desert is the South African veld. Jesus wept. Some people just can't bury their childhood."

Phil now turned to Henry amiably. "Discover any stone killers hiding on Hollis Street, Henry?"

"Not among the even numbers," Henry replied.

"I didn't get far with the odd addresses," Mohlman said. "What's Jackson doing now?"

"Stuck in the Second House, best I can tell. I like him. He's conscientious —"

Boog DeKlerk hated being left out. "I don't figure the husband for it, but he's the key to getting the killers."

Phil continued with Henry. "I did run into Ronald Devereau at Number 13, next to Jerry Proffet, one of the two-storeys. Used to be vice-president of the street group for a brief time. I got no further. But Boog has a point. Finding Tom Watson tops our priorities."

DeKlerk chewed on a zucchini stick while he waited for a chance to pontificate.

"Any sign of him?" Henry asked.

"Nope. Didn't show up for work. We issued a BOLO on the truck. Nothing. Chief Grady's office took care of getting the warrant out on Watson. Suspicion of homicide." ·

Boog grunted. "Should be for trafficking, that's the better rap.

We know he pushes drugs. This is pre-eminently a drug case, a gang making a point."

"A moot point if Watson is dead," Henry said.

"I'll buy that, preppy," Boog said. "Watson is in a dumpster somewhere in the Valley. His head may be in a different dumpster."

Phil, tiring of Boog's combativeness, waved him off. Henry noted that his partner often turned morose in the Black Rose. The restaurant had no connection to the famous Black Rose Irish pub down by Faneuil Hall, but Phil grew nostalgic for Boston whenever he drank here.

Henry reflected on the mentality of the three of them. The South African. The boy from Charlestown. The lapsed Mormon. They all lived in Utah and they weren't going anyplace, but still they positioned themselves as outsiders. It was an immature attitude, he recognized.

Henry was exhausted and wanted to get home to Theresa. His attention wandered. With its black lacquered bar backed by a big mirror, pinpoint red lights limning the mirror and baseboards around the room, the place resembled a Chinese restaurant more than an Irish pub. Due to another arcane state rule, there were no bottles of booze behind the bar. Larry the bartender was fed up with explaining that he wasn't Rocco, there never had been a Rocco, and no, he wasn't Irish. The bar/restaurant had trouble fixing on an identity — just like the community along Hollis Street, Henry mused. Maybe like himself, Phil, and Boog, too.

DeKlerk hammered on the drug argument. "I can get FLIR warrants on the units at Numbers 6 and 8."

Phil and Henry remained skeptical. Forward Looking Infrared spectrum analysis was a police tool derived from military technology. It registered the heat signature from a building, in this context the juice used by grow lights in a marijuana operation. Because of its lack of subtlety — planes flying low overhead — and the emerging controversy over drone surveillance, the courts were becoming restrictive in the warrants they granted. But police forces loved the technology.

"On two separate, unrelated houses?" Phil said. "Not enough grounds for a flyover. Any evidence risks being thrown out as unreasonable."

"Un-this, un-that. Hell, Phil, we'll have the judge onside. Blood's still wet."

Henry held his opinion back, but he was with the Drug Squad chief on the issue of authorization: in the aftermath of the discovery of a beheaded female victim, the court would be sympathetic to a FLIR scan warrant. He was more concerned about a breach of privacy allegation from an individual resident causing all of them to clam up. FLIR scans would increase the circus atmosphere on Hollis Street, when what was needed was calm, door-to-door police work.

Phil remained antagonistic. "The locals we've met so far tend to be snoops, old ladies and their equivalents, living their lives at the front curtain. I don't know, there's something about the residents on this street. You do a flyover — what, three or four passes? — someone is bound to call in a complaint —"

DeKlerk burst in. "I don't want my men knocking politely on the front door and trying the lock. Booby traps are a real danger."

"I've got a better idea," Henry said, taking the unlikely role of mediator between the senior detectives. "You have car-top scanner units, don't you?"

"Don't work as well. And with this heat, the contrast . . ."

"But well enough, I understand," Henry said.

Henry got the *other* look from Phil and Boog, not the Mormon Look, but the one that said, "You learn that crap in the FBI in Washington?"

Phil thumped the table and said, "Done! They'll blend in with the rest of the bullshit going down."

DeKlerk was satisfied. The drive-by unit looked odd perched on the roof of a vehicle, but a couple of passes up and down Hollis would be quick and minimally intrusive.

It was Phil who wouldn't let it go. "That's *all* we do on that front. Leadership stays with Homicide."

DeKlerk smirked. "Make it a drug case, Phil, and we easily explain the decapitation and the pipe bomb. I'll tell Grady the cartel moved a little farther north than usual."

"I don't plan to explain anything away," Phil lashed out. "I plan to solve it."

The Drug Squad chief sat back in the banquette. "Whatever. Grady wants us to wrap it up fast."

Henry had heard the refrain many times. "We have to wrap it up." It was a reference to West Valley's most notorious case. The tragedy of Susan Powell haunted every cop in West Valley, even those who had joined the force later. Susan Powell was a model wife, the mother of two boys, lovable and loved, who vanished from the Valley on a December day in 2009 and was never found. The case gripped the city for months. Half the citizenry had the husband for it, but as many wanted something else to be true, an abduction by an outsider, for example. West Valley, already in the shadow of Salt Lake, didn't need a reputation as an unsafe place for women, and the pressure to solve the kidnapping rose daily. The police force believed that her abductor had drowned her, but Henry had doubts, since it was almost impossible to sink a body in the Great Salt Lake, and the rivers up in the Wasatch Range are fast-flowing and unlikely to conceal a corpse for long. The killer had dumped her in the woods up near Park City, he believed. West Valley had its share of violent crime, but this one resonated, and as the case dragged on, the public started to suspect incompetence within the police department. In 2012, Susan's husband, who had relocated to Washington State, killed his two sons and then himself. The case was fresh in everyone's memory. Many a West Valley officer had been heard to say with gallows humour that it would have been helpful if he had left coordinates for finding Susan's body before he offed himself. The local chief, Grady, pledged to keep the case open. As if he had the choice. No one wanted a second Susan Powell.

"We got a profile of the husband?" DeKlerk asked.

"Watson. Age forty-two, no criminal record, two non-criminal citations way back for drinking in a public place," Mohlman stated.

"Employed as a journeyman electrician at Salaberry Electric in Salt Lake. Office says he didn't show up today, and his usual partner reports no contact since the day before, when he acted, quote, 'like all was normal.' No one so far on Hollis reports seeing him leave for work."

"No one saw anything," DeKlerk said. "Ya know, after a while, the cannabis starts to ooze out of a home factory like that. Somebody shoulda noticed."

"Like they're olfactorily deaf and blind," Phil added.

They were venting; they couldn't help themselves. Henry chimed in: "I agree. I've met less than half of them, but they all talk about 'standards' and 'neighbourliness.' Yet a grow house? Nobody paying attention when every house can see — smell — every other house, and you have to drive past the murder site to exit the street?"

"What's your point?" Boog DeKlerk said.

"We find it strange that nobody saw anything. What if the opposite was true? All the residents actually *knew* about the grow operation."

"And tipped off the Mob," DeKlerk tossed in.

Phil was unpersuaded. "Nice to see you two bonding, but one way or another, Tom Watson fled the scene and remains our top candidate."

The Guinness now tipped DeKlerk over into belligerence. It was no longer a matter of who had jurisdiction here — DeKlerk knew that he was far better plugged in to the convoluted drug trade than Homicide, and he only need bide his time. "So why can't you Eastern pantywaists find one bloodstained electrician in a van in a state of only 444,000 people?"

Phil never apologized for his Boston roots, especially not in the Black Rose, and especially not to the South African. "Get out of our way and we'll solve this."

"Why haven't *you* arrested anyone, Pastern?"

Phil won Henry's everlasting loyalty by bristling back. "My partner's the one who thought to look next door for the grow operation.

Otherwise, you'd still be walking around Number 3 Hollis with Al Pacino's dick in your hand."

Even Boog DeKlerk had to laugh.

The two senior detectives ordered another round. The zucchini had turned flaccid and the garlic sauce had coagulated. Henry excused himself and drove home to have dinner with Theresa.

CHAPTER 7

On most days, Henry made it home by dinnertime, although he often returned to work for a modified swing shift. Management expected extra effort from junior detectives. Sometimes Henry worked an all-night stint and arrived back on Coppermount Drive at dawn. The Utah desert was at its most beautiful when the first glimmer of morning crept in, and he loved pulling into the driveway in the quiet neighbourhood and going round back of the house to watch the sunrise. Often he would find Theresa dozing on the couch with the patio doors open a few inches.

Today, the Black Rose far down the highway behind him, Henry stopped in the driveway and felt oddly queasy. The feeling, he realized, had everything to do with the stark differences in neighbourhoods. Hollis Street presented a lurid contrast to Coppermount. It wasn't that the cul-de-sac was so bad, but for all the owners' efforts to keep up standards and sustain a cohesive community, the whole row had declined. Their paranoia, born of a desire to keep their little world static, had turned in on them. By contrast, Henry's street was brand new. It wasn't finished to the end of the block, although the last lots were marked and the piping and gas lines had only recently been installed, but once complete, Coppermount Drive would be more fashionable than the West Valley enclave could ever hope to be.

He locked the Subaru and walked around to the rear of the sprawling ranch house, intent on admiring the view. He liked to monitor the changes in light. By now, the desert plateau had darkened into ochre and rich browns, and the distant hills were purpling in the declining sun. Two firm truths struck him: the vista was perfect, and they had likely bought too much house. Oh, well, it was their sanctuary. Theresa wasn't healthy, but they had worked hard to turn this place into their dream home on the rim of the great desert.

He saw that the back doors were open. Theresa often turned the air conditioning off in late afternoon, even though the system filtered out the dust and sand that aggravated her throat. Henry entered the immense living room. He heard Theresa rattling dishes in the kitchen; the house was so large that she hadn't heard the family car pull up. At least she wasn't coughing. That was encouraging.

She came out of the kitchen and smiled at him. She wore a puffy oven mitt on her right hand. There was no doubt of her radiance and if her breathing problem had imposed a consumptive pallidness on her beauty, she still glowed and triumphed in the evening light. Theresa stood three inches under Henry's height, thin now but still almost statuesque; a mica-like fleck in her left eye often caught the light and gave her a mischievous look. As often happened lately, the first glimpse of her instantly called back to him, in abbreviated form, the story of how they'd met, even if these days the saga of their meeting — both of them native Utahans who'd had to move to Alexandria, Virginia, to find each other — seemed a cruelly short story, truncated by fate. Was he in fact fashioning a time capsule of anecdotes for a time when she wouldn't be here?

The FBI had historically liked Mormons, and all Utahans knew it. Even so, Henry was surprised when they accepted him straight out of university. He may have been the only applicant ever with a fine arts major and a criminology minor. By his third undergraduate year at Brigham Young, he had convinced himself that he wanted a lifetime career with the Federal Bureau of Investigation. Like much else in his youth, this was a murky choice that lured him because it bridged the straightlaced certainties of a Mormon upbringing and the uncertain rebellion represented by a career beyond the State of Deseret. "Perhaps over-enthused," one member of the recruiting panel wrote in his interview file. Henry got in, but his lack of focus bore consequences: when he started at the academy, he made the rookie mistake of saying that he would take "any assignment" in his novitiate years, and so, with Bureau logic, they sent him to Art Crime.

The Art Crime team back then contained only fourteen FBI special agents, and while the work could be exotic — once, Henry consulted with Interpol in Lyon — it wasn't exactly street policing. Much of the time, the agents collaborated with museums and conducted their investigations online, governed by the processes and protocols surrounding the National Stolen Art File. Once a purloined painting or rare document made it onto the computerized NSAF, or to the international list maintained by Interpol, the team opened a case file, provided they found a strong American connection. Henry soon had his own lengthy list of stolen items to monitor. Most days, the process was dry and plodding, but at least he got to work in the J. Edgar Hoover Building on Pennsylvania Avenue.

He and Theresa met at a party in Alexandria while he was still a trainee, on the day after he was informed that he would start in Art Crime. Their attraction was the usual American combo of coincidence, defiance, and optimism, and their respective moves east made their meeting feel preordained. It didn't bother her that she was a year older, or that his corn-fed blondness (though in fact Utah doesn't grow much corn, and he had shaved his head) made him seem even younger. His good looks, sincerity, and Mormon neatness gave her a package of sexy, if conservative, virtues to latch on to as she neared thirty. Henry played his self-deprecation card on their first date, making her laugh: "A fine arts degree from BYU requires writing your graduate thesis about velvet paintings of Elvis."

Theresa had moved to D.C. three years before, from the Ogden domain of her mother, Ruth. Her father, Mitchell, had moved there many years earlier. She was independent by nature and remained proud of the fact that she had won a position with a prestigious accounting firm without his help. Had she come to Washington for the accounting job, or to reconcile with her father? Henry was never sure; perhaps it was both. Mitch was high up in the federal government, probably CIA, and Theresa had lived with him for the first three months in D.C. Her parents had divorced when Theresa was ten, and through her teen years she saw her father fewer than twenty times. They later developed a correspondence, augmented by brief visits east, and her yearning for more contact built as she graduated high school. He supported her choice of the University of Denver for accounting, while her mother had to be content that Theresa hadn't demanded to attend a university in D.C.

Living with her father produced the reconciliation she craved. She eventually moved into a place with two girlfriends, but it was close to Mitch's penthouse. Their relationship continued to thrive. When she and Henry hooked up, Mitch took no offence as the couple put more distance between him and his daughter. Henry didn't know that he slipped $1,000 a month to Theresa for living expenses.

The idyll had ended sixteen months ago, when Henry and Theresa moved out of their one-bedroom in Alexandria and trekked back to Utah. It was a parody of the Mormon diaspora, he always thought. Her formal diagnosis was degenerative emphysema. After a year of testing and runarounds in D.C., the sureness of the label gave Henry a cause to hold on to: like a good FBI man, he resolved to manage her case. Henry and Theresa remained stalwart, and decisiveness became their way of resisting misfortune.

Emphysema wasn't sexy. Her cough irritated co-workers at the D.C. insurance firm where she had taken up a job in management. There were some complaints, and regular queries about her coping. Within months, her affliction rendered her dysfunctional, a humiliating and cruel invasion. People didn't understand: lung cancer, even from smoking, they could fix on, but not this sad, tubercular wasting that seemed melodramatized from an old Edwardian plotline. For a while, Henry comforted himself with images from the television ads for COPD. The drug companies urged him to believe that chronic obstructive pulmonary disease was controllable; the patient would soon be tossing a football on sun-dappled lawns. Only, it was never that way for Theresa. She took extended sick leave, and her doctors recommended a drier climate. In this age of drugs for every disease, such advice struck Henry as quaint. Thousands of Easterners had moved west in the nineteenth century seeking the dry cure — Doc Holliday, for example. The Mormons had set up sanitariums and outpatient clinics for hundreds of tuberculosis sufferers in the nineteenth century. What was old was new; Utah still welcomed its share of health seekers, even prodigal sons.

Theresa feistily rationalized their return, and Henry went along. It was necessary, so let's get it done. We know the Beehive State; we will be welcomed back. We'll have jobs. It was all very rational. Her cloying mother was her biggest problem, treating the return of her daughter as a victory in her tug-of-war with Mitch. Theresa bridled against the LDS community, which her mother promised to mobilize in support of her return. To Theresa, the church's aggressive comfort was another form of motherly oppression. There would be no re-embrace of Mormonism.

But Henry grasped the real point: their move back to Utah was permanent. He approached his superiors in the Bureau, and they were sympathetic. Salt Lake City had its own regional office and he could transfer, though he might have to take a drop in pay grade for the first year. Henry balked at the offer. The Bureau applied ineluctable rules to field officers, and Henry, as junior man in SLC, could be required to participate in investigations just about anywhere. Inter-agency collaboration, especially on terrorism dossiers through Joint Terrorism Task Forces across the West, made travel inevitable. In the end, Henry had taken the second job offered, a starting detective position with the West Valley force.

"Dinner's almost ready," Theresa said.

They kissed, and he followed her into the kitchen.

To Henry, who had learned to take Theresa's COPD day by day, she appeared much better than average. When her coughing abated and she stood up straight, you knew she had to have been a runner. Theresa couldn't run a hundred yards now.

Henry watched her lean down to the oven and take out a beef tenderloin, which sizzled in the pan and sent garlic and rosemary vapours his way. A rasping fit caught her, and Henry moved quickly to grasp her hand in the oven mitt and guide the pan to the counter. She recovered and turned to give him another kiss.

"How much time've you got?"

"An hour," Henry said. "But I'll be back by eleven thirty."

"How was your day?"

"Interesting. Interesting. I'll tell you about it."

She smiled again. He didn't always share his job life. "Can we eat out on the deck?" she said. It wasn't really a question.

Henry glanced at the kitchen table, which was covered in loose papers and ledgers. Theresa was a tax accountant now. Since moving back to Utah, she had built up a steady freelance business in the Salt Lake City area, doing individual and small corporate returns and setting up payroll records.

They ate slices of the tenderloin with mango and avocado sauce, a salad, and rolls. Henry never took booze, and her condition made wine a bad idea, and so they drank ice tea. The landscape beyond the patio remained still and hushed. They had only three neighbours along Coppermount and, as usual, none of them were outside.

The state of Theresa's lungs constrained their conversation. She had once been the talker. Only recently had Henry embraced the reversal of roles, but he wasn't a natural Scheherazade.

"I tagged a murder today," he said.

That caught her full attention and, a bonus, suppressed her impulse to cough. The burden shifted to Henry to carry the conversation, and she grinned to encourage him. Against the desert backdrop, silent except for one bird who chirped in anticipation of nightfall, he launched into a twenty-minute monologue. The story gushed out. He covered the beheading of Gabriella Watson and described the bizarreness of investigating the double crime scene at Numbers 3 and 5 Hollis, where both killing floors remained awash in blood. He covered the quirky bits and the gore, his own suspicions, and the tension between Homicide and the Narcotics Unit. He finished by expressing his unease with the residents of the street and with the defunct street association.

"The rule on Hollis is: nobody knows anything." It had already become a refrain.

Theresa had nodded him along, but now she said, "Henry, I'm having trouble figuring out whether the gaps in your story are because you're dodging them or because you don't know all the facts and won't speculate."

"What do you want to know?" He thought he'd been thorough.

"Where was her head found?"

"You get to the heart of the matter fast."

Theresa raised one eyebrow. "*Head* of the matter? Did the killer leave it next to the body?"

"No, as a matter of fact. Why do you ask that?"

Her look showed that she considered the answer obvious. "The killer wasn't in a hurry. He took his sweet time. That's curious. Where was it found?"

"In a plastic trash bag under the sink."

"Why do you think he left it there? It was a strange thing to do. Why be neat and tidy about it, if you've already spread blood all over the living room?" Theresa fetched a bottle of wine from the fridge, giving no hint that she was asking his approval.

"Two living rooms, in fact," Henry said. "This is all about sending a message. The beheading was an execution. This is about the drug business."

Theresa looked dubious. Saying nothing, he let her work through her logic. His joy at her good health made him patient. Theresa's affliction frustrated her in many ways but also made her more reflective: she didn't trust her lungs, so when she spoke she prepared her statements carefully. To him, her smoky voice was seductive.

"What are you going to do when you drive back to Hollis Street?" she said.

"I hope the rest of the people on my list are home so I can complete my share of the interviews and start on Phil's list. I'll hook up with Phil, if he's around. This is the slogging phase of the investigation."

"No, I don't think so," she replied, startling him. She bore a contemplative expression, almost mystical in the desert light.

"Huh?"

"I think you're already near the heart of the case, Henry. You might find the killer tonight. Be careful."

He almost laughed. "If you insist."

Henry hadn't seen this oracular side of Theresa before. *When you are constantly short of breath, your short sentences all sound like pronouncements. She's clearly into the mystery. Perhaps she possesses a better instinct for wickedness than I do.*

"The residents?" she asked.

"Typical of 'he was always such a quiet man' neighbours," Henry said. "More than the average number of busybodies. No one too broken up about the murder."

"The street association?" Theresa said.

"What about it?"

"What binds these people together, if anything? It's important."

Henry had to go. He took a deep breath and checked for signs that her coughing was cycling back. Theresa seemed to be deep in thought — or she was fighting to control her lungs. "What's that Agatha Christie story, Henry?"

Although Agatha Christie wrote dozens of mystery tales, Henry knew at once the one she meant. Sometimes they read each other's thoughts.

"*Murder on the Orient Express?*"

"That's it. The passengers on the train conspire to eliminate a nasty guy."

"Why would the residents on Hollis Street band together to slaughter their own neighbour? Why not just call the police?"

Theresa shrugged. There wasn't time to debate her theory now. "Drugs arriving on their peaceful street. Indifferent but pretentious neighbours fearful of outsiders. Seem like a recipe for murder to you, Henry?"

Henry prepared to go. He often gave the treasured desert landscape a final look before returning to work, but tonight his thoughts roiled with excitement and he rushed to his car. Even so, he paused there in the driver's seat to contemplate his moves. He shouldn't have discussed an active case with his wife, but he had no regrets. You don't say no to an oracle.

He had to share his exhilaration.

Henry got out of the Subaru and tried his smart phone there in the driveway. Sometimes reception was feeble out on the desert's edge. He found the coordinates for Chief Inspector Peter Cammon in England and keyed in a text message.

Peter Cammon, more than twice Henry's age and with vastly more experience, was the greatest detective he had ever encountered; Henry idolized him. They had met in Washington during Henry's biggest FBI case (his only big case) and had kept in touch since, emailing every month or so and talking three or four times over the past year. They had batted about the idea of Henry and Theresa visiting England but hadn't followed through, and in fact the younger man wasn't quite sure where the relationship stood now. Henry recognized that Peter in retirement was a reluctant mentor, having seen just about every kind of crime — and too much blood — over almost five decades of police work. Henry could understand the need to push all that violence into the past, but he always felt, even at that great distance, that his British friend was restless in retirement. Peter claimed that he was busy working on his father's personal papers down in his renovated air raid shelter — Theresa was amused by this image — but Henry dared to wonder out loud, "Why isn't Peter working on his own memoirs?" More, he sensed that Peter Cammon still had something to contribute, something to prove as a police detective. Just as Henry Pastern did.

"Hi Peter! Hope UR keeping well. How are the memoirs? Just to let you know, I have latched on to a good case. More to follow. Cheers." Henry pressed *send* but was a bit unsure whether the message had connected.

At the cottage in Leicestershire, where it was the middle of the night, Peter Cammon read the email and snapped off an unintentionally formal reply: "Keep me informed. Peter Cammon."

CHAPTER 8

Henry returned to Hollis Street with a brilliant sunset at his back, but he ignored it, never glancing in his rear-view mirror. His chat with Theresa had put him in a buoyant frame of mind, and he sensed opportunity. There were homicides and there were homicides. His murder cases thus far had been ordinary domestics or vehicular manslaughter. Now he was working in the centre ring of the Watson extravaganza. His aim tonight was to complete as many interviews as possible, including some of Phil's "odds." He would make himself the go-to expert on the Hollisites.

It was near dark when he passed through the gates. A morbid hush reigned on the dead end street; the neighbours had gone to ground. Jackson's cruiser sat in front of the grow house, a warning to the curious. The Second House remained taped up and dark. Jackson himself was likely in Number 3. A lurid homicide had cleared the street, but the ghouls and rubberneckers had yet to find their way to the perimeter.

Henry parked behind the cruiser, locked the Subaru and walked down to the home of Albert Torrent at 16. Torrent, a widower, was about seventy and dyed his hair a walnut brown, which came across orange in the setting sun. The interview was perfunctory. He had seen nothing, having slept through the night. He had never served on the street committee and only attended the annual barbecue because the "damn organizers" insisted on holding it at the Wazinskis', next door. Did the detective know that the committee had been defunct "for months"?

Henry moved rapidly on to Number 15, where Mr. and Mrs. Bross had resided from the day the street opened for business. He was Barney, she was Althea. Henry learned nothing new. The Brosses paid their street dues, but neither had ever served on the Hollis Street executive. They had seen nothing suspicious. "Be glad to continue helping," Barney Bross said, but he wasn't smiling as he said it.

Henry pondered the two-storey at Number 13, which his map identified as belonging to Ronald Devereau. He hesitated, knowing that Phil had mentioned a brief contact with Devereau.

His mobile rang and it was Phil. "Where are you, Henry?"

The front lamps along the street came on, all except the bulb in front of the Second House. Hollis Street was marginally more attractive at dusk.

"Standing alone in the middle of a deserted street. Did my last interview of the evens. No confessions," he joked.

"I finished Starr, Henneker, and Devereau. I hoped Starr might have seen something, living next door to the action, but wouldn't you know, he took a sleeping pill that night. With my mastery of interview technique, I established that he took two pills."

Henry's spirits sank. He had hoped to finish the witness list and control the summary report. But his optimism, and his sense of camaraderie, rose again as Phil said, "I'll feed you my notes and you can write 'em up. Follow up, too. I've got Boog to take care of. Where's Jackson?"

"Down at the Watson place. I'll check on him. What's new?"

"You know that the last couple to live in the death house were both dance instructors? Obviously not Mormons."

Henry ignored the feeble humour. "Any thoughts at this point, Phil?"

For all his joking, Phil was in a downcast mood. "It's shaping up to be a gang hit. Tom Watson will be found dead, I predict. Then the battle with DeKlerk will start in earnest. He'll maintain that this is all drugs all the time. I'll argue a double homicide makes it mine. Well, let's hope for bodies."

Phil hung up but called back a few seconds later. "Sorry, Henry. I should have said 'ours,' not 'mine.'" He didn't wait for Henry to acknowledge his apology. "And Henry, if you see the FLIR wagon go by, text me."

Henry prepared to walk back up the sidewalk to find Officer Jackson, but as he turned, he caught sight of a figure at the bottom of the cul-de-sac, in front of Number 11. It was a man, lean and tall but otherwise obscured by shadows. It seemed to Henry that he had positioned himself midway between the pools of light from the lampposts so as to conceal his face. Henry approached. The figure remained stock-still, left hand in his pocket.

"Good evening. I'm Detective Pastern."

"Investigating the killing?" The voice was gravelly, and Henry judged the man had a cold or other throat infection, perhaps from smoking.

"Yes. Are you Mr. Devereau?" Henry guessed.

"Yup."

"So my colleague, Detective Mohlman, spoke with you earlier?"

"He did." The man had yet to move. There was no hostility in his posture, but his voice was a different story, projecting, in only a few clipped words, contempt and dismissal.

The point had come for Henry to run down his list of generic police questions, but he hesitated.

Devereau said in a flat tone, "What qualifies you to investigate this street?"

"Pardon me?"

"No, I don't mean the West Valley Police lack authority to be here.

But do you know this community personally, officer?" Devereau spoke in a monotone. He seemed indifferent to any response Henry might give.

But Henry didn't bother to answer this patronizing question, merely allowed a silence to take over. He had enjoyed having the whole street to himself, and in his territorial mood, he wanted Devereau to know that the Homicide Squad ran the show. He was already tired of the residents. Wooski had said that Devereau might be Mormon but the man betrayed no sign of it. Henry observed the strange fellow as best he could. Devereau could claim a handsome face, a cowboy's face, weathered and tempered by outdoor work. So why was he living in suburbia?

"Do you like living on the street?"

"Sure."

"I have to move on, Mr. Devereau."

"Okay."

Henry took a step towards the stone-gated entrance, but turned. "Sir, did you see any unusual activity in the days leading up to last night?"

"No, Detective Pastern, like everyone else, I wasn't aware."

No smile, no inflection. The man hadn't moved an inch.

He isn't aware. Henry almost challenged him to justify his presence on the sidewalk, but he knew what Devereau would say: he was a Hollis Street resident merely taking the air on a summer evening. *It's all part of the street's collective indifference,* thought Henry.

Henry expected to find Jackson in his patrol car or else in the Watson home but as he approached, he spotted a silhouette in the Second House. Henry dodged under the yellow tape and entered, only to be pushed back by the bitter residual smell of blood and bodily fluids. Young Jackson came out of the kitchen. He wore pale blue rubber gloves.

"Detective, you see the lamp out front?"

"Somebody smashed the bulb. Yeah, I saw it. All the other lawn lamps are working."

"Concealed the hit team's arrival and flight, I'm thinking."

Henry came farther inside. The room offered no place to sit down, and the reek of blood only got worse. Though the technicians had mopped up the liquid, the stain in the centre of the living room would never come out of the wood floor. The house now felt haunted.

There didn't seem to be a reason for Jackson to be in here. "What are you up to?" Henry said.

"Hoping to figure out why and how the killers slaughtered Gabriella Watson next door, then brought her over here. Did they wrap her in plastic? Where's the plastic?"

The stripped-out house was loathsome and dispiriting, and Henry saw no point in staying inside. The Utah State Crime Lab would complete the preliminary DNA work within twenty-four hours, but the volume of blood made it obvious: two people had bled out in this room. Henry would have preferred that Jackson leave the crime scene alone.

But the patrolman wouldn't be denied. "The slicer was right-handed. Tom Watson is right-handed."

"How'd you know that?" Henry said.

Jackson moved around the room to the far side of the bloodstain. "Detective Mohlman called a few minutes ago to update me."

But he didn't bother to brief me with that detail twenty minutes ago. Was this a snub, or was Mohlman simply trying to lock in Jackson's loyalty by confiding in him?

"What else did Detective Mohlman tell you?"

"The taxes and power on this place are being paid by a finance company in Denver."

"Denver?"

"According to Mohlman, no one in the Denver office seemed aware of the condition of the house or what it was being used for."

Henry looked at the barren walls. "Jackson . . ."

The young cop noticed Henry's change in tone.

"Yes, sir?"

"Why kill anybody? Why not do the opposite? Rat on the Watsons with a phone call. Now the gang has multiple police forces coming down on them."

"For that matter, why not just torch this house to make your point? Skip the executions."

Henry nodded. "The ledger doesn't balance, as my wife would say."

Jackson had heard about Theresa's illness. He skipped a respectful beat, then retrieved a sheet of paper from his breast pocket. "Oh, Detective, the techies left an inventory of the pipe bomb parts."

Henry scanned the typed list:

Low-grade improvised explosive device/pipe bomb

Custom pine box, 12 by 16, machine buffed, screw holes
    at corners, screws missing

2 12-inch wrought steel pipes, threaded both ends, with
    tight-fitting caps

C4 or equivalent explosive compound (to be verified)

Military-style detonator, detonation cord

Red electrical wiring, some with alligator clips, some with
    soldered ends

Two small plastic/polymer custom carved pieces belonging
    to detonator trigger

Inner plastic lining (soft)

Soft gel pad suffused with chlorate

Cheap digital clock/timer

Henry was carried back to his trainee classroom at Quantico. This bomb was an amateur's work, inexpensive and limited in its ambition. The parts could be bought at a hardware store, while the detonator was an easily obtained mail-order item. With a second read-through, Henry decided that the bomber would have been lucky to set the house afire with this device. The room had been empty of flammables, and he had used no accelerant. The forensics team would try to trace the serial numbers on the detonator and the timer, but everything about the bomb was generic, almost primitive. The timer was simple, yet the bomber had fouled that up, too. He should have been able to set the clock at his leisure after he was done killing, yet he had botched it.

It felt late. It was time to desert this Caligari house before it closed in on them. "Let's go, Jackson, or our dry cleaning tab'll be huge," Henry said.

Henry's cell phone chimed. Jackson retreated to his cruiser while Henry took the call in the vestibule.

"Henry?" Theresa's voice was thick.

"Are you alright?"

"I had a premonition." Theresa's meds delivered exotic nightmares, but never had she called him at work. "Are you safe?" she said.

"Safe? Why wouldn't I be?"

"Where are you?"

"In the grow house."

"See? You're in a danger zone."

"The bad guys are long gone. I'm almost ready to come home. Are *you* safe, dear?"

"Sure." He sensed her calming down. "What is it your English friend says, Henry, 'safe as houses'? I dreamed about him."

"Peter Cammon? You really are having weird dreams . . ."

But then a figure of the aging British detective, as clear as the Utah night, hologrammed before him. Oh so suddenly, he wished that Peter was by his side. *Why did I never take up the firm invitation from his wife, Joan, to visit England?*

"Yes, Henry. He and I were on a viewing stand next to Hollis Street when a flood swept through those stone gates. It gained speed and crushed the houses all in sequence, drowning the neighbours and turning over cars."

"What happened when it reached the bottom of the cul-de-sac?"

"I don't know. I woke up."

"Funny you should mention Peter. I sent him a text earlier . . . I'll be home in an hour."

"Are you safe?" Theresa repeated. She was calm now.

"Yeah, of course."

Henry hung up and prepared to abandon the fetid house at Number 5 Hollis. A pair of bright headlights swept the vestibule, but before he could get outside, the vehicle was past and on its way to the bulb of the cul-de-sac. Jackson was waiting by his car. The square truck turned at the end of the street and slowly rolled back towards them. Steel rods poking up from the roof rotated to face the houses along the "even" side of Hollis as the FLIR wagon charted the neighbourhood. The truck halted before Number 8 and the antennae swept the façade; the scan was repeated before the empty house at Number 6.

"How subtle is that?" Jackson sneered. "If the neighbours weren't on the alert before, they are now."

Henry trotted down the sidewalk and crossed the street. He held forth his ID as he went. There was no point in getting a pistol pointed in his face. The driver motioned for him to come around to his side. Lord knew how many technicians were in the dark back of the cube.

"Valley Homicide," Henry said.

The driver nodded. "Quiet night." He wore navy overalls. Henry wondered if he occasionally posed as a cable repairman. "Just the way we like it for an uncontaminated scan." Somehow it was important to the driver that he project cool as he piloted what resembled a Brink's truck bred with a robot.

"Just doing these two houses?"

"Yeah, well, whatever," the driver said. "We'll make one more pass. These two *are* vacant, right?"

"Yes. Did you guys already get any readings for 6 and 8 from Utah Power?"

"Yup. No excessive consumption at either place. That's why this is a waste of time. Don't tell DeKlerk I said that." He pulled away and turned around at the mouth of the street, and as he made his second pass he waved to Henry, who was already double-thumbing a text to Mohlman.

The night was quiet, as the cynical FLIR tech had said. It was also hot and dry, with no tsunamis in sight.

CHAPTER 9

Three days later, a fisherman found Tom Watson snagged in a tree in the Lower Provo River, up in the Wasatch Range. By then, West Valley Police knew he was dead; the lab people had verified that nine tenths of the blood soaking the living room floor at Number 5 Hollis was his.

"We're lucky he's got his head," Phil Mohlman said when he summoned Henry over the phone.

It took Henry ninety minutes to drive to the right spot along the river. As a child, he had fished the Provo with his father, and he knew that man-made obstructions segmented the watercourse into three distinct stages. The third portion, the Deer Creek Reservoir, formed the Lower Provo, and farther along, it emptied into Utah Lake. Along this section, where the body had been found, the shore alternated between the steep walls of Provo Canyon and the flatter, accessible stretches favoured by fly fishermen.

Police and rescue vehicles cluttered the dirt road access to the river, and Henry had to walk the last hundred yards. Two state police cars, an ambulance, and Phil Mohlman's plain Buick blocked his view of the river until, approaching around the vehicles, he caught sight of both the water and the corpse. In the shallows, mostly out of the river, bloodless, perched Tom Watson in the branches of a drifting tree, stranded like a scarecrow on a barbed wire fence. Henry saw that the killer hadn't dumped the body here; it had to have floated from upstream.

Phil turned to greet him, a self-satisfied smile on his face because he knew that Boog DeKlerk had no claim over this homicide scene. Of course, the Staties, as Phil called them, represented a fresh jurisdictional threat, and accordingly Phil was working the cluster of troopers on the riverbank. Henry was surprised to see them, after a lot of nodding, crowd into their two cruisers and leave. He saw why. Phil turned to caucus with a familiar figure in blue coveralls and hip waders, a senior techie named Collins, with whom West Valley Homicide often worked. A pathologist, he was a Bostonian, like Mohlman, and revered for his expertise and his willingness to get his hands dirty in the field. More important, Collins was fair and wouldn't automatically pre-empt control of the investigation to the benefit of the state police. For now, the troopers were content to let Collins secure and explore the crime scene.

He began to stretch out police tape along the shore, and Henry moved in to help.

Collins's rescue team began to dislodge Watson from the tree, and the pathologist himself waded out to join them. He trod carefully so as to minimize footprints in the mucky pools between the rocks. The ambulance waited up the bank, its roof bulb turning.

Henry noticed that Watson's truck was not among the parked vehicles.

"Goddamn crucifixion," Mohlman said cheerfully as Henry joined him. Tom Watson's arms were spread, and a bullet, maybe two, had opened his breastbone. A small branch had penetrated his left side. Not really a crucifixion, was Henry's thought; maybe St. Anthony's agony.

"No sign of the truck?" Henry said.

"We'll find it. The fisherman found the corpse three hours ago."

"He wasn't dumped here," Henry opined. Their talk was even-toned and only mildly speculative. They were content, this particular morning on the damp riverbank. They contemplated the tree, which now entangled a struggling Collins.

"Surprised it took so long to discover the body," Phil stated. "This part of the river is lousy with fishermen."

Henry added, "Yeah, the killer took a big chance of being seen by some super-keen angler out on the river before dawn, vying for the best spot."

"They catch brown trout here, so I'm informed," Phil said. Fly-fishing was an alien and effete hobby, not for urban East Coasters.

"I used to fish here myself. Brown, rainbow, and cutthroat trout." Henry didn't reveal to his partner that the last time he had fished these parts was the summer before embarking on his two-year Mission with the Church of Jesus Christ of Latter-day Saints. He hadn't gone out on the river since.

Collins and his team had the body now and were pulling it out of the shallows.

Phil grew tired of pretending he was interested in fishing. "So where the hell are we, Henry?"

"Well inside the Wasatch Range. Between Deer Creek Dam and the Olmstead Diversion."

Phil waited, deferring to Henry, the native son, as he worked through the logic of the river and the mountain range. Phil prompted: "Less than ninety minutes from town, you'd say, Henry?"

"Yeah. That was the appeal, quick disposal. But he took a huge risk. There's a surprising amount of private waterfront land along the Lower Provo, and everybody has a gun in these parts."

It had started to rain lightly. Collins and the attendants man-handled Tom Watson onto the pebbly shore. They took their time carrying him to the ambulance. The irritant wasn't the river bottom or the rain, but rather the clouds of midges that had settled in with the moist air. Everyone gathered around the back of the ambulance and an attendant uncovered Watson. The first feature that struck Henry was the whiteness of the body. The bullets had penetrated the heart, likely nicked the lungs too, but the gusher had been caused by a prior slashing of a stomach artery. It was evident that Watson's executioner had attacked in a frenzy with gun and knife. The head showed bruises, but these didn't amount to major trauma. The fish had left the eyes intact.

The ambulance departed, leaving Collins and the two detectives standing in the rain. The body would be taken directly to the morgue, but Collins was staying behind to comb the shallows for any bits of evidence that might have fallen from Tom Watson's body. Since he was the only one with rubber boots, Mohlman and Pastern could only offer solidarity by waiting on the shore. They took refuge in Phil's sedan.

"Think we'll find the spot where they dumped him in?" said Phil.

"We have to search," Henry sighed, "but it's the truck we want."

"If the killers abandoned it, how did they get back to town?" Henry noticed that Phil referred to killers plural, while he had fallen into using the singular.

Henry turned to his partner. Both men wanted to be in a warm coffee shop somewhere. "Let's back up. It's likely the killer — killers — used the truck to get back to the highway, yet I still think it's important to try to find the dumping site. The selection wasn't as easy as it might seem. This area is getting crowded. Fisherman and tourists, but also new residents. Park City is just a few miles off. Why trek up here at all?"

Politics had just invaded their calculations. In winter, when visitors came to the Wasatch Front for the Sundance Film Festival and for the skiing, the population of Park City grew several-fold, and Utah promotional brochures switched from desert to snow scenes. Tourism was huge for the state, and no one wanted to see lurid headlines like "Sundance Murder!"

Henry continued. "There's more to think about. The mountains around here are full of old silver mines. A much better place to make a body disappear. Why didn't the killers use them?"

"Because they weren't familiar with the mountains?"

"Maybe, but it bothers me that they took the risk of running into early risers, including security patrols coming to and from the Canyons Resort and other rich housing developments. And there are game wardens out there watching for hunters jacklighting deer."

"Maybe they just didn't care. They would have been heavily armed. Maybe they're simply chancers, damn the hazard."

Henry nodded. "I'm beginning to think maybe so. Guys high on their own product aren't always worried about resistance or collateral damage."

They sat there in silence for five more minutes, watching the clouds of insects on the river. Collins finished his investigation and started packing up. The bands of yellow tape were already drooping. Emerging blue patches in the morning sky encouraged them all to move out and head for Salt Lake City. Phil started his engine and Henry got out the passenger side.

"There's another possibility," Phil said through the window. "Maybe they panicked."

They found the truck twenty minutes later, after taking the paved mountain highway out from the Provo River. Henry's instinct that they might pick up a clue to the killers' route was nothing more than a wild hope, but there it was, ten miles down the highway. Henry saw it first and honked, and put on his left turn signal. The truck, labelled "Salaberry Electric — Install and Repair," squatted half-hidden at the rear of a grim, low-slung restaurant and bait joint set back from the road on a crumbling asphalt parking lot. They stopped near the entry so as not to disturb any tire tracks. A red CLOSED sign had been slotted in the front window of the building.

They got out and scanned the parking pad. "You can see from the mud that fishermen and hunters use this place to turn around," Phil said.

Henry added, "They congregate here, it's a staging point. But not deer hunters. It's not the season for large game."

His partner fumbled in his coat pocket for his mobile and searched out a number. Henry heard the faint ringing; Collins answered on the third chime. Phil ran through their coordinates and demanded that Collins join them.

Henry walked over to the façade of the shabby roadhouse. Cobwebs had formed on the CLOSED sign. He turned and looked up and down the highway. Hydro wires ran along their side of the road, and an offshoot line stretched from a main pole to the frame building. Anyone driving by might well assume the truck was there to repair the feed.

Collins arrived ten minutes later and the three investigators walked Indian file to the truck. They took a few minutes to tiptoe around it, looking for obvious evidence. Phil picked up a flattened cigarette butt, though he had no reason to conclude that any of the killers had smoked it. Collins shimmed open the driver-side door.

There was no blood to be seen on either the driver's seat or the shotgun side. But there was blood to smell. And marijuana.

Collins got behind the wheel and hit the hatch release, while Phil and Henry walked around to the rear and lifted the door. Tom Watson's professional gear, tool belts, cables, voltage meters, and spools of wire had been repainted in red. The tech team had reported that eighty percent of Watson's blood had drained onto the grow house floor, but the killers must have quickly moved him into the vehicle, where the rest of his fluids drained away. Although the odour of weed was sharp, Henry found no plants; he looked closer and spied seeds and desiccated stems among the blood and equipment. It was a horror chamber on wheels.

The detectives contented themselves with a cursory examination of the vehicle, while Collins called for a full forensics unit. Soon there would be two red cube trucks parked on the rotting asphalt lot. Phil opened the glove box and removed the papers but found only the registration documents, a few customer invoices, and a pencil flashlight.

Anxious as they were to tear apart the truck, they had no choice but to wait for Collins's experts. Once again, they retreated to Phil's car, sitting in the front like parents waiting at the schoolyard. Phil asked the question of the moment: "What were the killers thinking when they left the body by the river and then left the truck back here?"

Henry turned to him. "The killers didn't mind the stiff and the vehicle being found, but not too quickly. They figured to buy a delay of one or two days, and they succeeded."

Phil looked at Henry with respect. "You got it right, I think . . . At least we know now there were two or more perps."

"How so?" Henry said.

"Somebody must've picked up the driver here when he discarded the truck."

"Yeah, can't be any other way," Henry conceded.

Phil got out and peered again into the back of the truck. "Well, partner, now I understand why they didn't take away the two bags of weed. They didn't have room for them in the back of the truck."

"I dunno," Henry said. "They might have stuffed them in."

Phil grimaced. "Not with that mess all over the trunk. Can't get anyone to buy two bloodstained trash bags of grass, no matter how good the quality."

"I keep coming back to the killers' strategy. How can they not have realized the likelihood of being observed? What's the basic mindset of a fisherman, Phil?"

"Mind-numbing boredom?"

"Right! You're out there before dawn, nothing to do. Think there might be bears. You consider trying a few casts in the dark to fight off the tedium, even knowing that's a good way to break your leg. You're bound to be on the alert for any interruption. Nothing like headlights on a truck to raise your trigger-happy paranoia . . ."

"Hey, didn't Robert Redford do a movie about fishing?"

"*A River Runs Through It.*"

"Liked fishing that much, huh? So he makes the movie, decides to set up a film festival down the road."

"No. Sundance predates the movie. He loved the book. I don't think Redford loves fishing particularly."

"Too busy being a movie star."

"And director, producer, and festival founder." Henry and Theresa had attended Sundance the previous winter.

"Just looking for connections, Henry. They filmed it on that river back there."

"No, they didn't. The book is set in Montana, and they filmed it in Montana. A few scenes in Wyoming, I understand."

Phil turned fretful as the rain started again. "Henry?"

"Yes?"

"Did you see that stomach wound?"

"Mm."

"One drive to the guts. I bet the blade went right through our Mr. Watson."

"So?"

"Consider this theory, Henry. The executioners — that's what they are — stabbed Gabriella Watson. That was premeditated and organized. Cut her head off, waited for the husband to come home. They decided to leave the wife behind, so it didn't matter what they did to her, but the husband had to be loaded in the back of the truck, transported into the hills, carried to the edge of the river, and tipped into the water. Why gut Tom Watson in his living room if you know he'll be bleeding out in the truck?"

"You making a point?" Henry prompted drily.

"I'm not sure. The first execution might have been controlled, however nasty. The second stabbing wasn't. The knife man panicked. I'm also betting he was shot after being stabbed to make look like an execution."

Before Henry could comment, a state police vehicle, lights flashing, pulled into the roadhouse parking lot. One of the troopers from the river got out and waved Phil over for a chat. A minute later, a red cube truck arrived, followed by another cruiser. Even the DEA showed up. Henry and Phil spent the next two hours arguing jurisdiction in the rain while Collins's people did their work. They never left the parking lot, except to pee in the woods behind the restaurant.

By afternoon, they were in such a jumpy state that they were sure Boog DeKlerk had sicced the feds and the Staties on them; if he couldn't have the case, Homicide couldn't either.

Phil placed a call to update Chief Grady. Every police agency and media outlet in Utah would soon latch on to the significance of their discovery. The double stabbing and the attempt to dispose of a body in the fishing grounds of the Wasatch made Hollis Street a major case, potentially bigger than Susan Powell.

CHAPTER 10

That night at dinner, Henry wove the fulsome saga of his misty day in the Wasatch. He knew that he was revealing too much but he convinced himself that Theresa, a tax accountant, understood discretion. In truth, Henry had begun to rely on her common sense commentary on the investigation. The fact that the Hollis Street puzzle seemed to revive her only encouraged his disclosures.

Theresa nodded at everything he said, until he reached Phil Mohlman's theory.

"*Panic?* Henry, don't you see? Nobody panicked. Psychopaths don't panic."

By now they had moved from the dining room to the patio, which faced west onto the raw and seemingly infinite desert. They often sat there until nightfall, and they had become connoisseurs of sunsets. The desert had grown into Shangri-La for Theresa. With the move to Coppermount, they had uncapped a wellspring that comforted her each day. Now, in their tranquil refuge, it did not seem at all odd to Henry to talk about the Hollis murders.

Without telling his wife, Henry had consulted her physician in

Alexandria. "I have never been to Utah in my life," the white-haired diagnostician declared as he stared at a climate chart for the Beehive State, "but be careful where you choose to live. The Goldilocks principle applies. Nothing extreme. High mountains in the . . ."

"Wasatch."

"That altitude may be too dry, leave her gasping for air. But the desert can be too much, too. Moderation, Henry. I note something else. The pollution in Salt Lake City has become very bad, according to National Institutes of Health numbers. I guess climate change is operative everywhere."

The respirologist's jumbled advice actually pleased Henry, for it meant that Henry had to make the big decision, and he resolved to impress his wife with his determination. He glanced out the window of the doctor's office at the concrete and glass wasteland of Alexandria. Yes, Utah was what his wife needed.

Not that their firm decision made the next steps easy. Both of Theresa's parents recoiled, in their own solipsistic way. Her father was heartbroken: to move east, he felt, should mean never moving back west. Theresa's mother's decline complicated their move even more. For Ruth, Theresa's announcement that she was coming home should have been a triumph over Mitch. But a month later, a stroke robbed her of victory, rendering her near-catatonic. Mitch, hoping to win back some favour from Theresa, set up an account to cover the costs of the nursing home. "The guilt keeps piling on me, doesn't it?" Mitch said. Henry, swamped himself by all the affliction swirling around him, in his morbid moments wondered if his mother-in-law's flash of triumph had triggered her stroke. But all in all, he could cope with in-laws. What chilled him was the possibility that his wife was going home to die.

They pursued the standard home-hunting ritual of young couples, looking at everything in the Salt Lake market in order to figure out what they wanted. Theresa was shrewd about real estate, in a minute sizing up the potential of every kind of house — new and old homes, traditional and adventurous designs, dull neighbourhoods versus trendy communities. She took ten seconds to reject Hollis Street. In hindsight, it seemed inevitable that they would embrace the desert. Still, she surprised Henry by her final choice. They drove west from Salt Lake City one afternoon, not intending to locate that far out, and she instantly fell in love with Coppermount Drive, even though it displayed mostly vacant lots and no human residents. Coppermount, Henry observed, was a last-chance-to-gas-up outpost in the desert, except without the gas pumps. It had been started in the boom era but had stalled with the recession, like so many other housing projects in America.

"That's it!" she had declared.

"I didn't know that 'potential' meant 'not finished,'" he said.

"Look at the view from the back patio," she argued.

"You mean the patio with no railing and no steps that trails off into infinity?"

"So you have to jump into the desert. Consider it some kind of metaphor for our new adventures."

"What are we buying into? The builder is likely bankrupt."

Theresa brightened at the rumble of a front-end loader. "Henry, there's a tractor rolling down that street over there. Someone's working." The machine approached the limit of civilization at the end of Coppermount and turned out of sight behind the last, partly built house. Henry held back from remarking that it might be fleeing the neighbourhood.

The incompleteness of the project held no terrors for Theresa. The agent understood that she had a sale and permitted Henry and Theresa to spend a night in the house with sleeping bags and takeout dinner. Theresa yearned to see the sunset. Later, Henry concluded that what clinched the deal for Theresa — that night they seemed to be alone on the windswept street — was the spectral sight that emerged on the western horizon. As the setting sun burned deep red and prepared to flare out, a figure in a black suit strode out of the desert towards them. He paused two hundred yards away and, almost deferentially, moved laterally away to the north. Theresa, perhaps hyper-alert for omens, smiled at the stranger. Even with the blinding sun, Henry knew a Mormon when he saw one.

The next morning, Thomas Abraham Tynan, black suit, string tie, grinning like a salesman, knocked on the front door and introduced himself. "I'm building on the last property down the slope. It's a folly, but it's my folly."

Tynan became their first friend in their new life.

"What *panic*? I don't see that the killers panicked," Theresa reiterated. She finished her allowance of wine for the evening and twirled her glass as she waited for him to challenge her.

Henry took his time responding. He disagreed with his wife and bought into Phil Mohlman's theory. The whole killing process had been cumbersome and largely improvised.

"So you think they had it all planned and under control?"

"No, not all the details," she said, "but the killers always planned to kill both the Watsons. They were decisive on that point. And they were sending a message, like you agreed."

"Right."

"And that doesn't mean they were very efficient or neat about it."

"So what are you saying?"

Theresa stared, as she often did, into the desert horizon. "Look at it this way. The killers didn't care about the risk."

"Oh, really?"

"I take that back. Put it another way: they were willing to take their time. Time to sever a head, remove a body, plant a bomb, drive up to the Wasatch, and transport the victim to the edge of a cliff."

Henry tried to sound neutral. "All calculated to send a message?"

"Yes."

Henry smiled. A product of the evolving roles in their marriage as they began a new life on the "frontier" (his word) was Henry's growing awareness of his own increased affection for her. Theresa needed him more than ever, and that was good for his ego. At the same time, his debriefings on the Hollis file had brought out a shrewdness in her that he could only envy and indulge.

"Henry, two contrary things can coexist. That's why they invented accountants. You think they panicked, because all you see are the mistakes they made. Assume for a minute the killers didn't panic, even if they didn't necessarily act in their own best interests. The problem I have is this: the slaughter of the wife and then the husband might amount to an elaborate plan to send a message to rogue drug traders, but wasn't it all incredibly . . . exhausting?"

"Mexican police recently found several dozen heads by the highway near Monterrey. *That* would be exhausting."

"Don't be facetious. Forget about planned-versus-impulsive. How did the killers on Hollis Street sustain their bloodlust?"

"Desperation?" Henry said.

"Nope. It was something else."

"So, my love, what sustained them in their demented work?"

Theresa walked out to the edge of the desert and turned to her policeman husband.

"Deep anger."

CHAPTER 11

For three weeks, despite a maximum hand-in-glove effort by Mohlman and Pastern, they got no closer to the killers. The detectives knew what was at stake, and the importance of speed. Murders weren't frequent in West Valley, and double homicides were unthinkable. The execution of the Watsons would stick in the headlines until resolved, and the echo of Susan Powell upbraided them every day.

Chief Grady's method of pressuring the Homicide Squad was to convene two-hour meetings every other day and harangue the detectives. "I need a storyline for the media," he stammered. "Is it terrorism? Drug lords? A disgruntled brother-in-law?"

Grady understood the need for a focused media line, and "drugs" remained the simplest theme. As the days passed, Phil and Henry felt control shifting more and more towards the Narcotics Squad. "We will keep the big-city scourge of illicit drugs back from our peaceful community," Chief Grady vowed at one press conference, with Boog DeKlerk, rather than Phil Mohlman, standing beside him.

DeKlerk faced his own challenge from the relentless insinuations of the Drug Enforcement Administration, the Bureau of Alcohol, Tobacco, Firearms and Explosives, and the FBI. It was too big a drug case for West Valley, they argued. Their subtext was that federal agencies could better handle its cross-jurisdictional dimensions, despite no evidence so far that the killers came from outside Utah.

The onslaught by the feds temporarily muted the rivalry between the West Valley Drug and Homicide Units.

"It's like a game of three-dimensional chess," Boog declared at the Rose one afternoon.

"Three-dimensional checkers," Phil answered. "Don't let's flatter ourselves."

Henry assembled a binder of profiles of every Hollis Street resident, including the previous owners of vacant units 6 and 8. For each owner, he charted his or her location at the time of Gabriella's murder and the estimated moment of Tom Watson's death and removal. Phil and Henry, with support from Jackson, followed up with the locals to lock in the details. They put up an impressive collage of the street layout in one of the interrogation rooms at West Valley headquarters, using a blueprint of the lots as a backdrop, and when that space was needed by other detectives, Henry reinstalled it in his cubicle.

The forensics labs offered few fresh leads. The bodies had given up most of their blood on the killing floors, and despite testing of samples throughout the two houses, no new DNA strings were identified.

Hollis Street itself remained in sad limbo. Henry tried to avoid the strip, since it depressed him. When he had to drop by, to follow up on a point with Jerry Proffet or take additional pictures, he encountered a creepy resistance. No one offered him lemonade or gossip, and expressions of pity for the Watsons were perfunctory. The denizens were waiting for the two suburban properties to be cleared of yellow tape and window blacking, so that the homeowners could sink back into complacency. Until then, Number 3 and Number 5 would haunt them, almost as much as they plagued Henry and Phil.

Midway into the third week, a crew came in to fumigate and scrub the blood- and drug-permeated homes. A crowd of rubberneckers gathered, resulting in West Valley Police blocking off the street entrance at the stone portals for the afternoon and checkpointing residents in and out through trestle barriers. Phil and Jackson came in to help. When Jerry Proffet and the Wazinskis bitched, Phil commented, "Well, you always wanted a gated community."

The Homicide detectives began to get along better with DeKlerk and his people, in part because there was so much legwork to be done. Drug-related inquiries broadened to nearby states, while national databases were scanned, including records of drug-financed domestic terrorism incidents. All the while, Boog and Phil put on a unified front against suggestions by the feds that the DEA should take over the case.

The lack of results only increased everyone's yearning for a breakthrough. Phil summed up their frustrations over lunch one day at the Rose. Sitting in the regular booth, he referred to a page of notes he had made. "Tom Watson either sold the bulk of his product to a single dealer somewhere in the state, or he spent his nights wholesaling small batches to scads of petty street vendors in Salt Lake City and Provo. It's unlikely that he ventured as far as Nevada in one direction or Colorado in the other, journeys that would have burned up his profit in gas expenses. Odds are he handed off the whole monthly output to a single middleman. Not likely he retailed the marijuana on street corners himself."

Boog DeKlerk was in attendance at the Rose that day but merely nodded noncommittally, causing Henry to wonder if Boog was concealing something about Tom Watson's business.

The following week, DeKlerk turned up a dope dealer in Sandy City, only a few miles from Hollis Street, who had been a seller of Tom Watson's product, and he was held in an interrogation room in the West Valley precinct for a full day. The promising lead soon hit a wall; the man knew nothing about Watson's broader links to drug networks.

The Utah Department of Public Safety welcomed calls (anonymous or not) from the public on its confidential drug tip line. Nothing useful came in from the citizens of Utah.

One night, a cool evening in the third week, a day after the cleanup crew had signed off, Henry drove to Hollis Street and parked by the curb between 3 and 5. He had reached a low point, no longer believing that the case was a career-maker. The residents had outlasted the cops. But he would plug away for a while longer, cobbling together help from Theresa, Phil, and anyone else who offered. He sat there in complete silence, not even crickets to be heard. The sweet odor of cannabis lingered in the dry Utah air.

The breakthrough came in the fourth week, from a source that no one, but no one, in the world of Utah justice could have predicted, and led to one of the most reverberant ploys in the annals of the police community.

It began one afternoon at the Rose, where Boog DeKlerk was holding court in the usual booth. Although Chief Grady still refused to transfer the Watson case to Narcotics, he had appointed Boog to be West Valley's delegate to a multi-department anti-drug committee that included every imaginable federal agency. Boog had just arrived from an all-morning session of the group.

"No one on this committee is naive about the drug trade," he affirmed, and from beneath his placemat slipped out a twelve-by-twelve-inch plastic-sealed map of the western states. He stabbed a fat finger wildly at the grid. "Six states we gotta consider." To Henry, it seemed that Boog was launching one more attempt to browbeat Homicide. Henry rolled his eyes. "Bear with me, Pastern. You can't understand the drug trade in West Valley without knowing the ins and outs of the drug flow across Utah. The big organized operations are all run by the Mexicans."

Henry examined the map. Two large states, Arizona and New Mexico, squatted between Utah and the Mexican line; add California if you wanted an additional buffer. Most of Utah's population lived in the northern third of the state, creating more insulation. This plastic map didn't change the fact that West Valley lay a great distance from the international border.

Boog moved his index finger to and fro. "Don't be deceived, my Homicide friends. All that land between us and the border is hardly a hindrance to smugglers and dealers when Interstate 15 provides a straight shot from Tijuana to Salt Lake and back. The Mexican gangs are masterful at running the trade in cocaine, heroin, and meth-amphetamines. Marijuana is a messier business, with regional/local variations in price and quality, and lots of small entrepreneurs, but it's profitable. The gangs assert control over the distribution networks, less so over the grow ops themselves."

Henry wondered where this lecture could possibly be headed. This wasn't news and, had the DEA been at the table, they would have recoiled and told Boog to get to the point.

"The Mexicans don't like publicity," Phil prompted, picking at a zucchini stick. Henry had the sudden feeling that his partner had been forewarned by Boog.

Something is coming.

Boog DeKlerk glowered at Henry. "We share a problem with the Watson murders. We all want West Valley to hold on to this investigation — and I've got a strategy. College boy, have you ever heard of Avelino González?"

Henry frowned. The name rang a distant bell but he couldn't place it.

"Tell us," Phil said.

DeKlerk's preamble and Phil's encouragement sounded rehearsed. *Phil knows the punch line.* Boog proceeded. "He's a drug lord with tentacles reaching across those six states. For the last three weeks, every U.S. police force with an interdiction mandate has been pressuring his distribution networks in all these localities, scooping up grow ops, cashing in informants to take down meth labs, big and small, and hassling small-timers at the interface point with street users, dime bag by dime bag. My squad has been as active as any of the federal agencies."

So that's all? Boog wants us to know he's on the job?

The big man paused and Phil nodded for him to continue. "This morning it all paid off. González controls half the marijuana trade and all cocaine sales in Utah. He's hurting. A few hours ago, he called me."

"Did he sound worried?" Phil queried, a note of sarcasm there. Henry remembered now: the Mexican was a particularly vicious cartel figure. González, who was rumoured to cut off his rivals' heads, wouldn't be fazed by any Hollis Street blowback.

Henry noted uncertainty in DeKlerk's voice, and it wasn't caused by the Guinness. If he had a plan involving González, it was by no means a lock.

"Tell us the deal," Phil said.

"González wants to meet. One time only. The deal is, he'll tell us everything he knows about Tom Watson, and keep us informed about anything new that comes up."

Henry rushed in. If Phil wasn't going to plant a flag for Homicide, he would. "You — we — can't promise to lay off his network."

"You think I don't know that? Sure, he hopes we'll back off a bit if he helps us, but no concessions."

Henry didn't understand the transaction. What kind of a deal was this for either side? The drug lord couldn't expect police agencies to back off on enforcement or give a pass to his distribution networks while targeting his competition. González was probably warranted under the RICO statute for half the offences in the drug code. He was a murderer. DeKlerk was pitching a meet with an unequivocal bad guy.

And there was another fundamental question to be addressed.

"Is it possible that González's people took out Tom Watson?" Henry said.

Boog scowled at him. "No, it wasn't him."

Henry glared back. He inferred that González knew who committed the killings on Hollis Street, but what did the drug lord want in return? What kind of a side deal had DeKlerk engineered? It all sounded like high-risk freelancing on DeKlerk's part.

"Will Grady go along with this?"

"I talked to him an hour ago. He's copacetic, as long as we convene a meeting with the agencies and get everyone's okay. I'll set it up for the day after tomorrow."

"It will be hard to keep this a one-off," Phil said. "The feds will want to use the meeting to pressure González on interstate drug trafficking, all kinds of issues."

"Hell, they'll try and Taser him right there!" Boog said. "González is ready to talk but not to the feds. He insists on only two police reps in the room. One state, one local. We can manipulate that to our benefit. You and Pastern can come with me this week and we'll hang tough with the feds and the Staties. This is an exceptional operation, and it's gonna be *ours*."

Henry grasped why González preferred to have only one state and one local delegate at the meeting. "He hopes to sidestep the bigger trafficking issues," Henry said.

"More important, college boy, he wants to get goddamn Hollis Street off the table." DeKlerk took a deep swallow of Guinness.

"If we get our way, that means a Valley Police rep and someone from the State Bureau of Investigation," Phil said.

"Where does González want the meeting held?" Henry asked.

"Wendover," answered DeKlerk.

Henry laughed out loud.

"What'd I say?" Phil sputtered.

Wendover was a tiny place smack on the rim of Nevada. A border town. To get there, you drove straight west on Interstate 80, threading the sprawling Utah Test and Training Range, up to the Bonneville Salt Flats and the Utah–Nevada state line. Henry laughed again. If Avelino González chose to escape, he could simply hop the border into the casino hamlet of West Wendover, Nevada. Utah police would be reluctant to follow.

CHAPTER 12

The planning session was set for two days later, at the shared police facilities on Amelia Earhart Drive, where the State Bureau of Investigation and the regional wings of the FBI and the DEA were lodged. The West Valley detectives expected a full house, with reps from the ATF, the Homeland Security–linked Joint Terrorism Task Force for the area, and the Utah State Major Crimes Task Force. Everyone would be defending turf. Phil Mohlman warned Henry to watch out for the DEA man, named Rogers, and the JTTF delegate, Walter Frommer, both known to despise municipal police.

"Neither has any good claim to take over the Hollis case, but it's in the nature of the federal agencies to pre-empt us local yokels . . ." said Phil, then realized that Henry used to be an FBI special agent and fell silent.

Henry wanted the Wendover plan to work. He and Phil had stalled, and it was time for a radical move. More important, though he discussed it with no one, Henry considered whether, as a former FBI man, he might serve a conciliatory role at the table and impress his colleagues with his fastidious prep work. Over the two days, Henry toiled on a detailed study of the drug lord, Avelino González, that he might provide to Phil and Boog for the session. Most of the core information, such as González's NCIS rap sheet, was available online on secure servers, but Henry also tapped the detailed files kept by the DEA.

Henry decided not to share the full report with Theresa — she would be alarmed by the Mexican's history — but he did ask her impression of the mug shot of González taken by Mexican police.

She stared at it for a full minute. The drug lord stared back. He appeared exceedingly relaxed in the photo, given the occasion of his arrest, Henry mused. His face was lean and disciplined. If, like many a cartel leader's, his eyes were cold, Henry concluded that this was a posture of contempt he had adopted at the time of the photo; indeed, candid photographs of Señor González were rare. "He's handsome, for a mass killer," Theresa said. "Sexy . . . or is it politically incorrect to say so?"

Even armed with this profile, Henry wasn't sure that he had a complete portrait. On the surface, González was a typical drug kingpin. He was born in the northern state of Sinaloa and rose from abject poverty by joining the Mexican Army Special Forces. The arc of Avelino González's adult life could be traced by flashpoints of greed and death. The Army employed him in the U.S. border zones, where he provided security for the maquiladoras, factories run by rich entrepreneurs in favour with Mexico City politicians. As a soldier he learned skills that proved essential later, in the drug trade. He fought on the government side in Chiapas, where as an enforcer he burned settlements and executed Zapatista captives in jungle clearings. This labour demanded total loyalty to the national government, but the moment young Avelino began to listen to the weeping of women in the Chiapas villages, he was done.

Next, the Gulf Cartel recruited him to shepherd overland ship-ments of cocaine from the jungles of southern Mexico to the Pacific coast, and as he established his reliability he moved into management. It was a smooth transition, and if he had to kill competitors along the way, that was better than killing peasants under the oppressive rationalizations of the PRI government. For five years, he oversaw all the cocaine routes for the Gulf Cartel.

So far, Henry viewed this as the standard life story of an avaricious drug lord, but he remained alert to any special factors in the biography that would explain why González might take the risk of parlaying with the police. He ticked off the unusual watershed points in Avelino's peripatetic career. Twenty years ago, entrenched in the unforgiving world of Mexican drug smuggling, he achieved a leap upward in the guise of a sideways move. Tiring of his routine and the squalid jungles of Central America, he made a deferential and unprecedented approach to his masters: he asked for a transfer. The Gulf Cartel often partnered with the Sinaloa Cartel in the north, and the two operations — unlike the Zeta organization, which hated everyone — seldom clashed. González made the transfer to his home state. The rest was blood-spattered history.

Drug bosses don't mellow, and they rarely die in bed. There was nothing in the police records to show that Avelino González, passing sixty now, ever felt remorse. Over the years, he had ordered the deaths of dozens, if not hundreds, of men. He had never been arrested inside the U.S., although the DEA monitored him each time he ventured north to organize his distribution network. Henry finished the file review without feeling that he had gained much insight into the passions of Señor González. And none of the American law enforcement agencies had him down for the Watsons.

Henry called a pair of friendly sources at the Bureau in D.C. He knew that federal agencies, including the DEA, commissioned detailed psychological portraits and character studies of cartel leaders. He was soon in possession of a ten-page bio of González.

The fact that the report remained sketchy intrigued Henry in itself. Despite the best efforts of the federal agencies, the Mexican remained as unfathomable as a businessman in a Sinclair Lewis novel by way of Mario Puzo. Henry combed the study for trenchant details. González was his birth name, but he had switched Christian names six or seven times, from Juan to Pedro to Chico, and so on. Drug dealers like to invent new reps for themselves, but his were not nicknames, for the most part; no one called him "the Fox" or "the Wolf" or "the Killer of Chiapas," although the file sometimes referenced him as "the Man"; perhaps a bland moniker contrarily won him respect and fear. González reportedly had three, perhaps four brothers, but, oddly, investigators could not verify where they lived or if some of them might be dead.

He had flirted with revolutionary movements in Mexico over the decades, said the report, but his drug dealing and three early years devoted to suppressing the Zapatistas in Chiapas made him seem a less than committed revolutionary.

Henry drove to the planning meeting with Phil, while Boog DeKlerk arrived on his own. Neither Homicide detective knew how Boog planned to finesse the federal and state agencies. There were too many officials around the conference table for Henry's comfort and he saw right away that it would be hard to achieve a consensus. None of the agencies would welcome a one-off interaction with a murderous drug lord. Henry recognized only half the reps. Ugly drapes on bangled curtain rings decorated the two walls of windows, and when someone slid them noisily along their rails, shutting out the sun, Henry felt that a bad movie was about to start.

Boog repeated the strictures set by González himself, adding, "González refuses to have any feds in the room."

The federal officials all recoiled at Boog's promise. Bad ploy on Boog's part, Henry thought; instantly, the feds in their unrumpled suits were unified by indignation. The JTTF delegate, Frommer, was first to mutter his disapproval, but DeKlerk tried to ignore him. Henry noticed that Rogers, the DEA man, maintained a sanguine neutrality at the far end of the table from the West Valley contingent.

"He's restricting the negotiations because he thinks he won't have to address trafficking issues," Frommer said in a pinched voice.

Boog took a blunt, hard line. "He won't anyway. That was never our deal."

"Why did you make the deal without our go-ahead?"

"Don't give me that rhetoric, Walt," Boog said. "I'm here today to get your approval on a strategy, not to renegotiate the ground rules."

DeKlerk let the discussion range all over the map. Henry understood. If he used up enough time on the particulars, the broad concerns of the feds might dissipate, or the clock would run out. The truth was, no one wanted the vanguard position in any encounter with González, lest they be tainted as the officials who "negotiated" with the enemy. Boog had good odds of keeping the meeting under the aegis of West Valley and within González's conditions.

Frommer, a loudmouth, took a cheap shot. "Use the opportunity to arrest him. It's your choice."

"No, we have a *deal*."

"A devil's bargain, and I don't see the benefit. Makes us look bad."

"Us?" Boog flashed.

Bureaucrats in a pack tend to become tiresomely aggressive. Henry saw that the feds were focusing their smug opprobrium on the West Valley contingent, and it wasn't working.

"Has he stated he'll give us the name of the Watson killer?" said the JTTF liaison.

Boog was almost home, but there was no easy answer to the last question. To Henry's surprise, Rogers intervened. "We keep it narrow, in my view. There are no big opportunities here. We aren't willing to set off a task force blitz against the upper echelons of the drug trade because of our problems with a local murder containing a drug link. We have a small opportunity. We take the shot, see what comes out of it."

Frommer persisted. "How do we know this wasn't the first in a series of hits by the González cartel, designed to consolidate the street trade in grass?"

"Because there hasn't been a second incident," Boog answered.

It was at this point that Henry began to suspect that Boog had done some effective lobbying in advance of the meeting. The federal and state officials squirmed each time Boog spoke of yielding to the Mexican's terms, but none openly denounced the setup, with one exception — Frommer never knew when to stop. He tapped his wide knuckles on the desk. "Why not seize the chance to wring some concessions from González? His gang's active in trafficking in umpteen states. Tell him you're considering arresting him. Lay down a marker."

Henry watched as DeKlerk, Phil Mohlman, and Rogers exchanged looks. González was not a crime lord whom you threatened to his face. Henry finally figured out Rogers's gesture: he had been seconded recently to the State Bureau of Investigation, and that put him in the running for the Wendover meeting. Rogers had negotiated with DeKlerk to be the second man on the team.

"González is approaching us, so let's see what he has to say," Rogers continued in a mollifying tone. "We don't know what he has to offer. Obviously, he's feeling some pressure. Let's keep it low key, look for openings."

The objections subsided as all began to absorb the fundamental point: this was about one case. No one knew why González wanted the meet, and curiosity was justification enough.

There was a final, uncomfortable pause. Boog said, "Look, there are local, state, and federal interests to be represented. I also acknowledge the interests of the Joint Task Force, and the Narcotics Task Force down in Iron and Garfield Counties, which couldn't make it today. González insists on only two officers present, and frankly, that's probably wise from our side. Otherwise, it gets crazy in the room. This has to be kept subtle, not become a negotiation of surrender. Therefore, I suggest our contingent include Rogers, covering state and federal narcotics concerns, and Henry Pastern, who knows the immediate case. Henry has background with the FBI and as well has the local perspective."

Henry tried not to let his jaw drop onto the conference room table.

On the way home, Phil driving, Henry looked over at his partner. "Am I right that Rogers supported us because he knew he would get to be one of the two in the room with González?"

"Yup. The fix was in. But the love-in with us is temporary. Watch that Rogers doesn't turn on you out there. He wants to do the talking."

Henry stared out the window at the broad Salt Lake City avenues. He turned to Phil again. "Why didn't Boog insist on being the second rep?"

Phil made eye contact and pulled over to the curb. "Because, Henry, Rogers and the State B of I folks believe Boog DeKlerk is in Avelino González's pocket. Boog knows this."

CHAPTER 13

"Is it safe?" was Peter Cammon's first statement when Henry stopped talking.

It was late afternoon in England, but Peter had already started on his third beer. He had welcomed the interruption to his dull day and listened with amusement to Henry's long summary of the multi-agency session.

"It's not safe at all!" Henry blurted.

Peter was determined not to laugh — he knew that Henry had called for serious advice — but it was a strange thing about the telephone, Peter thought: it's hard to conceal a smile.

"What do you really want to know?" Peter said soberly.

"I want to know why González requested the visit. I want to know the risk of meeting with him without backup."

For a few seconds, Peter hesitated. He wasn't particularly adept at the fatherly aspect of mentoring young detectives but Henry's passion was infectious. Peter went out to the veranda and sat down in his favourite Adirondack chair. He took in the familiar garden and the entrance to the old air raid shelter. Jasper, his old dog, didn't rise when he came outside. Joan was off visiting their son and daughter-in-law in Leeds. Henry's call was the only interesting thing that had happened that day. Peter felt old stirrings of the game afoot.

"Henry, you aren't worried about risk. You've already decided to take it."

"So, what do I do to prepare?" Henry responded, his tone ingenuous.

Peter became all business. "Try to figure out the first question you posed. What does the drug dealer want from you?"

"To relieve the pressure on his drug operations."

Peter harrumphed. "I wonder. You need to psych out the situation better. Then maybe we'll see his motive. Is he taking a serious risk that one of those alphabet soup federal agencies will try to arrest him? You said he refuses to have any feds in the room."

"There was talk at the meeting of taking him down. The man I'm going to Wendover with is actually a DEA guy assigned to Utah state police. He's aggressive with drug lords."

"You say the rendezvous spot is in the desert, near the Nevada border?"

"I think so. We're examining the GPS coordinates González gave us."

"What's the air space like? Mountains?"

"Yeah," Henry said, "But the big thing is the Utah Test Range. Spy planes, drone testing, and such. The feds can't fly choppers through a restricted zone."

"There's your answer. González knows the desert, and better than you do. He holds the cards. I advise you to go in unarmed."

"Take our chances?" A macho tone had crept into Henry's voice. Peter understood that this was about more than Henry advancing his career. This also concerned bravery, boldness, and self-control. The personal risk was substantial and Henry craved guidance. Peter had survived violent confrontations with men as wild as this drug czar, and Henry knew it.

"Henry, you can do better than just winging it. Think about it. Why should a big-time Mexican drug lord care about Hollis

Street? Don't go into this lion's den expecting definitive results, but remember every word González says."

"I think he knows who the Hollis Street killer is."

"Maybe, and maybe he has his own issue with the killer."

The conversation wound down. Henry flagged the corruption allegations against Boog DeKlerk as something he would like to explore further, after Wendover. Peter promised to be available to consult.

"Thanks, Peter."

"Call me after," Peter said blandly.

Both men hung up in a charged mood. Peter could tell that Henry could hardly wait for his great adventure to begin.

But on the veranda in the silent evening, as Peter put down the phone and began idly to scratch Jasper's old head, a worry began to creep into his mind. Instinct instructed him that somewhere in this adventure Henry was going to run right up against something evil. He wished that he had said more to his young friend. He promised himself that he would proactively call Henry after the meeting in the desert.

CHAPTER 14

Early the next morning, in the driveway on Coppermount, Theresa hugged Henry extra-hard. He hadn't given her the details of the Wendover caper, but somehow she understood the potential danger. There was so much to say that finally she said almost nothing. In a grim echo of Peter Cammon, she whispered, "Stay safe, Henry."

Henry and Agent Rogers set out for Wendover in an unmarked black sedan, with no evident entourage. That seemed about right to Henry, to cross the moonscape desert surreptitiously to a meeting with a killer, everything rendered nameless. He was thrilled, optimistic.

They didn't exactly travel unarmed or without backup, but they wouldn't win any gun battles. Phil Mohlman had the brainwave to persuade DeKlerk and Rogers to let Officer Jackson serve as driver, leaving the two detectives free to focus on negotiating. Young Jackson was equipped with two handguns and a short-barrelled shotgun slotted in the passenger-side seat well. No one had any illusions. If it all went wrong, he might get off a shot and a phone call before the Mexicans' AR-15s and MAC-10s cut him down.

Back somewhere towards Salt Lake City, three fast cruisers waited.

Jackson wore his uniform while, coincidentally, Henry and Rogers both had on white shirts, black pants, and beige windbreakers.

Henry felt the need to add a touch of formality to the encounter with González, hence a narrow black tie. He might have been a delegate heading for a day of peace talks on the thirty-eighth parallel.

González had provided GPS coordinates that showed the meeting happening inside Utah's boundaries, but the territory remained rugged and confusing. Jackson was told to proceed cautiously.

Henry hadn't driven Interstate 80 in a decade. The Great Salt Lake stretched off to the horizon on their right like some biblical wilderness, and indeed here was a world for ascetics, in which settlements were few and grudging. Sometimes the brine from the lake crossed the interstate, leaving it a floating causeway, and when the water retreated it left a rime of sodium chloride. The south side of the highway remained mostly parched desert, where the salt blew in and stunted all life.

The Utah Test and Training Range occupied 2,645 square miles of restricted terrain flanking Interstate 80, both north and south. As a boy, Henry had been disappointed not to see jet fighters and Nike rockets by the hundreds overhead, or arrayed in the mysterious desert ready to be launched. Now, as then, the military had done little to the landscape — Henry still wanted to believe that a massive secret base lay out of sight only a few miles from the highway — and there were few road signs acknowledging the military's presence. Henry hoped for at least a drone sailing overhead, but the best he could see was a lonely white weather blimp five miles off to the north. If González chose to make an escape, he would flee neither north nor south but west, into the Nevada hills.

Henry guessed correctly that they wouldn't rendezvous in Wendover itself. A few miles before the town, as the test range ended and the Bonneville Salt Flats took over the landscape on the right, Jackson made a left turn onto an arid tertiary road. The plumes of dust raised by the black sedan were entirely of salt. The desert here was featureless; mountains lined the distant western horizon like a palisade.

Rogers muttered his discontent as barren scrub land opened before them on the sketchy path. After two miles, a cracked wooden sign appeared: "Portal, Utah."

"Ghost town," Rogers stated accurately.

It also confirms we're still inside the state line, thought Henry, who remained watchful for hints to their destination.

"You staying alert, Officer Jackson?" Rogers said.

Jackson muttered and picked up speed, flinging up more salt-laden dust in his wake. In three more miles, they spotted a black SUV parked before a Quonset hut a hundred yards off to their right. The prudent approach would have been to slow down, but Jackson, perhaps reacting to Rogers's condescending question, barrelled straight into the parking area and halted forty feet from the SUV. A huge Latino man in opaque shades stood unconcerned next to it. It took a full minute for the dust curtain to settle.

Jackson stayed in the sedan and turned off the engine as the detectives emerged into the sun. There was no need to try to impress the Latino man, but Rogers took off his sunglasses anyway to demonstrate that he was unintimidated. The bodyguard-driver said nothing.

Bypassing him, Rogers led Henry to a small door in the wall of the Quonset. Henry presumed that González waited somewhere inside the awkward structure, perhaps with a larger entourage of gunmen. He removed his shades, anticipating the dimness within, and suppressed his excitement.

It took only a sentence from Rogers for Henry's hopes to shatter on the desert hardpan. Just before entering the hut, the agent stage-whispered, "You've been allowed into the heart of a criminal enterprise, a unique and high-risk gamble, so let me do all the talking."

Henry Pastern realized, at the second he crossed from searing brightness to stygian gloom, that he had been set up. He was West Valley's rep — DeKlerk's proxy and Grady's spokesman — but the DEA would happily blame him for any and all screw-ups. As he adjusted to the light, Henry further grasped the forces arrayed against him. Rogers intended to push the Mexican hard and Henry provided deniability for Rogers if it went south. That's why DeKlerk hadn't wanted to be present.

Now fully inside, Henry absorbed the worst news. Rogers would try to manipulate González both ways. If the Mexican revealed the Hollis Street killer, the State Bureau would take him into custody on the spot for aiding, abetting, lying, obstructing, and whatever other adjective they could find. Rogers, it was now evident, saw an arrest as a distinct option. The choppers were probably already in the sky, damn the agreement. Henry wondered if González knew the danger he faced.

The interior was a vast, hollow space with an office table and three chairs set up at the far end. A whirring fan stood on a tall pole near the middle; it would have been more useful closer to the table, but Henry understood that it would have drowned out conversation. Two dozen light bulbs shone from rafters that cross-hatched the dome, whose sections of corrugated steel pinged in the heat. González had chosen the venue well. The oversize enclosure signified neutral ground, unapproachable without warning, and shielded from drones and telescopes. No matter that it was an artificial, otherworldly place that no one would ever want to endure for long.

At the table, a man in partial shadow looked up as the detectives entered. He stood and waited for them to approach.

González was over sixty but appeared younger, and the difference was important. He was wiry, supple, muscled, disciplined. He wore chinos and a denim shirt, and new Johnston & Murphy loafers made him appear as relaxed as a Napa Valley vintner. But he was Mexican through and through, and his proud demeanour told them he would not be patronized as a supplicant or a guest or any kind of interloper to this desolate part of Utah.

"*Madre*, it's the Men in Black. Could they have sent me two whiter guys?"

Rogers marched the length of the hut. Everything about him was tight, knotted, demanding — not, in Henry's view, the way to hold yourself in a hollow space like this where, if you exhaled, your aggressive energy would puff away into the high dome. Most important, the Mexican entirely controlled the venue for this meeting. It occurred to Henry that González might keep track of government drug agents and would figure out that Rogers was DEA; if so, there could be hell to pay. Rogers seemed to expect González's bodyguard to burst through the tiny door at the other end, in which case, Henry thought, first they would hear him killing Jackson. Reasoning that Rogers carried a concealed weapon, Henry was ready to try to disarm the agent if he pulled it. González evidently had no weapon on his person, nor under the table. Henry was unarmed.

"It's your meeting," Rogers shot back. "You *are* Avelino González?"

González frowned at Rogers's abrupt effort to seize the agenda, but recovered. "Most certainly."

Now Rogers frowned melodramatically. "We have you as Juan Chico González."

"I changed it to Avelino," González answered.

They sat down, Rogers first. Henry remained standing behind him. He understood that the DEA man would be on the attack the whole time. This was going to be dicey.

"What possible reason would you have for changing your birth name? Insecure about something?"

The pause was embarrassing. Henry was sure that a single insult, real or imagined, could scuttle this encounter. The drug dealer was a proud man. González stayed calm, almost Zen-like (if a killer can achieve such composure). Henry had absorbed the file. He knew that the drug chief smoked, and now would be the perfect time for him to light up the cheroots he favoured. Sure enough, González took out a pack of smokes but left them on the table.

Henry had twigged to the name change. "Puerto Rico?" he muttered.

González shifted his gaze and smiled at Henry, and back to Rogers: "Forget it, señor. Let's get this done."

"Why are we meeting in this shithole?" Rogers said.

Henry paid close attention. González wasn't provoked. "I like the borderlands," he answered mildly.

"Borderlands? You think the state line will stop us from hunting you down?"

"I wasn't aware that you were here to arrest me."

"I repeat, *you* called the meeting."

"Your police forces have been pushing hard on everyone's operations . . ."

Rogers interrupted, "And we will continue to do so."

González hadn't looked at Henry again. Addressing Rogers, he became formal, his tone stiff, perhaps dangerously so. "I certainly hope not."

"Then tell us what you know about the murders of Gabriella Watson and Tom Watson."

"*E bien,* I can only tell you what I don't know."

"You mean you have no information."

"In this case, nothing can mean something."

Rogers sneered. "You're a philosopher, González?"

Sometimes the precise truth can be the worst kind of affront, Henry judged. The Mexican raised his eyebrows. *If he likes to play philosopher, Rogers, you son of a bitch, let him. We've both seen his sheet.* González had been a killer for four decades, a devious drug pusher ready to use violence to keep his empire together. He wouldn't be confessing today.

"Okay, tell me about the murders, and I will tell you what I think," said González.

Henry thought it politic to take over, and he presented the important details of the events on Hollis Street and the discovery of Tom Watson hung up in the floating tree in the Provo River. He followed with an account of the frustrating investigation over the last three weeks, and was relieved that Rogers didn't interrupt.

A couple of times, González posed quirky questions: "Detective, did you see the severed head of Mrs. Watson?" "Did Tom Watson die slowly?" At first Henry supposed the Mexican was wallowing in morbid detail, but then he sensed that he, like Henry himself, was struggling to climb into the killer's mind.

"The blood in both houses was . . . excessive," Henry said.

"I understand," González said solemnly. "Why would a rival operator, simply trying to take out a competitor, bother with all this formality? This . . ."

"Ritual?" Henry said.

"Yes!"

Rogers's gaze had stayed belligerent the whole time. He squirmed in his chair, hating to cede control of the interplay. "You tell us, González. You are the drug dealer. What do you know about Watson's dealing?"

"Small-time, sold only in Salt Lake and Provo. Rumoured good-quality weed, I dunno, I never tasted it. Watson didn't know what to do with it even then. He used unreliable street hustlers," González growled.

"Come on, señor," Rogers interjected. "You don't want even mom-and-pop sellers in business against you. Maybe you took him out. On principle."

Henry watched the Mexican fight for control. He had an elegance to him, but the hearts of elegant men can turn particularly cold. "Officer, I am telling you that this massacre isn't the style of the *hombres fuertes* in this area."

"Not *your* style?"

"Not our way, no."

"That's rich, sir, coming from you."

González took a deep breath. He wasn't about to offer a wiring diagram of the cocaine and heroin trade simply to make the point that the marijuana business in Utah was small-time and always would be. But the question hung in the air for all three men: What bothered González about Hollis Street?

He continued. "There's business, then there's individuals. You have to ask, why would we drive Watson up into the mountains, all that comedy with throwing an already dead man into a fly-fishing river?"

Rogers tilted back in his chair, his look contemptuous. More, he seemed to feel that he had the upper hand. *How wrong can you be?* thought Henry. He wondered again if Rogers and the state police had a contingency plan — helicopters, for example. If so, there would be three dead cops out there on the parking pad, and Henry one of them. The bodyguard in the sunglasses wouldn't bother with beheadings.

González leaned forward. "We were not involved. We don't need the aggravation from you cops. And I repeat, it is not my way."

"And I repeat, that's rich coming from you," said Rogers.

"Did you ever read Dante's *Inferno*, officer? Dante condemns hypocrites to the eighth circle of Hell. Ruby Ridge. Waco."

For the first time, Henry heard real anger from the Mexican, but the weighted references to the botched government ops were red flags on both sides of the table. The DEA, FBI, and especially the ATF, which screwed up mightily at Waco, recoiled any time Randy Weaver and David Koresh were thrown in their faces.

Rogers's retort was blatant, and cheap. "We have reports of your people cutting off the heads of your competitors by a roadside in Xuahaca two years ago."

González's voice turned hard. "Señor, I want to talk to this man alone."

"What the hell?"

"He is the officer with — what do you say — carriage of the case? You are DEA. I said no feds."

Henry felt panic and elation, and it seemed wise to suppress both. *Is it possible he expects something special from me?* González had revealed almost nothing of his motives.

Rogers persisted. "This situation is a lot simpler than you think. We can trade . . ."

González tossed a baleful look at Rogers, a final dismissal. The agent stood, unbelieving; he shot a warning look at Henry and strode to the other end of the steel building. González waited until the Alice-in-the-rabbit-hole door closed, and turned his chair.

"Sit down. You understood Puerto Rico, señor. How is that?"

Henry's voice cracked unimpressively. "Research?" He recovered, took a breath, and tried frankness. "While researching you, I noticed that Avelino González, a figure in the drug business, was just released after serving seven years for robbing an armoured truck with $7 million in it. I went back and looked at the case. He called himself an activist in the Puerto Rican independence movement."

González smiled; his posture was benign, and he had all the time in the world.

"I have had many names over the years. It is my nature to change shape, starting with my name. But my birth name is Juan Chico González. A dull name, right? I heard about Avelino González and found him inspiring. That was the inspiration to change my name."

"You've got my colleague confused."

"I don't like your colleague from the drug police. He thinks of Mexicans only as illegals, aliens, and outsiders. If anyone has got a claim to the old Wyoming Territory, it is Spanish-speaking people. Coronado rode up the Camino five hundred years ago, when everything was called Old Mexico. You know, Boog DeKlerk is the only one I can talk to in your shop."

"Meaning?"

"No, Detective, DeKlerk is not in my pocket. I mean, I can talk to him because he admits he is an outsider, a South African. Utah is a place for outsiders."

He fell silent to let Henry work it out. The Mexican, Henry understood, was saying that he did not defer to the DEA or any gringos.

"Take your people."

"You think I'm Mormon?" Henry replied.

"That clip-on tie you're wearing isn't fresh out of the box. We are all immigrants, all outsiders to this land. Who should say who should make the rules?"

"Let us be clear, Señor González, you deny any connection to the deaths of the Watsons?"

"I never heard of them before. I had no reason to care about their marijuana business."

"Do you care at all about the marijuana business in Utah?"

González treated this frontal assault with proper contempt. "I will not be confessing all my sins today."

González was entirely composed, yet Henry perceived that he wanted something from this confab. The FBI file recorded that he regularly smoked twenty cheroots a day, though he had yet to light up. He seemed to have abandoned other features of his profile: no sidearm, no hovering bodyguard. *Is he toying with us?*

González broke into Henry's reverie. "Besides, few love to hear the sins they love to act."

"Shakespeare?"

The drug boss nodded. Henry was flattered that the man wanted to impress him with erudition; then it occurred to Henry that González might have done some background research on him. He idly wondered about gaps in the police bio. Did González have children? Were there four brothers or five? Was he sixty or sixty-eight, or in between? Had he become bored with the drug business and that, somehow, was why they were meeting?

Henry knew that Rogers would re-enter the hut soon. González's sentinel might try to waylay him; a tussle in the blazing sun could easily cause a shootout. Time to press the case.

"Señor González, who do you believe killed the Watsons?"

"I told you, I don't know."

"But there's something you came to tell us? That's why you're here?"

The Mexican tilted back in his chair. "I can tell you this about the executions: the violence was not suitable to the problem."

"What was the problem?"

"Someone didn't like a grow house on their street."

The circular responses were getting to Henry. González wasn't used to revealing himself when every disclosure was potentially probative against him, yet he wanted Henry to know certain facts about

110

the Watsons. This wasn't helpful. Henry recalled one fact that the Mexican hadn't acknowledged: the Puerto Rican Avelino González had been the self-appointed leader of a gang called the *macheteros*, men who used machetes.

"You have to give me more, Señor González."

"If you show me your work files on the murder, your study of where they lived, the situation, I can tell you who killed Tom Watson."

"You said you didn't know the killer or the victims."

González clearly didn't want to answer and only said, "It's a puzzle."

Yes, it is a puzzle.

"Give me a takeaway, señor."

González stood and paced, came back to the table. *Is it still a negotiating table, or are we done?* His voice was flat, declamatory. "I know the killer. He has killed before. Show me the blueprints of his bomb."

"I can't release the whole file. The forensic reports, maybe . . ."

"No."

"The whole file?"

"Yes."

"I can't do that."

They paused. The room reverberated with the Mexican's power and all the possibilities of violence.

Henry heard Rogers open the door behind him. Before the agent gained earshot, Henry rushed to say, "I'll do my best. I'll be in contact."

González stood behind the desk and leaned on his fists. "Young man, we are in the presence of evil here. Be careful."

Peter was mildly surprised that Henry called so soon after the Wendover meeting, but he was also very pleased. Henry had been on his mind much more than he had conceded.

"What was your impression of González?" he quickly asked.

"He was self-controlled . . . confident," Henry said carefully. "A bit . . ."

"A bit old, like me?"

"Not that. But he reminded me of you in other ways."

Peter understood what his friend was getting at. Old men tote irreversible burdens, and the drug dealer could no more dismiss the ghosts of the men he had executed on Mexican roadsides than Peter could easily forget the men he had killed in the line of duty. Peter wanted to help Henry. He found González's approach to the police an extraordinary gesture — there was no precedent, and there had to be something personal behind it. Peter had the young detective run through every detail of the conversation.

"Then he quoted *Pericles*. He had courtly manners. And he wore beautiful shoes."

"Don't sentimentalize him," Peter countered. "Let me think about this."

Peter tried to visualize the Mexican. What did González need from Henry Pastern? Peter felt his old detective instincts welling up. The man had tentacles into six states and much of northern Mexico. He always thought big, yet Hollis Street was small beer. Peter thought it unlikely that the dead Watsons, whom González professed not to know, held the key to the fate of González's drug empire.

"Peter, are you there?"

"Yes."

"What do you make of him?"

Peter worked it out as he talked. "There is only one explanation for it. I don't want to prick your balloon, but he doesn't plan to reveal his operations to you. González's angle on Hollis is personal."

"A trade for our files, maybe? He indicated . . ."

"Think it through, Henry. He was jerking your chain on that, wasn't really offering anything in return for your file."

Henry sighed. "I can't give him any details anyway."

"Don't be tempted. It would end your career."

Peter realized that his advice thus far had been discouraging, and he moved to a more upbeat subject. "You know, Henry, that you've just earned yourself a reputation . . ."

"The cop who went up against the drug czar?" Henry sounded skeptical.

"More or less. You can use it to your advantage. You say that DeKlerk is trying to poach on Homicide's territory. Use this with your superiors to keep him back."

"But meanwhile, stay away from González."

"Yes . . . unless he calls with some real information."

Peter sounded firm, but he was equivocal. The Mexican's final statement had conjured up an image of "evil" that still lurked on Hollis Street, and that piqued his interest for unknown reasons. They were all trying to enter the butcher's mind. Perhaps González, even if he could not yet name this evil, knew the killer best. If the Mexican's motive was personal, it could only mean one thing: he was seeking vengeance.

They chatted for a few more minutes. "Call me anytime, Henry, but especially if González reaches out to you," he said. Peter thought that this final gesture would be enough.

It wasn't.

CHAPTER 15

Odd things happen to cops who obsess on a case. They shed weight, or perhaps they put on weight. They turn edgy and stop worrying about offending others, especially "civilians" — that is, anyone with nothing to contribute, which is pretty much everyone. In this, they become as insular and defensive as the fugitives they are hotly pursuing.

Over the next two weeks, Phil Mohlman and Henry Pastern forged a solid team as they got back to the hard slogging on Hollis Street. Initially, the González meeting was judged by everyone in the policing fraternity as a washout, but the Mexican's adamant denial that the gangs had taken out the Watsons impelled the detectives back to Forest Vale with renewed resolve. And so, as Henry was to recollect many times, perhaps González had achieved what he set out to do.

Chief Grady kept up the pressure with talk of "quantum leaps" and "clearing the ledger." But Phil and Henry preferred to think of their case as a jigsaw puzzle. The pair arranged and rearranged constellations of forensic details, time sequences, and witness statements on the wall of Interrogation Room Number 5. They expressed confidence that Grady would have his killer soon.

"A Rubik's cube with a magic solution just around the corner," Phil promised, punchily churning up the metaphors.

Grady remained supportive of Homicide but demanded an update every third day. Henry and Phil bonded over their conviction that the key to the Watson killings lay inside the Hollis Street cordon, and they strove to complete a detailed dossier on every one of the residents. They became dreaded figures on the cul-de-sac as they forced the pace of their visits.

They worked to fashion a truce with their law enforcement critics, except Agent Rogers, who reported to Grady that Henry's tête-à-tête with González was a screw-up, that Pastern had been gulled by the Mexican. But he wasn't party to the conversation, was he? The chief, who was cautious by nature, kept the bigger picture in view and remained hopeful that González would funnel leads to Pastern or DeKlerk. He was inclined to believe Henry's assessment that González was being honest when he professed no involvement in the local murders.

If the other federal agencies had ever sought control over the Watson case, they now abandoned their claims. The Wendover meeting was hardly a success, but no federal agent had ever managed to face the notorious drug dealer one-on-one, so there wasn't much they could denounce. An outlandish episode turned into a nascent legend, and Henry gained considerable street cred. The glances he received when he visited the federal and state offices on Amelia Earhart Drive were now semi-respectful. Rogers rationalized the DEA's pullback from the Hollis murders by dismissing the blood-bath as a localized incident.

As for DeKlerk, Henry and Phil dug a moat around Hollis and warned him not to cross it without permission. Staties and feds should not bother trying to enter the stone gates, either.

But the drug angle remained a raw issue. Rogers continued to assail DeKlerk for what he regarded as a humiliating fiasco in Wendover, and he persuaded his colleagues at the DEA in Salt Lake to minimize their collaboration with West Valley Police. Conduits dried up.

Henry tried to compensate by spending long hours on various crime databases looking for parallel incidents. He was soon convinced that Boog DeKlerk's re-involvement was essential.

"I trust him as far as I could throw a hogshead of Guinness," Phil said.

"Sure," Henry said, "but it will be faster to track down reports on drug incidents through Boog than on our own. I also need his advice on contacting González."

"Stay away from González, I told you. Besides, I don't know that he has Boog in his pocket, but you don't want your voice appearing on a tap related to some Internal Affairs operation."

"Do you believe Boog is regularly contacting González anyway?"

"I doubt Boog will risk dancing with the devil anymore. Grady and Rogers are suspicious."

Henry still hoped to consult DeKlerk about the use of pipe bombs in the drug wars, but it was DeKlerk who ended up making the overture with a phone call one afternoon.

"Pastern, I called to confirm the tests on the two bags found at Number 5. High potency, if not highest quality, all of it. Superbud-standard. White widow, northern lights strains."

The jargon was intended to impress Henry, which it did, prompting him to ask his "bomb" question. "Should I give González the list of components from the pipe bomb? He was interested in that."

Henry paused while Boog assessed the dangers in dealing with González under the table. "I wouldn't. The Mexican is no one's ally in this case."

Considering this unusual expression of caution by the South African, Henry called his partner. "What's with Boog's almost-friendly tone?"

"Yeah, Boog still hopes to rehabilitate his career, even though Grady has shifted him sideways from his job," Phil stated. "Internal Affairs is starting an inquiry into Boog's interactions with the Mexican. Boog needs friends."

The flow of tips from the public dried up. Nobody had seen anything. Nobody knew much more of anything.

One afternoon as they climbed back into Phil's sedan after another re-interview, Henry asked, "What now?" Phil drummed the dash with his hand and then shrugged.

They couldn't sustain this two-man charge without results, and Henry began to search for fresh perspectives. Every day, he was tempted to contact Avelino González, but he knew that the furor would be too great. He considered phoning Peter Cammon again, but he was pretty sure Peter would tell him to stay patient.

He turned to Theresa. He let her read his final report to Chief Grady on the Wendover mano-a-mano. "I can't figure out what González expected from me," he said.

"Just a guess here, Henry," she said, "but I don't imagine he was a foaming-at-the mouth drug user when you met him alone, right? He wasn't needy in any way?"

Henry, in part annoyed at himself for breaking all kinds of police rules by blithely handing her his report, as if demanding she edit the thing, transferred his pique onto her. "What's your point?"

"What are you consulting me about?"

"You're mad I didn't show you the Wendover details before now."

"No. You're being tight-assed on the biggest question of all. Why did he talk to you? I'm a tax accountant. You're like a tax avoider who flunked his audit. Fine, this report is what it is, but where's the personal detail?" She halted before a coughing fit hit her and sipped from her ever-present water bottle. "For example, how many brothers does he have? Are they all dead? Has the Watson thing some personal connection to his family? Where's your bottom line on González?"

"DeKlerk thinks his brothers, whether two or three, are in fact dead."

"Tell me all your *own* reactions, Henry."

Henry recounted every word of his conversation from the

Quonset hut, trying to recall the quirky turns in his interchange with the Mexican. She unnerved him by jotting notes on a steno pad. After an hour, she got up and gave him a sloppy kiss and returned to her chair.

"My brave husband," she said, though the compliment was spoiled by a wracking coughing fit. Henry read her list:

Severed head
Name changes
Sins
Cigars
Shakespeare
Evil

"What do these items have in common?" Theresa said.

Henry floundered in policeman mode. "They don't help us in finding the murderer?"

"Think again. This criminal kingpin has shared his personal preoccupations with you. He reached out. Some indicate change in his life. Some focus on violence and evil. Others imply feelings of guilt. Personal change, confession, concern with violence. How about that?"

"You're not an accountant, you're Mrs. Freud."

Theresa padded around the huge living room. "González is a man facing change, and he's apprehensive. He vibrates with his own history, and, I believe, everywhere he goes he finds echoes of his own sins."

"Which he won't confess."

"He's not into confession but he finishes his conversation with you with talk of 'evil.' Mr. González wants to tell you something, but he doesn't believe that his hypocrisy disbars him from passing judgement on the tragedy that unfolded on Hollis Street. Why this posture?"

"I've thought of calling him up. He left the door open to me."

"Beware, husband." Theresa had repositioned herself in her chair so as to take full breaths of the dry air on the patio. She disciplined her breathing, each inhalation measured, her movements slowed down. To Henry, she seemed more like the Delphic oracle than ever.

"Here's how I imagine him," she continued. "González is like an old vaquero probing the canyons in Old Mexico. An *imperialista*, unafraid to invade white-bread Utah and wander where he pleases. A drug entrepreneur, lord of the frontier. A Mexican patriot but an enemy of the establishment. Rogers was right, he's a philosopher, too. A fanatic for Diego Rivera, you mention here, and Shakespeare. But listen to me: I can romanticize him, but don't you dare, Henry. Something more is going on with Señor González, and he wants you to know it."

Theresa sat back to regain her breath.

CHAPTER 16

Phil threw his pen down on the chipped table, which was bolted to the floor in Interrogation Room Number 5, and declared, "We're driving the neighbours nuts."

They had shuffled the fourteen bulging folders, one per house, for the tenth time, and one of them, "Anderssen No. 12," had slipped to the floor. "When the file gets dog-eared," Phil said, "shoot the dog."

It was a bad joke, Henry thought, but the right one. Phil recognized that they were bouncing off walls. The street kid from Boston was ready to deal some rough treatment, and Henry fed in the straight line. "What do we do, then?"

"We drive just one of them nuts. Proffet."

Henry was happy to be doing something. "Okay, let me clear out this stuff so we can bring him in."

Phil wasn't through venting. "Jesus, Henry! They've closed ranks against us. The neighbours show more affection for Puffles the Dog than the Watsons. What if Theresa's *Orient Express* theory is right and we've got a big, fat case of collusion here? They took collective action against what just happens to be the first house on the block. Nice."

"Phil, have you got your notes on the community association handy? Before we call in Proffet, let's look at who served over the years."

They had a file on this, as they had on most facets of life on Hollis Street.

"Okay, twelve years back. That's when HASA was formed," Henry said.

Phil read. "First president was, no surprise, Jerry Proffet. Vice-president was Ronald Devereau, at Number 13. Term was one year, but renewed."

"So the president and vice-president lived next door to each other. Little power centre forming?"

"That often happens in condo-type associations, doesn't it?" Phil said.

"I guess." Henry checked the master list of presidents (which they weren't sure was complete) against the individual evens, while Phil did the same for the odds. "Carleton Davis at Unit 10 was the prez . . . for a single term. I'm guessing he chose not to run again. If you'd sampled Davis's personality, you'd see why."

"Didn't like local politics?" Phil said.

"Doesn't like people, I'd say. Maybe I'll interview him again."

Phil picked up on a theme. "You think maybe it was Jerry Proffet who turned him off?"

"Could be. Proffet returned for another double term. The next president was Devereau for one, maybe two terms, then — guess who — Jerry Proffet again."

"The Grover Cleveland of Hollis Street."

Henry scanned the list:

Jerry Proffet: 2 Terms
Carleton Davis: 1
Jerry Proffet: 2
Ronald Devereau: 1? 2?
Jerry Proffet: 2
Stanley Chambers: 1
Jerry Proffet: unofficial

Henry pointed to the bottom. "The most recent *official* president was Stanley Chambers at Number 6, one of the now-vacant places. Served one term, then the community committee dissolved. That was eighteen months ago. Has Proffet really explained why?"

"Said no one wanted to pay the annual levy any longer. They weren't a condo community, and there was no legal requirement to pay into a contingency fund. Contingency fund for what? Why didn't they levy a special fee to complete those stone gates?"

Henry and Phil began flipping pages as if competing to find the key to the history of Hollis Street. Eventually Peter returned to Stanley Chambers. "Picture this: Chambers lived right across from the Watsons but claims no knowledge of the grow house. He saw nothing, smelled nothing. But HASA went defunct after his term as chairman, and he sold out a year and a half later. Close to the crime, linked to the executive. He might be the best witness we have."

"Even if he wasn't living on the street that night."

Phil and Henry trundled their notes into the precinct boardroom and took over the whiteboard, as they had done many times since the González meeting. Phil scribbled out every resident's service on the HASA executive — *President* and *Vice-president*, after which he began a new heading: *Treasurer*.

Henry scanned the notes. "Interesting. Six different treasurers: Davis, Chambers, Bross, Anderssen, Devereau, Henneker — though Anderssen and Henneker now deny serving."

"Geez. Bureaucracies," Phil said. "But just about every resident contributed to the running of the street at some point, even the Watsons. And nobody but nobody saw a thing. I come back to that Big Possibility, partner. What if everybody saw everything? Maude Hampson and Carleton Davis saw the activity across the street at all hours and ignored it. Stan Chambers tired of the smell of marijuana and put his house up for sale. Nurse Anderssen ignored the light leaking from the factory at the Second House every time she came off her shift. Maybe the executive knew all about it but tried to wish it away, until . . ."

"And that begs another Big Question," Henry said. "Did Tom Watson ignore an explicit warning from the street committee?"

"Let's call in Jerry Proffet." Henry grunted assent. Phil added, "Coolest cucumber on the street, our boyo," and left the interrogation room to make the call from his desk.

The detectives skipped the hard-cop/soft-cop approach — every TV watcher knew that game — and launched straight into hard-cop/harder-cop. Beforehand, mulling over Proffet's problem with his body thermostat, Phil queried, "Should we turn up the air conditioning?"

"No fooling around, Phil. We simply push him hard to come clean," Henry said.

Phil summoned Proffet to the station and set the meeting for 11 a.m. Proffet arrived wearing a heavy argyle sweater, and they shook hands; Phil made sure his were cold.

Phil raised the stakes almost at once. "Jerry, thanks for coming. We feel we've talked to the residents as much as we can, but tell us, why do you think Tom Watson thought he could get away with marketing marijuana in your quiet neighbourhood?"

Proffet fell for the sucker wording built into Phil's question. "He wasn't *marketing* on the street. He slipped his bags of grass out at night . . ."

"Not those last two bags of top-quality weed," Henry chirped. "Premium Mary Jane."

That was a little fact Jerry, presumptive supervisor of Hollis Street, didn't know. Phil leaned in. "He brought in the seeds, the paraphernalia, the grow lamps, the fertilizer. He must have spent hours unloading it all, hours more crossing back between houses. He loaded his truck with product every few days and came and went in the dark, but nobody saw a thing. Nobody smelled a thing."

"I understand that it was a small operation. A few bags at a time," Jerry pleaded.

"How would you know?" Phil fired back.

"I never had an inkling of what he was doing."

"Did any of your neighbours ever buy from him?"

"Nobody knew about him."

Henry took a shot. "You had four or five association presidents over twelve years, out of a pool of fourteen households. Why not more inclusive?"

"We opened the election to all. Besides, the lesser executive posts were taken by others."

Lesser? Phil ignored the gaffe and played soft cop for a moment. "Jerry volunteered his services for six whole years as president, Henry. Cut him some slack." Both detectives knew that Proffet's tenure added up to more than seven years, if one counted his ad hoc service. He had always been the street czar.

Proffet asserted, "We've given everyone a chance who wanted it."

Henry counterpunched. "Did Tom Watson ever run for president?"

"He expressed interest a few years back, our third election, I recall, but I don't believe he would have been elected."

Henry remembered, from his classes on interrogation at Quantico, a lecture called "pedalling backward." The term lacked precision, but the idea was to disarm a witness by revisiting questions that had already been answered, thereby making him wonder if the interview would ever end, if the interviewer would ever be satisfied.

"Why'd you call it HASA?" Henry said, setting up the next line of attack.

"Why wouldn't we?" Proffet threw back, mustering indignation.

"It's Hollis *Street*. But the Hollis *Avenue* Street Association? Confusing. Redundant?"

"It sounds better," Proffet countered lamely.

Phil jumped in. "Why didn't you run for office yourself in year eleven, extending your chairmanship?"

Proffet arched his back, then adopted a stiff military posture in his chair. "Like I said, to give others a chance."

Phil's anger was genuine. "Were you afraid Tom Watson would beat you in a knock-down contest?"

"What? Knock-down?"

Henry piled on. "You were having trouble getting participation, weren't you? I think people were reluctant after a while to get active in street affairs when you and the clique refused to close down the marijuana operation."

"Clique?"

The detectives' grilling was intended to prompt Jerry's memory about what he thought he didn't know: *who was capable of the killings*. He couldn't win: If he was the keeper of standards on Hollis, why didn't he notice the grow op and take action? If street solidarity was firm, why not proceed to carry out the collective will?

Henry shifted in his chair and looked at the clock. "Okay, Mr. Proffet, why are there no pictures of the annual barbecues?"

Taken by surprise, Phil stared at Henry with admiration for this perverse little question.

"There aren't?"

"I talked to Wooski. Says he never took any. Someone, he can't remember who, didn't want any group photos."

"Well, I'm sure Selma snapped a few. I'll ask her when I get home."

Henry had hounded every resident on his side of the street and, even though the barbecues had stretched from the era of Instamatics to digitals to cell phones, all his interviewees were certain that they had left their cameras at home.

"Mr. Proffet," Phil continued, "we need you to state for the record that the street executive never had any suspicion that Tom Watson was running a grow operation out of Number 5. And that no resident ever lodged a complaint or a concern. This includes the recent period when you were serving as ad hoc president."

Proffet hesitated, knowing he was being put to an affidavit. "We were bothered by the houses going empty at 5 and 8, and then Chambers at Number 6," he began.

Henry's calculated explosion startled even Phil. "Come on,

Warrant Officer Proffet, a less lukewarm statement, if you don't mind. We're asking what the committee knew, what steps they took to verify the goings-on at Number 5, whether the committee contemplated taking action, and if Watson ever threatened you. You are the only real president the street's ever had."

On the word *threatened*, the ex-soldier winced. Henry caught the fright in his eyes and the contraction of his mouth. What had Tom Watson done to cow his neighbours?

Don't let up.

"Come on, Jerry, what did you know?" Phil said.

"Detective, I personally began to get suspicious when Tom Watson volunteered to maintain the grounds next door. It was right there, he said, no problem to cut the grass. The place had been vacant six months at that time, and the executive had failed to find out anything about the owners' intentions. Some subsidiary mortgage company from out of state."

"You told me that when we first talked," Phil said, his tone falsely kind.

"Right. We couldn't think of anything else to do to pressure the owners, so we accepted Tom's offer."

Henry pressed. "But Watson didn't do a complete job. You might say he did the opposite, letting the side yard grow over, and leaving toys and junk in the weeds to obscure the water line and power cord between the houses. Why didn't you take him to task?"

Proffet looked shamefaced. "I should have known. The previous owner had no kids and neither did the Watsons. Where did the toys come from, I wondered?"

Phil threw him crumbs. "He did it to fool the police, Jerry. Maybe they wouldn't suspect a grow op or a crack house if a family lived there."

"Did Watson ever threaten you?" Henry said.

"Never. Detective, the old executive gathered and considered sitting down with Tom and asking whether he was doing something illegal at that end of the street. We decided we had no proof and we backed off."

"Who was at that meeting?" Phil asked.

"Myself and Ron Devereau, and Selma, my wife, sat in. We recognized the crisis on the street. By then Stan Chambers had announced he was moving, and Mr. Starr at Number 7 was contemplating a sale."

Henry flashed on Theresa's dream. Indeed, a flood had crept through the stone gates and swept up the road.

"You were getting concerned about property values?" Phil said.

"Yes. Not that anyone at our end of the block was anticipating selling. That's as far as it went."

Phil pinned him with a hard-cop glare and faked a sigh. "So you never got proactive about your suspicions? Never asked Tom to let you inside Number 5?"

"Why would I do that?"

Henry, flushed from his own hard-cop performance, said, "You might have liked it. Would have been the same tropical temperature as your place, ex-Warrant Officer Proffet."

CHAPTER 17

It was closing in on one o'clock when they finally freed Jerry Proffet from the precinct. Had they continued, Phil might have openly accused him of plotting violent retribution on the Watsons. As it was, he couldn't resist a parting shot. "Thank you, Mr. Proffet, but please don't leave town for a while."

Proffet, who seldom left Hollis Street, departed in confusion.

Seconds later, Phil jumped up and shouted, "I'm hungry, need a drink. Let's do the Rose."

Phil's dusty sedan piloted itself to the bar, although Henry remained antsy about the choice of the Rose, not only because its boozy atmosphere made him feel like a temperance scold but also because it was Boog DeKlerk's home turf.

When Phil was stymied he turned profane. "Jesus, Mary, and Joseph. Do we have enough to arrest Proffet?"

"Nowhere near," Henry replied, hoping to dial back his partner's zeal.

"You're right, I agree. So, partner, let's work on a *search* warrant."

"For every house on Hollis Street?"

"Now there's a great idea!" Phil bellowed, and banged on the steering wheel.

They had almost reached the turn for the Rose when Phil shouted again and swerved back into traffic. "We're on the wrong track!"

"You don't want to search Proffet's house?"

"Oh, yeah, I think there's a good chance we'll find blood traces in the Proffet mansion. No, what we need, Henry, is to write a better story to hand Grady so that the chief can be the one to apply for the warrant. I know a perfect place to work."

Henry looked over from the shotgun seat. Had Phil bought the modified *Orient Express* theory, in which Jerry (Selma, too?) planned the vendetta and lured selected neighbours into carrying it out?

The perfect place was another Irish-themed pub, nothing special aside from the list of single malts posted behind the bar. Business was quiet. Phil knew the owner, who assigned them an entire back room, featuring a dart game with a slate scoreboard. Phil went over and erased the chalked number 501 on the board and replaced it with "Dog."

The owner of the pub entered and asked about drinks.

"Henry, you'll have a shot?" said Phil.

Henry had tried brandy and red wine, and an occasional glass of burgundy, inescapably, during his Mission in France (yes, like Mitt Romney), and once a bourbon at the FBI Academy in what amounted to a hazing ritual. Phil himself didn't drink all that much, but merely talked about fine scotch to put down the Utah rubes. But now his fervour persuaded Henry, and they welcomed two glasses of single malt from the taciturn owner, telling themselves that it would fuel their decision-making.

Phil said, "So, why didn't they kill the dog?"

"That one I've got," Henry said. "They didn't kill the dog, because they had nothing against the dog."

Phil smiled. "Compassion for the mutt but they behead the owner. Gotta love that."

"Respectfully, Phil, can we address the bigger scenario? Try this: one of the neighbours observed Tom Watson getting his product ready to move. It put him in a rage. He expected to find Tom when he rang the bell, but Gabriella answered. He overreacted . . ."

"Overreacted? I'll say."

"He killed her, spared the dog, had no time for the bags of grass, and moved on to house two. He had plenty to do loading Tom Watson's corpse into the truck and getting off the street before Nurse Anderssen arrived home from her overnight shift. What does this tell us?"

Phil rapped on the nearest bar stool. "The killer not only knew the habits of Tom Watson, he knew the patterns of the *other residents on the street.*"

"Right!" said Henry, grimacing as he sipped his scotch. "He wanted to do his grisly business and get out of there before Mrs. Anderssen came down the street."

Phil held the chalk like a baton. "Jerry Proffet had the most at stake on the street . . ."

"You're obsessed with Proffet."

"He has the motive. He worried about property values, and he resented the demise of HASA. People were selling out. Tom Watson was a provocation."

The booze fired up Henry, even as it nauseated him. He craved action. "I'm going to place another call to Stan Chambers. He lives down in Sedona now. He was the last elected president of the street association and lived the closest to the death houses, except for Maude Hampson. I want to know if there was ever a confrontation between Jerry and Tom Watson."

"Should we go for the search warrant for Proffet's house?" said Phil.

"Still not sure we can meet the threshold," said Henry.

"Good chance there's Tom's blood in there, maybe in the garage."

"If we blow it, find nothing, we won't get permission for any other property on the block. Why don't we just ask? Appeal to the better angels of his nature."

"Hey," Phil said, "we forgot to eat!"

But they didn't eat in the crypto-Irish pub. Henry insisted that Phil come over to the house on Coppermount. It was early afternoon, but

Henry uttered the universal words of invitation in Utah: "I'll grill us a couple of steaks."

Phil knew right then that his drinking was done for the day. He and Theresa got along — they called themselves "Easterners" — but he knew how sick she was, and he would avoid anything that might aggravate her disorder. Theresa would offer to open a bottle of wine, but he would refuse. From Henry's end of the call to Theresa, he understood that there were plenty of steaks in the Eastern freezer and company was welcome. Phil had been divorced for years; he lived alone and was quick to accept Henry's invitation. He hoped that their buoyant mood would carry through the evening, and he assumed that they would avoid further discussion of the Hollis Street murders. He was wrong on both fronts.

When they reached the desert house, they found Theresa resting on a chaise longue on the patio. Even this far back, Phil could see how pale she was. As the men crossed the broad living room, Theresa turned and looked through the open doors. At the same moment, a dark figure intersected their path and almost dropped the jug of ice water and the pills he carried. "Oops!" the man said.

He was all in black, and Phil's natural thought was that a Roman Catholic priest had come to take confession.

"Phil Mohlman, uh, Elder Tynan, our neighbour," Henry said, taking the water and putting it on the floor next to Theresa. He crouched down by his wife. Phil noted that Tynan wore a black suit but wasn't sweating — echoes of Jerry Proffet. He had the demeanour of a priest, standing with hands held open like a presiding pope and displaying a beneficent smile.

"Thomas Abraham Tynan."

As a choirboy, Phil had been taught to show respect to all priests, even if they were called Mormon elders. He half bowed and backed away as Theresa explained to her husband through coughing spells that she had summoned Tynan from up the street.

"What meds have you taken?" Henry said. The desert was scorching. Tynan diplomatically held back with Phil.

"I'm fine," she wheezed.

Henry enveloped her with his long arms and she seemed to recover miraculously, getting out of the chair and rising to full height as if to prove her fitness.

"Hi, Phil," she said.

Phil Mohlman had always liked Theresa, but he didn't want to be here. He no longer felt convivial. This was a time for husband and wife to be alone, and he was about to beg off and flee to his car when the strange man in black said, "Theresa, you're in good hands now. I'll go."

Theresa smiled warmly and gave Tynan a tight hug. Phil — and Henry, too — was surprised at the degree of affection. Was Theresa demonstrating her full recovery, or had she called the Mormon before? Henry was like any husband, alert to his wife's trust in other men.

"I should go, too," Phil said.

"No, no," Theresa said, her voice rising an octave. "Stay. I'm really fine."

To avoid a standoff, Phil said, "I'll walk you out, Tynan, and allow these folks a moment."

Phil and Tynan paused by the unmarked police sedan in the driveway. The sun was well past its zenith, and they looked up, as if to assess the impact of the searing heat on Theresa's well-being.

"She looks not so good, or am I wrong?" Phil said.

Phil appraised Tynan as honest, perhaps sage, a little of the mystic in him. Tynan said, "I'm not a doctor, but I think she's getting worse."

"What was that all about? She seems almost hyper now."

"She called me because she was choking. She could hardly get the words out. Her raw throat is heightened by inflammation of the lungs, and phlegm builds up. That's the obstructive pulmonary disease part of COPD."

"What's she on?" Phil said.

"The full range. Antibiotics, bronchodilators, prednisone at a low level because she doesn't want to gain weight. I think she should have an oxygen tank beside her at all times. Neither of them will hear of it. It's as if it would signal her crossing over into the world of infirmity."

Phil nodded. He liked the man. "Has she been coughing up blood?"

"She denies it, but I looked in the wastebasket in the bathroom and, yes, there was bloody sputum."

"Elder Tynan, you'd make a good detective."

In the ensuite bathroom on the far side of the house, Henry and Theresa were having a parallel conversation. Henry checked the array of pill bottles and inhalers on the sink. A new puffer contained albuterol; they had switched from salmeterol, which gave her a skin rash. A stronger antibiotic had been delivered that day by her usual pharmacy. It was backed up by a bottle of Ventolin, a corticosteroid. They had agreed to keep all her medications in one place. Henry worried that he was losing track of her pills-of-the-week. His anxiety reflected an ineluctable thought: *my wife is getting worse.*

For now, she was much better, almost frenzied as she ordered her husband to bring Phil back out to the patio.

"We'll talk about D.C. in the old days, when Henry and I met," she said to Phil as he returned.

But they didn't talk about Washington. They excavated Hollis Street.

Henry launched into a lengthy debriefing as soon as they sat down to their steaks, baked potatoes, and guacamole salad at the outdoor table. Phil begged off beer and wine.

Theresa wasn't impressed. "You guys fixate on the dog and the bags of marijuana, but two things jump out at me."

"What two things?" Phil said, bemused by his hosts' Nick-and-Nora act.

"The blood and the inside of the truck."

"The truck stymies us, too," Henry said encouragingly.

Theresa proceeded, her voice unblemished. "Guys, you need to think about the blood in the houses, outside the houses, in the truck. The murderer was efficient, in his own loopy way. He stabbed Gabriella and hauled her across the lawn, where he cut off her head, but he didn't waste time painting words on the walls like Charles Manson. No hesitation, am I right?"

"Yes, it was relatively quick and decisive," Henry agreed. "She wasn't tortured, but a message was being sent. But a simple beheading — I can't believe I'm using these words — is typical of the Mexican drug cartels. They're experienced. It's about sending a message."

"The drug gangs can get sadistic," Phil added.

"But González told you it wasn't *business*. There was no one who needed to receive a message. González is saying Tom Watson didn't deserve this."

Phil licked his lips, craving a shot of scotch. "Theresa, your problem is this: Why didn't he leave Tom Watson lying there on the floor of Number 5? Did he panic? And, if it wasn't business, in what way was it personal?"

Theresa got to her feet and paced once across the patio and back. Phil could see that it was her way of proving her passion and her vigour. She turned to face the men, her face pale and drawn. "It's like he wanted to exact the same biblical judgement twice. Who does that?"

"So much blood," Phil said. The conversation was turning morbid.

"Shakespeare again," said Henry.

"The blood," Theresa confirmed. "There was so much blood, yeah. It's the *way* he killed them that scares me. Henry told me there was a bucket of it inside the truck, even after Tom Watson supposedly bled out. Look for blood on clothing, in the vehicles of your suspects, anywhere. He wallowed in it. It might be the killer's biggest error."

Phil nodded at her pitiless summary. She had spoken too long, and now her face darkened alarmingly. Phil, preoccupied as they all were with images of blood, hoped that blood wasn't rising in her ruined lungs. He leaned in, inches away. "Theresa, do you think the folks on Hollis Street helped eliminate the Watsons?"

"I honestly don't know. But all you have to do is look for the source of the rage, Phil."

CHAPTER 18

Phil left and headed straight for the Rose to get a scotch and a beer chaser. He half hoped to run into Boog DeKlerk, even if the South African was a pain in the ass. Boog would bitch and argue, but he would finally support Phil's radical plan. Hell, Phil would barely be able to keep him from riding along.

Tonight.

Phil Mohlman intended to press Jerry Proffet hard, just one step short of arresting him; two steps, actually, since Phil had neither a search warrant nor an arrest warrant, and little prospect of talking a judge into authorizing either kind at eight o'clock in the evening. He had a scotch at the bar, ordered a second. Persuasion was the key. That would be ideal: talk the Proffets into a look around the house, casual, maybe lie a little bit and say he wanted to familiarize himself with the layout of the two-storey model on the street. Find a reason to examine the garage. Look for the blood Theresa imagined everywhere. Then give the impression he was wrapping up details. Come back to Jerry and Selma's living room and less gently ask how the conflict between Tom Watson and the ex-executives had come to this pretty pass. "Pretty pass" was a phrase Phil's mother often used.

He had floated the plan, without specifics, with his partner before leaving Coppermount Drive. Henry had promised to come along in support, but the moment he acquiesced, Theresa's flaring cough distracted him, and they had no time to work out the details.

Phil stepped out of the Rose to call Henry, but when he reached the empty parking lot, he speed-dialed Jerry Proffet by accident.

"Yes?" Jerry answered with military gruffness. Phil could sense Selma in the background. Maybe it was the scotch, but the fact that he had Jerry on speed-dial seemed portentous. He recovered quickly.

"I'll be by at nine."

"But why?" Jerry said, more fear in his voice than Phil expected.

"We've pretty much interviewed everyone about everything," Phil stated. "But the details don't add up in a few areas. Nothing serious, Mr. Proffet."

"What does that mean?"

"Nine sharp."

Now he stabbed the correct number, and for once the connection to the desert was clear. Theresa was feeling fine, and Henry cheerfully echoed Phil's own words to Proffet: "Nine sharp. I'll be at the gates."

Phil drank alone in the bar. Boog hadn't been there and wasn't expected, and nobody else from the West Valley precinct entered. He ordered a third scotch. He had the paradoxical feeling that he had been plodding for weeks but now he might be moving too fast. *Frustration will give you that feeling,* he observed. He wondered about Theresa Pastern and what had made her so . . . psychic. Her preoccupation with blood was an amateur's obsession, and morbid, too, yet she had convinced him that the blood spillage contained the signature of the killer's rage. Proffet had panicked and let his full fury spray across the rooms of both murder sites and, as Theresa had reasoned, generated a flood of malice along Hollis Street, house to house, up to its dead end.

The killer had driven into the hillside fog with Tom Watson's last fluids seeping into the spools of wire. In his own gruesome mood, Phil imagined blood raining down on the forest and river world of the Wasatch. He was a city boy, and he worked to envision the exhausted executioner hoisting a blood-sodden body by flashlight to the river cliff. The scotch was getting to Phil. Was Jerry Proffet a woodsman? He was military, but what difference did that make? Never mind, there were bound to be outdoorsmen among the neighbours. That guy next door to Proffet, Ronald Devereau? Jake Wazinski? That loner Henry interviewed, Davis? Which one had volunteered to help?

Phil's thoughts remained with Theresa. He found her beautiful, special, and a prize for his partner, Henry. She was more than that, for her illness had turned her otherworldly in an enchanting way. Her failing lungs forced her to disburse short sentences and, he had noticed tonight, often these swathed pearls of insight. She was radiant, with shining alabaster skin, but as his mother would say, she was a consumptive beauty. Of course he would obey her insights — he longed to be in her thrall.

The Rose was still, the bartender having retreated to the back. The silence rushed over Phil, and the recollection of Theresa's smoky voice beguiled him again.

A revelation came raw-edged from her to him: he must go searching for blood, *literally*.

He stayed patient as long as he could. He skipped a fourth scotch, went out to his plain sedan, and began to drive in the direction of Hollis Street, but then slowed to keep from arriving more than five minutes early. The plan was to rendezvous with Henry out on the avenue in front of the stone pillars at 8:55.

Henry was late. Phil held back at the false gate until 9:05 and eased onto the street, halting in front of Maude's bungalow at Number 4. He had tried to keep away in recent days, so as not to further alienate the residents; he didn't need Chief Grady getting complaints of harassment by his Homicide detectives. Now, with the low-angled summer sun fixing the street in amber, the ranks of silent houses spooked him. Susan Powell haunted him, too. Had the killer of Tom Watson tried to play off that tragedy by removing Tom's body with a sleight-of-hand flourish, convinced he could make the corpse disappear forever, like Susan?

He moved on to the bottom of the cul-de-sac and parked. The garage door at Number 11 was up, but dusk concealed much of the interior. He identified the trunk of a shiny white Toyota Corolla parked on the left side of the wood structure. Did the Proffets have two cars, or merely a two-car garage, the spare half a man-cave? No, this had to be Selma's vehicle.

Lights glowed in two rooms of the house, one up, one down, but the front door and garage lamps hadn't been switched on. Solar-powered bulbs lined the front flower beds but had barely begun to glimmer. The post light on the lawn was off. Next door, a single orange desk lamp glowed from a window of the Devereau house. All this oblique under-lighting made Phil suspicious, but still he kept his Glock holstered. He glanced back up the road. The air was fusty and Hollis Street began to close in on him, as if it were producing its own weather system. He looked around for something reassuring and glimpsed Jerry Proffet's pinyon tree in the easement near the house. It was the only sign of natural life on Hollis Street.

The garage gaped, beckoning the veteran detective. The warm night and the booze he had put back made him sweat, and he thought of Jerry Proffet shivering somewhere nearby.

Why was the garage door open?

Phil was known to be a little slack about his equipment, forgetting extra ammo clips when he went out on a Code Delta or leaving his vest at the precinct. Tonight he was armed with his Glock 17 and reloads but lacked a flashlight. He tapped his mobile and held it up, creating a torch and, bonus, giving him access to speed-dial. A quick scan of the garage and he would knock on the front door, pretending that he had freshly arrived.

He paused at the opening. No stained sink or bloody mop waited, and no sticky lake of blood coated the cement floor, but what did he expect? He flanked the white car and padded to the back wall, making sure not to bump against a ceiling-high rack of rakes and tools. Even in the shadows he noted the perfection of the storage array, all the handles of the rakes and garden implements aligned plumb vertical. He paused. The screen of his mobile cast only diffuse light onto the floor, and he knelt down for a closer view.

In spite of his offhand prediction to Henry, Phil did not really expect to find blood traces in the concrete, but there they were, five or six drops of red spoiling Jerry Proffet's perfect suburban pastiche. Phil somehow knew that this was Jerry's own blood; it was too fresh to be Tom Watson's. It was all happening again. Theresa Pastern had asked, "What's the one thing that's hard to believe about this madman?" Now Phil knew: that the lunatic was willing to spread so much blood around. And what was her last admonition? He should search for the source of the killer's anger.

Phil killed the phone and took out his weapon. He considered texting Henry to warn him, but the blood on the cement changed his plan.

He eased around the grill of the Corolla and managed to miss all the hanging tools. Looking back into the garage, he fathomed the obvious: Selma had parked her car hard by the left wall of the garage to leave room for Jerry to pull in. But where was the husband's ride? Phil had a vision of the killer fleeing up into the Wasatch Mountains in Jerry's tidy SUV, a body or two oozing in the back.

Looking down, he found a red smear on his pants. Blood had transferred from the bumper of the Corolla onto his knee. He was confused. What had happened here, and was he heading into another living room slaughterhouse? The killer had likely taken Jerry prisoner and forced him inside from the garage, where he planned to do . . . what?

The garage connected to the house by what in the East was called a breezeway. In this configuration, the walk-through ended at the kitchen entrance. To knock, or not to knock? Phil thought again of calling Henry. He turned back to the garage and noiselessly took an old-fashioned garden spade from the punchboard rack. He laid the shovel on the hood of the white car so that it became an arrow for Henry to follow down the passage to the kitchen.

He opened the kitchen door.

The antechamber offered two ways to go, a short hallway off

to the right into the entertainment den, or the full kitchen straight ahead. He could make out a giant television in the den. He paused, evaluating the danger, but quickly saw that the kitchen was unoccupied, and so he went that way. It was almost a relief not to find bodies on the floor or blood smeared on the cupboards. The closed-in humidity of Jerry Proffet's home got to him. He regretted that third glass of scotch.

The main rooms on the ground level lay beyond the next doorway; this route would take him full-circle through the living and dining rooms to the den and its flat-screen monster. In the heart of the kitchen now, he tiptoed around the chopping-block island in order to advance on the main corridor. The front door off to his left was deadbolted; far to the right, sliding doors exited to the backyard, and they appeared to be locked, too.

He circled right, coming to the entertainment room. The TV — it had to be a sixty-inch — loomed at an angle across one corner, and although the space was in heavy shadow, he could make out a boat-size couch facing the television. The den was large, but the furniture, including a La-Z-Boy chair, filled it. When did they start making everything so big?

Phil's eyes adjusted to the gloom, allowing him to make out the bodies of Jerry and Selma Proffet on the carpet before the La-Z-Boy. He tiptoed forward and knelt down. Both were dead, though only Jerry displayed a wound, a deep hole in his throat. Phil had the feeling of being watched and held his gun higher.

The watcher moved out from behind the flat-screen. He halted in the silence, waiting. Fifteen seconds. Twenty. Thirty. Ronald Devereau, one-term president of the Hollis Street executive committee, pointed the gun-shaped Taser at Phil Mohlman's back. The detective spun about, a quarter turn only, but enough to recognize his attacker. Fifty thousand volts launched Detective Mohlman face-first into the rug. Before passing into darkness, he remembered something Theresa had said to him: *What's the one thing you can't believe?*

Devereau wasn't intent on killing the policeman with the Taser, but he was perfectly willing to jolt him again if he somehow came awake. Devereau's thoughts drifted, bright pictures splaying out from his memory. Watson had needed two jolts to keep him down. Maybe the sight of his wife's head had made him brave. Whatever it took.

The detective didn't move, and Devereau was content to stare down at the grouping, fortuitously arrayed, in his fierce view, like icons of a triptych, two dead flanking one unconscious.

He considered restaging the room to make it appear that the cop had killed the others, but none of these scenarios played persuasively. How could anyone reasonably interpret the flight of Jerry Proffet from the garage (screwdriver in the neck) to the den (boot heel on the throat), and Selma's demise (choking in front of *Antiques Roadshow*) so as to incriminate the cop?

He stuck to his initial plan, though he had to hurry now, for others were coming. He dragged the detective by the heels from between the Proffets to the dining room. As Devereau reached to slide open the patio door, the cop moaned and began to revive. His captor dropped his feet and took a stride back into the room. Phil turned his head to one side and spat a gout of blood, thick as phlegm, onto the rug. Devereau drove a foot into his face and then stomped on his left knee joint.

Ronald Devereau credited his survival in this world in equal parts to shrewd planning and benevolent forces outside his control. It was his version of humility. He'd been blessed. Never arrested, let alone charged. Never fingerprinted. Never wounded in battle, though most of his life had unfurled around guns and explosives. His good fortune was bolstered by the precautions he took. Most important, he declared to himself, he possessed Luck. He had endured for twenty years in anonymity because he made smart decisions and Fate rewarded him.

Until now. With these rash killings he had set his course for the Void (he loved to put capital letters on big-concept words). Rather than castigating himself, he asked: can the Void, Destiny, and Luck merge? He paused in the silence by the sliding doors and looked at the side of his house at 13 Hollis. His plan had been in place for years, and now he stood at the cliff edge of freedom. Reconciled to his own extinction, he drew strength from the certainty of his Fate and savoured the potential gifts of Luck.

As he dragged Detective Mohlman from the patio to the lawn (*bump, bump, bump*), he amused himself by counting his lucky moments that evening. Benighted Jerry Proffet had come to see him, all clammy-skinned and worried. How fortunate that it was *Antiques Roadshow* night and Selma was guaranteed to be in the TV room, just waiting for him after he dispatched her husband. Blessed, certainly, that the older detective, the one he had met three times, had dropped by alone. And lucky that had been ready with the whole neat plan, a full can of gasoline waiting in his own garage.

A pair of headlights sweeping across the lawn between his house and the Proffets broke his reverie. Caught out in the open like an escaping jailbird, he looked away to avoid the blinding beams. But he didn't drop the detective's body, and certainly didn't panic. He knew who was coming to get him.

CHAPTER 19

Henry arrived late, though only by twelve minutes.

He and Theresa finished clearing the dishes, and Henry walked out for a view of the desert light show. He knew why he loved the West. Others talked about the witching hour or the flash of green on a sea horizon, but all Utahans were intimate with the march to sunset, when the desert sky worked its way across the colour spectrum into indigo blue, purple, and black. Henry shared his wife's dislike of Hollis Street: it was dark territory, and it didn't feed off the beauty of the Utah light the way the house on Coppermount did.

Tonight he would miss the close of day, so he lingered an extra minute.

He heard Theresa starting to rasp again. He crossed the patio to look for her new inhaler but remembered that the tray with all her prescriptions had been moved inside. He found her on hands and knees in the living room, heaving, engulfed, and he ran to the bathroom for her pills. In the crisis, it didn't matter to either of them that she had taken her limit of Ventolin. Back in the main room, she rolled onto her side on the Navaho carpet, elbows clutched to her ribs, hands shaking, lips turning blue. All the while, she tried to spit out what wouldn't come.

The Ventolin calmed her lungs, or perhaps, Henry thought, the outburst had exhausted itself. Theresa remained on her side, and so, as he had many times, he crouched down to wait for her cue that she was recovering. It came as a wan smile and a fluttering of her eyelids. Had Henry been attentive to deeper clues, he would have seen her look across the carpet to the closet in the hallway, where the oxygen tank was stored.

Relief swept over him as his wife levered herself up from the floor without further straining or croaking. She smiled. That was something she couldn't fake.

"Follow Mohlman," she directed, her voice as firm as Corrine's on the 9-1-1 desk at the precinct. For emphasis, and to demonstrate her sinew and will, she squeezed his arm and held him to her side. "Go. Stay safe."

Henry took in the placid look on her face. She was magical to him. Theresa had been making pronouncements all afternoon, and he and Phil had found every magisterial statement convincing. She understood the murderer. Henry knew that she was right to highlight the anger and the unhinged mind behind the Watson killings.

"Do you want to go to the hospital?"

"No, no. Let me relax. It's passed. You have to help Phil."

"At least let me call Tynan to come over."

Henry expected his wife to demur, but she said, "Okay, just for a few minutes to watch the sunset with. I'll wait up for you, sweetheart."

Theresa wasn't okay and knew that her paroxysms would return in an hour or two, but she understood how important it was that Henry join Phil and participate in the arrest of Jerry Proffet. With all her misgivings, she insisted he go.

She accompanied Henry out to the car and made sure he left with his .45 on the floor on the passenger side.

Theresa lounged alone on the patio, enjoying the birdsong at sunset. The new inhaler had kicked in, staving off the tightness in her chest. She dozed, in and out of the world. Elder Tynan was suddenly there, striding from the evening horizon. They had an understanding that he would announce his arrival a hundred yards out whenever he arrived out of the sun. Now, when he was the requisite distance from the patio, he *ahem*ed theatrically. She opened her eyes and smiled at him as he came in and took her hand.

"Henry called me," he said, in the even tone of a visiting pastor.

"You didn't need to come," Theresa said.

"No, but I did. Henry's worried about you."

Theresa valued his friendship, in part because he remained calm at all times and she could learn from his self-possession. Even-tempered men sometimes irked her, but Tynan had helped her master patience. She also trusted his weirdness. He patrolled the red rock formations to the west, monitoring who knows what, for his own purposes. She liked to watch him on his desert prowls. He wore white shirts, like a minister, which he surely was, and they reflected back like flags or sails in the rippling heat. What had Jesus accomplished in his forty days in the wilderness? She had forgotten.

They spoke little as they waited for night. Twenty minutes into their vigil, the Pasterns' phone rang. They'd had trouble with their landline but for once, the reception was good.

"This is Theresa Pastern." She gave her name up front while she had the chance; a coughing jag might surge at any time.

"I'm looking for Henry Pastern. This is Stanley Chambers. Your husband called me earlier, said it was urgent. Sorry, I was out."

Theresa wasn't privy to Henry's call, but she made a guess. "Mr. Chambers, do you live on Hollis Street in West Valley?"

"Not anymore. But I resided at Number 6 until a few months ago."

"In fact, Henry's over on Hollis right now. I don't know what he called you about."

Concern tinted Chambers's quick reply. "I do. He wanted my opinion on something. Who's he planning to visit?"

"Mr. Proffet."

"Okay, then." Theresa felt him working through Henry's query. "Can you pass him a message, Mrs. Pastern?"

Theresa picked up on his edgy tone. "I can get him on the phone right now." She turned feverish. She didn't tell Chambers to call Henry directly.

"He wanted to know whether Tom Watson and Jerry Proffet ever had an open fight."

"And?"

"Not between those two that I'm personally aware of." Chambers had an accommodating, almost courtly style but his statement seemed vague to her.

"Between Tom Watson and someone else?" she probed.

His voice turned steely. "I'm talking about a fight between Jerry Proffet and Ronald Devereau. You see, they both knew about the marijuana."

"You should have told Henry before. He couldn't believe the community association didn't confront Mr. Watson in some fashion. No one admits it."

Chambers paused, avoiding a direct response, letting Theresa work out that he had put his house on the market because of the grow op across the street. "I was president for a while. I quit because I got tired of the politics of the committee. They wanted to regulate everything. They say there's nothing nastier than street politics, and this was like that. No one but those two residents wanted to continue HASA. Devereau and Proffet live next to one another, and they tried to run the place from their end of the block. They were the only ones who knew about Tom. But two people doesn't make a quorum."

Theresa went for broke. "Did Devereau and Proffet know about the grow house from the *beginning*?"

"Not at the outset, no. It was recent. Otherwise, they wouldn't have entrusted Tom Watson with contacting the Colorado company that owned Number 5."

Theresa now understood why Chambers had failed to report all this to Henry. He had known about the grow op before any of the other members of the executive and was ashamed.

"Did Devereau ever threaten you?"

But Chambers was gone. Theresa was unsure whether he had hung up or they had lost the link; she cursed the phone service in the desert.

Instead of calling back, Theresa called Henry's mobile. It kicked over to his message box. She considered leaving a lengthy account of her conversation with Chambers, but kept it short, allowing her panic to carry the message: "Watch out for Devereau."

The Mormon elder had been listening.

"Tynan, is your truck working?" she said.

"Never not working. Where are we going?"

Tynan always dressed in black. His tractor was black and so was his truck. Theresa had watched him barrelling down Coppermount many times, the vehicle coated in desert grime. She ran outside towards Tynan's house, the Mormon in tow, but by the time they traversed the hundred yards to his driveway, she was winded and he had to prop her up against the frame of his garage while he entered the door code. The door flipped up to reveal the truck. Theresa realized that she had never been in his vehicle, his house, or his garage, which like every other part of the property stood unfinished.

Tynan backed the truck out and helped her into the passenger side. The seats were leather and he had polished the dashboard with Armor All. The GPS affixed to the dash was state-of-the-art and came on with the ignition, maps swirling, options blinking all over the screen. The AC cooled the cab in thirty seconds.

"Where did you buy this starship?" she rasped.

"Military," he said unhelpfully.

The engine rumbled and settled into a forceful hum. Everything under the hood seemed powerful. Tynan typed in "Hollis Street," and the GPS lady advised them to follow her detailed course. He listened for only a few seconds and slapped a red button on the GPS screen; it seemed right to shut her up.

They fell silent. Tynan made all the turns unerringly up to the Hollis Street entrance and swooped through the stone gates, halting in front of Maude Hampson's address to reconnoitre. The clock on the display showed 9:32. Given the drive time from Coppermount to Hollis, a little slower for Henry than Tynan, Theresa calculated that Henry was already here and had connected with Phil within the past seven or eight minutes. Tynan turned off his headlights and crept in the darkness towards the two vehicles parked down at the cul-de-sac.

"I don't know Devereau's address," she said.

"We'll figure it out."

She examined the houses, imagining she could smell blood mixed with marijuana. Tynan pointed to the Proffets' lawn sign and pulled to the curb. Theresa gave a thumbs-up and whispered, "Chambers said Devereau lives next door."

They emerged from the big truck and appraised the houses. The setting was oddly familiar to Theresa, whether from the one time the realtor had taken them by or from Henry's Scheherazade tales.

"Do I smell smoke?" Tynan said. Theresa shrugged. She didn't dispute Tynan's senses but rather doubted her own: the drugs had dulled her olfactory system. There was no visible smoke.

They had to choose and might have moved closer to probe Devereau's two-storey, but the light from the Proffets' kitchen and the yawning garage lured them onto the same path Phil and Henry had chosen through the garage.

Reaching the kitchen door, Theresa felt the danger. Tynan held up a cautionary palm and pulled her around, manhandling her back out the garage to the truck. Rooting behind the cab seats, he brought out a .357 Magnum and a military-grade flashlight. He tossed the torch to her; she read "JetBeam Raptor" on the casing.

On their second pass through the garage, they missed the blood drops on the cement and the smears on the bumper of the Corolla. Theresa, taking the lead, turned to Tynan in anticipation of advancing on the main house, and eyed the Magnum. *Guns lead to gunfights*, she reflected; the large pistol might generate a reflexive shot from Henry or Phil inside. Tynan seemed to understand and lowered the weapon but kept the safety on.

She hissed, "I think we should announce ourselves."

Tynan took the risk and called, "Henry! Phil!"

They entered the kitchen, but instead of tracking Phil Mohlman's route, they made a hard right into what Theresa knew real estate agents labelled a "family room." She made the call to turn on the torch. Its powerful LED ray caught the glint of blood streaming from Jerry Proffet's throat wound. Next to him, in a fetal clench, lay Selma Proffet.

Tynan whispered, "These can't be anyone but the Proffets. Should we call 9-1-1?"

"The police are already here," Theresa said. *Call the fire department, too, if you want,* she thought. The threat was here, now, and Theresa was manic to find her husband.

Tynan raised his pistol again. He slipped into the kitchen and was back in fifteen seconds, shaking his head. "Follow me."

Theresa understood that he was clearing each room in sequence while trying to figure out the path Henry and Phil had taken. The choice now, both realized, was to search the upstairs or proceed around to the patio doors. A sweep of the flashlight revealed no more corpses in the family room, and they passed into the carpeted living zone. Theresa almost stepped in the upchuck of blood and scotch that Phil had deposited on the rug inside the glass panels.

Theresa took the vanguard position out the door, abandoning any effort at stealth. Smoke drifted towards them across the side lawn. Theresa headed across the grass to Devereau's patio, which was the match of Jerry and Selma Proffet's, but found the door lock on. Seeing this, Tynan diverted course around to the front of Devereau's two-storey, his goal the front door. Darker smoke belched from a vent on the side of the house.

Theresa caught up to Tynan on the cement steps before the solid oak front door. He tried the handle, stood farther back and fired a single booming shot into one of the narrow glass panels flanking the entrance.

Tynan stepped back, startled by his own gun. He looked at Theresa.

"Now we'll see if everyone on Hollis Street is truly deaf," she said.

A single shot responded from the interior. Tynan reached through the narrow window gap and unlocked the door. The smoke, billowing now, had turned black, and the smell of gasoline was strong, promising an explosion. As Theresa attempted to rush into the hall, she staggered from a convulsion that her adrenalin fought to suppress. Tynan rushed past her and in three strides reached the far side of Devereau's kitchen, where one glance revealed the source of the fire as the basement.

Theresa was down now, incapable of moving any distance. Tynan, gasping himself, carried her to the open front entrance and onto the stoop. Even this spot wasn't clear, for pitch smoke continued to snake out the door from the kitchen stairs.

Tynan made several wild calculations. Henry and Detective Mohlman were in this house and one of them had fired the shot. He also guessed that the killer might like symmetry and that the detectives could be in the den of the Devereau house. Keeping low, but running, Tynan circled the downstairs rooms and arrived at the far end of the den. It was almost bare of furniture — no massive TV — but he could find few reference points through the poisonous mist.

"Mohlman and Pastern," Henry's disembodied voice panted.

"Where?" Tynan called.

The crack of Henry Pastern's .45 drove Tynan backward. The shot produced a sulphurous flash in the far corner of the den, letting him place Henry.

"Take him. I can't walk," Henry pleaded.

Tynan groped around the den and found Phil Mohlman on the carpet. He was unconscious. Blood coated his left eye.

"Be back for you, Henry."

Henry wheezed, "I'll try through the garage."

"No," Tynan said, "the fire's coming up the basement stairs. Use the front hall. Where's Devereau?"

Henry began choking, and Tynan didn't wait for an answer. He had already decided to work his way through the den and the hall to the front. Let Devereau come after him. Tynan began to drag Phil by the feet out the doorway. *Around the corner now, ten more steps, don't drop the Magnum. Don't shoot into the smoke unless you're sure it's Devereau.* He reached the open front door and found the air unimproved as smoke rolled out onto the landing, thicker than ever.

But now hands were reaching out for his burden. The tenants of Hollis Street had finally come forward to help. Tynan tripped on the top step and a red-haired figure caught him. Recoiling, he almost shot the man. A little old lady moved into view and began to clean the blood from Phil Mohlman's eye with her shawl.

Theresa lay on the lowest step, fighting for oxygen as neighbours propped her up and bathed her brow. Behind her, halfway down the corridor of the house and out of sight, a man retched and began to cough, as if mocking her affliction. Finding new strength, she fought free of the residents holding her and stumbled up the steps into the fog.

Tynan, reviving, followed but at once encountered disorienting smoke. It occurred to him that the ceiling sprinklers should have gone off; Devereau must have disabled them. In the darkness at the edge of the family room, he tripped across Theresa, who was attempting to drag her husband by one shoulder along the hall. Tynan knelt and saw that a gunshot had torn up Henry's left thigh. He positioned himself at Henry's other side and heaved him up with both arms.

At the front door, Jake Wazinski collected the semi-conscious policeman and handed him off to his wife and Maude Hampson. Wooski then helped Tynan out the doorway. Sirens announced the passage of fire trucks through the stone gates. The sound grew closer, reflecting off the bungalows along Hollis Street. Tynan turned and went back inside for Theresa.

CHAPTER 20

Three weeks later, Theresa Pastern died in the University of Utah Burn Center, her lungs scarred beyond repair, a double transplant ruled unsurvivable.

Across town, in another Salt Lake City hospital, the sight came back to Phil Mohlman's right eye. The left would have to wait another month.

The ceremony at Parkland Cemetery had ended, leaving Henry at loose ends, looking for something or someone in the crowd who might relieve him of his obligation to accept sympathy. Then he sighted Peter and Joan fifty yards distant. Henry's father had died years ago, and now he realized that he had always wanted more than just professional guidance from Chief Inspector Cammon. Not a father exactly, but the availability in his life of a serious man whose honesty was unrelenting, whose goodwill was unstinting, and whose experience was unequalled by any other policeman Henry had met. Thus, when Henry beelined towards Peter, it was not for sympathy or overt sentiment, but guidance.

It was Peter who showed emotion. He was filled with sadness and regret, for he was ravaged by guilt that he hadn't offered more help in those brief interactions with Henry over the preceding months. Joan walked beside him and held his hand. She had been the first one to suggest a visit to England by the Pasterns, and now she, too, was guilt-ridden that the trip had never happened. As they crossed the sun-blasted lawn, Peter saw expectation in Henry's chilling look. The Utahan wanted something, and now Peter knew what: retribution. Was this what was meant by Blood Atonement?

Joan embraced Henry and moved away to let the men talk.

"I can't have my revenge," Henry rasped. They hadn't hugged, but Peter held on to his hand with a strong grip. "What do I do, Peter?"

"Henry, this what you do. You write everything down, every detail. It's a story you must tell."

It was not quite that easy, of course, but the two, both trained policemen and English majors, understood that telling the full story could exorcise a policeman's demons and provide its own form of revenge on evil.

After getting used to walking with a cane, Henry Pastern returned to Hollis Street hoping for some measure of closure. Officer Jackson drove; they had become friendly.

Henry would have burned Number 13 to the ground again, but only a charred cavity and Devereau's garage remained at the spot.

"The basement is barely cold," Henry said, as Jackson pulled up in front. "Not much left to clear out."

For once, Jackson felt that he could speak as an equal. "Henry, man, you don't have to do anything, except your duty to your wife to remember every damn thing that happened on this cursed street."

Jackson's words echoed what Peter had said at the funeral, and Henry felt a chill.

The fire had been intense, four gallons of accelerant exploding and searing everything in the basement, igniting the upper storey and leaving only a black pit. To Henry it was a tragic place, profane, like everything Devereau had done.

There were surprises in the police report. Devereau's body had cooked and crusted in the basement inferno, but it remained intact, and the CSI excavators extracted a whole bullet from his chest. He had used a .25 calibre pistol on Henry and then on himself; it was a very lightweight gun for a man bent on slaughter, but sufficient to blow through his own heart.

Henry said nothing the rest of the time he and the patrolman were parked between 11 and 13 Hollis. Jackson respected Henry's silence but couldn't resist one more comment. "Funny that he shot himself in the chest. Most suicides go for the head."

Over the next months, Henry began a report chronicling the deadly events of that summer night. When Phil called Jerry Proffet that evening, Jerry must have panicked. He contacted Devereau. The detectives were coming, Proffet warned. *When? At 9 o'clock sharp.* Devereau instructed Proffet to wait. *It'll be okay. Stay calm. Exactly 9 o'clock, you say?*

The killer followed his final plan to the letter. Having arrayed four red gas cans in the cellar under the stairs of his own house, he trickled the contents around walls — one can, a second. The other two made effective bombs, as he knew from previous experiments with arson. Who knew how long Devereau waited before strolling across to Jerry's garage, taking the screwdriver from the pegboard and knocking on the kitchen door? There was no hesitation, Henry imagined: invite Jerry out to the garage; drive the tool into the gullet; head for the big TV.

Devereau's charred body was found in the basement. DNA tests revealed that his birth name was Jim Riotte, and he had a criminal record for buying restricted chemicals and was suspected of aiding domestic terrorism a decade ago. Since then, Hollis Street had been his hiding place.

Case closed.

Until the day Henry Pastern and Phil Mohlman met for the first time on the patio on Coppermount Drive after Phil got his "new eyes" and limping was no longer impossibly painful for either man. They both drank beer. They had all afternoon; they were on sick leave, extendable as "discretionary administrative" leave. Nothing was said for a long time, until Phil expressed chagrin that he hadn't twigged to Devereau/Riotte during his three interviews. Henry opened the thick case file for a last look, and Phil, with his glasses on, examined the front-view/side-view jailhouse portraits of Jim Riotte from his arrest in 1994, a man he was willing to swear he had never seen before, with either his old or his new eyes.

PART 2

PETER

*The English have a great hunger
for desolate places.*
Feisal to Lawrence, *Lawrence of Arabia*.
Screenplay by Robert Bolt and Michael
Wilson.

CHAPTER 21

Peter Cammon, Chief Inspector (retired), was a great detective.

Everyone said so. His career was inevitably labelled "distin-guished." New Scotland Yard threw him three retirement parties. He had killed seven men (or was it eight? — his colleagues had begun to forget as Cammon slipped into semi-legend) over four and a half decades in harness, and none of the internal departmental reviews had affixed any blame. And so, untarnished, fabled, he had faded into retirement.

The late spring day the padded envelope arrived at the cottage in Leicestershire, Peter was firmly re-established in the depths of the renovated air raid shelter in the garden. He had lost count of the months he had spent on his family project, and now that the weather had turned fine, he had rushed back to these ascetic surroundings determined to finish off the task. His brother, Lionel, had died of a stroke, leaving a request of his only sibling: delve into a memoir left by their father of his War years, and perhaps get it published. The subtext of Lionel's posthumous petition had been that Peter would discover a heroic truth about their father. Peter had started out excited. Orderly stacks of family papers now lined the cement walls of the uncomfortable air raid bunker.

George Frederick Cammon, named in a lapse in judgement by his father after the German composer George Frideric Handel, had been a prominent solicitor and, throughout the Second World War, a trusted intelligence officer with the British government. Until Lionel's bequest, Peter had known only the first part of his dad's biography. GF's dramatic memoir, typed on yellow paper, covered his entire war experience from 1939 through 1945, and a bit before and after, and Peter rushed through the text in one go, as a good son of Britain would take in any thrilling story of the Empire. As Lionel intended, Peter was carried back to his father's knee, awestruck by what he had never known. It might indeed make a thrilling book.

George Cammon's role leading into the War had been to think up ways to counter the radical British fascist party and hound its leader, Oswald Mosley. After the declaration of war, the lure of the fascist view in Britain, though diminished, continued, and Mosley's network remained a thorn in Churchill's side. Throughout the conflict, George Cammon risked beatings by pro-Nazi thugs and endured threats to his family as he monitored the remnants of the British Union of Fascists.

Lionel's somewhat coy entreaty promised that Peter would discover a secret, swashbuckling deed within their father's account that would change Peter's view of their old man. And there it was, popping up on page ten of GF's saga. In 1929, Oswald Mosley had married Diana Mitford, one of six sisters in a prominent English clan. George was asked by the Home Office to watch the couple under the ruse of providing liaison between the government and the Mitfords on legal issues, very vaguely defined. George, according to his own notes, became a regular presence in the Mosleys' drawing room, "although," he wrote, "I never stayed for dinner." If Diana wholeheartedly embraced fascism and, with her husband, kept in touch with Hitler throughout the 1930s, her younger sister, the scatterbrained Unity Mitford, idolized the Fuhrer; she may have slept with him. While in Germany in 1939, the unstable Unity tried to commit suicide by shooting herself in the head. Winston Churchill personally dispatched George Cammon to Munich to verify the news reports and recommend a course of action. Ultimately, the well-connected Mitfords were able to transfer their daughter back to Britain with a minimum of scandal. For his efforts, George Cammon came close to execution by a German bullet.

Lionel had a Good Cold War working in the Home Office in the fifties, sixties, and seventies. He was, to sum up, some kind of spymaster. George always favoured his elder son, and Peter and his father had had a bumpy relationship. GF seemed a cold, uncommunicative figure to his younger boy. Later, as Peter, straight out of Oxford, embraced a career in the Yard, he was made to feel substandard by his father. Police work was too "straightforward" a career choice, George pronounced. It never occurred to young Peter that George Frederick Cammon was a snob.

George's roughed-out autobiography made Peter feel that his own career had been hollow, without any equivalent triumph on his record. It was a sign that the son was still in the intimidating shadow of the father that, as Peter toiled in the air raid shelter, he failed to ask some obvious questions. Why had he never been told these stories, and was Lionel's request entirely benign? On this point, Joan, happy that her husband had retired from his "life of crime," understood what he failed to see: that a distinguished detective must expect to encounter ghosts — including family ones — and learn to live with them.

As months rolled by, Peter saw no end to the project, and the tedium and complexity of editing the manuscript only increased his unease with his own recently completed career. He had told himself, and his father's and brother's ghosts, that his task was to set the record straight on GF's heroic contribution. He now admitted to the concrete walls and to his golden retriever, Jasper, that he wasn't sure where he was going with the reams of notes and documents he had assembled.

He spent too much time in the claustrophobic shelter, and Joan looked for an opportunity to point out his declining sense of proportion. The one time he confided his sense of inadequacy to her, she didn't hesitate. "What do you mean? You helped capture the

Yorkshire Ripper, the Kray gang, that Unabomber fellow, and how many other killers and terrorists?"

"Yes, but I killed men along the way. Offset by what?" Peter countered.

Joan, never receptive to self-pity, treated this as the non sequitur it was. She encouraged him to abandon that gloomy hole in the ground for the renovated shed at the rear of the garden. The bomb shelter, she said, had become a metaphor for "bombardment-by-kinfolk."

Peter turned a bit dopey. He began to latch on to small auguries. One evening, they went out for dinner at an Italian place, and he noticed on the menu: "Try our signature veal parmesan!" *That's what I lack, a signature accomplishment as a career detective.*

To Peter's credit, he soon pinpointed his dilemma, although his insight did not bring him much closer to finishing the manuscript. George's and Lionel's exploits had imprinted the idea of *evil* on his mind. Oswald Mosley and Joseph Stalin, fascism and communism — they had been wicked. Thinking back over his career, Peter couldn't swear that any of the men he stopped had been purely evil. Not like Mosley or Stalin.

When the post arrived with the Salt Lake City address and the outline of a mountain on the upper left corner of the envelope, Joan had Jasper carry it out to the air raid shelter. She knew it was important. She had been at the funeral of Henry Pastern's wife in Ogden and, not always telling Peter, had chatted with Henry at length the few times he had called England over the winter.

The retriever sat at the top of the stone steps with the package in her jaws and waited for her master to notice her. Jasper no longer kept Peter company in his bunker; it was too boring even for a loyal dog. Peter called her down, took the envelope, and kissed Jasper on her head. He hefted the padded mailer and noted Henry's name on the return label. He climbed the steps and strode — a little faster than he might have, Joan noted from the kitchen window — to his work shed. Jasper trotted behind Peter to the building, which had once been a chicken roost. "We flushed out the chicken shit," Peter would tell people, "and I keep my own in it now." They christened it Hispaniola; his side was Haiti, and her potting shed next door, the Dominican Republic. Now, in the pleasant and spacious room, he pondered why he had bothered to work in the cramped underground shelter; no one was going to buzz-bomb his father's records.

Jasper jumped onto the long trestle table by the window. She was an old dog, and the effort strained her joints. Peter looked again at the outline of the mountain on the package. He regarded Jasper, slobbering and pleased with herself, and felt his excitement growing. Jasper had never leapt onto the table before, but now she posed with her ears perked up. *If I need a sign, my dog hears the high notes I can't.*

Peter spread the contents out on the work table. There wasn't much: a police report stamped with a Utah state police logo, a head-shot photograph, and a drawing of a man's face. The latter, Peter noted, was a police artist's sketch, a face-on portrait. There were two photocopied affidavits, one Henry's and the other signed by Detective Phillip Mohlman; Peter remembered the wounded cop from Theresa Pastern's funeral. Finally, Henry had included his own typed ten-page narrative, and clipped to the last page was a stiff card with the hand-written plea "Can you come to Utah?"

He read through Henry's narrative before examining the other materials. It summarized the blood-soaked chaos on Hollis Street, the manhunt, Theresa's death, and the demise of Ronald Devereau; the González meeting in Wendover had been dealt with perfunctorily. Peter understood that Henry had begun the gruesome tale with the hope of achieving some form of catharsis, but that it now climaxed in his request to his old British friend.

Peter also caught a whiff of his father's story in Henry's violent account. George Cammon's wartime career may have amounted to a Gentleman's Lark most of the time, but his memoir was honest about the dread he had felt in confronting malevolence, and Peter tasted that horror in the tragedy of the Pasterns. He moved the police report out of range of Jasper's drool, but at key points in Henry's chronicle he scratched the retriever's noggin and muttered affectionately to her.

161

Henry's notes were rumpled, he hadn't used spell-check, and he seemed to have lost the shift key. Peter concluded that the typist had been drunk at the keyboard. This bit of fussy detection made Peter feel better.

He turned to the police report, which he merely scanned for now.

He laid out the two pictures side by side. Two men with similar faces stared out at him, both with neutral expressions. The photo was an arrest mug shot of a clean-shaven Caucasian man in his mid-forties. On the back, someone had jotted "James Riotte, taken June 13, 1994." The sketch was of a different man, whom Peter judged to be age fifty-five, quite possibly older.

Peter got up from the table to gain a better perspective on the pictures. Jasper barked at him. The sketch, said Henry's notes, was of the man responsible for the death of Theresa Pastern, and on the obverse of the drawing Henry had written "KILLER = RONALD DEVEREAU." Peter's detective powers might have been rusty, but his instincts were available to him, and his synapses made an astonishing connection. The KILLER portrait was remarkably close to the famous wanted poster of the Unabomber issued nationwide by the UNABOM Task Force in 1994, though the KILLER figure was much older and did not sport a hoodie or aviator sunglasses.

With trepidation and a sense of fatefulness, Peter went to the filing cabinet next to his desk and pulled out his Unabomber file. He riffled through the dossier and removed two pictures, adding them to the identity parade on the trestle table. One was Peter's copy of the famous Unabomber poster from 1994. He shivered as he looked at it for the first time in eighteen years. Devereau, as portrayed in the KILLER sketch, shared the aquiline nose, thin lips, and sharp jawlines of the man in the wanted poster. The other image in Peter's dusty file was a police drawing of yet another man. Here were four similar-looking suspects: James Riotte, Ronald Devereau, the Unabomber, and a fourth one. But, for Peter's practical purposes, and accounting for age differences, they amounted to a single portrait of evil.

At the funeral in Ogden, Peter had got the feeling that the Hollis

162

Street case wasn't over, wasn't complete. He was right, the evil hadn't been expunged.

He gathered Jasper in his arms and helped her down. With the old dog in tow, he shut the door to his side of the shed and crossed the garden to lock the portal to the air raid shelter. He walked up the steps of the cottage to the kitchen. Joan stood in the centre of the room.

"We need to talk," he said.

Joan nodded. She saw the change in his face, the fading of worry and guilt and the arrival of grim determination.

And so, at that moment, he became once again Peter Cammon, Chief Inspector, New Scotland Yard (no longer retired).

CHAPTER 22

"I'm flying to America as soon as I can book a ticket. I expect I'll be staying a month."

Peter sat Joan down at the dining room table, which struck her as overly formal given how much she already knew about Hollis Street. She was slightly annoyed at his non-negotiable utterance. She wasn't invited, and he wasn't contrite about his abandonment of the cottage, her, or the dog.

But Joan saw the new spark in his eyes. She had watched Peter trudge to the shelter every morning to work on his father's papers. She had worried that he was falling back into old, reclusive ways. No, it wasn't exactly that. She admitted that Peter was amiable enough once he completed his morning's work. But retirement had not changed him the way it should. He needed to break cleanly with the past. For example, he owned six identical, stuffy black suits, and he had retired only three of them; it was an example of half measures. He even refused to toss out his bowler hat.

Peter produced the two pictures from Henry's package.

"The mug shot photo is James Warder Riotte. West Valley Police say he killed the Watsons and the Proffets, attacked Henry and his partner, and then committed suicide by shooting himself through the heart while burning down his house. This picture was taken in 1994, when Riotte was arrested for buying large amounts of fertilizer and trying to sell it to a militia group in Colorado. He disappeared without a trace in '95. Investigators believe he took the name Ronald Devereau and bought a house on Hollis Street in 2002, just after the neighbourhood was built."

"Where was he between 1995 and 2002?"

"No one knows. The police have given up on all aspects of the case."

"But why does Henry believe that Riotte didn't commit the killings?"

"Because the police sketch of Devereau, this one here, is a different person. It's based on Henry's recollection of Devereau, as well as the efforts of Phil Mohlman and two or three residents on Hollis Street. Riotte and Devereau are — were — different people."

"You don't find that a bit thin? The second face isn't too far off the first. Except the second man has a mole on his neck. You believe Henry?"

"Yes, but the authorities don't, except his partner."

Joan sat back, waiting for Peter to expound his own theory. The faces were similar, very close if you factored in aging. She worried that he was getting carried away by this new puzzle. She had seen Henry Pastern in mourning, seen Theresa's father at the gravesite. No matter how intriguing this emerging manhunt was, a cloud of bitterness hovered above Salt Lake that perhaps distorted common sense.

There was something else in play here. Peter's last case, the Carpenter Affair, had drawn in the whole Cammon family, exposing Maddy and Michael, Peter's son, to considerable danger. Peter had understood this, and he subsequently opened up to Joan about his police work in a dozen or more conversations at this table. This time, she was wary of his reticence to include her. Did he know that she wanted to accompany him to Utah, that her talks with Henry gave her a stake in the matter? Also, he seemed unaware that leaving England without consulting Maddy, their daughter-in-law, would certainly give offence. And was there another dimension to the case, a factor that rendered it personal?

"There's something else, isn't there, Peter? Another reason to reject the official scenario."

Tapping the sketch labelled "KILLER," he said, "Does this face remind you of anyone famous?"

She picked up the picture and set it down again. "Not really."

Peter juxtaposed the Devereau sketch with the Unabomber wanted poster. "Remove seventeen years or so and add sunglasses, you have the Unabomber."

That's it? Joan thought but did not say. She was confused. The Unabomber was in custody. *That* case was closed, and so was Hollis Street. One man locked up forever in a prison, and the other immolated in a house. Peter was running off to chase phantoms, and who knew what mental state Henry Pastern was in.

Peter launched into his theory of the Unabomber. "Ted Kaczyński sent or planted sixteen explosive devices between 1978 and his capture in 1996. From the eighties on, there were rumours that Kaczynski had help in manufacturing his bombs. He was a second-rate carpenter and, we can never forget, hostile to technology, so, allegedly, he must have had assistance. In 1994, the investigators generated this sketch on the basis of an interview with a bystander in Salt Lake City at one of his target sites. Everyone in the world got to know this face. Now, Joan, look at this fourth portrait."

"Who's that?"

"It's a witness composite from another case." He hesitated. "From the Oklahoma City bombing."

Joan saw distinct similarities among the four pictures, also some differences. Devereau, the man in the wanted poster, and the fellow in Oklahoma could be the same man. The one in the photograph, said to be Jim Riotte, was different. She didn't even want to consider the final picture, with its implication that Devereau was involved with Timothy McVeigh in the Oklahoma City tragedy.

"Ted Kaczynski's brother turned him in, and the FBI made the arrest in Montana in 1996, which is not long after Jim Riotte disappeared. What if Riotte and Devereau, fearing they would be tied to Kaczynski, disappeared together?"

"And there's more to this trip than consoling your friend, I'm assuming?" she said, almost to prompt some form of confession from her husband.

"I believe Henry when he says Riotte died in the fire and Devereau is out there, and I have an idea how to find him," Peter said.

Joan was suddenly anxious about his intentions.

"But you don't know who this Devereau is."

The pause seemed endless to her. "I know two things. I know I can find him, and I know that he's evil."

Fear for Peter's safety, for what was to come, made her bold. "What exactly are you planning on doing?"

"I'm going to kill him."

CHAPTER 23

In the main concourse of Salt Lake City International Airport, Peter encountered his own reflection. A spectral figure in a black suit and white shirt, no tie, stood by the luggage carousel, looking his way. He offered the benign smile of a religious shill, or someone knocking at the door with a vacuum cleaner to sell. Peter wondered at his own harsh judgement, for the man seemed open and friendly enough. It took Peter a moment to make an important connection: not only did he recognize the fellow from the Ogden funeral, but he concluded, correctly, that this was the Mormon elder, Tynan, whom Henry had mentioned in his report, the one who for reasons unclear had driven Theresa into West Valley that deadly night. Peter, his brain funked from five thousand miles of flight, continued checking the arrivals throng for Henry Pastern's shaved head.

Against Joan's advice, he had worn one of his remaining black suits out to Utah. He eyed the desert sun blasting the glass walls of the air terminal. He was out of sorts from his London–Chicago–Salt Lake relay and expected to bake in the heat outside. But, he told himself, as his daughter Sarah said, sometimes his uniform was what held him together. He felt a tad better at this thought but then realized that he had left his trademark bowler hat at home. *I am befuddled*, he decided.

The man in black stepped forward, and Peter prepared himself for a homily of some kind. He was being unfair; he reminded himself that he knew nothing about Mormon clerics.

"Mr. Cammon?"

They shook hands. Bemusement inflected the corners of the Mormon elder's smile.

"How do you do," Peter said. "You're Elder Tynan. You live next to Henry?"

"Down the road. I would have addressed you as 'Chief Inspector,' but I wasn't sure if you appreciated the title."

"Right. Well, I am retired."

"Me too."

The smile broadened. Peter began to like the man.

"We don't usually apply the honorific," Tynan continued. "Henry just calls me Tynan. But I am ordained in the LDS." They collected Peter's valise, and Tynan said, "But you weren't really asking if I was an elder, were you?"

"What was I asking?" Peter replied.

"What a Mormon churchman is doing picking you up at the airport instead of Henry."

"Do you always try to get out ahead of questions?"

"Sometimes. When I'm addressing a chief inspector who Henry says is the best detective he ever met."

"That's flattering, coming from a churchman who likely faces tougher sinners than I do."

The banter had turned cute, and the two old veterans of life's wars fell silent. It was odd they hit it off at all, Peter reflected. He didn't go for religious types, found their agendas obvious, and there was an undercurrent of the proselytizer about Tynan. But Peter, who anticipated a lonely pursuit of Ronald Devereau, was quick to embrace allies, and he felt a kinship taking seed. *It will be interesting to watch Tynan's demeanour with Henry*, he thought.

"Excuse me," Peter said as they reached Tynan's grimy truck, "but is Henry well?"

The smile did not vary. "Henry is what we teetotalling Mormons call indisposed."

As Tynan drove onto Coppermount Drive, the airport and the city far behind but the Wasatch Front still visible like a movie set backdrop, Peter realized that he would need to rent a car to get around. "Isolated" did not begin to describe the neighbourhood into which they were heading. The streetscape was doing battle with the desert and wasn't necessarily winning. Most lots were marked out, wired and plumbed at the foundation level, with crude address posts but little more. The windswept emptiness had begun to absorb several parcels. The asphalt ended abruptly a hundred yards down the slope from Henry's house, where a last home, far from complete, anchored the street as best it could.

"That's my place, end of the row. The patches in between me and the Pasterns have been in legal limbo since the recession."

"In distress?"

"I'll say. Figured I should make the effort to finish mine. There's always hope that the development will be fleshed out."

"You're doing the work yourself?"

"Sometimes Henry helps with heavy lifting."

The Pastern estate was a sprawling, horizontal ranch model, plenty of glass and oversize rooms. Peter's first reaction was that the house was far too big for a widower. Peter and Tynan entered the vestibule; Peter noted that the front door was unlocked — whether out of hospitality or slackness, Peter wasn't sure. But Henry did not appear, and Peter started to fear that there was something seriously amiss with his young friend.

Tynan, irresolute, hung back by the rim of the broad, open main room, allowing Peter to absorb the panorama out the back windows. *It would be easy to get lost out there,* was Peter's lambent thought.

"Do you find him roaming in the desert?" Peter speculated.

Tynan seemed to find this a perceptive comment. He half smiled. "Sometimes. I keep my eyes open for him."

Yes, thought Peter, *you are monitoring Henry. Why? Just how much of a missionary is this Mormon elder?*

Peter noticed with some amazement the green bottle sitting on the granite bar. It prismed the sun, projecting an emerald beam across the big room. He recognized the unique green of absinthe. Peter had a lit degree from Oxford and knew that Henry had studied fine arts and literature at Brigham Young. No one reads English without a flirtation with Baudelaire, Dowson, and Verlaine, who were perhaps the most famous of the absinthe-drinking poets. The Green Fairy. The Wormwood Frog. The Goddess. Absinthe had ruined many an artist. It lured the morbid, the poetic, and the self-destructive. If Henry Pastern wanted to give offence to his abstemious religion, he could not have chosen a more alien contaminant.

The paraphernalia of the absinthe ritual were laid out along the bar. A polished salver held a set of Pontarliers, the sundae-shaped glasses used by devotees. A pair of flattened, slotted spoons lay nearby, with a bowl of sugar cubes. An ice bucket completed the gear, the ice melted but the sweat on the outside testifying to recent use. Absinthe turns mystically cloudy when ice water is added, and the effect on the drinker is a fog induced by alchemical interactions. It is the perfect destructive potion for a man in hopeless mourning.

"The tray was a wedding gift."

Peter turned to be greeted by a gaunt beanpole of a man, hollow-eyed and struggling to stand at his full height. Henry was hungover, though near the sober end of a drinking cycle, Peter concluded. His usually shaved skull was stubbly, and he scratched at a scab.

They embraced. Henry managed a generous smile.

"Want a drink of this, Peter?"

"No, you know I prefer beer."

"But absinthe is the preferred libation of the greats. Oscar Wilde and Edgar Allan Poe. You know your writers, Peter."

"So do you. Brigham Young University, I recall?"

Henry flopped onto a set of cushions. "I really could use a drink. Oh, hi, T."

Tynan stepped in from the vestibule. He was no longer smiling. "I'd better go work on some Sheetrock," he said, and left by the patio doors without looking at Peter.

Peter sized up Henry's state. He was in worse shape than expected and required a full-time nurse, or at least a minder. Peter had no intention of taking on the job. On the flight, he had resolved to make a quick start on his re-investigation of Ronald Devereau. This search, wherever it led him across the West, might take a month but shouldn't be allowed to stretch into two. The quotidian challenge of squatting in this remote house and catering to his friend ran up against his intended method — namely, rambling wherever the clues led him, with or without Henry in the passenger seat. He considered asking Tynan to drive him to a hotel.

Peter hauled his Gladstone into the big room and extracted a sheaf of notes. He wasn't interested in the absinthe ceremony. Henry started to drift off, and Peter raised his voice. "You want to get started? Let's sit at the table."

Henry stared at the bundle. After a stunned minute, he took an exaggerated breath, clapped his hands, and kipped up onto two feet. His smile this time was bright and open. "Right! We're in business. Do you want to change out of that black suit? You and Tynan are like the Smith Brothers cough drop twins, without the beards."

The relief Peter felt was only that of the sober man hoping the drunk will snap out of his addiction, but he grabbed onto it. He was willing to posit that constant motion — no lingering in this haunted house — could be Henry's deliverance, even if Henry didn't know yet that the heavy work would start with a visit to Hollis Street.

Peter opened his bag wide and dug for the red-and-lemon-yellow Hawaiian silk shirt that Joan had packed. It was the shirt he had planned not to wear. He changed right there in the living room.

Henry grinned. "I can see you drinking beer on the back patio."

I see a man on the verge of pouring his next dose, Peter thought. "No thanks." He went over to the bar and tucked the bottle of absinthe out of sight. "Let's work at the table," he repeated.

And so the cop in the jogging shorts and BYU T-shirt and the one in the improbable floral Hawaiian shirt took seats at the dining room table. Peter decided to start with fundamentals. "Where are you on the hunt for Devereau?"

Henry shrugged and shook his head at the same time. "Phil Mohlman and I have both sworn affidavits that James Riotte and Ronald Devereau are not the same person. I sent them to you."

"I wondered about that. Shouldn't it be easy to verify? He must have left a paper trail after living ten or more years on the same street."

"It's amazing. He covered his tracks. Oh, there's the arrest photo of Riotte from twenty years back. I sent *that* to you, too, but Devereau's a self-styled ghost. A grainy driver's licence and one candid photo from a street party five years ago. He remains a cipher."

"He bought a house. Doesn't the real estate agent or his banker remember him?"

"Real estate guy died. Mortgage banker has only a vague recollection. Devereau made all his payments online."

"Facebook page? Internet habits?"

"Facebook? You kidding? Nope. His service provider resisted our requests for his Google search log. Fought it in court, can you believe. Judge said case was closed, what did we need the records for?"

"Eyewitness statements? You have some, you said."

"The residents of Hollis Street remain tight-lipped. A couple — I can provide names — looked at the Riotte photographs and agreed it wasn't the same man but refused to swear to it. I tell you, Peter, our saying about the residents is: nobody on Hollis ever knows anything."

"What about the Bureau?" Peter knew that Henry had approached his former colleagues in Washington.

"They blitzed their databases as a favour to me. Looked through all their terrorist lists, also serial killers, highway killers, left-wing and right-wing groups, militias, and drug gangs. But without fingerprints for Devereau and *with* Riotte's fingerprints there already in the files, there was never an incentive to look very far. The ATF and DEA made a token effort."

"In other words, they didn't believe you and Mohlman."

Henry shot a longing glance at the bar. "Remember, Phil's only recently gone back full-time. I'm on admin leave. We aren't at the precinct every day to push this."

Peter understood that no one at Henry's workplace would tolerate his obsession for long. And why should they? He wondered if Detective Mohlman had given up.

Bitterness deepened Henry's voice. "West Valley and the Utah Bureau of Investigation consider the Watson murders solved. That means the case file is just about sealed."

"There's no doubt in your mind that Devereau killed both Watsons?"

"No doubt."

"He acted alone?"

"The actual killings, yeah. But we never figured out how he got back home after ditching Tom Watson's truck in the Wasatch."

Henry's report was entwined with these forlorn questions, but Peter didn't expect easy answers. The breakthrough would be achieved through ponderous analysis and re-interviews. Still, he appraised the list of questions he himself had made on the plane. How did the killer hide so effectively? How could he be that lucky? Why were there no photos of his face? He was on the street executive, even served as president, and attended the annual barbecue, but no one had really befriended him. Grocery store checkout clerks didn't recall him, and he did all his car repairs on his own. No prints were found in the ruins at 13 Hollis.

"Henry, let's visit Hollis Street."

Henry winced, almost tipping back onto the floor. "I haven't been on Hollis . . . for a long time."

"Just one visit, to help me visualize it." Peter didn't specify "it."

"No, I couldn't endure the neighbourhood."

"It will perk you up."

"I don't think so."

"What if I told you I have an idea where to look for Devereau?"

Peter had noticed that Henry's moods cycled quickly through anger to resignation and back to morbidness. He required a lot of attention. Peter's cajoling was hit-or-miss.

"If you tell me the truth about one thing, Peter," Henry said.

"I will."

"Do you believe the killer is out there? Do you believe me?"

"I came five thousand miles because I do believe you."

Henry nodded, quickly accepting this pledge, although he was lucid enough to sense that Peter might also be in Utah for his own reasons.

CHAPTER 24

When Henry insisted that Peter take the wheel of his Subaru, Peter thought it wise to comply, given Henry's probable blood alcohol level. He drove conservatively, acclimatizing himself to North American traffic rules. Henry slouched in the passenger seat and fell asleep several times, and Peter had to nudge him for directions to Hollis Street.

Henry came alert the moment Peter slowed through the stone gates. Proximity to death broke through his dreaminess. "This damn street is doomed. It . . ."

Peter stopped at the curb, thirty feet inside the gates. He took in the padlocked bungalows at 3, 5, and 8, and the barricaded lot at the far end. "You were going to say, 'It always was doomed'?"

"My God, Peter, that's exactly what I was about to say. I knew you were psychic . . ."

Peter drove a little closer to the Devereau site, and that diverted Henry. Peter began a running critique in an even tone, like a medical examiner dictating autopsy impressions. "There are signs of house-pride on the street, but the two murder houses still have police locks and no FOR SALE signs. Number 8 was on the market at the time of the fire, you said, and no one has moved in. You said the residents here keep their mouths shut. Who can blame them for feeling defensive? Not hard to believe they were cursed from the outset on Hollis Street."

Peter's spiel was in part an effort at distraction, but Henry, fidgeting, remained fixed on the Devereau ruin ahead.

Henry tried to delay the inevitable. "You want to see inside the grow house?"

"Not necessary. The police reports seem complete." He edged the Subaru closer to the cul-de-sac.

"Really? I remember you telling me, Peter, you love nothing better than spending time at crime scenes. 'Wandering the killing floor,' you put it."

The absinthe had made Henry jumpy, and Peter could do no more than address each of Henry's thoughts as it popped into his mind, even if he had to dissemble. "I consider this whole sad street the crime scene."

"One thing Phil and I wondered, why do you think Devereau opted to leave behind the two bags of weed?"

"Because he didn't need the income."

"It was premium weed. He could have sold it down the street in a flash."

Peter shook his head. "If he wanted money, he could have blackmailed Tom Watson for half of the action. Maybe he did. Marketing that small amount to street operators would make him memorable. Too much risk. Devereau was super-careful."

"Super? He was about as subtle as a flash flood."

Peter's long trip and his frustration with Henry made him snappish. "You didn't collect a single fingerprint from either house. Devereau gutted the Watsons but never stepped in their blood. No photos of him exist. That's the most fastidious killer I've ever heard of."

"If he wanted to keep it simple, why not burn down the grow house? He decided to torch his own place."

"Before then, he still had hope."

"Of what?" Henry persisted.

Peter was drifting into pontification, and he slowed down. "Of redeeming the street, I guess. The first time, he planned to stay, so he didn't burn down 3 or 5. He'd been hiding on this street for ten years, and he had grown to like it. He clung to an idealistic greeting-card view of suburban bliss. Label him the Hallmark Psychopath. The second time, when he killed Mr. and Mrs. Proffet, he was trying to get away, and he adopted a scorched earth strategy."

"What about the pipe bomb?"

"Was it powerful?"

"No."

Peter grunted. "It wasn't designed to burn down Number 5 but only to wipe out any evidence. He still had hopes for the street."

Cammon parked the Subaru in front of 13 and stared at the detritus.

"What are you expecting to see, Peter?"

Resoluteness was the way to keep Henry moving. "I'm expecting to see ashes. I'm hoping to find clues. Let's do it."

The arson squad's report had highlighted the fierceness of the blaze, which caused the upper floors to buckle and collapse and every flammable object in the basement to implode. Peter smelled damp soot as soon as he exited the Subaru. The police had erected a pressed-board fence around the property, but panels of it were already sagging. If someone didn't bring in a bulldozer soon, the place risked becoming a permanent eyesore. The Hollis residents had reason to worry about their property values.

Peter peered around a sheet of plywood into the abyss, where greasy water had collected. Henry forced himself to look.

"Nothing left bigger than a Buffalo nickel. Except Jim Riotte's body survived mostly intact," Henry said.

"Why do you think that was?"

"Don't know. Burned all the skin off his body," Henry said. "Bastard."

Peter was intrigued by the condition of the body, given that everything else in the basement was consumed, but he moved on to examine the last remaining structure.

The garage endured, scorched on the outside but otherwise intact and currently strapped in police tape like bad gift-wrapping. The makeshift fence hooked up with the back wall of the structure, leaving no entry point. Peter rattled the slide-down garage panel, now sealed by its internal mechanism. He could jimmy it or have Henry call in for the key.

"Let's break in, Henry."

"You sure, Peter? What'll we see?" Henry leaned on a corner of the garage. Grief and too many doses of the Green Fairy had undermined his stamina.

But Peter was in a mood, too. "Henry, you seem to expect me to play Sherlock Holmes every five minutes. Ronald Devereau left no signatures, no testament for posterity, no suicide note, no documents at all. He burned up every shred of his persona. We'll take it as it comes. If we see anything off centre by a millimetre in this garage, I'll consider it probative."

"How do we get in?" Henry said.

Peter began to circle the double garage. If the door at the front was impenetrable and both sides were solid, then the rear offered the only way. Around the back, the collapse of the breezeway had left a hole, and Peter started to push aside a slab of composite board that the police had clumsily nailed over the opening to the garage. Henry followed; picking up on the chief inspector's impatience, he aimed a kick at the board and split it in two.

They entered gingerly. Rectangular windows high on the south wall of the wooden box provided light for their search. There were no cars in the garage, and the vanishing of Devereau's Buick remained a puzzle. The state police had issued a BOLO alert, but the Utah tags never resurfaced. Along one side of the frame structure, garden tools hung in their proper places, while a red lawnmower, a well-maintained electric model, stood on its outlined spot on the floor. There was no barbecue — thank God, it would have blown out the walls — but everything else bespoke American suburban normal, Peter concluded. A full-size white freezer dominated the non-automobile half of the garage.

"Should we guess what's in the Coldspot?" Peter asked. Henry didn't pick up on the gallows undertone in Peter's manner. Did he not grasp that Devereau had stored Jim Riotte's body in the deep freeze, Peter wondered?

"Empty. It would be standard procedure to clear it out and unplug it," replied Henry.

And so it was, except Devereau was the one who had cleaned it out. Peter, pleased that the investigators hadn't locked the unit, tilted up the lid. The empty whiteness was discouraging; only a blue ice pack and some kind of deodorizer were left inside.

Henry leaned against the far wall, mildly amused and still unaware of the freezer's recent use. "Are you about to present me with a Poirot moment, Peter?"

"If you insist. Why not? This is the last-but-one resting place of Jim Riotte."

"Say what?"

"Why do you think that the body survived as a solid mass, like baked Alaska? Everything else was devoured by fire. Devereau poured accelerant all around, dumped acid into his three computers. He kept his doppelganger on ice and transferred him to the cellar to roast in the fire he was setting. Murdering Mr. and Mrs. Proffet smells of panic, but who knows how far in advance he had Riotte in the icebox, ready for a post mortem performance?"

Peter's effort to shock Henry out of his lethargy was working. A brightness came into the young man's eyes, displacing the alcohol in his system as he began to re-engage.

"Maybe not long, Peter. I reckon Riotte was the one who picked up Devereau in the Wasatch. Then Devereau killed him."

"Sounds about right. On the other hand, that freezer's been sitting here for a while."

"I'll get a team to scour the interior for trace . . ."

"I wouldn't bother." Peter saw little importance in the timing of Riotte's execution.

He pivoted back to the freezer and fully opened the broad lid. An image had stuck in his short-term memory. Leaning half inside the appliance, he stretched down to the corner where the ice pack lay. Levering back out, he held up a tiny figurine. It was four inches long, moulded in off-white plastic or Bakelite, but it had no moving parts.

It was Yoda.

"A toy," Henry said.

"Maybe."

Peter closed the freezer and pocketed the figure. He shifted his attention to the narrow metal shelves that covered six feet of the south wall of the garage. The racks above held handsaws and power tools; some of the plastic grips had melted, but none had fallen off its perch. Peter dropped to one knee and felt along the floor-level shelf, conscious that even obsessives allow junk to filter downwards. Feeling in behind a container of WD-40 that somehow hadn't exploded in the conflagration, his fingers rolled over a pair of objects, neither larger than the toy Yoda. He fished them out and held them up for Henry to see.

They were airplanes, oddly shaped, each made of the same material as Yoda. One crumbled to dust in Peter's hand. The other stayed together, although Peter observed that it was missing half its starboard wing.

They picked up fried chicken at the Chicken Yard on Highway 15.

"Last stop before cardiac arrest," Henry announced.

The mood in the SUV wasn't exactly light, Peter assessed, but at least Henry wasn't catatonic. Hoping to keep his friend talking, Peter took the Yoda figurine from his pocket and balanced it on the dash.

"No, Peter," Henry said. "For the record, I never had a dashboard Jesus in my car."

But once they were back in the house on Coppermount Drive, the atmosphere changed for the worse. Yes, the young widower had every reason to wallow in his misery; even so, Peter had thought he'd made progress, having persuaded Henry back onto Hollis within hours of arriving and started a discussion. But the trek to West Valley had amounted to a concession to a guest, little more. Henry homed in on the granite bar and brought out the silver tray.

"Ever had an absinthe, Peter?"

Peter, jet-lagged, had a sensation of rewinding. He was ready for a nap in the desert air, but now his gains with Henry had been reversed. They hadn't truly reacquainted. Peter represented a distant world known as the Past; he was an old friend intruding on a newly bereft household. Peter didn't even know which bedroom was his.

Henry began the procedure of mixing the absinthe, while Peter stood on the edge of the living room in his ridiculous shirt and watched. It took Henry twenty minutes to mix one glass. This was a sad ritual for the departed. It reminded Peter of nothing so much as a cooking show on the telly. Absinthe contains thujone, a stimulant, and alcohol, a downer. It is a self-contained speedball yet is not a fermented drink like the uninitiated usually believe. Worse, more alcohol in the form of brandy is often added. Peter knew from the French and English poets he had read that the Green Fairy produces a euphoric cloud in the drinker and heightens perception, eventually pushing the user into terrors and depression.

"It's very much a bohemian thing, Peter. Your English poets used it for inspiration. Try one, my friend?"

Peter shook his head. How did a Utah resident get hold of obscure French grog? A drive out-of-state, no doubt, and an up-yours to the Mormon church and state liquor laws.

Henry uncapped the tall bottle. "This is *Le Perroquet* — the Parrot. Good stuff."

The harsh herbal scent, mixed with the grease from the bucket of fried chicken, was nauseating. Literary allusions floated to the surface of Peter's mind. Melville had Ishmael in the Spouter-Inn tavern observe the sacrament of pouring the liquor into "villainous green goggling glasses." That was about right. The accoutrements on the granite bar were fashioned for the ceremony. The Pontarlier glasses had been etched with Plimsoll lines to show the dosage; Henry poured carefully to the first mark. Next, he sat the leaf-shaped slotted spoon across the rim of the glass and put a single cube of sugar on the spoon, as if placing the final card atop a card house. He dripped green liquid onto the sugar and set fire to it. Peter was aware that purists avoided the flaming, but men like to set fire to food, and Henry was enjoying himself. Peter observed in silence, almost dozing off.

Henry rambled on. "The timely addition of ice water clouds the absinthe into a mixture known as a 'louche.'" Henry raised a toast to Peter. "Thank you for coming."

The sun outside the big patio doors was beginning to lose its force, and the evening loomed. Peter gathered cutlery and placemats and arranged the dining room table while Henry brought out the chicken. Glum about the chances of finding beer in the kitchen, Peter opened the fridge anyway and met a six pack of Bud Light, with Tynan's note taped to it: "Don't know from beer. Seen the ads for this one. Told me green beer is only for St. Patrick's Day."

The dinner was unpleasant. On the table, the emerald absinthe clashed with the iridescent green coleslaw, and Peter lost his appetite. He sat the Yoda figurine and the crippled airliner between their plates. They felt to Peter like childish mascots.

The carb-heavy food revived Henry momentarily, and he went to his bedroom and retrieved a bundle of files, which he brought back and plunked down on the table.

"This is everything I have."

Henry seemed annoyed, and Peter understood why: he suspected that Peter was hiding a personal agenda. His reply to Henry's package had cryptically mentioned the Unabomber. Despite Henry's visible irritation, Peter began to doze off.

"What the hell's that about?" Henry broke in, his speech slurred.

"What, Henry?"

Louder, Henry said, "What does the Yoda mean, Peter?"

"I don't know yet, but it meant something to Devereau."

"He isn't the whimsical type."

"I agree."

Henry himself suddenly fell asleep. Peter propped him up against the table. Five minutes on, Henry came awake and cried out, "Do you know who Devereau is?"

"Sleep on it, Henry. We'll start our search in the morning. Where's your room?"

"Down there. Yours is the other direction." He stood and drained the last quarter inch of the green syrup. Peter aided him along the hallway.

Peter returned from Henry's room intent on sleep himself, but the sunset performance outside the patio doors caught him up short. Yellow and orange bands of sky backlit vermilion and mauve wisps of clouds. The borders of the cloud layer blurred, and within minutes darkness overwhelmed the darts of light with a last flare. The sunset felt decisive, night complete.

He was no longer sleepy. The light show had invigorated him, and now the hollow, dark house spooked him. Feeling mildly paranoid, he removed his laptop from his valise and cued into Henry's Wi-Fi to check his email. He wondered if somehow his former boss at New Scotland Yard, Sir Stephen Bartleben, had got wind of his expedition to America. This was unlikely, and Sir Stephen had no residual control over Peter, but still he chewed on it. Peter didn't doubt that Homeland Security would be complaining to London sometime before all this was over.

He sent a short email to Joan and Maddy, telling them he had arrived safely. Joan would expect nothing more, but he felt guilty about his daughter-in-law. Maddy had helped him during the Carpenter investigation, and although with the baby she couldn't have accompanied him to Utah in any case, he should have briefed her before he left. He sent a separate message to her: "Will call or Skype in three days to update. May have research for you. Okay?"

He unpacked in the guest bedroom, placing his own notes and the new bundle from Henry on the carpet under the bed. Dipping further into the bag, he was surprised to find a folded document. Joan, no doubt at Maddy's suggestion, had slipped in the map of the

United States that had hung on the wall of the garden shed at the cottage during the Carpenter Affair. He was glad he'd sent the email. He and Maddy had often gathered in the shed to speculate on which of the fifty blue-bordered states the murderous fugitive Alice Nahri had chosen for sanctuary. He found some tacks in the kitchen and pinned the map to the bedroom wall.

Still restless, he lay on the bed and pondered the map. The pillowcase gave off a fusty odour. Peter was likely the only guest to use the room since Theresa's death; perhaps she had last made this bed. The condor-eye map pleased him, and he decided that in the morning he would buy a packet of labels and annotate the map with known "terrorist" occurrences that bore any resemblance to the incidents on Hollis Street. Including the Unabomber's many attacks, the array would touch Utah and a half-dozen nearby states. Oklahoma had to be featured, and McVeigh and his co-conspirators had committed crimes in Arizona, too. Painting with a broad brush would draw in Idaho, for Ruby Ridge, and Texas, for the Waco disaster. The Homeland Security Office of Domestic Terrorism could provide Peter with dozens more incidents — should he decide to reveal his presence in Salt Lake.

Peter hadn't informed Henry of the potential link between Hollis Street and Tim McVeigh, nor had he fully explained the Unabomber connection. He believed that two decades ago, Devereau, or whatever his real name was, had styled himself the Unabomber's tactician, perhaps his intellectual mentor. Peter was less confident of a link to the Oklahoma City plot. After the Murrah bombing, which had occurred only five months prior to the publication of Ted Kaczynski's *Manifesto* in the *New York Times*, investigators found indications of a spectral character who had hovered around McVeigh and Terry Nichols as they planned their attack. Peter suspected that man was Ronald Devereau. Back in the nineties, a few contrarians had tried to link these monstrous plots, but as McVeigh's accomplices went to ground and a few arrests and convictions were registered, no one listened any longer. Now a key player had surfaced on a nondescript street in West Valley.

There were several ways to hunt down Devereau. He appeared to hate drug dealers, but did he steal drugs in order to finance his terrorist plans? Peter would get Maddy searching for telltale drug incidents in the western states. He believed the arson angle also held promise. Devereau's pipe bomb and his torching of his own home had been perverse and well planned, signs of a criminal pattern. Did he have a history with fires? Finally, almost eighteen years in hiding had not soothed Devereau. His crimes bore the marks of an unmitigated psychopath.

Peter turned off the light in the guest room. Lying there, he realized what was agitating him. How do you find a ghost? He craved momentum, knew he had to move fast — faster than Henry was capable of going. The expanse of Hollis Street, with its sad houses, formed an elaborate crime scene. How could there be no fingerprints? No group snapshots? The investigators had given up on Hollis too easily.

His jet lag swept over him and he fell asleep above the covers.

CHAPTER 25

Between 1978 and 1996, the Unabomber, Theodore Kaczynski, mailed or planted sixteen explosive devices across the United States and caused twenty-two injuries and three deaths. He stands as the greatest solo act in American domestic terrorism history.

Ted was both lucky and moderately skilled. Most of his pipe bombs detonated on schedule, although a few did not or were defused before they could explode. He was observed twice in the act, but neither occasion led to his capture. Never did the FBI find a fingerprint or trace a component from any of his box bombs.

He dispatched his devices to targets from coast to coast, to Illinois, California, Michigan, Utah, Connecticut, New Jersey, and Washington; he shipped a package on an American Airlines flight out of Chicago. The authorities christened him the UNABOM for his attacks on universities and airlines, although Peter Cammon always felt that he should have been called the "Postal Service Bomber," since he used the mail so much. The U.S. Postal Inspection Service was a main player in the task force set up in 1979 to solve the "UNABOM" case, as it was known at the beginning, and during that period Peter came to believe that law enforcement would find him by analyzing his use of the postal system.

Ted Kaczynski lives in the federal Supermax prison in Florence, Colorado.

Some would maintain that the Unabomber was hard to catch because his targets were haphazardly chosen — they didn't truly represent the technological society so hated by Kaczynski — and because he demanded nothing from his victims. Ted's motives remained obscure. His attacks were irregularly spaced over eighteen years and followed no rational pattern. More significant, until Ted won publication of his *Manifesto* in 1995, he never seemed to be aiming for any particular result other than wanton harm to individuals. In *Industrial Society and Its Future*, he stated, "Until the industrial system has been thoroughly wrecked, the destruction of that system must be the revolutionaries' ONLY goal." In Peter Cammon's view, Kaczynski was a petty, small-time terrorist.

A typical Unabomber device was a pipe bomb in a carved wooden box, most of the components homemade and untraceable, and the whole package compact enough to mail through the nearest post office. The Unabomber was a Luddite who nonetheless used mechanical, electrical, and chemical technology in his devices. Some on the task force thought it possible that his homemade bombs were artfully rudimentary and deceptively naive; but, Peter wondered, what would have been the point of that? Kaczynski's devices weren't unsophisticated if you considered the objective. He had created havoc with them, and almost brought down a plane. They got the job done.

Peter's first exposure to the case came in 1985, just after Kaczynski had killed for the first time. His victim was a passerby who unluckily picked up one of his pipe bombs. That was in Sacramento, and the attack is known as Incident Number 11. In that year, the UNABOM Task Force invited Scotland Yard to sit in on its weekly conference call, and Sir Stephen Bartleben anointed Peter as his rep. The reason for his assignment was always unclear to Peter. He had visited the States twice on other files and worked with the FBI on one joint investigation, but that hardly qualified him to comment on the Unabomber. Someone, he heard, had told the Americans that he had contributed to the Yorkshire Ripper case and figured he could help in profiling the postal killer.

Deputy Director Lattner from the U.S. Postal Inspection Service chaired the conference call, which included a dozen police agencies. Even over the phone, Peter felt the frustration in the room. There was much discussion of where the Unabomber lived, with a consensus that he resided in the West or in California, although it was evident that he ranged widely. It must be remembered that this was before DNA, the internet, the Twin Towers, and the formation of Homeland Security. One tool the authorities did have was profiling; law enforcement had fallen in love with profiling techniques after Son of Sam in the mid-seventies.

Peter had studied the task force dossier on the Unabomber and was unimpressed with the profiling effort. When his turn to speak came, he said, "If I were you, I would look at the connections between where the bombs exploded and *where they were sent from*. The map of the latter is quite different from the former. We're all asking ourselves where the Unabomber lives, urban or rural. If you look at the postmarks on his packages and analyze the bus and train routes to those post office locations, I think you'll find he lives in a rural setting."

Eleven of the devices had been mailed or planted up to that point, and his theory came across as glib to the Americans in the room. Deputy Lattner, seemingly offended by Cammon's alien English accent, snapped. "Okay then, Inspector" — Peter wasn't a chief inspector yet — "what do you think the Unabomber *wants*?"

"I don't know," he said, sounding too dismissive, "but we all agree that he's a recluse who spends a lot of hours carving and moulding parts to fit into his box bombs, all of which are customized to some degree. I also think there might be two perpetrators. The bomber may be a recluse and have a co-conspirator who eggs him on and assists with his devices."

He had ignited a flare in the room from thousands of miles away. Lattner asked him to elaborate, and Peter backtracked a step. "Well, we are all drawn to the lone-assassin premise, and it seems to apply here. The bomber hasn't been in a hurry, has no distinctive timeline. And, the most infuriating factor of all, he doesn't appear to have a set of demands. So he's a loner, neurotic, lacking affect, taking his sweet time. But I'd be worried. We've all seen crimes where the culprit has been pushed by someone else to act out his grievances. However haphazard the Unabomber's bombing schedule, it seems to me that he's building to something. I don't know what. But what if he does have a partner?"

He had posited at least three wild theories in his screed: that the Unabomber lived in a rural setting, that he had help, and that he was getting more aggressive in his bombing pattern.

Lattner spoke up righteously. "So what if he does?"

Peter responded, "If he's not entirely alone in this, then the chances are that his partners are in the terrorism business, with a more coherent agenda than our man. That's worrisome. I recommend you follow that angle."

He was telling them that an individual madman's grievances could be exploited by terrorist groups, but they weren't ready to listen to this speculation in 1985, before Ramzi Yousef, Timothy McVeigh, and Osama bin Laden showed how cataclysmic terror could be. Nothing came of Cammon's theorizing, and everyone forgot about the consult.

But someone must have remembered his sermon. By the end of 1994, the task force had begun to despair of tracing the pipe bombs back to their demented creator. More innocent Americans had been mutilated and two more had died. Feelings about terrorism had progressed, too. Ruby Ridge in 1992 and Waco in 1993 showed how off the rails anti-government agitation could get, while the detonation under the World Trade Center, masterminded by Ramzi Yousef, signalled the vulnerability of America's infrastructure. Against this evolving backdrop of fear, the quirky Unabomber pursued his solitary campaign and became the symbol of the feds' investigative inadequacy.

In 1994, Deputy Director Lattner called Sir Stephen Bartleben,

Peter Cammon's direct supervisor, and explained his needs: could New Scotland Yard spare Cammon for a month to work for the task force in Denver, Colorado? At first Peter balked, feeling no different about the thin evidence. But the Unabomber had struck several more times, and Lattner played on his dilemma in his follow-up call directly to the chief inspector. "That time — nine, almost ten, years ago — you raised a theory that seems almost prescient now. You suggested that the Unabomber was building to something bigger, more destructive. Well, he took a break for six years after Salt Lake City in 1987, then he struck again in California in June '93, twice, and again just last week in New Jersey. They were especially nasty packages, did a lot of damage."

"I threw a lot of theories into the mix," Peter said with self-deprecation.

"Yes, and I have a growing appreciation of their shrewdness," said Lattner generously, "but now you have more examples to test them on. For example, I'd like to know if you still think he lives in a rural area, and in what state."

"I'll come," Peter said "but I need a month to shut down a current investigation here. Meanwhile, send me the details up to today."

As it turned out, Peter did not make it to Denver until late February, although by then he had absorbed the files thoroughly and revised his main theory of the Unabomber's whereabouts. He had settled on a strategy for answering another question: did the madman have assistance in planning, fashioning, and delivering the bombs?

Denver immediately became Peter's home base, but he spent little time there, for his plan required him to visit seven — eight or nine, if he had time — of the bombing locations and the cities where the Unabomber was known to have mailed his packages. With a Calgary cop who was on secondment to the FBI's Denver office, Peter drove to Evanston, Chicago, Nashville, Ann Arbor, and Salt Lake City, and flew to Berkeley and San Francisco. The Canadian and the Englishman wandered the Midwest and the Far West for almost a month.

By the second peripatetic week, Peter felt the presence of a shadow, a more intelligent shaper behind some of the attacks. The Unabomber had crossed a line when his opposition to government and corporations began to express itself in the rash targeting of strangers. Someone had been there, particularly in the early years, pushing him up to that line.

Tiring of the road, Peter hived off from his Canadian partner, returning to Salt Lake City for a week to take a closer look. He still had faith in his idea that the place of mailing was as important as the place of impact, and Salt Lake loomed large in this theory. He noted that Kaczynski planted his fifth bomb at the University of Utah in 1981 and a few months later sent his sixth device from a Brigham Young University post office; similarly, his tenth mail bomb derived from the Utah capital. Also, if the Unabomber lived in a rural setting in the West, as Peter believed, then Salt Lake provided a convenient hub for highway or air connections across the country.

But the February 1987 bombing, Incident Number 12, remained by far the most intriguing one of the bunch. The target had been the owner of a computer store in a Salt Lake mall; the reasons for selecting him were obscure, likely irrational. The Unabomber's tactics made it probable that someone else would be injured when he planted his contraption in the parking lot. Peter knew that the bomber didn't mind blowing up strangers, but this effort seemed poorly planned. Although the Unabomber had previously deployed bombs in person, Peter wondered: Had he planned to take a bus somewhere else that day but panicked? Had he started out for the post office and ditched his package along the way?

Less than fourteen months before, the bomber had committed his first murder-by-mail, the owner of a computer rental store in Sacramento. Now he was wanted for a homicide and the Postal Inspection Service had increased the reward, raising the pressure a notch. Perhaps he was extra-nervous that day in Salt Lake.

Incident Number 12 occurred on a sunny but cold morning. The device, disguised as a road hazard, lay on the asphalt, and coincidentally the computer store owner arriving for work was the first driver to see it. In removing the contraption, he tripped a spring lever switch, causing the bomb to detonate. While it caused severe and permanent injuries, it did not kill him. The big difference this time was that there was a witness. Minutes before the explosion, a secretary in the store saw the Unabomber lean down and plant the bomb by a parked car. She offered a description to the FBI, who quickly released a police artist sketch. Tips began to pour in to the task force hotline. The subsequent release of the police sketch and increase in the reward must have alarmed Kaczynski, for he did not attack again for another six and a half years.

If there was one matter that Peter had needed to revisit during that distant winter, it was the witness sketches. He tracked down the computer store secretary and quizzed her on the accuracy of the three pictures that had been done of the Unabomber. The first one had been little used, but the second, painted in full watercolour, served as the reference image for investigators. The problem, as Peter well knew, was that this portrait had produced no sightings of the suspect in more than six years, resulting in the task force commissioning a revised poster in 1994, this one adding sunglasses and a hooded shirt. Peter queried the secretary about all the images of the suspect. She was now weary of the whole manhunt, but she remained firm on the main features, conceding only that perhaps that the hair was too curly and the chin too strong. (After Kaczynski's capture, Peter was not alone in pointing out that the notorious wanted poster did not closely resemble Ted.) The man she had seen was indeed the man in the picture.

The lack of tips from the poster nagged at Peter. Investigators in 1987 found a waitress in a nearby diner who claimed to have seen the man in the hoodie and shades on that day. The restaurant was located less than two blocks from the parking lot, and thus the bomber might have had his breakfast and strolled with his nailed-together boards in a canvas bag to the target site. Now, in 1995, Peter located the waitress and she confirmed her sighting: the man in the poster had been in the diner.

Everything changed for Peter on April 19, 1995. He had been in the United States for more than the one month promised, and he was winding down his efforts in anticipation of going home by April's end. The Unabomber hadn't struck again while Peter was in the country, and except for locking in his belief that the terrorist lived close to Salt Lake City, Cammon was no further ahead than any other investigator. But on that date, Timothy McVeigh and Terry Nichols blew up the Murrah Building in Oklahoma City. Panic ran through the federal law enforcement agencies, already on edge because of the Unabomber's months of silence, and it did not take long for the task force to look for links between the Unabomber and OC. The bomb attack in 1993 on the World Trade Center had fuelled ongoing fear of foreign terrorists going after domestic targets and perhaps led President Clinton to jump to the conclusion that Islamist terrorists had blown up the Murrah.

The same day, Peter got a summons from Deputy Director Lattner. "Cammon, you offered the opinion to the Unabomber task force that the bomber might be hooked up with domestic terrorism."

"I thought this was Middle East terrorists," he replied.

"Not foreign, never was," Lattner said. "Arabs in Oklahoma City? Not likely. Knew it was domestic the moment I heard 'Ryder truck' and 'fertilizer.' Thousands of half-baked local revolutionaries know how to make a fertilizer bomb, doesn't take a hundred-plus IQ. We are swamped with leads and phone-ins. One thing we want to be absolutely sure about is that the Unabomber has no connection whatsoever to Oklahoma City. What can you do for us, Chief Inspector? You're the man with the theory."

Within a day, it became clear that foreigners hadn't detonated the truck, and the president withdrew his statement. Peter was about to drive from Denver to Oklahoma City when he heard the name Timothy J. McVeigh for the first time. McVeigh had been apprehended by a highway trooper and charged. The relief felt by all the federal agencies produced a call from Lattner cancelling Peter's trip. Peter protested but was firmly ordered to "stay home."

But home for Peter was England, and he had a hard choice: fly away or fashion a credible new theory to keep him in America. Conspiracy theories received a boost when Terry Nichols and Michael Fortier, both tied to radical militia movements, were connected to McVeigh, but nothing in the Unabomber's history linked him to the plot.

Peter learned that the night before the Murrah Building explosion, Tim McVeigh had stayed in a motel in Junction City, Kansas, parking the infamous Ryder truck behind his room. FBI special agents found a delivery man who claimed to have seen McVeigh in the motel. Before leaving for England Peter obtained a copy of the witness sketch. While the face did resemble the Unabomber, by this time Peter had lost faith in the accuracy of the widely distributed wanted poster, which had produced few good tips. He kept a copy of the sketch but never did make it to Oklahoma.

Five days after the Oklahoma City attack, a parcel from Kaczynski arrived by mail at an address in Sacramento, blowing up a timber company executive. At Lattner's request, Peter flew to California to investigate possible connections to McVeigh, but it turned out that the Unabomber had mailed his device from Oakland a day or two before McVeigh carried out his nasty deed. There was no connection.

Peter Cammon remained convinced that he almost had Kaczynski. The bomber was getting more aggressive and taking greater risks, as Peter had predicted. The reward had reached a million dollars. Somebody would have ratted on Kaczynski if his brother hadn't done so a few months later. After the 1987 Salt Lake attack, the Unabomber had vanished, not striking again for almost seven years, but between 1993 and 1995 he struck four times. He was building to something. Peter guessed that he would soon demand a response from the authorities and from the society he was attacking. The bomber was growing frustrated with himself, having achieved notoriety but not public acceptance of his philosophy.

Kaczynski issued his *Manifesto* later that fall, and the big papers published it. There was a short period between the publication of the *Manifesto* and his brother turning him in where Peter might have nabbed him. But Peter was back in England when they caught Ted.

Peter took the portraits of the Unabomber and filed them, until that morning the padded mailer arrived in the post from the widowed Henry Pastern.

CHAPTER 26

Peter woke up in the dark. His watch, adjusted to Mountain Time, read 4 a.m. He listened for snoring, bird sounds, maybe wolf howls, and imagined coyotes patrolling just beyond the glass patio doors.

He half expected Henry to be pacing the house, perhaps drinking again. He used the bathroom next to the guest room and flushed, but Henry didn't stir. In the living room, Yoda and the fractured airplane sat between the plates on the table. He considered tossing the chicken bones outside but then realized what a bad idea that was. Clearing the mess, he went back to the bedroom for a notepad and pencils and brought Henry's files to the table. He began to read.

In two hours, he ran through Henry's material three times. Police authorities had conducted a token inquiry, but obviously no one believed Henry or Mohlman. Terrorism wasn't mentioned in the state police report. Details emerged and he jotted notes for follow-ups, such as the curious facts that Devereau owned three computers and that fine metal tools were found under the ash in one corner of the basement. Peter sat back and rotated the Yoda in his hand. Add one more line of inquiry. Who fashioned the polymer toys, and why?

At 7 a.m., Henry was still in bed, no sounds coming from his end of the house. Peter chafed to get on the road but decided to give

Henry ten more minutes. He slid open the door to the patio and stepped outside. The morning air stimulated him, speeding up his metabolism and increasing his impatience. He had been bored at the cottage, unmotivated by the open future called retirement and the well-trodden pathways of Leicestershire. He recalled that he had dreamed in the night of restless heroes from his childhood: crossing the Negev with T.E. Lawrence and questing with Burton to the source of the Nile. The dreams carried messages of yearning from the wastelands of Old Age.

He looked out to the dunes and scrub desert and saw a figure in motion. It occurred to him that it might be a mirage. He made out the Mormon cleric, white shirt and black trousers, no tie, striding towards the horizon, oblivious to everything but the desert. Peter gazed on until Tynan disappeared.

Peter had understood from the outset that he would need the help of government authorities, including all three levels of police, but he was determined to delay his approach as long as possible. Once he invoked a terrorism link to the Hollis murders, Homeland Security would co-opt the investigation. This wasn't necessarily a bad thing, but for now there were quieter avenues to explore. The American politician Tip O'Neill had said, "All politics is local." All crime was local, too. A wife dead. A neighbourhood ruined. Seeds of distrust sown on a dead end street. Devereau was a terrorist, but first and foremost he was the scourge of Hollis Street.

Peter waited another hour and rang up Phil Mohlman at West Valley police headquarters. Henry had said that his partner's injuries kept him tied to his desk. Phil invited Peter to come right over.

Henry still showed no signs of life. Peter took his host's keys and went out to the Subaru.

Although Phil Mohlman was seated, Peter could tell that he suffered a limp and endured pain in his left leg. The veteran street cop leaned back a few inches in his hard wooden chair, creating the angle necessary to allow him to stretch out the leg. Mohlman faced a practical problem. He had to remain in denial about the limb, since it wouldn't do for management to catch him limping to his desk. Peter guessed that he told everyone that he was on the physio path to a full recovery. Until then, management had limited his fieldwork. If his colleagues were smart, no one on the West Valley force would call him a gimp.

Peter smiled and shook his hand. Mohlman skipped the smile. Although Phil had chauffeured Peter and Joan to and from Theresa's funeral the previous fall, they had avoided discussing professional matters. It was time for a fresh introduction.

"Henry speaks highly of you," Phil began.

"He speaks very highly of his partnership with you," Peter said.

"Enough of that. I haven't seen Henry in over a month, and he storms in the other day and tells me you're coming to town with a theory of who Devereau really is, and how you're going to trap him. Is that about right?"

Peter said nothing.

"I checked you out, Cammon. You were here in '95. For the record, that's long before my time in Salt Lake City. It says you were on the Unabomber task force for a while. Also, you liaised with the Oklahoma City investigation. Is that your theory, that Devereau has a connection to domestic terrorism from a decade and a half ago?"

Mohlman squirmed in the stiff chair and his leg banged against the desk. No doubt this cop invested his talents fervently in every investigation, Peter concluded. His hair was more grey than Irish black, and each etched line in his hound dog face charted a different case. Peter wondered if Phil's nagging injuries would drive him back to Boston.

"Possibly. I'll explain, if you like," Peter said.

"Before you do that, let's be crystal clear. If you have evidence linking Devereau to domestic terrorism, you're going to need the regional Joint Terrorism Task Force's help. You know this. Henry is still hooked in with Washington, and I presume you still have old friends at the Bureau there. So the big question I have is, why are you coming to *me* before approaching Homeland Security? Answer? Because you don't quite believe Henry Pastern when he swears that the body in the basement on Hollis isn't Ronald Devereau."

"I believe it," Peter said.

"But you want to see if I'll confirm what Henry swears *before* you go to the Bureau. You think you might look like a fool."

Peter, miffed, leaned forward. "I've looked the fool before, Detective. I don't need to come all the way to the middle of nowhere to look foolish again."

Mohlman suppressed a smile. He recognized Peter's allusion to the insult levelled at Mitt Romney by British prime minister David Cameron regarding the Olympics. "Okay, Chief Inspector, what's your plan?"

"I want you to look at some pictures without telling your superiors you saw them."

Phil scanned the array. He shook his head. Here was this short, ancient, retired English cop in an inappropriate black suit, thousands of miles from home, looking to stir up a bunch of shut-down investigations. "Devereau is the Unabomber?"

"No, Devereau advised Kaczynski. The witnesses fingered *Devereau* in '95."

"Now you're telling me, Inspector, that you think you can find Devereau without involving the Bureau, ATF, or DEA."

"I'm doing it for Henry."

Mohlman absorbed the truth. "You plan to kill Devereau!"

Peter conceded nothing. "Henry's your friend, too."

Phil Mohlman stretched his bum leg and said, "Taser messed me up. Here's the deal. I'll do it your way until it all goes to hell. I'm as sure as Henry that Riotte and Devereau are different men. I met Devereau three times and Henry encountered him just once, so maybe my conclusion is more credible. But the bottom line is, we'll stay lonely. No one is going to believe us, and there's plenty of ways the higher-ups can browbeat us into letting it go. Henry, for example, won't be allowed back until he gives it up. Also, the moment we shift the case into the realm of counterterrorism, the JTTF will swoop in and snatch control. So take your shot while you can, Peter."

"I could use your help."

Mohlman painfully levered himself up. He took a business card and scribbled on the back.

"This is where I'd go next. Jim Riotte's charming brother."

Peter took the card. He agreed, nodding. But Mohlman was still staring at him.

"Okay, Cammon, you want me to do something else, don't you? It could get me in trouble, right?"

"Yes. I need you to access the Unabomber files. I'm looking for a witness. A waitress named Alma May Recve."

It wasn't yet noon, and Peter took his time returning to the house. He was enjoying Henry's Subaru, and he considered arguments he might employ to borrow it for a trip to Kansas the next day. He planned to travel early and alone; he feared that Henry might assault Mark Riotte, and that would certainly be counterproductive. He set the GPS for Temple Square and swung the Subaru into a U-turn on the broad avenue, up to North Temple, past Brigham Young's gravesite and the cathedral and out to the Great Salt Lake Desert.

As Peter turned onto Coppermount, he saw Henry pacing in front of the house, his stubbly pate turning red in the noon sun.

"Where the hell have you been with my car?" he said before Peter was out of the vehicle.

There was no avoiding the truth. "Sorry. I went to see Phil Mohlman."

"Without me?"

"Without you. You were asleep."

Henry was keyed up, probably into the absinthe already (one

glass of the concoction could swing the drinker from euphoria into militancy), but it was tepid anger. Henry sat down on the asphalt driveway and started to weep. "I thought someone had stolen it."

Peter let him recover on his own. "Sorry. I need to rent a car."

Henry wiped his bleary eyes. "Why would you want to do that? Just ask me, or Tynan will lend you his truck, I bet."

"I have to go to Kansas tomorrow to interview Jim Riotte's brother. I'm going alone."

Tynan's dusty truck jerked to a stop at the end of the driveway. He got out but didn't try to help Henry to his feet; if Cammon had failed to reach out, Tynan wouldn't presume. Henry stood up without aid and Peter handed him his keys.

To Tynan, Peter said, "I need a car."

"You need a truck," Tynan countered, and Henry appeared to agree. "Randy," Tynan said.

Henry perked up. The announcement of Peter's solo trip hadn't upset him, Peter noted, but a visit to "Randy" sparked real enthusiasm. "I'm coming. It's out on the desert road, Peter. I've never been there but I gotta see it!" Peter would have to get used to Henry's mood swings.

"Peter, you'll want to wear that flowered shirt of yours," Tynan said drily.

"I'll drive," Henry pledged, if only to assert that he was sober.

Randy's Rides lay thirty miles out west in the desert. It sprawled along a two-lane that appeared to have no purpose other than to bring errant car nuts to Randy's lot. The vanishing point ahead ended in misted, isolated mountains, increasing the impression that this was a road to nowhere.

The first thing Peter noticed about Randy's Rides was that it used up a lot of desert. Cars and pickups of all vintages had been parked across corrals where horses once were confined, and there were enough tires, in beanstalk towers, to equip them all twice over. Randy's notional office was a weather-beaten shed, and Henry honked for him to come out, which he did with no urgency. The eponymous owner displayed two weeks' growth of beard. Navy tattoos of women decorated each bicep, and his stomach bulged like a steam boiler. He nodded to Tynan with evident respect, and Peter made a guess as to whether Randy was Mormon. He thought not. Randy made Henry for a cop and Peter for what he was.

"You're an Englishman. I got a Rolls somewhere out there."

"I had a rugged sedan in mind," Peter said, knowing he was feeding a straight line to the Utahans.

"He wants a truck," Henry said.

"He wants a truck," Tynan chimed in.

"I got a nice 1999 F-150. No serious collisions," Randy stated.

Peter tried again. "To rent."

Randy clapped him on the back. "Mr. Winston Churchill, why rent when you can buy? Or, as folks say out on this stretch, why rent when you can steal? My price is a few farthings. We sell gift cards, too."

"Give him a deal on a rental, Pastor," Tynan said. Peter raised an eyebrow and Tynan explained. "Randy is an ordained minister of . . . what faith is that?"

"The Church of Perpetual Motion. Keep moving fast enough and the Devil can't corner you. Used to be the Keep on Truckin' Church."

They went outside to examine the truck, but evaluation was a minor issue, since Randy assumed he had a deal. Now he was more determined to show off his "church."

"Come along with me."

The four men strode through the salty desert for about five hundred yards to a semicircle of Lincoln Town Cars that emerged from the sand like leaping ocean leviathans.

"You like whale watching? Look at these humpbacks," Randy proclaimed.

"Where have I seen something like this before?" Henry said.

"They got Carhenge off in the high plains, in Nebraska, I think, and Cadillac Ranch down in Amarillo, but those cars fire down *into* the ground. Look like they're crashing out of the sun."

"I know how that feels," Henry said.

"But these luxury vehicles are reaching for the stars. Ain't nothing like that in Great Britain."

Tynan volunteered to head back to Coppermount Drive in the Subaru while Peter and Henry tried out the truck, which all agreed was a bargain at $600 for a month's rental, insurance included.

"The deal's renewable, or don't even bother," Randy stated. "Bring 'er back when you can."

A mild celebration seemed right. Peter drove the F-150 with Henry in the shotgun seat, while Tynan followed in the car. Henry guided them to a Mexican restaurant in a shopping plaza in the West Valley on the edge of Highway 15. After lunch, Peter walked across to a Shopko and purchased a Magellan RoadMate GPS. At a nearby Walmart, he bought a pack of blank rectangular address labels and six Sharpie pens.

Peter's energy remained high, even if Henry had by now conked out in the passenger seat. *Here I am*, he mused, *in a mud-spattered pickup truck in a Walmart parking lot in Utah, with a Mormon drunk and a desert mystic.* Why did he feel the need to reinvent himself each time he came to America? *Because America is always surprising me.*

He sent Henry off with Tynan and, alone, drove around the city for a while. He was extraordinarily restless, thinking of the interstate to Kansas. The snow-tipped mountains that pincered Salt Lake City from three sides both enlivened him and made him feel hemmed in.

When Peter reached the house, Henry was washing dishes. The act of domesticity failed to dispel the gloom. Theresa Pastern's spirit wandered the desert house as surely as the ghosts of the Watsons vexed Hollis Street. The green bottle was out of sight.

"Do you like your new truck?" Henry called.

"Yes. Many thanks."

Henry finished the dishes and drifted off to his bedroom. Peter waited five minutes and went to his. He broke out the labels he had bought, and for the next hour he annotated his U.S. map to reflect his research. If Devereau's breakout from Hollis Street signalled a return to his terrorism career, it would be useful to clarify where he might slot into the modern world of "domestic terrorism."

Peter broadened his labelling effort to most of the country:

Georgia: Atlanta Olympics, 1996 — bomb
Michigan: Michigan State University, 1999 — arson
Various: anthrax letters, 2001
Various: mailbox pipe bombs, 2002
Kansas: abortion clinic, 2009 — shooting
Arkansas: recruiting office, 2009 — shooting

There were more. Judges assassinated. Prosecutors taken out answering their front doors. Caches of weapons seized. He also parsed the list by organization and motive: anti-abortion fanatics, anti-government militias, animal rights radicals (the arsons by the Earth Liberation Front in Michigan and Washington), Aryan Nations, other religious extremists. Method counted, as well: bomb, anthrax, gun, kidnapping.

There were intentional absences, too. He ruled out attacks by radical Islamists and episodes on the East Coast. For the moment, he wanted to believe that there was a distinctly Western take on terrorism.

Henry entered the guest bedroom and glanced indifferently at the wall map. He was sober, but his face was pallid. "You know, I don't mind your going alone."

"Thanks. I'd like to review the files with you as soon as I return."

"Peter, do you know what they say about you in the training course at Quantico? They say you would have found Kaczynski if his brother hadn't turned him in first."

Few police colleagues knew the full story of Peter's exploits. "But I didn't find him, did I?"

"I wish I'd been there," Henry said in a self-pitying tone.

There was no answer to this, and Peter, impatient to get on the road to Kansas, had no time for such self-absorption. He gathered his files from beneath the bed. "Here. Study these while I'm gone."

"Peter, I'm not sure I can kick the Green Dragon."

"Do your best. I'll need your help very soon."

"You know the French loved the stuff? Rimbaud, Verlaine, Toulouse-Lautrec."

"Verlaine, as I recall, referred to the 'green pillars' of absinthe," Peter threw in.

"Rimbaud used to mix it with Jell-O. Green Jell-O, presumably. Think of it, Jell-O shots made with absinthe."

Peter was uneasy. He wanted to connect with Henry, but the common ground of a long-past literary education was a shallow premise. The French poets and painters were a far too morose bunch for a grieving husband to adopt as models. For another thing, Peter wasn't ready to sink into his own history. He thought like a cop and not a professor of literature. There had been a point at Oxford when he had almost ditched his plan to join the Yard. He might now be a retired teacher, never having killed anyone.

Never planning to execute anyone.

Henry noticed Peter drifting. "Looking for patterns on your map, Peter? Here's one. Ernest Hemingway shot himself with a Boss & Co. shotgun in 1961 in Ketchum, Idaho, just up the road from here. J. Edgar Hoover had been tapping his phone for years. Oh, yes, Hemingway was a heavy absinthe user."

CHAPTER 27

Peter rose early to the lure of the eastern sun. The night before, he had set the GPS to the quickest route into Kansas, and he was pleased with it: head north first, to Wyoming through the Rockies, then let the I-25 guide the truck south to Denver, and from there run a straight line on the I-70 to the Sunflower State.

He loaded his valise with a night's clothes and selected papers, including the Unabomber and Hollis Street sketches, and placed it on the passenger seat of the F-150. He sat the GPS on the dash, flanked by the polymer figures of Yoda and the broken plane.

Peter felt comfortably solitary. Never did he get bored on the road. He listened to weather reports, country music, and abstruse talk shows about growing corn ("How to keep your cobs standing up"), and absorbed the view as it shifted from magnificent mountains to flat, peaceful plains. At 6 p.m., he reached the turn for the hamlet of Crispin Breach, although the immediate horizon offered nothing that qualified as civilization. The cornfields and amber waves were soon relieved by a shallow gorge cutting through nubby, sunburnt hills. Flash floods must be a constant concern, Peter judged.

Crispin Breach, forty miles on, turned out to be a two-sided row of clapboard buildings sitting on dusty ground. He stopped at the gas pumps on the edge of the hamlet to ask for directions to the Friendly Trailer Park, which he had expected to see from the road. Flatlands stretched infinitely in three directions. The gas station operator, a grizzled philosopher from central casting, pointed him to the fourth, a dirt road winding into the gentle hills.

He picked up on Peter's accent. "You a tourist, or an anthropologist, maybe? Looking for the Friendly Trailer Park, you must be a digger for old bones. Half-alive bones. Beware of any American business with 'friendly' in its name. The place is rude and mean."

Peter thanked him for the string of non sequiturs.

"You are welcome, my English amigo. My name's Crispin."

The Friendly Trailer Park crouched less than two miles away, sheltered behind some small hills. No one challenged or welcomed him as he entered via the never-locked front gates. He drove slowly down the gravel lane and scouted for Number 17. Several trailers seemed abandoned. Mark Riotte's pale blue double-wide stood at the end of the path. There was no one around to ask regarding Riotte's whereabouts, and so he honked lightly. No one emerged from the unit, and he got out and tapped on the aluminum door, then again.

The younger Riotte brother was thirty-five or so, wiry and about five-foot-six, and mangy overall. Peter at once wondered if Jim had been as short. Hollis Street consensus put Ronald Devereau at just under six feet, but Peter could not call to mind Jim Riotte's height as recorded on his arrest sheet. Short enough to fit into a freezer, Peter supposed.

"Who're you? You police?" said Riotte through the door.

"Yes. About the death of Jim. I need to pin down a few loose ends."

Peter was always surprised at how the direct approach got him through doors in America. Riotte let him inside. The place was as jumbled and unsanitary as Peter expected of a trailer park bachelor; also, it was larger than the few trailers Peter had been inside before, almost too big for one slovenly squatter. Riotte shifted a pot of Kraft Mac and Cheese to the back burner of his narrow stove, as if this gesture would improve the décor.

"You can have a seat, if you can find one."

Peter stood. He scanned the room for guns. "When was the last time you saw Jim?"

"I told the FBI agents. It was just after Oklahoma City went down. Middle of 1995."

Peter had to be careful. The more he prodded, the more likely Riotte would demand to see his credentials. He tried to avoid any hectoring tone that would imply an "active" investigation. But young Riotte seemed neither surprised by the visit nor afraid of cops. But he might be afraid of Devereau, Peter speculated.

"No contact at all since then?"

"I was only eighteen back in '95. He weren't my role model. Didn't make me think one way or 'nother when he went missing."

Peter was never sure what Americans meant by the expression "gone missing." Did he mean that Jim Riotte had made a choice to disappear, or had he been forcibly removed from the scene? It was hard to believe that the brothers hadn't made contact. Then again, the hermit life seemed to be a Riotte specialty.

"Is it Marcel? Should I call you Mark?"

"It's both . . . either. Are there loose ends?" His look suggested that he was worried about something. Peter tried to see his point of view. The FBI agents had braced him already about his sibling's disappearance. Perhaps, therefore, he should be afraid.

Peter was sure that the cops hadn't hammered on the theory that Devereau and Jim Riotte were different people, but Peter counted on them having mentioned it. He handed Mark Riotte the police sketch of Ronald Devereau. "This is a police artist's rendition. Does this man look familiar?"

Riotte cast him a condescending smile. "Mister, you know what 'rendition' means? It's what they do to terror suspects."

Peter was torn between provoking this redneck and asking diversionary questions to keep him from challenging the unexpected arrival of a British-accented cop in his trailer park.

"Your name is Marcel. Was Jim's birth name Jacques or Jean?"

"Jacques. Our old man was from the north of France, came over after Normandy, after the Liberation. I speak some French."

Peter resolved to keep him off base. He spoke faster. "Was it here you saw Jim for the last time?"

"No. Over in Denver."

"Were you living here then?"

"No way. Drive from here to Denver? Shit, no. We was in a house in Pueblo."

"Your family home?"

"Yessir. Lost it to the bank after Jim vanished."

"Look at the picture, please."

It took a minute, but Mark Riotte began to nod. "That man is Shaw. Older now. Chin's wrong. Eyes definitely off."

"First name?"

"Casper. Met him just two times. The second time was in Pueblo . . . No, it was in Denver. Jimmy's truck popped a gasket and I had to tow him to Denver . . ."

Peter was breathless. Mark Riotte had just given a name to Theresa Pastern's killer.

"Did Jim tell you much about him?"

"Really, not much at all. But Jimmy respected him. Called him inspiring. Talked about the Posse Comitatus, World Government. The Trilateral Commission. Sounded like a lot of empty theory, but Jim wouldn't hear criticism of the guy."

Peter took a chance, saying, "But maybe it went beyond theory. They both disappeared after the Murrah bombing."

"Jim wouldn't have blown up children."

Young Riotte was growing touchy at all these probes, so Peter employed the interrogator's technique of taking the subject into his confidence. He laid out the theory of Devereau's betrayal of Marcel's brother, culminating in the gruesome defrosting of his corpse in the cellar at 13 Hollis.

Marcel recoiled at these images, moving to the door of the trailer and opening it to let in fresh air. "I never saw anything good about their bein' friends."

Peter shifted tack. "Do you remember anything else about Shaw?"

"Yes. He loved technology. Was a whiz, Jimmy swore. Cameras, weapons."

"Maybe bomb making, too?"

"Yeah, maybe."

"Did your brother ever mention him in connection with the Unabomber?"

"Kaczynski? Never. Didn't the Unabomber oppose technology?"

"You said his eyes were wrong. What's that mean?"

"Scary eyes. One moment they were fixed right on you, like he was making a big point, the next he was lookin' all around, crazy-paranoid, like."

"Fixed on you? I thought you met him only twice. Did you have a conversation with him?"

"More that he gave me a lecture. That time with the gasket on the truck, like I was trying to tell you, he helped fix it. At one point, he found a baggie of weed under the front seat of my truck. Started ranting about how drugs are bad for you and the police should raid all the dealers. Sounded like Nancy Reagan."

But young Riotte had no idea of Shaw's address from 1995 or any other core information regarding his brother's intimate friend.

Peter flipped over the picture with Devereau's name on it. "Ronald Devereau. Ever hear of him?"

"French. But Jim wouldn't have used that name. It's not good French. He'd have known to add the *x* to it."

Peter considered running straight through to Utah from Crispin Breach. He could stay awake at the wheel for twelve hours, and nighttime in the mountains didn't faze him. But he wasn't about to risk challenges from a state trooper about his temporary tags, his

English origins, or his scribbled field notes, which contained such words as *terrorist* and *UNABOM*, followed by many question marks. His credentials for investigating Devereau were shaky, and this was the age of paranoia on both sides of the terrorism war.

Up by the I-70, the straightest interstate he'd ever been down, surreal at midnight, Peter booked into a cheap motel. The Paradise was shabby and he was one of only two customers, but the door to his room had a solid Yale deadbolt and the air conditioner worked. A sign by the office warned of rattlesnakes nesting under the ice cooler.

He should have slept, but a hollowness overwhelmed him, as empty as the black sky outside his locked door. He had no next move. He had hoped for more from Marcel Riotte. The lad had confirmed that an unhinged figure was involved with his brother Jim at the time of the 1995 Oklahoma City bombing, but really, what did he have? Casper Shaw. Another unresonant alias on an expanding list.

And the Kaczynski link? Marcel Riotte had confirmed Shaw's love of technology. The forensics people had found shattered computers in the basement, damaged by sulphuric acid. The clumps of wire and aluminum framing seemed to have no practical use. Devereau/Shaw had retrenched to live the quiet life on Hollis Street, that much was known, and possibly he had become bored and, Peter bet, chagrined that he was contributing nothing to the battle for hearts and minds in the West. He watched the broader world getting crazier as the millennium turned. The U.S. government's powers over the ordinary man were increasing, and he could neither speak out nor meet up with old allies to plan new blows against growing tyranny. And then it invaded his street. The obscene grow house on his home turf. How long had he suppressed his anger in the basement of the two-storey, fiddling with his machines?

He was turning into that fool Kaczynski.

The freezer? Had he always planned to place Jim Riotte inside for when the authorities got close? Or was it conceivable that Riotte had lain there for ten years?

Thoughts of the freezer brought Peter around to the figurines. He unlocked the motel room door and fetched the Yoda and the airplane from the dash of the F-150. He sat on the bed, examining the objects under the bedside lamp. Yoda was a cheap statuette, with poor facial definition and no sharp edges. Everyone knew that George Lucas had shrewdly retained the merchandizing rights to the *Star Wars* characters, but this one seemed to be homemade, or perhaps from a cheap kit. It was fashioned from a yellowy substance, monochrome but ready to be painted by some collector. It bore no labels. The aircraft, while of the same material, was more ambitious, yet the attempt at detail in its wing and tail elements had left it brittle. Peter examined the underside of the plane and was able to make out three letters etched into the polymer: "SLS."

L for Princess Leia? Luke Skywalker? *S* for Han Solo?

Peter booted up his laptop, but there was no internet reception. He didn't bother moving to the open door to search for a signal. Instead, he called Marcel Riotte.

"Sweet Jesus, man, why didn't you ask me those questions when you were just here? I'm sorry I gave you my number. I've got things to do. It's 2:45 in the morning."

Peter later regretted not asking what Riotte's urgent plans were.

"It just occurred to me, Marcel, did Jim's friend collect anything? Did Jim say Shaw had any kind of hobby?"

"What the hell? You called to ask me that? What kind of hobby? Guns?"

"Sure. Or did he collect toys, *Star Wars* memorabilia?"

"How would I know, I never got to know his ass." The pause that followed was eerie as Riotte projected back in time to the man who might have immolated his brother. "He was a fitness freak, Jim told me. Hated drugs. Can't see him collecting *Star Wars* toys. This guy wasn't into kid's stuff. He was a tough, cold bastard." Peter let Marcel's bitterness take form. "He was 'fire and ice,' Jim said."

"What's the 'fire' part?" Peter said.

"Didn't I tell you? The weirdo liked to set fires."

"So you do buy into my theory, Marcel?" Peter replied.

"That he killed Jim and set fire to the house?"

"Yes."

"Yeah, probably. Either way, if I see him ever, I'll kill him, even if he is Darth fucking Vader."

The sky was opaque, not even the suspicion of morning chasing his back, when he reached the Colby Oasis Travel Center on the Kansas-Colorado border. Violating his travel plan, he had rushed along the bleak interstate in search of a Starbucks with Wi-Fi service. He bought a venti coffee and a bag of pecans, most of which he would save for the long rush to Coppermount Drive. He retreated to a booth, started up his computer and Googled "SLS abbrev."

He hit the first listed site and forty-two suggestions leapt onto the monitor.

"Self-Locking Systems." "Side-looking Sonar." Neither was helpful, even if the latter was the most popular notation. "Statistical Load Summary" was promising but it dealt with aircraft capacity. "Spider Lamb Syndrome" afflicted sheep — eight-legged lambs? ("Ares Brotherhood"? He was getting punchy.)

"Symbionese Liberation Society"? No.

Then it jumped out at him from the screen: "Selective Laser Sintering."

This was a manufacturing process used with 3-D printers to make machinery parts from ceramic and metallurgical compounds. High-powered lasers employed SLS to form shapes in computer-programmed layers. The geometrics were complex, but not beyond a bomb aficionado with a huge amount of time on his hands.

Riotte, the brother, had said that Devereau obsessed on technology. Now the phantom was fashioning bomb parts using a 3-D printer.

Peter got in the truck and drove west. For the first time since arriving in the States, he felt truly discouraged. Shaw had disappeared. Peter had to draw in the counterterrorism professionals soon, and once that happened, he and Henry Pastern and Phil Mohlman would lose control of the pursuit.

Maybe there was another way to find the shadow man. The Unabomber could be insane, Peter thought, but a visit to the Supermax might be helpful and timely.

CHAPTER 28

Peter reached the Coppermount house by late afternoon. The roughed-in street with its incomplete homes offered little comfort. He glanced down at Tynan's worksite but detected no progress, and he wondered if the elder had ever invited Henry into his work-in-progress. For that matter, had Theresa ever been welcomed inside?

Peter's expectations for Henry's sobriety were low, but when Peter came into the living room, there he was, clear-eyed, perusing his thick file on Ronald Devereau. Papers fanned across the table. The green bottle and all the Pontarlier glasses had disappeared. That was a relief.

Henry looked up and smiled. "How was Kansas?" he said blithely.

Peter, stiff and road-worn, went to the kitchen and took a bottle of orange juice from the fridge. Henry had washed the absinthe glasses and organized them on the kitchen counter. It seemed another half effort to kick his habit. If Henry were serious about giving up drinking, he would put them in the cupboard, or smash them. He filled a glass with juice and returned to the living room.

"You look whipped," Henry said. "What about Riotte's brother?"

Peter sat down, his back to the patio.

"He met our man in 1995, or maybe late '94. His name then was

Casper Shaw. Nothing much more. No address, no photographs or signed papers. Marcel said he harboured grievances against the government. Shaw was good with technology and hated drug dealers, but so what?"

"That could tie him to Hollis Street."

"In our view and probably nobody else's. What are you doing there?"

"Oh, looking through the files again. Peter, can I speak frankly?"

Peter, on edge, wanted to say that they should have been having frank conversations from the moment of his arrival in Utah. He nodded.

"Are we any closer to identifying him? These files aren't getting us to the next level. We're going to need help from somewhere *official*."

Peter's frustration burst out. "I'm here to help. Isn't that enough for you?"

"Whoa! Don't get mad. I'm trying."

"Okay." Peter rubbed the grit from his eyes. "I'm sorry. I agree. We have to draw in some of the agencies. Soon, I guess."

Henry, imitating Peter, rubbed his eyes hard against the heels of his palms. "Are you ever tempted to give up? I worry we'll never find him."

Peter wasn't in the mood for more whinging from Henry, although he was unsure of the source of his own anger. "We know that Devereau exists. Therefore he can be found. That's all we need know to advance to the next stage."

Peter was on the edge of losing control, his voice rising with each sentence. He realized that he was venting his pique on someone who was trying hard, whom he would need for that next step. But it was Henry who backed off.

"Sorry, Peter." Henry held up a slip of paper. "Phil Mohlman called. With an address. Do you know someone named Alma May Reeve? She works in Provo."

If the Green Fairy had been sitting in the bar, Peter would have added some to his orange juice. Alma May Reeve was the waitress who had seen three men in a Salt Lake City diner in 1987 on the day of the Unabomber's parking lot attack. Peter now believed that the three conspirators were Ronald Devereau, Jim Riotte, and Theodore Kaczynski. Peter had interviewed Alma in 1995 and showed her the famous public sketch of the Unabomber. She had responded, "He was one of them."

He had misinterpreted her words at the time. Alma was truthful when she said, "He was one of them," but he had failed to understand her meaning. Peter hoped Phil Mohlman could find her. If there was a single motivation for Peter being in Salt Lake City now, it was this: to apologize to Alma May Reeve.

"Henry," Peter said, "I'm going to put a frozen pizza in the oven, maybe two, and then I'll tell you about the waitress and the three killers. Tomorrow, we'll visit Alma."

Over dinner, Peter mused on the Unabomber's sins. "It was Salt Lake that caught my attention. I'd developed a crude scale based on adding up where a device was hand-delivered to or where it was mailed from. Salt Lake City scored six events. For example, Kaczynski mailed his sixth and tenth bombs, in 1982 and 1985 respectively, from Salt Lake post offices. His eleventh device, planted in Salt Lake City in 1987, interested me for a lot of reasons. It was the heart of winter, a strange time to launch an attack. I asked myself: Did he rush this one, change his plan because of the cold? He had been working away in solitude in some hovel, carving components, connecting wires, setting triggers, and now perhaps he was impatient. That winter, did he take a short ride — not to the far-off state capital in California, but to a closer capital city in nearby Utah — so that his gratification could be almost immediate?"

"And so that he could watch it blow up?" Henry contributed.

"Alma saw him that day. She may know something," Peter said.

"I like the strategy," Henry said the moment Peter finished his tale. Peter regretted his earlier tirade. He needed a partner, even a flawed partner, and he could only hope that Henry stayed sober.

"We'll head over at mid-morning, once the breakfast rush is done."

"Thank you, Peter."

"I need you clean."

Henry got up from the table and approached the bar. "Let's throw out the bottle now."

Another ritual, thought Peter. He ducked behind the counter and removed the bottle of absinthe, the slotted spoon, and one sugar cube. "Okay. But I recommend one last drink. I'll fix it."

"I'll do it," Henry said.

"No, I'll do it." Peter had no idea if this was a good or bad idea, but he was committed to the cathartic purpose of the ritual Henry had initiated. Henry watched as his partner fetched a Pontarlier glass and a jigger of water from the kitchen. Peter clumsily poured the absinthe and water into the glass. He set fire to the sugar cube resting on the spoon and they watched it burn off. All the while, Peter mused on the silliness of his friend's exotic choice of indulgence. Why pick this odd, cloying drink, as opposed to scotch or bourbon? "Henry, is there a reason other than your English lit degree you tried absinthe?"

Henry took a sip and grimaced. "It tastes terrible, I admit." He raised his glass. "Because it hardly earns a mention in the Book of Mormon, that's why." He brought the bottle to the kitchen and poured it down the sink. In his enthusiasm, he returned for the glass, took a tiny swallow and dumped the dregs into the drain.

"I'm going to bed. What time are we out of here tomorrow?"

"Up at eight for nine?" Peter said.

Peter usually slept well before a challenge, but not that night, and regret over Alma May Reeve was the cause. Had she suffered? Had the Unabomber case, some part of it unresolved, tormented her? It had certainly worn on him.

He got up at 2 a.m. in a vague state. He tiptoed to the station in the living room and checked his emails, and for once there was nothing from home. He considered his address list.

His message to Maddy, his daughter-in-law, was plaintively short. "Are you up?"

Five minutes passed.

"Yes. Call?"

Him: "Yes, please. Me to you. Wake the baby?"

Her: "No. Love to talk."

Mobile reception was erratic inside the ranch house and not much better in the surrounding desert. A report in the *Deseret Star* suggested that activity at the Utah Testing Range farther west had fouled everyone's signal, but this struck Peter as tinfoil-hat paranoia. He went out to the driveway — a hot spot, in his experience, but only if he stood in the bed of the F-150 and faced east. He punched in the number for Maddy and Michael's home in Leeds.

Maddy's warm voice answered immediately. "Where are you, Dad?"

"I'm standing in the bed of a pickup truck in the Great Salt Desert," Peter said.

"So you're fitting right in, then. Is that what they call a tailgate party? I wish I could be there."

Maddy was left to interpret the flicker in Peter's reply: "That would be . . . nice," he said. Was it possible that he was homesick? Or was he feeling guilty because he had rushed away from England without having said a proper goodbye to her? During his last case, the Carpenter Affair, he had brought her in early, asking her to undertake an intense probe into Alice Nahri's background. She had succeeded magnificently, to the point of tracking down Alice's mother to Henley-on-Thames. He had every reason to rely on her.

Like Joan, Maddy worried about Peter's safety but knew to approach the subject obliquely. "You have your American map, and I put up a new one in the shed the day after you left." The implied offer was that she was ready to track his adventures and provide support from afar. "Have you any idea where to find your killer?"

Affection welled up in both of them. "I owe you an apology, dear. I should have fully briefed you beforehand. Maybe it was the sight of young Joe on your hip that night after dinner. I worried . . ."

"That's okay, Dad," she interjected. He didn't need to apologize. Everything between them was fine.

"I could use your research skills, dear, if you have time."

"I have time." She wasn't about to explain that Joe pretty fully occupied all her waking hours, nor the counterweighing truth that she ached to be with Peter on the manhunt. She would be there for her father-in-law, and he wouldn't challenge her again, she was sure. They were back on respectful ground.

"I'll follow up with emails, but here's the essence. I want you to poke into any databases you can find listing major arson incidents in the United States between 1990 and 2012. Include charges and convictions, also any news reports implying a link between the arson and drug dealers. I'm particularly interested in fires in crack houses and marijuana grow ops. Don't ignore incidents where small-time dealers accuse their competition of setting the fire."

"Geographical parameters?" Maddy said.

"Western states." He listed twelve states, including all that bordered Mexico.

"There's more?"

"Yes. Note any drug and arson cases with a mention of domestic terrorism, the Unabomber, or the Murrah Building."

Maddy said, "How about we also frame the terrorism search using Homeland Security categories? They're likely divided by domestic versus foreign-linked incidents. They must be time-delineated, pre- and post-9/11, for example."

"Yes, and both eras are of interest exactly because of the different perspectives. The eighties up to mid-nineties form Reagan's war-on-drugs period, and I'm curious about that. By the by, it sounds like you've been doing research already."

"Joan told me about the grow op murders in Salt Lake. I was curious."

Peter didn't have to tell her that her initiative pleased him.

"And that raises a key question," she added. "A lot of the details and cross-references will only be in secure police databases. You want me to stay away from them?"

"Hold off. Don't pull a WikiLeaks on any Homeland Security files."

"When should I call?"

"I'll ring you tomorrow night. My battery's running out, or the reception's just plain fading. I have to go, dear." Peter sometimes forgot the human dimension. "Oh, how's Joe?"

Peter's battery faded out, and he failed to hear Maddy's chuckle as she pictured him standing in the back of the pickup.

CHAPTER 29

Peter awoke at six thirty. At seven thirty, Henry rousted himself from his mattress and spent thirty minutes in the bathroom getting ready, as if he were trying to scrub away his experiment in dipsomania. They left at nine in Peter's truck.

Phil Mohlman's note gave an address up in Provo, an almost straight shot from Salt Lake City on Highway 15. Alma May Reeve worked at the Spector Diner. The note gave no more details.

Henry hadn't fully expunged the alcohol from his body, but he kept himself under control. And he kept the banter light. "Why would you call your place the Spector Diner?"

"Wall of sound."

"What?"

"Phil Spector. Girl bands of the sixties. Chiffons. Also, Righteous Brothers. 'You've Lost that Lovin' Feelin'"?"

"Not my era, Peter. I grew up with Nirvana — and yeah, even Mormons listened to Nirvana."

"Okay, then. I like all music."

"You like the Strokes?"

"Who are they?"

"A band, Peter. You know: five guys, three guitars, some drums."

"Three guitars?"

Henry smirked. "Even the Beatles had three guitars, Peter."

"Maybe they've changed the name of the place to the Strokes Diner."

The issue remained moot. The address was right, but the name had changed to the Blue Horizon Café. Phil Mohlman's information was out of date, so the police must not have interviewed Alma lately.

"Blue Horizon," Henry affirmed, getting out of the truck.

Peter led the way inside. Only three tables had patrons, all of them clustered on the sunny side of the restaurant. The breakfast rush had dissipated, and a waitress and the rotund fry cook chatted by the kitchen door. Alma wasn't in evidence.

The cook made them for cops as Peter approached.

"Alma May Reeve?" Peter said.

"Don't know that name," the fat man replied, but a flash of recognition crossed the woman's face.

The hinged door to the kitchen opened and Alma came out with two full plates in her hands. She looked grey and harried, the stress lines in her face deep. She looked at Peter and dropped both plates.

The cook, who appeared to manage the place as well, came forward to steady her.

"It's okay," the other waitress and the man said simultaneously.

"It's okay," Alma parroted. Peter saw that her nametag read "Dawn."

Henry pressed forward and began to pick up broken crockery. "I'll get that," he said.

"Don't," Peter whispered, unnecessarily harshly. Offering that form of kindness to Alma at this point wasn't the way to go. She was tough in her own fashion, Peter knew, and would reject condescension.

"I can do that!" she said.

The chef took over and instructed her to take her break. Without looking at Peter, she said, "Let's go to the park. I can smoke there."

As they walked down the street, Henry trailing, Alma said in a husky voice, "My name is Dawn Lewis now. Please use it."

Seldom had Peter been more anxious to re-interview a witness. For almost two decades, Alma had held in a fact that went to the core of the Unabomber case and that might well have driven the investigators to rechristen it the Unabomber Conspiracy. The trio reached the park, and Peter sat down next to her while she smoked. Henry stood apart. "You knew I'd be back someday?" Peter said.

"I knew that you or another cop — or one of *them* — would return. Strange how one event can flow through your entire life. You're damn right I've been waiting."

Peter leaned closer. "Dawn, I'm here because I know I got it wrong. I apologize."

She said nothing for a long minute. Peter remained calm but wished that Henry, fidgeting nearby, would go back to the truck.

"Events that haunt our lives," Alma said as if looking down a tunnel into the past.

"Yes," Peter said. "When the police first interviewed you, you said you had seen three men at a table in the diner around the corner from the computer store. They showed you the wanted poster for the Unabomber."

"With the sunglasses and the sweatshirt, yes. It was two weeks after the bombing. They seemed to know which man they wanted, understand? I told them, yeah, I had seen the guy in the picture, that was him."

"But the one you identified wasn't Kaczynski," Peter said.

"You made the same mistake when you came by years later and asked me about the poster."

"Yes, I did."

"The man on the poster was someone else."

"And he was at the table that day?"

"Yes, he was."

Peter allowed a diplomatic pause, but unfortunately Henry jumped in. "So, you did see this man?" He showed her the Devereau sketch. She nodded but turned to Henry with some irritation.

"Who are you?" said Alma.

"I'm the husband of the woman this man killed less than a year ago."

Alma swung towards to Peter. "He's come back? That's why you're here?"

"We're on his trail. It would help us if we went over your recollections."

"It would help if you tell me you'll stop this man in his tracks. Where's he been all this time?"

"Living under different pseudonyms."

"I know what that's like."

Henry sat down on the bench on the other side of her. This time Alma looked at him with sympathy. "Miss Lewis, why are you so certain you're in danger from this man?"

"Young man, I'm sorry about your wife. But you're still young and you don't get it. I don't really think he'll come after me but one encounter with an evil person can permeate your entire existence." Alma turned back to Peter. "There was craziness in his eyes. That face haunts me and I don't mean the Unabomber."

"Tell us about that morning," Peter coaxed.

"The three men were having breakfast at a corner table. Kaczynski was extremely antsy. He was shabbily dressed and had the look of a loser. Didn't eat his breakfast. The one in the sketch, the one we're talking about, did all the talking. I overheard words like 'government,' 'justice,' 'effective deterrence.'"

"He was agitated?" Henry said.

"Yeah, but not loud. He was very intense."

"What about the third guy?"

"He kept quiet. The interesting thing 'bout him was he looked a lot like the one you're after."

"I don't want to be argumentative, Miss Lewis," Peter said, "but how do you know that the suspect in the poster wasn't the third guy?"

Alma looked at Peter and smiled for the first time. "Because the third guy wore a bushy handlebar moustache that day. Obviously fake."

"Did all three men leave together?"

Peter and Henry waited for the rest of her story.

"I have to get this off my chest, so let me tell it my way. They'd been sitting there a while. The intense guy was doing most of the talking, but Kaczynski didn't like whatever he was saying. You get a sense with customers. They were building to an argument. Kaczynski got up to use the bathroom. Then the serious guy suddenly picked up a canvas bag from under the table and walked out. Kaczynski came back and got all upset that the bag was gone, and the man in the silly moustache tried to calm him down."

"That explains why Devereau and the wanted poster are so similar," Peter said. "It was Devereau the secretary in the computer store saw planting the bomb. Did he return?"

"No. After twenty minutes Kaczynski and the moustache character left."

Peter said softly to Alma, "I know you couldn't come forward afterwards. The police were convinced they already had the right suspect in Kaczynski . . ."

Alma snapped back, "I was flabbergasted when I saw they arrested the hermit. Looked nothing like the one in the poster. But you see, what did I care which guy they arrested? But mister, *Kaczynski wasn't the one in charge at the table that day.*"

Peter spoke. "You've been waiting all these years for us to come back to see you. I'm sorry."

"I've been waiting for . . . I don't know what. Maybe I was responsible for a killer getting away."

Alma seemed to shrink, becoming tiny. She was holding something back.

"Did you see something else, Dawn?"

"There was a book on their table. By someone called Turner."

"*The Turner Diaries?*"

"I think so. What are they?"

"A favourite novel of the anti-government militia groups."

"I always wondered," Alma said. The information did not appear to lift the burden of her bad memories.

"Did they leave anything else behind?" Peter then said.

"You mean other than no tip?"

"I mean anything."

Alma stubbed out her cigarette. "You know, Detective, I've been waiting for someone to ask me that. None of the cops wanted to listen back then; they were committed to their scenario. Come with me."

Alma led the two men three more blocks down the street. In her apartment, she ordered them to wait by the door while she went to the bedroom. They heard her tossing boxes around. She emerged with a dog-eared sheaf of typewritten text.

"The man you want left this behind."

"What's that about?" Henry said.

"It's Devereau's manifesto," Peter stated.

"It's about how a crazy man might blow up the world," Alma said.

Peter held on to her hand. "If he hasn't returned for it by now, he won't be coming back."

"I really hope not," Alma May Reeve said. There was relief in her voice.

CHAPTER 30

On the way back home, Peter stopped at a Staples and had six copies of the Devereau manifesto photocopied and bound.

In the truck, Henry flipped through his copy and offered a running critique. "Maybe thirty pages. Funny, the thing is typed but the title is handwritten: *Fire and Brimstone*. A screed denouncing the U.S. government . . . all governments in general . . . Lots of quotes. If only there were signatures on it."

Peter glanced over at the crudely typed manuscript. "Henry, we need some help on this."

"Time to call in the cavalry, Peter?"

"Well, the quiet kind of cavalry. Can you think of someone back in Quantico who might give the manifesto a discreet review?"

Henry understood where Peter was heading with this. "You want to know if the guy who wrote this thing also wrote Kaczynski's *Manifesto* back in '96. Well, there are guys in Art Crimes who know text-comparison software. I could ask, but the atmosphere is tight these days in the Bureau. Sidebar work is heavily discouraged."

Peter knew that every law enforcement agency in Utah would hear about their query within a day. "You're right. I have a better idea."

At the house, Henry went off to read his copy of Devereau/Shaw's diatribe while Peter checked his emails. Maddy had yet to respond with research results. He was pleased to find a clear dial tone on Henry's landline and he punched in the number for Leeds.

Alma's memories had not disappointed, but it was crucial to maintain momentum. Peter's plaguing fear wasn't that Devereau would return to attack Alma but that he was planning to vanish soon, either into the impenetrable underground of militias and domestic agitators or, more likely, back into another suburban identity. Peter assessed the various scenarios. The deadliest hazard was a fresh terrorist attack by Devereau, in which case Peter and Henry would pay heavily for failing to plug in the agencies in advance. Peter was ready to freelance for a few more days, but not much longer.

"Hi, Dad. I'm sending you a pile of stuff," Maddy began on the phone, without more greeting than that.

Had she been up since dawn? Peter could only guess at the volume of material about to flow across the Atlantic. He let her run with her news; it was always wise policy with his daughter-in-law. "Send it to Henry's email. Give me the headlines now."

"All right. You wanted me to find cases involving arson and drugs, with any notations on terrorism. I went for the 1980-to-2012 bracket, a bit wider than you requested."

"I almost hate to ask, dear, but did you break in to any restricted databases along the way?"

"'Break in' is a relative term, Dad. Most criminal-record data are organized by specific investigative requirement — terrorism, drugs, organized crime. The need shapes the data sets. There's a Homeland Security agency or sub-office for every topic. Absolutely amazing. Every little bureaucracy wants access to the stats. I had no trouble getting what I wanted online."

"Results?"

"Mixed. I found several hundred drug busts over the full period that involved fires. In most of these, the drug dealers themselves set fire to their inventory, or the police somehow caused a fire in the crack house. It was a lot harder to pin down cases of one drug dealer burning out another. Police forces like to take credit for the downfall of every pusher. My charts show the spread across eight states, and I'm still working on the other jurisdictions."

"Bottom line?"

"No bottom line. Patterns are broad. I've highlighted two dozen fires where 'rivalry' and 'vengeance' — or everybody's favourite, 'internecine drug war' — are mentioned. But look at page sixteen when you get the package. It shows a cluster of unsolved drug-related killings in the 1990-through-1993 period in Utah, Colorado, Arizona, and Kansas."

"Terrorism links?"

"Rarely are specific links made between drugs and terrorism. I marked six incidents of someone taking out a drug dealer where the police expressed puzzlement about the attacker's motive and thought some militia movement was looking to finance its operations. Nothing linking drug or arson cases to the Unabomber, other than the fact that his own bomb on that American Airlines flight in 1979 caused a fire."

"Okay, Maddy, I will read everything."

"Keep looking?"

"Keep looking."

"Anything else?" It amazed him that neither ever asked the other about their health or the weather. Maddy was all business.

"Yup. I'm sending you a document by international courier. I'd scan it in, but I prefer you examine the text in its original format. I want you to compare it to the Unabomber's *Manifesto* published in the *New York Times* and the *Washington Post*."

"I'll read it."

"Good."

"You want to know if the same person wrote both documents."

"Yes. Henry says there is text-analysis software available online."

"Put him on."

"What? Really?"

Peter fetched Henry from his bedroom. In two minutes, he was talking happily with Peter's daughter-in-law. The ease of it made Cammon feel very old. Henry laughed once, almost the first time since Peter's arrival in Utah.

"Maddy, they use three standard programs to compare texts," Henry said. "They always start with tagging software, measuring word frequency. They use a second program to evaluate sequence probabilities for parts of speech. Those are called Markov models. Finally, try what they call sentiment analysis. If you don't have the program, I can probably get it for you. Movie studios use it to assess audience reactions at sneak previews. All this gives a ninety percent accuracy rate on identifying stylistic similarities between texts."

They talked for ten more minutes, and Henry gently sat the phone on its cradle. Peter respected the pause but then said, "Should I have asked you to do the analysis?"

Henry shook his head. "She's beautiful."

Peter drove into town and shipped the coffee shop manifesto at a DHL outlet; he was promised delivery within three days. He took his time returning to Coppermount; he wasn't in the mood to hash out his next steps with Henry. He picked up Chinese food and drove around Salt Lake for a while, arriving at the house to find that his host had set the table for dinner. Henry had taped the various sketches and photos from Peter's rogues' gallery to the backs of the dining room chairs and was pacing the floor examining them. The effect was unnerving.

They chatted about the case, about Alma and the similarities between the faces in the sketches, and frequently got up to re-examine one or another portrait taped to the chairs. They agreed that the next day they would report their findings to Chief Grady at West Valley police headquarters.

While Henry cleaned up, Peter sent an email to Joan. On impulse, he sent an affectionate note to his daughter, Sarah. He thought she was on assignment somewhere along the coast of Scotland. Sarah was the true wanderer among the Cammons, her job as a marine biologist constantly taking her to the edges of Britain and Europe. They kept in contact mostly by emails and text messages. It amused him that both Sarah and Maddy were addicted to their smart phones and rarely let five minutes go by before responding to his missives. But tonight Peter was so exhausted that he immediately turned off his mobile and went to bed before Henry.

The next morning, Peter was brushing his teeth when Henry came in, the telephone extended.

"Phil Mohlman," he whispered.

Peter took the phone.

"Cammon, what the hell do you think you're doing?"

"What's happened?"

"Mark Riotte's dead."

"When and where?"

"Night before last, and I think you can figure out where. Stabbed through the heart. His place was torched. And guess what? A witness fingered a truck, an F-150 that showed up two days ago at the trailer court. She noted down the tags. The truck is leased to you, Inspector."

Peter experienced an odd thought: could the medical examiner determine the exact hour of death? He had called Riotte from the Paradise Motel at 2:30 a.m.

"Yes, that's right. What do we know at this point?"

"Here's what we know, asshole. You and Henry need to get down here this morning. A meeting is scheduled for ten o'clock. Me, DeKlerk, and Chief Grady."

"Why are you so angry? You think I killed Riotte?"

"No."

And then Peter understood. Blood and ashes. Knife and fire. Here was Devereau's Hollis Street signature. This gruesome thought slightly cheered Peter; this was a link to Casper Shaw. But why was DeKlerk inserting himself? "Did Riotte's death involve narcotics?" he asked Mohlman.

"Don't you get it? I got Riotte's address *from* DeKlerk. He did me a favour, and he took a big chance by not clearing it with Grady or Rogers at the DEA. Now that Riotte has turned up dead, they're giving Boog flak, asking what you were doing in Kansas, and why, once again, Boog handed off the case to West Valley Homicide. You have to explain to Boog and the Kansas police. I'm not carrying that weight."

Peter wanted to suggest that DeKlerk should be chastised for not warning him and Mohlman that Marcel Riotte was a dealer, thereby endangering Peter.

DeKlerk had once again manipulated West Valley Homicide to make them look foolish. Peter simply said, "Henry and I will be there at ten."

Phil became calmer. "Can Henry deal with the pressure?"

"Yes."

"All right, I'll cut you some slack on Boog DeKlerk, but he's gunning for you. To him, you're an illegal alien. You've opened a big can of worms. As soon as you go begging to the ATF, DEA, Utah State Police, or the Bureau for cooperation, which I know you're considering, you got a problem with DeKlerk. The only thing Boog hates more than you taking over a drug case is you letting the feds take over."

"We'll be there."

Peter briefed Henry on the drive into West Valley. Henry, sober and energized from a night's sleep, wanted to talk "strategy."

"Henry, since I'm the one who went to Crispin Breach without notifying anybody and pushed the Drug Squad's buttons, I'll take the heat on this."

The younger man smiled at him from the passenger seat. "You always knew we'd have to involve the rest of the police world sooner or later."

Peter smiled back. "This isn't exactly how I thought collegiality would kick in."

When they entered the conference room at the West Valley station, Phil Mohlman was sitting at the big table with Boog DeKlerk, but Chief Grady was absent. From their grim faces, Peter knew he was in deep trouble, and he moved to get out ahead of it.

To DeKlerk he said politely, "Peter Cammon."

The big man reluctantly gave in to English manners and shook hands.

But that was his only concession.

"Under what authority did you drive across the Kansas border to formally confront a suspect in an active investigation? Have you immigrated, Inspector?" DeKlerk said.

Peter had kept the Hollis Street carnage bottled up inside him for a long time. He decided to push back. "I was there to see Marcel Riotte. And isn't the Devereau investigation wrapped up?"

"*Marcel?*" DeKlerk spat. "The police hereabouts know him as Mark. He has a criminal record. And why didn't you inform the Hollis Street investigators of your visit? My Homicide colleague Detective Mohlman, for example?"

Henry tilted forward. "Peter informed *me*," Henry said.

"You're not on the investigation anymore," DeKlerk snapped.

"There is no investigation," Henry said. "Every police force in sight has suspended it or ignored it."

"Bullshit."

Peter watched the sparring, startled by the intensity of the South African's hostility. DeKlerk was ready to roll right over Henry Pastern, and Peter, too. He was overdoing it. He had dodged the Watson file, but did he want back in? Peter resolved to endure the big man's hypocrisy while he figured out these questions.

Phil Mohlman lost his temper. "I didn't know Cammon was planning the trip, but when you provided Riotte's coordinates, you might have mentioned he was a narcotics dealer."

It was a standoff for a moment, and then everyone regrouped.

"I'll tell you everything I did," Peter said reasonably, "but fill us in on Riotte's death."

DeKlerk quoted the report from the Kansas police. "'Residents of the Friendly Trailer Park were awakened by a fire in one of the units in the early morning, roused by the smell of burning cannabis.' Lots of it."

Peter tilted forward, trying not to sound combative. "I was in Riotte's trailer. There weren't substantial quantities of drugs inside that I saw — and no smell of weed."

Mohlman said, "Riotte owned a second trailer down the end of the row. Everyone knew he used it for illicit business."

Everyone but me, you mean.

"And no one cared if it was drug business," DeKlerk added. "Places like that are drug villages."

"Just marijuana?" Peter said.

"A local resident said Riotte dealt cocaine and heroin, too."

Mohlman added, "Kansas Homicide told me the attackers heisted narcotics from the second trailer."

Henry said, "How do they know for sure?"

DeKlerk shot him a look of contempt. "Because they got the drug squad out lickety-split to take a gander. In Kansas, Homicide *cooperates* with Narcotics."

Mohlman attempted to calm things by redirecting the conversation. "Cammon, why did you go to Kansas in the first place?"

"Devereau is a ghost. Nobody's owned up to knowing him. I figured if anyone met him from two decades ago, it might be Riotte's younger brother. I also hoped there had been fraternal contact more recently."

It sounded weak, and it was. "You were grasping at straws," DeKlerk fired.

Henry was in a mood to take on the Drug Unit chief. "Cammon is here because I asked him to come. You and the entire force have closed the file on Devereau. What do you care if someone delves into a dead investigation?"

Mohlman jumped in before DeKlerk could throw a punch. "Mark Riotte was thirty-five when he died. That puts him at eighteen the last time he *might* have met Devereau's 'ghost.' You can't work both ends of this, Cammon. You're trying to track down this nasty bastard by yourself, without drawing in the authorities. I know, you're going to argue that the authorities don't believe there is a killer out there, and don't care. Trouble is, you can't go any further without stepping on someone's official toes. Kansas Highway Patrol are pissed off."

DeKlerk said, "Come clean, Inspector, what did Riotte tell you in Kansas?"

"I went there for one reason, to see if he ever met someone *like* Devereau. I showed him the police sketch West Valley prepared. He said he had encountered a man like that. Called himself Casper Shaw."

"What else? Address?"

"No address. Marcel never saw where he lived. But there was one thing. Shaw hated drugs."

"What else did Mark Riotte tell you?"

"He said he would kill Devereau if he ever saw him again."

Chief Grady entered the boardroom in a rush. He was in his late fifties, skinny rather than lean, with the typical cares of a chief of police weighing on him.

"You're Chief Inspector Cammon?"

"Yes."

"Cammon, I may have to send you Topeka."

The four detectives in the room all understood that Grady's worries reverberated beyond the sordid killing of Mark Riotte in lonely Crispin Breach. The bigger police agencies were now irreversibly involved in the Hollis Street case and the manhunt for Ronald Devereau.

There was more.

"There was a major raid on a drug operation in Wichita last night. No one killed but four shot and the place burned out. Captain Brockhurst of the Kansas Highway Patrol demands to know if the attack is connected to Riotte."

CHAPTER 31

Peter and Henry returned to the house, neither man particularly chastened by Chief Grady's anger. Henry chattered about their defiance of Boog DeKlerk's effort to intimidate them, but then he announced that he needed a nap, and retreated to his bedroom.

Coppermount felt isolated. The urge for movement swept over Peter and he secretly — he wouldn't confide this to Henry — was pleased at the prospect of taking to the interstates again, no matter what grief this Captain Brockhurst gave him. He searched out Topeka on his bedroom wall map and found that it lay at the far eastern edge of Kansas.

He considered Henry's state of mind again. He allowed him his deep grief, but his uneven conduct — why suddenly depart for a late-morning nap after a solid night's sleep? — made him think that Henry might be about to go back on the booze. Joan, an emergency room nurse who had seen her share of addicts, believed in the "addictive personality," and Peter wondered if Henry's drinking went beyond normal grief. Peter had stated, perhaps rashly, that he was travelling to America to kill a dangerous man. It would help to have a reliable partner at his side when the time arrived. But for now he decided to make the trip to Kansas alone.

Presumably Devereau/Shaw had attacked the Friendly Trailer Park one night and a significant drug operation the next, both in one state. Why was he moving so fast? He was ripping off drug dealers and selling off the product to finance . . . what? Peter worried that he was racing towards some kind of terrorist assault, returning to his old ways. He had long wondered how they would trap Devereau, and now he perceived a weakness in the killer/terrorist's pattern. Times had changed in the West and across the country since 9/11. Drug dealers, perhaps including the Mexican Henry had encountered, had come to understand that they could no longer launch drug wars in the West with impunity. Homeland Security had effectively obliterated the distinctions among drug marketing, organized crime, and terrorist actions and were targeting every kind of criminal organization. Spreading carnage across the Kansas drug world two nights running reflected old, lawless frontier thinking. It would bring Devereau coordinated attention he didn't want.

You're out there, Devereau. Not far. But you're running fast now, aren't you?

Peter had Captain Brockhurst's number, and before dialing he pondered what to say. He supposed he would have to disclose his full theory of Devereau's links to the Unabomber in order to satisfy the Kansan. There was no other way to explain away his visit to the trailer park.

As he was about to ring up Brockhurst on Henry's landline, Maddy reached him on his mobile.

"Dad, can you go online? I've only a minute. Joe's on my lap."

Peter could hear his grandson babbling in the background. He went to Henry's computer to access his email. Six massive files from his daughter-in-law sat in his inbox. The volume didn't bother him, since she included an explanatory summary with each data set.

"Dad, are you there?"

"Six files. Next?"

"Open the one called 'Picture/95/15/04.' Call me when you can."

"Bye, Grandpa," Joe said.

Peter clicked the label, and the police artist's black-and-white sketch of Ronald Devereau from Junction City, Kansas, stared him in the face. No, it was *different*. Here was a refined version of the sketch generated by the bloke who had knocked on Tim McVeigh's motel room door. Peter sat back in surprise. This was new.

He read Maddy's caption.

Found this artist's sketch in Oklahoma City records (okay, in Alcohol, Tobacco and Firearms historical file system — semi-secure file system — hope you aren't sharing my hacking!). It is supposed to be Timothy McVeigh!!! On April 15, 1995, about four days before the Murrah Building explosion, McVeigh stayed at the Dreamland Motel in Junction City, Kansas. He ordered takeaway Chinese food, and the lad from the restaurant delivered it to his door, Room 25. This is a picture of the character who answered. Does it look like McVeigh to you? Here's the thing, Dad: later, the delivery boy swears it wasn't McVeigh who paid for the food. He stuck to his story. Does the chap in the picture look like someone we know?

Peter knew most of this already, but what the FBI had never told him was that they had re-interviewed the delivery boy and come up with an amended portrait — now staring him in the face — that looked even more like Ronald Devereau. Peter printed out the sketch. He now had five portraits of Ronald Devereau. He was running out of dining room chairs.

Keeping the picture file open, he rang up Captain Brockhurst in Topeka.

"Chief Inspector Peter Cammon, I'm presuming." Brockhurst's drawl was low and thick but, to Peter's limited ear, sounded like a Texas accent.

"I am retired, Captain. Private citizen."

"Not of this state. What the hell were you doing in my backyard two nights back?"

"Tracking a killer."

"Who's the victim, other than Marcel Riotte?"

"The wife of Henry Pastern, a West Valley detective. Plus a couple named Watson. Another couple named Proffet."

"Listen, Mr. Cammon, when Chief Grady told me who you were, I checked you out. You were here during the Unabomber mess."

"Yes, I was."

"Ever make it to Kansas back then?"

"No. I almost came to your state in 1995. There was talk of a possible connection between Ted Kaczynski and Timothy McVeigh, but I never made the trip."

Brockhurst grunted. "I was also involved in the Murrah blitz in '95, but I guess we didn't meet."

"No," Peter said neutrally.

"Any links between this week's drug raid and domestic terrorism or militia groups?"

It was Peter's turn to pause. "I confess, Captain, I think there is. Can you give me your email? I want to send you something."

It took only a minute to forward the fresh sketch of the stranger in Timothy McVeigh's motel room.

"Who is this?" Brockhurst said.

"Probably Ronald Devereau, also known as Casper Shaw, and likely the killer of Marcel Riotte." Peter explained the delivery man's testimony.

"Inspector, you've become suddenly interesting to me. I'm expecting you in Topeka. There are daily flights from Salt Lake."

"I'd prefer to drive. See the country," Peter said.

"It'll take you two days, but I suppose you could do it in one fifteen-hour stretch."

"I'll do it overnight. Oh, am I a suspect in the trailer park case?"

"Everyone's a suspect. This is America."

Peter left for Kansas within the hour, without Henry. He sensed that he might have an ally in Brockhurst, a cop willing to work with him. Of course, maybe this optimism merely reflected his longing for a partner of his own generation.

He crossed the Colorado border on the relentless I-70 and stopped for the night at the El Palomino Motel in Grand Junction (he liked the leaping horse on the sign out front). He could just as well have left Utah in the morning, but he was consumed by the need to press on, and driving always did the trick. After a restless sleep, he was on the highway at sunrise. The I-70 ran all the way to Topeka.

About 150 miles out of the Kansas state capital, a road sign startled him: "Fort Riley Military Reservation." Timothy McVeigh had been assigned here for a short spell. A second interstate marker promised "Junction City: 2 Miles" — the town where McVeigh had stayed at the Dreamland Motel.

But a gas station attendant in Junction City informed Peter that the Dreamland Motel had gone out of business. McVeigh had left no martyr's shrine.

Brockhurst had asked Peter to come by police headquarters as soon as he reached Topeka, "as long as the sun is up." The captain was in the office when Peter arrived. Peter instantly took to him. He carried the aura of a wily small-town sheriff, jowly, ruddy-cheeked, and dramatic in his every movement; his hair, barely thinning as he reached sixty, swooped past his temples to form a pompadour.

Peter soon learned that dramatic movement was the captain's hallmark. No sooner had Peter entered than he was up, snagging his jacket from the rack and brushing past his visitor with, "You drink rye?"

"I drink beer," Peter said.

"They have Guinness in this place."

"Coors will do."

That brought a smile. Brockhurst talked over his shoulder as they strode up the block to the restaurant. "You didn't bring Detective Pastern with you."

"I thought we might talk more frankly without the widower of Devereau/Shaw's victim in the room."

"Cold bastard, aren't ya?"

At the restaurant, the captain went right to a booth. "I'm a fixture here, and no one bothers to listen to me, so we can talk freely. Tell me about Crispin Breach, Peter."

Cammon covered the important points in twenty minutes.

Brockhurst ordered a second rye and ginger ale and sighed. "I want you to know I do accept that Devereau and Jim Riotte are different people. But you see the obvious problem I've got? Kansas can hardly issue a bulletin on Devereau without solid identification. No fingerprints were found in either of Riotte's trailers, nor in Wichita."

Peter waited until the waitress brought their drinks. "I understand the low-lifes in the park are sure Mark Riotte traded large amounts of heavy drugs, including heroin. It seems the killer looted the storage trailer before setting fire to it all."

The captain nodded. "Here's an interesting detail. The incendiary devices were homemade delayed-fuse bombs enclosed in wooden boxes. Our forensics team is looking at the remains now."

Peter described the bomb left at Number 5 Hollis. He removed the Yoda from his pocket and handed it across the table. "Captain Brockhurst, could you ask your people if they found any of this material in the wreckage?"

"Sure, but it's polymer resin. It tends to melt easily. But we'll compare the two devices."

Peter took out the sheaf of police sketches, which he had collected from Henry's dining room chairs, including the latest Dreamland Motel portrait. Brockhurst looked at the Junction City drawings and nodded. "I'm mortified to say I'd forgotten about this witness. The Chinese-food delivery boy. No one believed him. I was on the Oklahoma City liaison group at the time, and I remember the chaos that week. This got lost in the shuffle."

Peter laid out the sketches in a row. "They're all variations of Ronald Devereau."

"Or Jim Riotte. That's your problem, you see? Without a name and prints . . ."

Peter produced a bound copy of the *Fire and Brimstone* document. He explained that Alma May had kept it for two decades. "Ronald Devereau wrote this diatribe and left it in a diner where he was having coffee with Ted Kaczynski."

Brockhurst thumbed through the document. "Have you compared it to Kaczynski's *Manifesto*?"

"It's being done," Peter said.

"So you're saying your man was the theoretician behind two of the most nasty terror campaigns in U.S. history. You've got to take this to the Domestic Terrorism unit at the FBI."

"I'm hoping to find him first."

The Kansan shook his head theatrically. "The focus of Homeland Security on domestic terrorism is stronger than it ever was. They'll share their case files if you shape your argument right. They maintain an Extremist Crime Database, or ECDB, which records every case of a violent attack by white supremacists, 'patriot' groups, eco-terrorists, and animal rights extremists. Between 1990 and 2010, there were 148 attacks by right-wing agitators, including Oklahoma City. Most of these can be characterized as ideologically motivated."

"You stay plugged in to this area, I see," Peter said.

"There's another plus to gaining the cooperation of the Bureau and the anti-terrorism players. They have all kinds of new databases. Did you know they keep an index of highway serial killers? If you can win access to all this data, you may come across other plots inspired and influenced by our man."

Peter decided to push harder. "I'm interested in what you personally remember of the period we're talking about."

"We saw this kind of thing in the early nineties. A bombing in a crack house in Yuma in 1992, where pipe bombs lit up the whole place. Colorado Springs a couple of years later, with an incendiary device detonated in a grow house. Another in Denver. I always wondered if the criminals were ripping off the druggies in order to finance domestic terror plots."

"Was McVeigh's operation financed that way?" Peter asked.

"Most of these Western militia groups preferred bank robbing. The Aryan Nation in particular is known to have robbed banks in Missouri and Iowa. Taking down a bank fit their self-styled populist imagery. Banks are like governments, fair targets. Remember that scene in *Bonnie and Clyde* where Warren Beatty hands his gun to the farmer so that he can shoot his house, which the bank has just foreclosed on?"

"Did the militias avoid drug raids because of the cartels?" Peter said, thinking of Avelino González.

"No. They're about as macho as the Mexican and Colombian gangs. It just seemed easier back then to rob banks. Which makes me wonder about your man. Why is he obsessed with drug factories?"

"Money," Peter said.

"Right. Always the quick cash. And that, my English friend, leads us to the question of what he needs the money for. My concern is a new terrorist attack."

"Me too. But do you expect it?"

Brockhurst paused to sip his rye. "I don't know. The raids in Crispin Breach and Wichita were close to demented, showed a real hatred of drug dealers. Is our guy a true terrorist? If so, he's shown his incompetence so far. How could he forget his personal manifesto in the diner? And why not go back for it! I keep picturing him with his bacon and eggs. Kaczynski's five minutes from leaving a crude pipe bomb in a parking lot, where it's likely to kill some innocent pedestrian. Devereau, who is insecure enough to let a fruitcake like Ted get his goat, starts wondering what happened to his feature role in the revolution. He grabs the bomb and plants it himself. Sounds like a dreamer who tried to prove himself a tough guy."

Peter reinforced the point. "And he thought he could manipulate Ted by handing over his own manifesto and getting him to take all the risk."

"Maybe Kaczynski announced at the diner that he had already started his own manifesto."

"Jim Riotte was the third man in the diner and was part of the team," Peter said. "Let's assume that Riotte and Devereau reached the same decision. They both realized that Kaczynski was becoming unstable and that the FBI would sooner or later nab him. They decided to disappear. They needed enough money to set themselves up with new identities, completely new lives. Probably they had already been accumulating cash by ripping off crack houses and grow ops and burning them out."

"The Murrah attack and the 1993 and 1995 Unabomber incidents both had their imprint on them, a bomb in a box. The fertilizer in the Ryder truck was just a bigger version."

Brockhurst smiled at the waitress as she passed, but Peter knew there was no need to command a second, even a third rye. It would arrive unbidden.

"Chief, I think Devereau inspired every one of these attacks. One thing we can be sure of is that Devereau plans to disappear again. The question is, will he make a big splash first?"

"Right. And that means we're most likely to nail him during one of his fundraising raids before he commits a terrorist act. I'll watch the ticker for fresh cases."

"Does that mean you'll help me and Henry?"

"I consider it unfinished business. Oklahoma City and the Unabomber, both." Brockhurst looked amused. He nodded to a farmer in coveralls and waited until he was out of earshot before saying, "You know, Peter, Alma May Reeve was present for a moment in history, the sea change when Casper Shaw realized his own misjudgement of the Unabomber there in the diner. A rare thing, a psychopath recognizing his mistake."

"Kaczynski wasn't up to Devereau's standards as a terrorist, yet Ted was the one with guts to set bombs. That's what our man was trying to prove when he took the device and delivered it himself."

"And don't forget the duelling manifestos. Ted got published. This one sits on the slush pile."

"Consigned to the dustbin of history."

"Trotsky said that. Also Reagan."

Both men got up from the table. "Thank you," Peter said.

"You take care now, Peter. I forgot to tell you. There were four attackers at the trailer park. Six in Wichita. Be safe."

CHAPTER 32

In the ten days following his excursion to Topeka, Peter waited for an arrest, or at least the confirmation of a fingerprint from one of the Utah or Kansas crime scenes. Nothing so helpful occurred. Brockhurst called once, ostensibly to brief him on a pair of suspicious drug rip-offs he had heard about in Albuquerque, but really to explain that he had decided not to use the Mohlman-Pastern sketch of Devereau on the wanted poster for the Mark Riotte murder.

"What if everyone thinks it looks like the Unabomber?" Brockhurst said.

What indeed.

Maddy rang up to report. "Dad! I've done a first run on the *Fire and Brimstone* essay you sent me. There are many similarities with the Unabomber's *Manifesto*. I believe your man contributed significant elements to the Unabomber's rant. For example, a lot of the text in the chapter in the *Manifesto* on "The Nature of Freedom" is identical to Devereau's. But there are differences. The Unabomber hates technology, blames the Industrial Revolution and government for all our woes. Your man doesn't have it in for technological change."

Maddy's and Brockhurst's were the only friendly voices. Phil Mohlman and Chief Grady, dreading interference by the feds, remained hostile to any talk of a terrorism link to the events on Hollis Street. Peter kept his distance from West Valley. He was uncomfortable with Henry, too. Though the younger man was always polite and mostly even-tempered, to Peter he seemed on the verge of taking to drink again. Peter was careful how he raised unresolved issues about Hollis.

One afternoon, Henry turned from the dining room table, where he had stacked his interview notes, one manila folder for each house, and stated, "I've been through all the statements from the residents again. There's an anodyne quality to every one. Nobody seems surprised that the street went to hell. They really weren't astonished that a grow op functioned on their block for a year, maybe two. When we went over there, did you notice that nothing has been done to refurbish the street since the fire?"

"They've shut down their own American Dreams," Peter said.

It was perhaps the wrong turn of phrase. Henry had lost his own dreams, brutally, and the Coppermount house was as hollow as any building on Hollis Street. Peter was about to apologize when he perceived a hopeful glimmer in Henry's reaction. Like Peter, Henry was driven by the need to stop an evil force, and they would eventually find common ground in that. Both of them would show up for the final confrontation. They had found their connection. Henry expressed it first.

"Peter, I'm trying. I'll come round, I really will."

Henry went off to nap, while Peter sat on the patio with a beer. The Gordian knot principle had kicked in: the investigation was strangling itself from cross-purposes and miscommunication. Only a dramatic development could cut through the confusion.

The phone rang and it was Boog DeKlerk, calling from the West Valley precinct. "Cammon, I've got somebody who wants to talk to you."

"He must be the only person in Utah who does."

"Do you know who Avelino González is?"

Peter rushed to figure out what DeKlerk was up to. He assumed that the South African didn't know that Henry had relayed every detail of the Wendover meet to him.

"Yes, but he doesn't know me. You sure you meant to call *me*? If González is favourably inclined to confide in Henry again, why doesn't he call Henry directly?"

"He knows you're staying at Pastern's house . . ."

"Because you told him."

"Can you drive down to the precinct without Pastern?"

This was a terrible idea. DeKlerk was dividing and conquering, and Peter saw the risk at once. This screamed setup. And when Rogers at the DEA heard about any new plan to interact with the Mexican, he would have a perfect excuse to have Cammon deported.

"No. We can talk on the phone. Even then, I have to plug in Henry right away."

DeKlerk barely hesitated. The belligerent detective was nothing if not decisive. "Okay. I'll be open with Pastern, but first I need to clear some things with you. I'm only asking what González asked me. Is Henry steady enough to meet with González tomorrow in Castle Rock?"

"Colorado?"

"Yeah. González was firm about meeting in the afternoon."

Perhaps Boog knows me better than I figured, Peter thought. A session with González was intriguing, especially if he had fresh information to trade. It also occurred to Peter that González must have a powerful hold on DeKlerk for him to help set up a second meeting.

Peter said, "If I have the last meeting straight, González promised to feed us anything he learned about the Watsons. We've received nothing. That promise was made before Devereau killed the Proffets, wounded two detectives, and caused the death of Theresa Pastern. Do you think he has something new to offer that will tempt Henry?"

"I don't know how Henry views González at this point."

"Why don't you simply ask him?"

"I'd prefer you sounded him out, Cammon."

"DeKlerk, if you don't think Henry's up to it, send Mohlman. I don't need to go."

"González asked for Henry and you specifically. Hell, Cammon, you and Henry have the plus of being unofficial, off the books, not real cops."

"Thanks. If I get shot, explain that to my wife. Why does González trust me?"

"I told him you are staying at Pastern's house. González understands why you're there."

"Mind telling *me*?" *Butter wouldn't melt*, thought Peter.

"To make sure that Henry's revenge succeeds."

"Is that your theory or his?"

"The Mexican's phrasing, Peter. He also said that the evil that men do lives after them."

"*Julius Caesar*."

"Even I know that."

"DeKlerk, do you know what González wants from me and Henry in Colorado?"

"Just a meeting, that's your only commitment."

"I think he wants more. He knows Henry and I have been working 'off the books.' He believes we're willing to freelance some more. I bet he doesn't want us involving Colorado State Patrol or Brockhurst in Topeka. Which, DeKlerk, makes me ask why you aren't communicating all this to state authorities. I can see why you might keep your back channels open with a drug lord but . . ."

And then Peter understood the biggest part of the big picture.

DeKlerk paused and said, "That's why I'm calling you. I owe Avelino González, and he wants some killing done. That is why you came to Utah, isn't it, Peter?"

Peter was truly startled by DeKlerk's bluntness but he had no intention of answering this question directly. He acknowledged that DeKlerk had a keen insight into his motives for coming to the States. This could be a blatant sucker play by the Mexican but this was the second time he had reached out to the police and Peter was fascinated and beguiled by this unorthodox move. He stated, "You have to tell all of this to Henry. Now."

He walked to Henry's bedroom and handed the phone over; then he went back to the patio to wait.

"What do you think?" Peter said as soon as Henry returned.

"Peter, you and I have always seen this the same way. We're hunting a man with the intention of exacting punishment. As soon as we let the FBI or DEA or state cops in, we lose our chance. González may be a thin opportunity, but I'm willing to take it if it means getting to Devereau."

Nothing had visibly changed in Henry, but he seemed a touch more upbeat.

"Do you trust him, Henry?"

"Are you kidding!" Henry saw Tynan way out in the desert and waved. "But for some reason, González likes me, and I guess that's enough."

"But why does he like *me*?" Peter said with a half smile.

"Maybe he knows how many men you've killed." Peter threw him a dagger; Henry continued. "Boog is taking a huge gamble in brokering this. Colorado police get wind of it, he's toast."

"I don't know what he's thinking," Peter said. This was a lie. Boog DeKlerk was pushing this because he was on the take and González gave him no choice. DeKlerk was setting up Henry and Peter to take the fall if the plan shattered, thereby diverting attention from Boog's own sins.

They drove into the city for a Japanese dinner at the Naked Fish. Both of them skipped the sake. Back at the house, Henry brought out his pistol to clean it.

"Henry, I suggest you leave your service piece at home."

"Fine. I have another pistol I'll bring. It's a .45."

Peter didn't know which was riskier, carrying a Utah police weapon across state lines for a "private" purpose or bringing an unregistered handgun. But both men were excited. They would just have to drive within the speed limit.

Henry turned to Peter. "I know you British cops don't usually carry guns, but you should have a weapon for yourself."

"Bollocks. I expect González will have all the firepower I need."

CHAPTER 33

The expedition felt crazy in the light of day, Henry and Peter agreed as they headed to Castle Rock — but after days of frustration, waiting for something to break, the caper was irresistible.

Avelino González had instructed them to be at the Avalon Motel outside town by sundown. In all other respects, the invitation remained baffling.

"Peter, you know there are reports that González beheaded some of his opposition."

"What are you saying?"

"González is serious business."

He looked over at Henry. "Something else on your mind?"

"I'm wondering why you're not nervous. We're walking into a meat grinder, you know that."

Peter refused to explain himself. He was tired of mapping out the real world for Henry. He had no fear of González for the simple reason that he wasn't afraid of physical danger. When anyone, cop or civilian, asked him about the gun battles he had been in or the violent criminals he had faced down, the one factor he never discussed was his fear, or lack of it. It was impossible to articulate, since it would come across as arrogance, even stupidity, if he tried. At best, he would appear to be a cold bastard, which he was not. He feared for others but not himself.

Peter sidestepped Henry's probe. "Simple. The question we'll ask is the same as before: Does he know Casper Shaw's true name? If he won't answer that . . ."

Castle Rock turned out to be a pleasant reinvented tourist village with cute storefronts. It prospered as an adjunct to Denver, just far enough away to claim a separate municipal identity. The eponymous Castle Rock, visible from any spot in the area, pinned the town to the map.

"Drug dealers and motels go together like burritos and refried beans," Henry said as they parked the F-150.

The Avalon was modern and comfortable. A shootout here seemed unlikely, Peter estimated, but he asked for a room on the second level, with a view from the window of the highway approaches.

A half hour later, there was a knock on the door and Peter answered. A tall, fat-bellied Mexican man with a bolo tie stood back from the door, by the iron railing. "Ready to parlay?" He could have been the hospitality coordinator inviting them for wine and cheese in the lobby, except that he didn't smile and he displayed a large handgun on his hip. The big man led them outside.

Coincidentally, or not, González occupied a mini-suite six numbers down the same upper row of the motel. Peter then realized that the Mexican, a man who depended on elaborate precautions, probably wouldn't be in the same room overnight.

González was about sixty-five, Peter estimated, older than he had expected for a drug dealer; but then, the Mexican probably didn't expect to be dealing with a seventy-three-year-old detective either. His movements were slow, measured. He silently acknowledged the detectives. Peter sized him up: he wasn't high on his own product and his expression was alert, though he wasn't big on eye contact. This was a serious character.

The fat man with the impressive sidearm stayed by the door until González told him to leave. The drug lord put the chain on, a ludicrous thing to do given the security patrolling the balcony.

"So, the Mormon and the Englishman," he said, to let Peter know he had done some research. "I prefer a second-floor room. Allows me a view of the *camino*." He glanced at Peter. "I always used to rent the last unit in the row, so that I could hear my enemies coming up the stairs. Until the night they began firing their MAC-10s directly through the end wall."

"Why are we here, señor?" Peter said.

"You know Shaw's real name, or so you told DeKlerk," Henry added. Peter noted that any goodwill from the Wendover one-on-one had dried up, at least as far as Henry was concerned.

"I don't know his name," González said.

"Then we can't do business," Henry said, too brusquely.

"Just a minute," Peter said. "I want to talk with Señor González alone for a moment, Henry."

The younger man looked puzzled. Peter explained. "Señor González initially asked for me on the phone. I want to ask him why."

Henry hesitated but allowed everyone to save face. "Sure. See you back in the room."

"We need a mutual pledge of good faith," Peter said the moment Henry departed.

"What do you expect from me?" González said. They were two old realists talking, veterans of the criminal justice world.

"You don't know Devereau's name but you know where he's going to be, am I right?"

A flicker of a smile. "Yes. Tomorrow night. We will ambush him while he tries to rip off one of my warehouses."

"How many men are we bringing?"

"You, me, José, and Señor Pastern, and a few spotters."

"You could bring an army."

"This is personal. Are you in, Mr. Cammon?"

"Not so fast. If I commit, I'll need to know why you are taking such a risk. Did Devereau kill your cousin, like DeKlerk suggested to me?"

The Mexican pondered his answer for a full minute. "It was not my cousin that Devereau shot in one of his hijackings back then. It was my younger brother. I have three brothers, but to lose any one of them like that demands retribution. Revenge is always personal. Yes, I want to be the one to kill him."

"That was the attack just north of here, in 1995." Peter silently thanked Maddy for her research.

González looked over at Peter in surprise. "Yes, that one. Five dead men." He paced the room like a lion in a cramped cage. "The leader shot them point blank and burned the operation to the ground. Now I want my turn. But is it personal for you, Señor Cammon? Is it personal *enough*?"

Peter's answer came a little too fast. "I have no problem killing him . . ."

"I understand that you have killed seven men."

But Peter wouldn't allow González to find common ground in body counts. "I believe Devereau is evil, on the basis of his murder of the Watsons, the Proffets, and Henry's wife. There were also terrorist actions back in the eighties and nineties that qualify as indiscriminate killing and show a psychopathic mind, but it's personal for me because it is that way for my friend."

González smiled. "Revenge is a dish often served best on a cold case." He had discerned that Peter's resolve came from recesses as dark as his own. Peter was committed and the Mexican knew it.

It was time to change the subject to very practical matters.

"Was Marcel Riotte one of your people?" Peter asked.

"Yes, but small-time."

"Did he deal in cocaine and hashish as well as marijuana?"

"Yes."

"Heroin?"

"Yes."

"The Kansas police found only traces in Riotte's trailer."

"Devereau stole the heavy drugs. He sold them in Denver the next day. We are sure of this."

Peter leaned forward. "Which leads us to why we are all in Colorado today. How many armed men do you expect tomorrow night?"

"He has put together his squad very quickly, but it won't outweigh our firepower."

"I'm told four men took out Riotte. A team of six in Wichita," Peter said. "How easy is it for Devereau to recruit people from the militia movements?"

González shrugged. "Weekend cowboys."

Peter felt that González was being far too casual about the opposition. Was this some macho, daredevil expedition? "Nonetheless, I'd like to go over our preparations in detail."

The Mexican stood and shook his hand. "Tomorrow morning."

When the fat-bellied man knocked, González nodded to Peter, who slipped the chain and opened the door.

"Enjoy your evening," González said. "The place offers free Wi-Fi."

CHAPTER 34

A strange torpor afflicted the Avalon Motel. A swirl of warm rain came and went, steaming up the rooms. Everyone understood they were heading into a confrontation the next night, yet little had been discussed and the plan of attack remained vague. Peter felt his momentum peaking, and he itched to get going. A walking tour of Castle Rock seemed ill-advised, and so they asked at the front desk for a good Mexican restaurant. Before leaving the lobby of the motel, Peter noted the fat bodyguard slouching in an armchair and watching television when he should have been watching his boss. It took a minute for Peter to grasp that José was positioned there to watch Henry and him come and go.

At the restaurant, Henry and Peter drank Cokes. Peter ordered the mildest item on the menu, and they spent the rest of the evening checking email messages from their phones, as if electronic connections with the broader world might palliate the tension pervading the motel.

Maddy had sent more data packets, and opening them would overload Peter's phone, but she had included a cover note pointing to one item labelled "W/B: Coincidence?"

Dad:

Broadened my search this afternoon to look for events (I'll let you define this category) coinciding with the Hollis Street killings. Part of attached package. Do you know Whitey Bulger? Crime boss from Boston, killer of maybe forty people. Disappeared in 1994 and arrested in June of 2011. Period roughly coincides with Devereau. Expected to come to trial next year; Bulger case has been in the news last six months. Not suggesting the two knew each other but maybe Dev figured if Bulger could be caught after umpteen years under a new ID, then he was vulnerable too.

At 9 a.m., González sent José to fetch them. Peter noted that the bodyguard led them to a different room at the other end of the Avalon.

González was cheerful and recharged as he opened the door. Weapons covered the bed, which hadn't been slept in.

"Who wants to man up?" he said, sweeping his hand over the smorgasbord of weapons. There were pistols and revolvers, hunting rifles converted with military sights, semi-automatics, sawed-off guns, and a Taser. All the guns were suitable for an ambush, but at first Peter was unsure which one to select for himself.

"On TV," Henry said, "the weapons seized from drug deals always include gold-plated guns with giant silencers."

"Nobody *seized* this stuff, señor," said the fat man in a smoky, aloof voice. "No toys or bling. Any one of these guns will get you out of gold-plated trouble fast."

Henry gazed in awe. "Look at that MAC-10."

Perhaps because Henry sounded like a boy shopping for his first fishing rod, or because they had no idea what was coming, Peter adopted a no-nonsense tone. "Relax, Henry. I'm the one who needs ordnance."

"You want a pistol or a long gun, Chief Inspector?" José said.

Peter picked up the MAC-10. The machine pistol was popular

with drug dealers and their bodyguards, and remarkably compact. Peter hefted it and found the weight was balanced nicely over the grip and the magazine. "What kind of ammunition does it take?"

González answered. "Standard .45 ACP, or 9-millimetre. Have you used one before?"

"No. I've tried the Cobra. It looks similar." The Cobra "land defence pistol" had found favour with Rhodesian farmers back in the sixties. "What's the range?"

"Good at 200 feet, less good beyond 230," González stated. Peter noticed the threaded barrel on the MAC-10. "It is usually fired with a sound suppressor," González added. "Would you like to try it today?"

Henry's head jerked up. "Yeah! We don't have much else to do while we wait for tonight."

Peter remained cautious. "Where can we shoot?"

González looked over at the fat-bellied man, who nodded. "There's a place out in the desert. We've employed the range before."

"Don't we risk attracting attention?"

"Hell, it would be unusual if you *didn't* hear shooting in the desert. We'll try not to alarm the gringo condominium owners. You notice we haven't offered you the AR-15, which is a very powerful and popular semi-automatic. Not right for what we are about to do."

"Do you have shotguns?" Peter said.

"There's a Remington there on the pillow."

"I prefer the Heckler & Koch 12-gauge Tactical."

"An older gun, the 512 Auto. We can get one." The fat man nodded again and smiled a connoisseur's smile.

"And perhaps a light semi-auto carbine, the H&K German-type, as backup?" Peter said.

"We can try. Standard .45 ammunition, ten-round mag. We will definitely try."

Peter didn't relish shooting out in the desert with Henry, but doing something macho might calm him down; otherwise it would be a long day in the hotel room with bad television choices. Peter liked his own weapon selections. The German carbine would do for distance work, and he trusted the shotgun for close-up slaughter. The machine pistol was an indiscriminate firearm, and he left it on the bed.

It took an hour to reach the makeshift range in the desert. Peter and Henry followed González's matched pair of Cadillac Escalades into the open, undistinguished scrubland east of Castle Rock. José and two sunburnt Mexican assistants were already setting up posts at paced-off hundred-yard lengths. They came back and hauled green melons, one at a time, out to the posts and balanced them there like Humpty Dumptys.

González led Peter and Henry to the back door of one of the Escalades, where several guns, including the shotgun requested by Peter, were lined up.

Looking at the display with a wry grin, the drug lord said, "I am ready for anything these days. When you look in the back of a truck, you don't know whether you will see guns, drugs, cash, or bodies. All in a row, like *los espárragos*."

The helpers carried each man's weapons out to the firing line. González favoured a Glock 14, with a .45 in reserve. José gave instruction to Henry, who had fallen in love with a MAC-10, which this time came with a cylindrical suppressor screwed onto the barrel. Peter wondered if the silencer threw off the shooter's balance, but he judged that the overall package remained light and deadly. Henry fired off a few rounds, which kicked up dust ninety feet away and did no damage to the closest post. He pressed the trigger again in rapid fire mode and nicked the green-hided melon atop the stake. The machine pistol produced a gentle stutter. Peter could see why untrained bangers in the drug business liked to use the no-aim-required MAC-10 and MAC-11.

"Not for you, Inspector?" González said.

"We want to shoot one man, not erase the neighbourhood. Henry, you'd do better with your own .45."

José brought over the Heckler & Koch shotgun, and a beauty it was. Peter examined the action and felt the weight of the gun. He loaded the chamber with medium-size shells. He began to stride towards one of the posts, halting and firing his first shot, holding the gun at near shoulder level but avoiding any kickback that could wreck his upper arm or buck him in the chin. The shot went two feet to the left of the post. He lowered the gun to hip level and fired three more times as he continued walking. The second shot struck the post, sending the melon rocking, but before it could fall, the third load hit the target. Peter stopped twenty-five feet from the shattered mess and fired his next shell into the post stump, execution-style. The innards of the shattered melon coated the stunted pillar like blood.

Peter returned to the start line, grim but calm. His performance overwhelmed Henry, who sensed that it had been for his benefit. Peter didn't dare meet the Mexican's eyes, or both old pros would have laughed. Henry was now convinced that his partners at the OK Corral were lethally serious men; this had been Peter's objective all along.

Peter took a short turn with the carbine but otherwise was content to watch. While Henry and José continued practising, he walked a distance into the scrub and took out his mobile. He speed-dialed Maddy and reached her on one ring. Although blasts of gunfire could be heard behind him, he spoke as if nothing was unusual.

"Hello, dear."

"Am I interrupting anything important, Dad?" A particularly loud volley forced her to pause. "What's that noise?"

"I'm standing in the middle of the desert, shooting guns."

"So nothing new . . . You didn't respond to my last package. I've been worried about you."

"I'm safe."

"Surrounding yourself with guns doesn't make you safe. Americans!"

"I haven't had time to open your attachments, except the Whitey Bulger note . . ."

"Dad, Mom and I were both worried. We both had violent dreams last night."

Peter knew better than to discount premonitory dreams. "Is she there with you?"

"No, no, I'm in Leeds. You should call her tomorrow, let her know you're okay."

"I'm okay."

Peter returned to the carnage of fruit. The drug kingpin was full of surprises. His silent helpers had manhandled an easel and a whiteboard from the rear of the Escalade and erected it at the firing line. *This is like some corporate morale-building exercise, with semi-automatic weapons.* One helper brought out a building schematic and clipped it to the whiteboard. José, Henry, and Peter gathered round. Peter almost expected González to pull out a laser pointer.

González explained the layout of the drug operation and the way they would approach it that night. They would take up observation posts at the back. The complex was made up of three linked buildings. Hashish and marijuana were processed in a central building connected to a shipping room, which exited onto a driveway under a portico. A third building on the other side of the processing centre contained a marijuana storefront where college kids and small-timers bought their dime bags. Hashish, when warm, gives off a strong odour, and the centre processing room was equipped with powerful fans to draw off the smell.

"The noise from the fans works against us," González explained. "It may cover Devereau's invasion. But we're counting on sealing him *inside* the building from both sides, so that our team won't have to go in after him at all. When he comes out, bang!"

Henry put up his hand; it seemed appropriate. "Are you hoping he'll blow himself up with his own bomb?"

"It might be the best outcome, but I don't count on that result. The buildings will be kept almost empty. No cocaine or hash left inside. He won't bother with the grass this time. There will be many bags of powdered milk, however, for him to take."

Peter said, "Which direction will Devereau enter from?" His options were the entrance under the portico at the right, or the front desk of the marijuana store to the left.

"Ah, señor, you are wondering how Devereau can hope to deal with all the guards. Well, I have let it be known that the cocaine and hashish will be trucked tonight out the shipping room side, into the covered laneway. There will be only two inside workers in the central processing area and one token guard in the marijuana store. He will enter at the driveway on our right, snatch the false drugs and retrace his steps. We will be waiting."

Peter and Henry both saw the obvious flaws in the setup but said nothing. They exchanged glances. Devereau would arrive prepared to kill everyone who got in his way; better to have no one inside. Plans to trap him in the dark buildings gave Peter no comfort. Devereau would carry enough ordnance to blast his way out.

Peter owed Joan a call, as he had promised Maddy, even if it was only a heads-up that he and Henry were okay. This was a new era of spousal openness and communication, he told himself. But as he summoned the cottage number to the screen, he faltered. *If it all goes wrong tonight, is it better that I told her the risks, or that I said nothing?*

CHAPTER 35

They abandoned the Avalon before sundown. González's enormous Escalade barely accommodated the four men and their guns, with two pairs of night goggles adding to the heap; José's body armour took up a seat on its own. González drove and kept up a stream of orders over a headset, while José sucked on a jumbo bottle of guava cocktail.

To Henry's annoyance, they stopped at a burrito stand in south Denver. "Why the delay?" he whispered.

"Be patient," Peter hissed back. "We don't control this."

Peter was content with a taco salad, thus branding himself the least macho hombre in the vehicle. José tempted him with a cup of guava, but Peter declined; with his bladder, he would likely be peeing in the parking lot when Devereau moved in to attack.

Peter remained edgy, no matter his command to Henry, and he fortified himself for what lay ahead by checking his ammunition supply. He ignored the passing highway signage, since maybe it was better that he not remember too many details. The smart move was to take his cues from the Mexicans, who remained self-possessed and confident.

On a silent and anonymous street in South Denver lined with one-storey warehouses, González pulled over next to a beat-up Honda and an equally scruffy Chevy Impala, each piloted by a small

266

Mexican man. The soldiers got out of their junkers and transferred armloads of guns to the cars. González beckoned Peter to the Honda, while the fat man and Henry got in the larger Impala and drove out of sight. Peter and Henry said nothing to each other as they parted.

Within a few minutes, with their guns arrayed along the back seat in easy reach, Peter and the drug boss moved into position some two hundred yards from the trisectioned warehouse. Henry was somewhere in the darkness off to their left. A single spotlight flared on in the parking lot, accentuating the shadows and creating hiding places for anyone stalking prospective entry points to the drug complex. Peter assumed that the Mexican spotters were poised to attack from the surrounding block.

He recognized that his personal risk in this enterprise was high, in part because he hadn't winkled the full truth out of González. Did the drug dealer know what awaited them in the darkness ahead? Peter knew stakeouts and was in no rush to talk, despite his qualms about González's plan. González stayed serene. The air had cooled, and only a mild sweep of traffic could be heard from the street beyond the warehouse. The spooky quiet pressed a slow rhythm on the passage of time.

González spoke without altering his gaze. "Inspector, you know that this will be our last opportunity to get him?"

"You don't think he intends to get back into the terrorism business?"

"No. He is on the run. He will vanish after tonight."

"Even if he collects only powdered milk?"

"Yes."

"Then, señor, I will be disappointed. I hoped to confront him with his past. His terrorist actions are a disgraceful part of that past."

"Even worse than my brother, than Pastern's wife?"

Peter closely considered his answer. "Perhaps."

"Is there something you want to tell me, Inspector?"

"Yes."

Peter laid out the history of Devereau's involvement with

Kaczynski and possibly McVeigh, and his ambition to issue his own anti-government manifesto.

"Señor, you are a very perceptive policeman, but I have to disappoint you. From everything you tell me, Devereau, or Señor Shaw, was never a very good terrorist. Do you not see that? Was his heart ever in it? You police love to profile serial killers and terrorist bombers, but you do not understand this man. One obvious thing you seem to have missed: he gave up easily. Did he treat the Unabomber with respect? No. He let Kaczynski take all the risk. The same with McVeigh. Where was his courage? He worked behind the scenes but took almost no chances himself. His manifesto? He never finished it, you say. He wrote a few chapters and left the manuscript in that restaurant, and didn't bother to collect it. He thought he was too good for his proteges."

"You're convinced he will disappear?"

"Understand, Inspector, he is not a reasonable man. He is a psychopath. After his dreams rotted away, what remained was insanity. He may have fancied his own genius, but what does a psychopath do when no one listens to him? He goes *loco*. His lunacy lives in the space between his terrorist ideas and his quest for a quiet life."

Peter measured González's argument. Maybe he was right. Devereau had lost control each time he was affronted. He might have lived with Watson's irritating drug business or waited for the cops to pounce, but instead he lashed out. He was too quick to go after Jerry and Selma. Who understood the triggers of his rage?

"I think you're right," Peter finally said.

The Mexican tapped the dashboard superstitiously. "The executions. The blood. The bombs. The fires. He is moving fast. He cares about his own safety, not the objectives of any militia movement. He must be dreaded for that reason. He has gone *loco*."

Peter glanced into the back seat at the shotgun. "It's curious that we don't know his real name, yet we're willing to kill the man."

"Revenge. Trust it. It sweeps away doubts."

"I can live with that," Peter said.

There was a long pause. "Are we like Devereau?" González said.

"Evil?" Peter said.

"Yes."

"You want absolution for your sins, Avelino?"

González let out a bitter laugh. "No, it is too late for *la miseri-cordia*. You know about killing men, Peter. DeKlerk told me. To be honest, I invited you along tonight because you understand killing. Neither one of us is looking for a reprieve for our sins, not tonight. I want revenge for my brother. Maybe I just want to round out my destiny."

After a half minute, he added, "Like you, Peter."

They should have known better. The explosion came *fast*, and from the wrong end of the complex.

From the deep shadows behind the drug warehouse, Peter saw the top of a cloud rise beyond the section on their left. None of the three merged cubes presented a back exit, nor even a window anywhere along the rear walls, so the explosion wasn't easy to interpret. Until then, they had been monitoring the small door around the side to their right, where a feeble bulb lit the asphalt driveway. The false cocaine shipment, according to González, would emerge from there, and that would be Devereau's point of attack.

Too late, Peter realized how blind they were at their observation post in the rear. They had no line of sight on the marijuana store entrance, and González's two outliers on the far street had failed to report the enemy's movements.

On the avenue on the other side of the complex, customers had slowly realized that the cannabis outlet was closed for the night (it was not as though the hours of operation were posted), González having ordered the door double locked and all inside lights turned off. One man was left to monitor the back storage area, but he had nothing to do in the dark but get high on the merchandise. At about 11 p.m., a stream of college students and dopers began to arrive. They peered through the front door and pounded on the glass. By 11:20 a crowd had formed on the sidewalk. The mob rumour mill began to grind, accelerated by dopers quickly convincing themselves that something called marijuana withdrawal was raging through their systems. Screams of "Open up!" swept them forward.

A tall man in a grey hoodie and a large backpack moved to the front of the group and turned to address them. "Folks, there's no point in kicking that door in, there's just another one behind it."

"We want our bags," a kid yelled.

"Be careful, there may be someone with a gun behind that door," Hoodie Man replied.

Another kid called out, "Who are you, spokesman for the marijuana dealers defence league?" Pressure had been building in Colorado to legalize marijuana, but no one laughed.

Hoodie Man took off his knapsack and reached inside. Out came a sawed-off Remington shotgun. The crowd *ooh*ed, and some applauded.

"Gentlemen, I urge you to stand back. Let me go in first. I'll let you know when it's safe." Witnesses later reported that he sounded reasonable, a leader.

The crowd retreated from the door and formed a crescent, waiting. Hoodie Man levelled the shotgun at the door handle and fired. The blast obliterated the lock and set the interior steel panel swinging into the anteroom. The solitary guard in the back, completely stoned, heard the explosion as a surreal convulsion somewhere nearby. He got to his feet and stumbled around the dark room in search of his AR-15.

Hoodie Man — Ronald Devereau — hauled his knapsack through the wrecked doorway. The crowd pressed forward to follow, but two new shooters brandishing MAC-11 machine pistols stood in front of the entrance and gestured for the students and down-and-outers to hang back. The pair slipped inside, leaving the crowd staring at the yawning doorway.

Devereau knew the configuration of the complex. He dodged around the front counter and kicked wide the door to the storage area, where the guard was fumbling with his AR-15. Devereau could have erased him with a shotgun blast, but he moved aside to let one of his men do the job. The MAC-11 stuttered, and the guard flopped onto a low pile of marijuana-filled plastic bags.

The use of the MAC-11 was deliberate. Devereau knew that the distinctive sound would reach the street. It was the sound of professionals at work. The crowd respected it and stayed back from the door for the time being.

The three invaders halted in the first big room and assessed the doorway to the middle building, where the cocaine, heroin, and premium hashish were processed. Devereau verified that it was thirty minutes shy of midnight. It was possible that the hash and blow were already in the far building, but he didn't think so; the two guards would move it to the exit at the last minute. This was the moment of greatest uncertainty for the attackers. Their inside man had promised that it would be easy to penetrate the central factory, but that informant, who now lay in a mess of blood-smeared Ziplocs, had also greeted them with an AR-15. Treachery was to be expected at every step of this gauntlet.

Devereau calmly took a wooden box from his bag and went back to the counter area, while his two gunmen waited for his signal to assault the centre building. There were more bystanders on the sidewalk than he had expected. He slipped the box under the counter. Three twenty-year-old students watched him from the edge of the doorway. Devereau swiftly returned to the storage area, and thirty seconds later the bomb went off. It wasn't a large device, and was fashioned as much for its bang as its lethality, but the force of it splintered the vertical panel supporting the counter and drove a quiverful of wood shards into the inquisitive students, killing all three.

The breach of the middle door had to be finely timed; Devereau waited another few minutes, until his watch read 11:50. He had deployed a five-man team. Two of them, one armed with an Uzi and the other with a Glock 17, waited on the far sidewalk down at the end of the three linked buildings. They heard the bomb and saw the smoke roll out onto the street. They waited in the gloom, poised to attack the shipping door from outside at the ordained moment.

Out in the parking lot, Peter and Avelino González leapt from their car seconds after the first blast. Peter guessed (mistakenly) that the bomb was a diversion and that the main objective remained the shadowed doorway to his right. He opted to hold back one minute longer; meanwhile, he retrieved the shotgun from the back seat of the Honda, reasoning that in such darkness it would be the most effective weapon against the pending attack.

González blew off Peter's strategy before they got fifty feet beyond the car. "They're going through the front door. They're getting to the shipment that way." He gestured to the left, where the smoke from the bomb was still rising.

Peter was unsure how the three buildings were connected. Any guard inside would be smart to barricade the doors between the units. Peter then realized that Devereau knew all about the linking doors and likely would have a second bomb ready to blast his way to the centre. His outside crew would attack the exterior door by the asphalt driveway, catching the defenders in a squeeze. Either way, the door on the right offered the best opportunity to stop Devereau. Peter checked his shotgun load and made for the paved alley on a diverging vector from the Mexican.

Far off, he caught sight of Henry and José running for the narrow passageway that would take them around to the left, to the marijuana store. Screams reverberated overtop of the building and into the parking lot. Henry was running full tilt now, so fast that he had to slow down to unholster his .45. Peter guessed at his logic: with the panic on the street and the likelihood that the attackers were well inside the building, it might now be safe to break for the store entrance. Even so, the game would get trickier. Henry, José, and González each carried a pistol; Peter judged that they would need shotguns to overwhelm the squad inside the marijuana dispensary.

The Mexican had left a skeleton crew of two soldiers in the middle building, where the phony narcotics were stored. They might slow down the invaders, but Peter doubted that González could make a squeeze play work. Peter heard the machine pistol bursts from Devereau's team and concluded that they had the clear advantage in firepower.

Peter was almost at the driveway. He hesitated, scanned the dimly lit door beneath the overhang, and listened. Devereau probably had enough men to attack from both ends and work his own trapping manoeuvre, in which case Peter had to watch for a barrage from multiple directions.

As well, González's two spotters lurked somewhere out in the streets and at that moment must be trying to reach the boss and José on their mobiles. Peter had no doubt that their instructions were to shoot any gringo who tried to enter the shipping door. He wasn't about to ring the bell.

None of these scenarios transpired. Peter learned the details later. José and Henry reached the marijuana storefront before González. Three bloodied and inert students had been hauled out to the sidewalk by bystanders, and the crowd had re-formed and was pressing towards the façade. Wisps of smoke hung in the air outside the building; more drifted from the large round hole in the side panel of the counter inside. Henry was in the lead. So close finally to meeting his enemy, he fought for a clear line of fire, but González, abandoning caution, pushed past him and José and charged into the gloom, obscuring Henry's shot. González, Henry later reported, gave off the vibe of a gunfighter hell-bent on a face-to-face shootout.

Just for a second, Henry made out the shape of his ghostly target — *it* must *be Devereau* — ten feet away.

Devereau had brought along a specialized device to blow open the middle door. It resembled something manufactured by the Unabomber, the lab would later note; he had designed the blast to shoot forward and up to the level of the door lock. He planted it a mere two feet from the metal frame and with his two shooters retreated into the marijuana storage area and took shelter behind a pair of desks.

González halted by the marijuana stack, his pistol extended. The haze from the first bomb obscured the ambush. Henry thought he had the Mexican's back, but in fact Devereau was less than ten feet from González and Henry when the second device detonated, launching González backwards onto the dozens of crates of packaged marijuana. Fragments of steel and wood punctured his chest and throat in fifty places, killing him by the time his body stilled. In the flash, Henry saw Devereau clearly, and Devereau saw his face in the same instant.

The explosion pushed Henry back and onto the floor. A piece of shrapnel carved a groove across his forehead as he fell, stunning him. Devereau could have finished him off, but he kept to his plan. The bomb had blown the connecting door off its hinges, and he and his men, armed with their MAC-11s, pushed into the factory room. The blast rendered the token guards deaf and ineffectual in the smoke and heat. One of the attackers moved forward and sprayed the middle room with Colt ammo, executing one defender and wounding the other.

Outside, hearing the two explosions and the advancing gunfire, Peter guessed that the attackers were heedlessly blowing up everything around them as they moved through the cubes. He waited for a third explosion, but for a minute there was silence. Peter himself felt exposed to multiple angles of approach, so he moved to the bushes to wait, knowing it wouldn't be long.

The second detonation served as a signal to Devereau's two outside watchers. Peter tracked a figure carrying an Uzi as he arrived up the driveway, and crossed into the shadows by the door, where he hid. Another, hefting a Glock 17, provided backup, taking up an ambush position in the scruffy hedge less than thirty feet from Peter. Neither shooter saw him. Peter set his priorities. The Uzi presented the bigger threat, though the Glock man was lethal too, perfectly positioned to attack the Mexicans when they emerged from the building or came around the corner. Even without a view of their faces, Peter knew they were poised to attack when the door opened. He couldn't allow them the initiative.

He took a step out into the lane and aimed the shotgun at the one with the Uzi, who stepped confidently into the light with his weapon pointed straight at him. Peter fired one round and blew the triggerman backwards into the door, his body obstructing the exit. The crash, Peter hoped, would confuse the thieves inside, and if they panicked, they might run pell-mell out this way. Not hesitating, Peter dropped to the pavement and turned the German gun on the Glock man by the hedge — or where he ought to be in the darkness. The gunman fired first; Peter could tell he was using 9-millimetre ammunition. Peter shot from the ground and the man screamed.

Devereau and his two companions burst through the door. They stumbled over the dead Uzi shooter but quickly fixed on the position of their wounded man in the hedge, and then Peter, who was in the middle of the lane, madly loading fat shells into the shotgun. Devereau had a .45 in his hand now. He swivelled towards Peter.

What saved Peter was the white van that turned the corner and began speeding up the driveway. Peter was taken by surprise. He hadn't imagined that Devereau would carry verisimilitude this far: having a phony vehicle show up on schedule to pick up the load of drugs. *That's how he planned to persuade the guards to open the side door.*

But it became evident the young Latino driver hadn't been fully briefed. He wore earphones and nodded to his music as he completed the turn, oblivious of the bloodletting around him. His right front tire rumbled over the corpse by the door and came to rest on the Uzi and the dead gunman's left arm. Everyone but the clueless van driver took cover. Devereau's team pushed back to the wall. The wounded man with the Glock fell back into the hedge, where he remained a threat to Peter.

Peter rolled and scrambled to the hedge, some fifty feet from the tangle of gunmen. The van temporarily shielded him from most of the shooters but he realized that he was still in the line of fire of the Glock. He got to his feet and held the shotgun up where the van driver couldn't fail to see it. For a long thirty seconds the boy froze; when he gained focus on the shotgun, he reflexively crouched down below the dashboard. Peter shifted his aim; he wasn't about to waste a cartridge on a warning shot. He considered sending a double load Devereau's way to keep him at bay, but the van effectively blocked his aim. Instead, Peter waited for the driver's head to reappear and then waved him out of the van. The boy slipped out the door and disappeared back out to the street.

Peter had choices to make, knowing that he was in trouble unless substantial reinforcements arrived. Where were Henry and the Mexicans? But he remained unruffled: he had a pocketful of shells and would use them the moment any of Devereau's men showed a body part. He waited, thinking how sloppy the drug dealer's planning had been. The marijuana store — Peter could smell the grass through the cordite and ammonium nitrate — should have been more securely sealed.

The empty van offered shelter and a vantage point from which Devereau's men could cut down Peter where he crouched in the bushes. For a flash, he considered stealing the vehicle and leaving the attackers stranded, but that would take him out of the action. *The hell with that!* Yet there was no percentage in running back towards the Honda, since the shooters could hardly miss his exposed back. Peter stood and began firing at the wall of the building, cascading shards of cement onto his opponents. The wounded Glock shooter on the other side of the van was less of a factor now, since he would have to squeeze around the driver's mirror to gain a shot. Peter shifted another step to his left. Each shotgun shell illuminated the three men crouching by the door. One of them let off a wild burst from his MAC, but Peter remained unscathed.

José had waited for the smoke from the second bomb to clear. He verified that his boss was dead, then paused a minute before edging into the factory room. The roof fans made it hard to sort out who was shooting, but he understood that the invaders were killing everyone they encountered as they progressed to the end door. He, too, was determined to kill everyone *he* saw from that moment forward.

In theory, with Peter anchoring the far end of the complex and the fat man on the interior side, the defenders had achieved their squeeze on Devereau. In reality, as Peter grasped, they controlled none of this disputed territory.

Henry, meanwhile, had retreated from the scene of the second explosion. His bleeding head throbbed; a metal fragment had arrowed into his left bicep, leaving his arm dangling. As he exited the marijuana storefront into the foggy light on the street, he became delirious. A sign, askew on the wall, loomed in front of him: "Support Legal Medical Marijuana." Looking down, he blearily noted that his left leg was bleeding. But he still had his .45 in his right hand, and he began to limp down the sidewalk towards the far corner of the linked buildings.

Devereau's men knew to wait for Peter to exhaust his ammo. He had no choice but to use up his cache of shells, and for three minutes he blew the mortar above the door to pieces, showering the killers with fragments and pinning them by the van. He even tried a billiards ricochet into the narrow gap between the van and the wall, causing one man to fire a MAC-11 volley into the air in exasperation. Peter lost vital seconds when his fingers caught on his pocket as he reached for the last of his shells. Ronald Devereau stepped from the shadows and raised his large handgun. Peter recognized the police artist sketch of the man from 13 Hollis. He was also the figure in Alma's diner and the visitor at the Dreamland Motel. Devereau hesitated, puzzled by this old man with the incongruous shotgun in his hands, and Peter responded with a last double salvo.

Devereau's left ankle appeared to collapse. Peter saw a flash of fire under the white van. One of the Mexican scouts had finally entered the contest, having taken ten minutes to sort out whom he should be shooting. Cleverly, he had judged that the lines of sight for Devereau's men had a blind spot, the centre of the back panel, and so he pasted himself against the loading door of the van. It was risky to open the rear door, smarter to slip under the vehicle and wait. The first target that presented itself was Devereau's ankle.

Henry reached the far corner, and although he couldn't see Peter, he located Devereau and at once began firing. All three of the raiders fell back into the inadequate shelter of the doorway. Peter counted on González and José emerging from the shipping room. Devereau would be boxed in from three angles, though his man with the Glock 17 remained well sheltered on the driver's side of the van and persisted as a threat. Peter watched as Devereau and the Glock shooter appeared to achieve a silent consensus through the van windows. Peter was about to fire into the windshield when the Glock man opened the van door, using it as a barrier, and squirmed inside. At the same time, Devereau opened the passenger door and half pushed, half dragged his wounded colleague into the back seat. He also managed to toss the bundle of "drugs" inside. Devereau leaned out and snapped off six shots at Peter. None connected.

The Glock man turned on the ignition, while his boss ducked into the back of the van. The last member of the gang, crouching in the alley, fired his MAC-11 at Peter, missing. Henry shot him from behind and the body landed on top of the corpse of the first dead assailant. Devereau shifted into the front seat. To Peter, from his vantage point facing the van, Devereau appeared to lock his gaze onto Henry; Henry later confirmed the strange mesmerism of the moment.

The pair of corpses prevented Devereau from closing the passenger door. The wounded driver lurched forward, rising over the double hazard and slamming the driver's-side door against the wall with an unholy screech. José emerged from the shipping door and levelled his .45 at the side of the getaway vehicle, pumping four bullets into the door.

José and Henry swivelled to track the racing white van but managed only two more shots each, since they feared hitting Peter. The retreating vehicle was now almost surrounded by Henry at the rear, José on the passenger side, and Peter at its front. It accelerated across the sixty feet to where Peter stood aiming, in a target stance, at the windshield. Although he had a good angle on Devereau, he had no time. He dropped and rolled to one side of the road. The wounded driver, marvelling at the old man's alacrity, shouted "Fuck you!" and sped up.

José stood in the doorway and watched the vehicle scream out of the parking lot. Peter, bruised and filthy on the asphalt, signalled to the Mexican bodyguard, who turned to his two men and held up a restraining hand. They lowered their guns.

Henry was in the worst shape of the group. Blood soaked his thigh and his shoulder drooped, giving the impression that his left side was melting. The leaking furrow over his left eye caused Peter to begin estimating blood loss.

José ignored Henry's injuries and turned back into the building to retrieve his dead boss and decide how to carry him off into the night before the real cops arrived.

CHAPTER 36

"We're all tainted by this," was the first thing Henry said when Peter went to pick him up at the hospital, a full ten days after Denver. Official hell had broken loose.

Condemnation rained down on every policeman who could be connected to Denver: Pastern, Mohlman, DeKlerk, Chief Grady, Rogers at the DEA, and Peter Cammon. Denver Police, feeling abused by the bloody free-for-all in their capital city, cried the loudest, concentrating their outrage on Grady and the West Valley force. Grady's own man, Henry Pastern, even though he was only on administrative leave, had no business involving himself in a drug sting outside his jurisdiction. Then there was this mysterious British national: he might be a private citizen, but where was his firearms licence? And on that subject, why did Pastern and Cammon think they could borrow high-powered weapons from a drug dealer? And so it went as the Denver and Colorado State forces struggled to clarify the facts so that they could move indignantly towards a jurisdictional showdown.

Grady for a time considered protesting that Henry was operating undercover, but no one would have given the claim any credence. Bureaucratic remedies were needed. He was a veteran of cross-state and cross-agency wars, and made quick moves to allow both Denver

PD and his own force to save face. Most offensive in this context was Henry's participation in the raid, and the chief formally suspended him. He called in the Utah State Bureau of Investigation to independently investigate the origins of Henry's crazy alliance with González, hoping that state police involvement might shift the focus from West Valley's incompetence to the broader, multi-state challenge of narcotics, a concern on which all states and the federal agencies could find common ground.

The passage of time, Grady understood, would fog the details of the Denver raid, but one fact could not be ignored: the death of three Colorado students outside the Denver marijuana store. An altar sacrifice was required, and that would have to be Boog DeKlerk. Grady was ruthless. DeKlerk could be drummed out of the force without much fear of union appeal, while Henry, optics considered, presented as a handsome Mormon, picturesquely wounded in anti-drug combat. DeKlerk couldn't be rehabilitated, and Grady was disinclined to try.

Before confronting Boog, the chief took the surprising step of consulting Peter. He might have sought out Phil Mohlman, but the Boston detective hadn't been at Denver. Cammon wasn't such an odd choice. After four days of bureaucratic dodge ball, Grady needed to bounce his strategy off someone experienced in the internecine jealousies of police forces. At the same time, he could use the Englishman's vulnerabilities against him if it came to needing another scapegoat for Denver.

"Three dead civilians, Chief Inspector. One of mine seriously wounded. González dead plus at least one other bogie. And you appear in my office looking unscathed. What the hell?"

Peter could have displayed his abrasions from the parking lot, but that wouldn't address Grady's point, and he waited for the chief to tell him why he had been summoned. Grady's next shot startled the veteran detective. "I could have you deported for abuse of jurisdiction. I may be forced to do it."

That's clear! thought Peter. (Technically he would not be deported, but he might be declared *persona non grata*. In that case he would depart on the next flight out of Salt Lake International.) Peter still hoped to be present at Ronald Devereau's takedown, and so he argued. "I'd make a lousy scapegoat, since no one will understand my presence in Denver. But I am ready to meet with the Colorado police."

Grady smirked. "Will you tell them the full truth, Cammon? Because I don't think you've been open with *me*." Peter heaved a sigh and was about to mount a defence when Grady held up a hand in a peace gesture. "We'll get back to that. I want your counsel on something else. Your *honest* counsel. So, what do you think? How would you handle this in England?"

"For the police forces involved, the problem is clear enough. You need an institutional response. I presume you'll invoke Internal Affairs?"

"It's inevitable and it's already started. The IA investigators are Salt Lake City officers, to keep it objective. Their names are Furst and Ordway. But between you and me, Cammon, I'll try to focus them on DeKlerk rather than Pastern."

Peter nodded, understanding that DeKlerk couldn't be saved.

Grady proceeded. "Trickier will be the revived investigation of the Watson killings. I never closed the file officially, and I've mandated the new team to look into any and all dimensions of the case. I hope to divert them from the Denver raid. There's no way you or I or Pastern can ever explain what González was trying to accomplish in Denver. But Cammon, I want you to be available for the Colorado inquest. Tell them the whole truth, but don't even think of implying that West Valley was behind the sting."

Peter acquiesced again. The solution to bureaucratic friction was always more bureaucratic manoeuvring. The storyline had to shift to the drug trade and its disruption: the deaths of the three young men illustrated the dangers of the street traffic in marijuana. The demise of González didn't offset the loss of the students, but it was some comfort, and citizens were grateful when drug dealers killed one another. Grady could only hope that his Colorado counterparts bought into these broader themes.

"Is Henry Pastern up to all this?" Grady queried.

"Henry will recover," Peter stated, as if that were the point. "I saw him yesterday."

"Shit, Inspector, Henry may be the key to all of us surviving this storm. He was there with González one-on-one in Wendover and present when González died. He can make us look good. Our poster boy better perform."

Clean white bandages swathed Henry's head, shoulder, and left leg. The doctors continued to worry about infection but ruled that he could be ministered to at home. The two members of the new "Watson Team," Furst and Ordway, had dropped by the hospital twice. "I don't feel I had good answers," Henry reported. Peter knew from contact with Phil Mohlman that the two Bureau agents had largely held back any tough questions while they waited for Henry's discharge from hospital.

Peter had already journeyed to Denver in the F-150 and given a long statement to local investigators about his involvement. It had gone as well as could be expected, with a minimum of evasions on his part, and Peter was optimistic the afternoon he arrived to take Henry home to Coppermount Drive.

Over those ten days, Peter had visited the hospital daily, except for his Denver jaunt, and had grown used to his friend's depression cycles. Peter remained upbeat. "It's shaping up well, Henry. The new team is open to our evidence, and they're buying your view, and Phil's, that Devereau survived that basement, and that it was him in Denver."

Peter couldn't help his own buoyancy. Chances were Devereau would be nabbed in a dragnet somewhere in Colorado or Utah.

Henry waited until halfway to Coppermount Drive before commenting. "The question is: Will Devereau strike again before they get him?" He stared out the window of the truck as if he had never seen this view before.

"There are things we can contribute to the case review," Peter said. "He's following a distinct pattern. They'll welcome our input."

Henry shook his head emphatically, even though his pain flared. "I'll never be reinstated. God, my shoulder aches . . ."

Peter's tone was harder than he intended. "You wanted to engage the enemy, you've done that. Don't regret the costs. As for being suspended, you were already out of the action."

Henry whined, "As long as they don't have a name or prints, they'll fail."

They were entering a new phase, Peter saw. If they were to finally hunt down Devereau, a degree of cold-heartedness was necessary. They had finally achieved some progress, made eye contact with their prey. González's death was behind them. There was nothing Peter regretted about the Denver raid, not even González, and Henry's wounds were badges of honour. "You look like a hero from your Revolutionary War," he said, trying to lighten Henry's abject mood.

Henry wasn't to be cajoled. "We're done. Devereau escaped."

Tynan was waiting at the front door on Coppermount, as prearranged. Peter never quite got used to his strangeness. Today he carried a tool belt and a handsaw. He played it casual. "Doing some work. Thought I'd drop by."

Inside, Henry slumped on the sofa and eyed the hot desert beyond the patio doors. Tynan, uncertain, lined up the bottles of prescription pills on the bar.

"I'm going to nap," Henry announced.

"Sure," Peter said, "but I thought we'd review the municipal records relevant to Number 13 Hollis later today. Devereau paid his taxes on time annually, and there was no record of building permits applied for by the owner. Water, sewer, and electricity were paid online. There must be a signature or an ID card somewhere . . ."

Henry's look was indifferent. Tynan tried: "We should work out

284

your pill schedule, Henry." Tynan read the labels on two of the bottles. "Hydromorphone and diazepam."

Peter and Tynan shared the gloomy understanding that they would have to share monitoring of Henry's narcotics consumption. The painkillers could easily become substitutes for the absinthe that had once sat on the granite bar. Peter had few expectations of the home care visits scheduled for three times weekly: he and Tynan would be Henry's real nurses.

It wasn't surprising that, in fifty years of marriage to an emergency room nurse, and numerous wounds on his own aging carcass, Peter Cammon had learned a little about meds and their side effects. He checked the dosages of the drugs: the hydromorphone came in three-milligram pills; the diazepam had been prescribed in five-milligram doses, four times daily. Peter estimated that, as prescribed, there was little risk of Henry falling into addiction.

But that night Peter learned how bad it could get. A keening sound awoke him at 2:30. He rolled over in bed and listened for a repetition. The guest bedroom had been designed with a long, horizontal window high in the wall, and Peter often propped it open. He was used to the voices of night predators, but this wailing was unusual. It came again through the high window, with a dying fall of misery.

Peter got up and crossed the living room to Henry's bedroom. As he passed the kitchen he glanced in. Halogens under the cupboards lit the row of pill bottles that Henry had relocated to the counter. He lay crumpled on the floor. Blood had seeped through his shoulder dressing; his right hand was bloody, as if he had struck his own wound in an act of self-mortification. The painkillers hadn't staunched his grief.

Peter crouched next to him but didn't try to raise him to his feet. "What are we doing out here, Henry?" he said.

Perhaps it was Henry's wretchedness that turned Peter obdurate. He needed the young Mormon to return to the game — with luck, the endgame. Henry had suffered and he continued to wrestle with his grief. For Peter, his own pursuit of vengeance was complex: his decline into octogenarian status, the echoes from his father's life, and his brother Nigel's death were tied up in his decision to come west to the desert and, just as significant, stay for the conclusion of it all. Those were the givens underpinning his revenge plan. He understood that Henry had his own demons.

"We aren't close, Peter."

"We've come close, Henry. You and I looked Devereau in the eye. Nurse your wounds, my friend. Stop feeling guilty. Buy a dog."

Peter let his friend lie in his misery on the kitchen floor. There was no present answer to his self-pity. Peter raided Tynan's stash of beer in the fridge but did not offer Henry one. He sat down on the cool floor and began a long story about his golden retriever, Jasper, back in England, spinning it out until Henry fell asleep. Peter wondered what Scheherazade tale he would tell the next night.

CHAPTER 37

Peter did what he could to flush Devereau out of the chaparral, but his efforts were ineffectual. Devereau stayed hidden.

Grady suspended DeKlerk and promised dismissal, damn the union, but he failed to make the dismissal public. Everyone knew that Boog had been on a slide for a year or more, and although there was no proof that he had taken direct bribes from González, it came out that he had looked the other way quite a few times. He admitted that much to Grady when they met, both men knowing that the Internal Affairs team would dig up the truth anyway.

Peter decided to cooperate fully with Furst and Ordway, and he spent three days in the Salt Lake offices of the State Bureau, going over the evidence gathered by himself and Henry; Henry even joined in for an afternoon.

The lead on the manhunt was finally shifting out of the hands of Peter, Henry, and Phil.

Initially pleased that state police were throwing resources into the search, Peter, within a week of the appointment of "F&O," as Mohlman called them, began to feel his isolation from the hunt. "It's called authority," Phil rambled in one of their regular calls, during which Peter pressed him for inside information on the team and

Grady's latest machinations. "You don't have any. My advice? Don't go rogue on the Watson Team."

Peter, frustrated by Henry's torpor and the realization that he had truly handed off the less-than-hot pursuit, needed down-to-earth, trustworthy advice. He called the only country sheriff he knew.

It was as if Brockhurst had been waiting for his call. He picked up on half a ring and bellowed, "Peter, what are you still doing in Utah? Those fresh-faced state cops, what's their name, 'Four-Way' . . ."

"Furst and Ordway."

"Let them do their job. Come visit Topeka and justify your malingering in the Beehive State."

"Well, Bill, I was going to ask if you've stayed plugged in to the Hollis Street case, but obviously you are."

"Yup. I've always been interested in your killer. Devereau? Riotte? Shaw? Whatever name you give the Devil."

"I need your advice."

"I'm your reality check. And I have an idea!"

Peter asked Tynan to change Henry's dressings for the four days he'd be in Kansas. Henry's police benefits covered visiting care, but the nursing agency in Salt Lake had resisted driving out that far each day and had cut visits to once a week. Tynan consented. As backup, he said, he could use outpatient services at Utah General. Peter expected that he had an entire church to help, if needed.

The truck held up nicely on the day-and-a-half-long drive to Topeka. It was a sign of Peter's settling in to the West that he considered extending his lease indefinitely with Randy at Randy's Rides.

Peter and Bill Brockhurst rendezvoused in the same eatery as before.

"Nothing I haven't tried on the menu," Brockhurst stated, looking it over anyway. "Stay off the cheddar and broccoli soup, unless you're spacklin' a wall. How can I help, Peter?"

"Has Grady kept you plugged into his task force?"

"Nope. I know it's happening, and Grady keeps the door open. It's early days. What's the hurry?"

"Once he finishes ripping off the drug dealers in a half dozen states, Shaw'll be back to his plan."

"What plan, his manifesto? Remember, Peter, he left it behind in the diner two decades ago. He's shown no sign of testing out a terrorist strike. If so, you'd expect him to probe a military facility, a power dam, or take a potshot at a judge or a prosecutor. That's what terrorists do these days. There's a huge military base in Colorado Springs, just up the road from the narcotics factory he hit. But Peter, he hasn't attacked anything other than drug operations."

"Your point?"

"Do you have that Yoda toy?"

Peter took the figurine with him everywhere. He put it on the table. Brockhurst smashed it with his pistol, causing the waitress to look over. Peter recoiled from the granular mess on the Formica table.

"Change your thinking, Peter. You believe Devereau fashioned parts in a 3-D printer for use in Unabomber-like devices in Denver and Kansas and West Valley. He did use customized parts — we found polymer resin in Riotte's trailer — but we've seen no domestic terror conspiracy. He's small-time. He was just playing with the technology. I consulted some in-the-know forensics people. There's all kinds of loose talk about criminals using 3-D printers to make bomb and gun parts, but it's experimental."

"I didn't know that," Peter said.

"No, you didn't," said Brockhurst. "Times change, Peter. That's my point."

"You're saying he's stealing money and drugs in order to vanish, and no other reason?"

"Yes!" Brockhurst slapped the table and waved for another round. He got up and paced, and sat down again. Three beers was becoming too much for Peter, and he was finding it hard to keep up.

"We're both yesterday's men, I guess," Brockhurst said.

"So — you hinted you have an idea for dealing with the elusive Casper Shaw?" Peter asked.

Brockhurst appeared tired. He took a long time to respond. "You know why I like to talk to you, Peter? Because I've never killed a bad guy, and you have."

"Never?"

"Wounded three suspects while arresting them. That's it."

"That hardly qualifies me to advise on this case."

"It does when evil is on the table, Peter. You're not sentimental. You know what has to be done. That's what I'm saying. So what if Devereau has given up his terrorist objectives? He's still a son of a bitch. Home in on the evil that's still out there. That hasn't changed. Stop him because he's a psychopath, not because he's an ideology-driven terrorist. Stop him because you, not Henry, not the Watson Team, not me, are the one ready to kill him."

After a long pause, Peter said, "How do we trap him?"

Brockhurst had been building to this point. It was the reason for his invitation. "Unless we find his real name, it'll take a long time to nail him, maybe not before he goes into hiding. I've been reviewing the case files, including the incident with Alma May Reeve. Is it possible the Unabomber knows his real name? Can we ask him, do you figure?"

Peter took a long moment. "I'd thought of it, but how long to get access to the Supermax?"

"We need the permission of the Federal Bureau of Prisons for an interview, and for that the support of the Domestic Terrorism folks. Six months.".

"Too slow. Devereau will be gone by then," Peter said.

"Right. Well, let's speed things up. I see two ways. Kaczynski's allowed visitors once a month. First option, get an invitation from Ted himself. Second approach, tell Domestic Terrorism all about the Unabomber's and McVeigh's old buddy."

"Let's do both, starting with Ted," Peter said.

Brockhurst pulled out a note torn from a pad. "We give him this and see what he does."

The paper listed three names:

Jim Riotte
Ronald Devereau
Casper Shaw

"We need an ally in Homeland Security," Brockhurst said. "Someone who'll lever you into the Supermax fast by treating the visit as some form of official business."

Peter considered the obstacles to winning the support of federal law enforcement. He undoubtedly had a reputation now for his provocative interference in the Hollis Street and Denver affairs.

"I'm writing my memoirs," Peter said.

Brockhurst grinned. "*The Casebook of Peter Cammon.* You just need to check a few details with Ted. Now, who do we know in Washington?"

Peter left town with a hangover. He was much too old for this sort of thing. Since moving in with Henry he had cut back his drinking, and now he was paying for Brockhurst's hospitality. Six pints and broccoli and cheese soup.

For once, he drove the interstate without enthusiasm; the straight line westward promised only tedium. He had muddled things. González killed. Henry, the one he had come to help, wounded again. He had alienated law enforcement and dragged his daughter-in-law into a goose chase. It could take half a year to gain access to Kaczynski.

He continued in silence, not even country music for company. He saw the sign again for Fort Riley but wasn't tempted to divert from the I-70. Pulling into the Petro Truck Stop at Salina to fill the tank, he realized he had reached roughly the midpoint of the state, and then he remembered that the centre of the continental United States lay somewhere in Kansas. He couldn't be too far away.

A student working the cash told him authoritatively that the centre of the forty-eight contiguous states sat between Lebanon and Smith Center, Kansas, a half hour west and no more than ninety minutes north. Peter stocked up on sandwiches and bottled water for the pilgrimage northwest and set the GPS.

He took his time. The territory inland from the interstate proved more barren than the main highway, if that was possible, almost as if most of the settlers had spun away centrifugally from the centre point of America on an Oz-driven tornado.

Smith Center and Lebanon, neither more than a passing thought, both laid claim to the centre of America. What an American thing, Peter observed. In the race for municipal hegemony, Smith Center asserted an additional claim on a weathered plaque: "Birthplace of Roscoe 'Fatty' Arbuckle." Who knew?

He eased himself out of the truck at a cairn that told him he was at the Crossroads of the Forty-Eight. He hardly bothered to read the bronze plate — odd, since he had driven all this distance — and he wandered away from the husband and wife who had pulled over in their Winnebago and were scrutinizing the plaque.

Peter had sent an email to Joan and Maddy after the Denver shootout telling them that he was safe, but he had provided no details of the dangers he encountered that night. He knew that his reassurance must have rung hollow. Since then, he had failed to follow up with either Joan or Maddy. He wondered about phone reception out here, seeing no transmission towers on any horizon.

But before he could press speed-dial, his mobile chimed.

"Good news, Peter," said a sober-sounding Brockhurst. "You can see Kaczynski."

"When? How?"

"I cashed in a marker for you. A Texan friend of mine in the Bureau of Prisons did me a favour and looked into it, and it turns out Kaczynski has a constitutional right to visitors, and so does every inmate at the Supermax. But he has to agree to see you. And the reason for your visit

has to be legit. My contact suggests a 'legal investigation' category —
namely, you're clearing up loose ends on an old case."

"Will Kaczynski want to see me?"

"I don't know, but I passed on the three Devereau aliases."

"How soon?"

"He thinks as early as three weeks. Visiting day is Friday. I gotta
go, Peter. Call the warden's office."

Revived, Peter didn't hesitate to call England. Joan picked up
immediately. Her worried voice came clearly across the miles. "Peter?
Are you okay?"

"Yes. I'm calling from the dead centre of the United States."

He could feel her anxiety change to coolness. Perhaps he had been
gone too long. "The way you go on with your wanderings. Where on
earth would that be?"

"Kansas."

"Right you are. Well, you just missed the kids. They set off ten
minutes ago."

"How's Joe?"

"Right as rain. Teething almost over. Except he lives for your dog.
Cried when he left. Jasper herself is moping around now."

It was hard to avoid the reverberations. Jasper was his pet, but
he wasn't home to walk her, was he? And Joe had turned two. He
was missing an important stage in his grandson's life. Calling from
the windswept prairie of Kansas now seemed self-indulgent, falsely
romantic. He was far away from English hearth and home, trying to
impress his wife with an artificial tourist attraction.

"Have you pinpointed your man, Peter?"

"No. We thought we had him trapped in Denver, but he got away."

"Your note was vague. Were you in danger in Colorado?"

Peter noted the edge in her voice, but still he was tempted to
gloss over the raid. He didn't want to worry her. He looked down the
sun-baked highway. *Damn it, I'm seventy-three years old. It's time to be
forthright with my own wife.*

"Yes."

"Did men die?"

"Yes, there was . . ."

"How many?" she snapped.

"Five."

Peter faltered, not quite ready to confess that he had killed two of Devereau's gunmen himself. For her part, Joan hesitated to press for specifics. She deduced that he needed to tell her something important. On the crackling line, she felt that they had lost their wave length and she wondered how to get it back from an ocean away. From long experience, she knew when her husband needed support from her. Usually it took the form of reassurance — but once, a case down in Dorset, he had summoned her to view a crime scene and she had helped him with the evidence. But Peter had been in America well over a month now, and she was still peeved that he hadn't brought her along. And all his talk of evil . . .

And then she knew.

"You want me to come over there?"

He hardly hesitated. "I'd like that. The West is beautiful. We'll take a vacation in the desert."

"Okay."

Her tone was neutral, a bit cold, but he didn't pick up on it. "You can come over anytime," he said in that voice husbands use when they don't want to reveal any more details.

"How about Friday? That gives me time to arrange things. Jasper will have to go up to Leeds with Maddy and Michael, and I need some clothes . . ."

"That's terrific, but there is one thing I have to do in three weeks or so. It's complicated."

"What's that?"

"I have to meet with the Unabomber."

"Of course you do."

It was all surreal. Joan had already been wondering if she would be shut out of his mission. That was unacceptable at this point in their lives together. His approach to the Unabomber signalled that he remained in the thick of the hunt for the killer of Henry Pastern's wife, but where did that leave her?

Am I to be part of the endgame or the waiting game?

"You'll love the desert," he said.

"You won't be preoccupied?"

"As soon as you get here, I'll tell you everything I'm planning."

You'll tell me now. "What do you want from Kaczynski?"

"A name, that's all. I'll hand it over to the police, and a dozen agencies will track down the killer of Henry's wife. All that's left for me to do is get the name."

"I'll come," Joan said, "but on one condition. You have to tell me *everything* that occurred in Denver. And no, I don't care if your battery runs out. Tell me now. From the centre of the United States."

And so he recounted the tale of the Denver shootout, from beginning to end, and from the middle of nowhere.

Passing the truck stop in Colby, Peter made another decision: when Devereau/Shaw appeared out of the long shadows, when Peter and Henry dealt with him, someone would have to tell his twisted story.

Peter hadn't called ahead to give Henry his time of arrival, but when he reached Coppermount on the second afternoon, Elder Tynan was standing in the driveway. *How did he know when I'd pull up?* The Mormon appeared worn and worried, not his usual self; on the other hand, even a shabby Tynan projected an Old Testament willpower that impressed Peter.

Dusty and road-weary, Peter followed Tynan inside. "What's wrong?"

"Henry's off the wagon. A little bit," the Mormon said penitently.

The big living room was empty. Peter looked for the green absinthe bottle.

"I've been having trouble with the shoulder bandage," Tynan said.

Henry drifted in from his bedroom. He wore pyjama bottoms but no top; blood leaked through his shoulder compress.

But more striking was the powder on his nostrils.

"Hello, Peter. When did you get back?"

Henry moved in a robotic circle and disappeared into his wing of the house. Tynan went to the bar and gestured to a small wrought silver box sitting on a glass tray. "Pure White."

Peter wasn't sure what surprised him most: that Henry had latched on to a supply of cocaine or that Tynan was familiar with drug lingo. Pure White. Tynan was becoming a fixation for Peter. Perhaps he had a more complicated history than he disclosed. Walking the desert, building a house, mending the wounded. Was he striving for atonement?

Peter knew that cocaine produced ugly interactions with prescription painkillers, but he was too tired to press the matter with Henry or the old Mormon.

"Let him sleep it off. I need sleep myself."

But Tynan himself had issues and wanted to get to them, Peter saw. Having been subjected to lectures by both Joan and Captain Brockhurst, Peter wasn't keen on another. Tynan restlessly walked to the patio windows, gazed at the vast desert, and turned back to Peter.

"This vendetta of Henry's. It has to end sometime, Peter."

Peter's response was more glib than he intended. "Isn't that the nature of vendettas? To end?"

"I'm hoping Henry returns to the church someday."

Peter wasn't ready for this. He turned evasive, as he always did when religion came up. Religion was the antithesis of practicality, and Peter was always practical. "He has a long way to go, and the first stages of his recovery will be, I would say, 'secular.'"

Tynan smiled. "You're probably right. I'd at least like to get him into rehab, for both drugs and liquor." Despite the Mormon's tangent into religion, Peter liked and generally trusted him. Fortitude and loyalty were his virtues.

Peter considered going into Henry's bedroom to change his bandage. Instead, he said, "So, Elder Tynan, are you trying to convert *me*?"

Tynan joked, "Sure. I'll start with wise counsel, then see how we do . . . How is your investigation going, Peter?"

"I'm working out what to do next." Peter surprised himself by sitting down on the couch and laying out his current dilemma in detail. He covered the re-investigation of Hollis Street, Devereau's evaporation, and his own Unabomber strategy.

"You're still determined to help Henry achieve his revenge?"

"Yes, in a word."

"Don't get me wrong, Peter. I'm not trying to talk anyone out of anything. But is this manhunt wearing both of you out?"

Everybody's a critic, Peter thought. But he found his will collapsing, and he felt compelled to reveal his surfacing unease. Perhaps this was Tynan's clever doing, the first ploy in his effort to convert him. "I'm afraid that Devereau will turn out to be ordinary, not the arch-villain I had him pictured as."

"And you are sure that Devereau is the villain you encountered two decades ago in the Unabomber case?"

After a long minute, Peter said, "Yes." Tynan, recognizing that he was in the presence of an experienced criminalist, did not push.

"He was a terrorist — once," Peter added, recalling Brockhurst smashing his pistol down on the fragile Yoda.

They remained on the sofa, each man exhausted for his own reasons. Tynan turned directly to Peter. "You know the great thing about Mormonism? It gives us epic stories, all of them as intriguing as the Greek myths."

"What does it do for the devout?"

"It makes you feel part of an important larger story."

Peter wasn't ready to be dislodged from his tepid Church of England upbringing. "Any epics of revenge in the Book of Mormon?"

"Oh, yes. Do you think, Peter, that I would try to dissuade you from your fully justified plan for retribution? What I'm skeptical about is your commitment to your own strategy."

"Should I have to demonstrate more than I already have? Sorry, but vengeance versus balanced justice isn't an issue I plan to debate."

"I'm not asking you to buy into the metaphysics of the Bible or the Book of Mormon, Peter, but don't do this alone. You have to take a larger perspective than your pigeonholing of Devereau as evil. You and Henry need each other. Your journey is nothing without Henry beside you, hunting with you. As for Devereau, I'll concede he's irredeemable."

"I know how he fits into Henry's epic nightmare. That's all the metaphysics a policeman like me needs."

"Don't misinterpret me on the bottom line, Peter. It's a practical matter."

"You're saying I need to understand my enemy?" He looked at Tynan in puzzlement.

The Elder hesitated. He stood and again walked to the patio windows. He swept his hand across the horizon in a grand, almost imperious gesture that told Peter that here was Tynan's permanent home. Henry was entwined with it. He would defend this place and Henry, too. The Mormon turned to Peter.

"I'm not impugning your motives."

"What are you getting at?"

"Oh, wasn't I clear? I believe that Devereau is evil in every way."

"Explain."

"The worst betrayal of Theresa would be to wait around for Devereau to burst from hiding. You need to name the Devil and then deal with him. Be proactive."

"You sound like you believe in righteous retribution."

"I'm saying, Peter, you need to ratchet it up. Revenge should blaze white-hot."

CHAPTER 38

Peter had planned to sleep in, but as usual he awoke a few minutes after dawn. It was too early for his urgent task, calling the warden of ADX Florence, the Colorado Supermax, and he went to the kitchen to make coffee. Henry wouldn't be up for a while, he figured, and he could relax in solitude on the patio and consider where the Devereau manhunt stood.

On the way to the fridge, he looked for the silver box of white powder. He found it behind the granite bar. There was the glass tray, the cocaine, and a 500-peso note. He brought out the works and contemplated the white powder. On impulse, he rolled the banknote into a tube and clumsily leaned in to the line of blow set out on the glass. He drew a small amount of the powder into his right nostril.

Peter had tasted cocaine once, but never ingested. He was surprised at the instant high. It wasn't exactly euphoria; rather, it came on as a flood of clarity and cold fire. The living room lit up in fluorescent indigo and white. He padded to the broad windows, where the spectrum out in the desert broadened into canary-yellow, mauve, and orange waves of light. He went out to the patio. In his youth, he had embraced the pseudo-profound *Teachings of Don Juan*, with its hallucinations and sombre instructions for achieving personal insight. *Castaneda, you old phony: at least you got the hallucination part spot-on.*

The rush faded after twenty minutes. The feeling of supremacy had been compelling, but at the same time the coke had slipped a tincture of paranoia into his momentary rapture. He returned to the kitchen and made the coffee extra-strong.

He sat on a chaise longue on the terrace for an hour and free-associated. His greatest fear was that Ronald Devereau would disappear like a "wisp of smoke," as he had put it to both Tynan and Brockhurst in his recent conversations. *There is an element of cowardice in all terrorists, who think they can fight for grandiose principles while remaining anonymous.* Both Devereau and the Unabomber had drafted their windy manifestos without any intention of publicly defending them. There had always been strong odds that Devereau would quit the game again and slip away. Brockhurst's persuasive argument that Devereau wasn't the ambitious ideological radical he once was only added to the urgency for Peter. And so, however unimpressed he was by the work of Furst and Ordway thus far, he would continue to cooperate with them. They had the network and would likely be the ones to bring in the murderer.

But he didn't plan to tell them yet about his visit to the Unabomber.

As a priority, he had to address Henry's drug habit. From the day Peter had arrived in Utah, Henry had veered from depression to resolve, crashing in each cycle; he had offered inconsistent help. Peter wasn't naive: his friend's tragedy had poisoned his life but now, if Henry's cocaine indulgence came out, his career would be scotched.

Peter was considering this problem and contemplating going back to bed when Henry wandered out. He smiled as if nothing was wrong, and Peter actually felt relief wash over him. As Tynan had admonished, he and Henry inevitably remained partners in this vendetta, however fitful Henry's engagement.

"What's on our agenda, Peter?"

"Let's go for a walk, Henry."

It was a crazy thing to wander the desert in this heat; Henry did not even have to mention mad dogs and Englishmen. But he followed Peter out the patio doors without a word.

"Something's been bothering me, Henry. That night in Denver. Why did González rush into the marijuana store like that?"

They were a hundred feet beyond the house. Henry squinted against the sun. "I was behind González all the way into the warehouse," he began. "He barely hesitated. It was strange. José was with us, but he remained behind me. I figured he was trusting me to play backup, but maybe it was his way of being protective of me, on González's orders."

"What was González's mood?" Peter said.

"Determined. Fatalistic. He walked right into the bomb."

"And you said José came to see you at the hospital? Why?"

Henry took a moment, and when he spoke there was a new assuredness in his voice. "These Mexicans aren't sentimental people. I learned that from talking to González in Wendover. They kill their enemies without regret, and that was certainly Avelino's intention in Denver." Henry scuffed the pebbly ground. "José came to the hospital to bare his soul. He said something had changed in González last year. He had become obsessed with finding the man who shot his brother. When he heard about Hollis Street and the Watsons, he figured out, with details from Boog DeKlerk about the pipe bomb, that Devereau was the man he wanted. He was sure, José said, and he became single-minded, obsessed, and neglected his drug empire. When he convened the meeting out in Wendover, he took a liking to me, and he instructed José to follow up if anything went wrong with the Denver sting. José feels guilty about my injuries."

"And a silver box full of coke is his way of atoning," Peter said.

"Sure helps with the pain!"

"How are your wounds, Henry?"

"Not bad at all. I can drive myself now to the clinic."

Peter decided to leave the coke issue for the time being. "Henry, you asked about our agenda."

"Yup. What's our plan?"

"We'll put a notice in the *Deseret Star*. An ad for a killer." He handed over a sheet of paper. Henry read the scribbled words:

Insight into our modern dilemma!
Recently unearthed masterpiece, FIRE AND BRIMSTONE
Write for your copy, Free!
Pay postage only
Box 1234 . . .

"I like it!"

On their circle back to the house, Peter said, "I have two more developments to tell you about." He explained his plan to interview Kaczynski, and Joan's arrival.

This news appeared to revitalize Henry. They quickly refined the newspaper squib, and Henry insisted on calling it in to the *Deseret Star*.

No sooner had he placed the ad than Ordway called to say that his team had issued a warrant for the arrest of Ronald Devereau, also known as Casper Shaw, on suspicion of murder and arson. The Watsons were the only named victims. He and Furst had developed a new sketch in collaboration with Phil Mohlman. They emailed it to the Coppermount house, and Henry and Peter ruled it to be as good as any of the many past efforts by witnesses; Peter noted that the detectives had taken pains to avoid replicating the classic Unabomber hoodie-with-sunglasses drawing. What surprised and pleased Peter was the fine-print description of Devereau's sins, albeit a mundanely phrased reference to "known involvement in narcotics trafficking and possibly in domestic terrorism conspiracies." Inclusion of terrorism made strategic sense if the new team wanted to draw Homeland agencies into a dragnet.

"Do we retract the newspaper posting?" Henry asked after the phone call.

"I don't think so," Peter said. "At the same time, I didn't mention it to Ordway."

When Peter called the Bureau of Prisons office in Denver, he was told that neither the warden nor the deputy warden of the Florence Supermax was available to talk, and he was shunted to a Corporal Youngman in Special Investigative Services.

"I'm speaking with Chief Inspector Peter Cammon of New Scotland Yard?" The stiff voice of the corporal wasn't encouraging, but then: "The warden instructed me to extend every courtesy to you. It will be feasible for you to visit inmate Kaczynski under secure arrangements, but we require details regarding yourself and the active law enforcement process that supports your contact with him. Now, I am told that you're coming here under the auspices of Captain Brockhurst of the Kansas Highway Patrol."

Brockhurst had come through.

Peter carried the phone to the patio and allowed the morning to bathe him in brightness and warmth. The day was starting well, and he felt the manhunt accelerating. Reaching out to Brockhurst in Topeka and, likewise, embracing the Watson Team's fresh warrant had toppled the wall he had built around Devereau's terror-linked past. It was time to be completely open with the Unabomber's minders on the Kaczynski-McVeigh-Devereau connection. Peter took most of an hour to explain all this to Youngman, after which he artfully brought the tortuous saga back to the simple, distilled legal process of the Furst and Ordway warrant. "Obtaining the birth name will bolster the warrant, Corporal, hopefully enabling the capture of a man who has slaughtered two married couples on his own street."

Corporal Youngman asked few questions, other than clarifying the three names to be given to Kaczynski: Jim Riotte, Ronald Devereau, Casper Shaw.

"Of course, Chief Inspector, the inmate will have to agree to the visit, but . . ." Peter understood that Kaczynski would likely agree. Peter wasn't flattered: Ted would welcome human interaction with anyone. "Assuming he okays it for three Fridays from now, could you drive down to Denver this week for a security briefing and a few signatures? No need to travel all the way to Florence for these preliminaries."

Peter promised to meet Youngman in the Bureau's suburban office in Denver on the upcoming Thursday. Hanging up, he debriefed Henry on the latest developments, and they agreed that the case was picking up speed. Peter silently wondered how he would stay focused on showing Joan around the desert while he waited for his appointment with the Unabomber. But overall, the tumblers were clicking into place, and Peter was infused with the policeman's singular zeal that comes from the certainty that the investigative process is advancing.

Four hours later, Youngman called back with amazing news. Upon being shown the three names, Ted Kaczynski had insisted on meeting with the English detective as soon as possible. Ted didn't say why — indeed didn't have to, for he knew every nuance of his rights. The ADX warden lacked any reason to refuse a meeting with Peter on a regular visiting day.

"Indeed, Mr. Cammon, we see no harm in allowing a visit *this* Friday, if that suits you. To be honest, we prefer to give ground on the small issues and save our gunpowder for the bigger conflicts. He has no other visits scheduled that day."

Peter understood. "This is a good sign, Corporal. Mention of the names to Kaczynski triggered a strong response. It signifies to me that he knows the identity of our man."

"I agree," Youngman stated.

Youngman pledged to email a list of the rules for visitors, but they would skip the security briefing. Peter managed to reach Joan at the cottage and promised that Henry would pick her up at Salt Lake City International on Friday.

CHAPTER 39

For vaguely ascetic reasons, Peter drove from urban Denver to the ADX Florence without using the GPS; it seemed right to get semi-lost in the desert. Down the middle of Colorado, Interstate 25 eventually branched west onto the narrower Colorado 115, and he found himself for a few minutes out of sight of any settlement. He luxuriated in a broad landscape that was scarred only by a few wandering fences and wheel tracks that meandered into the horizon. The first road sign he met, and the next few as well, informed him that Florence, Population 3,653, lay up ahead, but he ended up bypassing the town without seeing it.

Peter's wife had always maintained that her husband was quite capable of excitement but that he was always careful about it. Now here he was, driving to consult one evil killer/terrorist about another one, and he was both excited and wary. He had begun this journey to America with an unbridled resolve to trap and expunge this evil, yet the facts had begun to chip away at his image of the killer as a terrorist mastermind. He wished that he knew more about Devereau, whose behaviour displayed pettiness and impulsive violence as much as diabolical control. Peter remained convinced that Devereau was a psychopath, frustrated and pathologically ever more desperate.

Could Peter still manage to kill this man? Would he be content with merely bringing him into custody?

The Supermax worked hard at creating a force field of isolation. It sat out of sight of the town of Florence, although a golf course bordered the prison grounds. Penitentiary facilities, in Peter's experience, mimicked ancient forts, with an outward calm and silence masking the expectation of a direful attack — except that no one had ever breached the Supermax, in or out. Peter pulled up to the long entrance road, with its small-font, mundane sign announcing "Administrative Maximum Facility, United States Penitentiary." He eyed the complex of low-slung buildings. An architect can only do so much to beautify a maximum-security prison. Rolls of razor wire topped double fences to confront any escapee with a steel maze, and cylindrical guard towers set up cross-hatched lines of sight across every foot of the grounds. There was no exercise track for the high-security inmates. All life was controlled. Here the prisoners endured in cruel amber.

Peter left the truck in the visitor's lot, which contained about forty cars. The layout of the complex channelled everyone to the reception room and commanded them to sign in with the institutional duty officer. Peter entered with a group of families, all of them hot and frazzled. He had to wonder how often they made this journey.

A six-foot-tall, barrel-chested African-American correctional officer was taking details from a weary woman and her mother. He looked up and made Peter for a cop. Finishing with the women, whom he buzzed through a heavy door, he wandered over, and Peter presented his ID. Calling up the appointment, the big man announced, "You have a Law Enforcement Interview scheduled. I'll give you an attorney-client room. However, since you are not the inmate's counsel, Chief Inspector Cammon, he will be in leg and hand restraints and a belly chain at all times. Your escort will collect you here. Please read these instructions while you wait. Shouldn't be five minutes." He inked Peter's hand with a rock-concert stamp.

Peter was startled by the arrival of Corporal Youngman in a fashionable suit; he had expected a Bureau of Prisons uniform. Youngman displayed a square jaw, cold eyes, and very controlled amiability. The Special Investigative Service officer smiled. "We must have almost followed each other down from Denver."

He reviewed the sheet of institutional rules with Peter but treated them cursorily. No contact, no cursing, no publication of inmate statements, and so on. "But you knew all that stuff, Chief Inspector, I'm sure. Here, put on this ID badge. Wear it at all times. I'll escort you to the interview space."

Peter followed Youngman through a dozen doors, buzzed open in sequence by anonymous hands. Soon he was lost, disoriented in a windowless world. That could be the point, he mused.

"We have to talk about one thing," Youngman said as they stop-started down corridors from one iron door to the next. "It's not happenstance that we're giving you a lawyer's room. We want Kaczynski to open up to you. He knows all his legal rights intimately, so he's certainly aware that attorney-client confidentiality doesn't apply when a police officer gets friendly. But he was extremely keen to talk to you, and we're curious why."

Perhaps because he's bored and crazy, Peter thought.

"You intend to record our discussions?" Peter prompted.

"Yeah, we will be doing that, sir. I admit, we're walking a legal tightrope here. Inmates know that any conversation is subject to recording, other than with counsel or a priest — that'll be the day with Kaczynski. We believe we're not misleading him by arranging this environment. What do you think?"

"I have no objection," Peter answered, although he knew that nothing he could say would alter the plan. He realized why Youngman had shown limited curiosity about Peter's questions. He would soon have it all on tape anyway. Peter had no idea what Youngman hoped for and didn't particularly care. Recording the interview wouldn't affect Peter's interrogation style.

The consultation room was a large concrete box with a table and two chairs and a small, square one-way observation window. There was a door at each end; as Peter took his designated chair, he understood that guards would usher Kaczynski in through the far portal. Youngman repeated the most important of the advisories: "Don't get physically close. Watch for mood changes. Don't make promises." He looked abashed at the last instruction, aware of Peter's vast experience as an interrogator. "Good luck," he said, and left Peter in featureless solitude.

Twenty minutes passed. Peter never wore a wristwatch, and the guards had retained his mobile, along with his truck keys, money, and comb. A number of vagaries, including a change of heart by Kaczynski himself, might nix the meeting. But Peter remained patient and intrigued: the Unabomber had pushed to see him at the first opportunity, and if all he had wanted to give over was Ronald Devereau's birth name, he could have mailed a letter (although, Peter considered, perhaps Kaczynski harboured an aversion to the U.S. Postal Service). No, Ted had an agenda. Twenty-three hours a day in solitary conditions, and you tended to conjure up elaborate agendas, Peter reasoned.

Ted Kaczynski entered in chains through the far door, a guard moving him along by the shoulder. The prisoner's orange jumpsuit surprised Peter, and with the restraints, it seemed punitive. Ted had resided here for many years and must have mastered the rules. Had he breached them lately? The tug and pull of small privileges doled out by the prison administration was important to the Supermax inmates, and Peter hoped that Kaczynski was in a benign mood.

The Unabomber was clean-shaven, and his face had thickened on all planes over the years, but he had retained his dense mop of wiry, uncombable hair, now gray — and he suffered inevitably from prison pallor, like a disease.

Ted's sidelong look at Peter began the dance. Peter knew that he wanted something, and he might well get it in return for the information he had to offer. Peter had prepared strategies to create a rapport.

He deliberately spoke first. "My name is Chief Inspector Peter Cammon, New Scotland Yard."

The Unabomber jangled to the other chair and sat down, waiting while the guard locked him to the ring welded to the table. Judging that all would remain peaceful, the guard left them alone.

"You're English. I like the English."

Kaczynski's voice was raspy (from disuse?) but Peter heard educated notes in the timbre. He recalled that Kaczynski had a Ph.D. from the University of Michigan. The prisoner made eye contact, although his expression offered little access to his thoughts. Peter let him talk and tried to concentrate on each word.

"I often listen to National Public Radio in my room at night. Early morning, it switches to the BBC, sometimes Radio Australia. I like the accents of the announcers."

Peter offered a wan smile. "You may be wondering why I'm here, all the way from England."

But Ted lived full-time in an elaborate memory palace whose geography did not include present-day England. "Do you time-travel back to the old days, Inspector?"

Peter adjusted quickly. "February 23, 1987. The incident in the parking lot at East 900 South in Salt Lake City. I investigated it."

Kaczynski nodded, with a touch of arrogance showing. "You worked the Yorkshire Ripper case. Scotland Yard loaned you to the FBI because of it."

Peter had fully expected Kaczynski to show off his intellect, but this was just internet research.

"Why did they equate me with a sex predator like Sutcliffe?" Kaczynski added.

Ted had a point — granted, he wasn't a pedophile like the Ripper — but Peter wasn't interested in rhetorical debates about long-faded issues. The Unabomber tensed and fought to conceal his anger from the watchers at the square window. Peter watched the cogs turning as the madman indulged his bitterness.

"The federal police are despicable, taking my house and possessions for selling." The Unabomber's mock-Thoreau cabin had travelled around the United States for years since its uprooting from the Montana woods, ending up in the Newseum in Washington.

Peter moved to insinuate himself into Kaczynski's memories. "February 1987. A cool and clear day. You took the bus down from

Helena to Salt Lake. You carried a device in a white canvas bag. It was pretty heavy, being made of two steel pipes and blocks of hardwood. Tell me, was the computer store your original target?"

"I did not intend to kill anyone," Kaczynski rushed to say.

Peter fell silent, allowing the bomber his tidbit of justification. No doubt the prisoner remembered that day well. The parking lot attack stood out in the evolution of his terrorist career, not to mention the deterioration of his mind. It had been as vicious as it was irrational, and Ted knew it. Psychopaths forget nothing; slights and blunders in particular lurk close to the surface.

Peter continued to call up the details. "I think you originally targeted the University of Utah, which lies just up the road. You'd tried there before, hadn't you?" The UNABOM, as he was then called by law enforcement, had planted a device in a corridor in the university complex in 1981, but police defused it.

Kaczynski was stolid as a tombstone. Any minute, Peter expected, the aging terrorist might cut off their conversation. Peter went for broke.

"But first, you had arranged to meet up with Jim Riotte and the man I know as Ronald Devereau, but you probably called Casper Shaw, in a diner around the corner from the computer shop. Why? Did they promise to drive you to the university?"

"No. Are they alive?"

"Riotte is dead. Shaw killed him."

"Casper Shaw is alive?"

"Yes," Peter said. "You never trusted Shaw, am I right? And it wasn't your idea to go after the computer store owner, was it?"

Peter readied himself. Now came the challenge to Ted's ego.

"No," Ted answered. "Shaw was weak."

"You knew him as Shaw?"

Ted, adopting a sly look, said, "Shaw? . . . We'll call him that."

Although they had only an hour, Peter let a full minute of silence pass. Kaczynski was embarrassed. His marathon of mail bombs and planted devices had been indiscriminate and heartless but the small computer business had been an odd target even by his standards. It certainly did nothing for his legacy. No one had been impressed by the attack, so petty and arbitrary.

And Peter knew what Ted was thinking. *Shaw is weak but I'm the one locked up in here.*

"It was winter. The diner was warm," Peter continued.

Kaczynski acknowledged this, but riposted, "You don't understand. My plan was to *mail* the bomb. I won't tell you where to. The diner was two miles from the post office. Shaw refused to drive me there. He tried to persuade me to leave it on the ground outside."

Peter leaned forward, but not within range of the dog chain. "There was something else. Who arrived at the diner first that morning?"

"I did. What does that matter?"

"You brought along a copy of *The Turner Diaries* to read in case you had to wait. The waitress saw it. Let's talk about the manifesto."

This time Kaczynski jerked back in his chair. A look of mixed anger and fear came over his pallid face. "I got it published," he croaked.

"That's not the one I'm talking about."

Ted pulled reflexively against his chains. The guard opened the door, sized up the dynamics, and went out again.

Peter had been allowed to bring in a soft bag to hold his papers. He took out Alma May's unstapled photocopy of *Fire and Brimstone*. The Unabomber gaped.

"Ted, am I right that one of the reasons you allowed Shaw to change your mind was his promise to give you his essay-in-progress? It was a cold day. You might as well leave the bomb around the corner, he argued. He invited you to collaborate on a revolutionary manifesto. Move the revolution forward. It was easy. He promised to be your ally, your first collaborator."

Ted snapped back, "Oh, I'd met him before, in Montana. He wanted to be my friend then. Lent me some books . . ."

His tone was defensive. From his years of interviewing witnesses, Peter knew that criminals with something to hide tend to fall into formal phrasing. Kaczynski gathered himself. "It is true that his short manifesto gave me, in part, the idea of writing and publishing my own statement of my philosophy. His never achieved publication."

"And it never will," Peter said, tossing *Fire and Brimstone* onto the table. Ted smirked. "But Ted, I want to know exactly what happened next. Let me see if I've got this in order. When Shaw arrived with Riotte and offered to give you one of only two copies of his treasured manuscript, you had a fight. He made an excuse to leave."

"I went for a piss. He was already out of there when I returned. He never asked my permission to leave. It wasn't the plan."

Peter thought he knew the sequence of events but wanted to hear it from Kaczynski. "What, then?"

"Detective Cammon, you're missing the big thing! While I was in the bathroom, Shaw took the *bomb* with him. He planted it in the parking lot. Cold bastard. Riotte confirmed what his buddy was doing. When Shaw returned, I was long gone, and with my copy of his essay."

"Why didn't you go after him when you came out of the loo . . . the toilet?"

Kaczynski looked embarrassed. "I was in the can fifteen minutes. I had a case of the runs. Diet up in Montana . . . Now you tell me he left his *own* copy behind, too!"

Peter fought to keep the rapport. "The witness saw Casper Shaw, but you didn't see him again?"

"No. I just took off."

"Shaw arrived that day wearing a hoodie, am I right?"

"I never wore a hoodie, and after that, made sure I never did. He had a pencil-thin moustache and shades, never me."

"I always wondered why the figure in the wanted poster looked nothing like you when you were arrested. I came across a sketch of Devereau in the context of two other crimes and realized that it was the wanted man from the poster. Or maybe Jim Riotte; they looked similar."

Kaczynski remained fixed on *Fire and Brimstone*. "Yes, they did.

But it was Shaw who wrote that half-assed document and Shaw who left my package out there."

"The waitress filled me in on the rest. Do you want to know?"

"Yes, I certainly do, Inspector."

"Riotte stayed behind in the diner after you left. When Shaw returned, he was angry and must have realized that he was in danger now that you had his manifesto."

Ted guffawed. "They gave me the photocopy and forgot the original from under the table. How's that for a Freudian slip? He leaves behind his only two copies! Some revolutionary. He came looking for me a week later, but I avoided him, hid away my duplicate of his essay. Can't call it a true manifesto . . ."

"Do you still have your copy?" Peter said.

"Nope. I used a few ideas from it in my *Manifesto*. Ignored it, mostly."

Peter knew from Maddy's thorough text comparison that this was a lie. He had borrowed extensively from *Fire and Brimstone*, no doubt infuriating Devereau. The Unabomber dodged him for the next decade. Devereau must have searched, but like everyone else, he didn't know about the one-room cabin in the Montana forest. The publication of Ted Kaczynski's *Industrial Society and its Future* in the *New York Times* and the *Washington Post* in September 1995 must have alarmed Devereau, but by then Ted was out of reach. Ted's rivals decided that their only option was to fabricate a new persona and vanish.

There was one more issue to cover, and both men went for it. Ted, apparently gratified that someone else now knew about the Utah mess, crossed his legs to the rattle of the chains. It was hard to appear insouciant in an orange jumpsuit, but at least he looked self-assured.

"What has Mr. Shaw been up to recently, Chief Inspector?"

"Murder. Arson. Aggravated assault. Misuse of firearms. Drug pushing."

"Anything in the line of what they now like to call 'domestic terrorism,' as if Islamists don't operate inside this country?"

Peter, struggling in the last minutes available to find a way to get Ted to offer up Devereau's birth name, didn't answer. He took out the broken-winged polymer plane that he had found in Ronald Devereau's garage and set it on the table, where Ted could reach it if he wanted. This risked the guard barging into the room.

"You like to carve things, especially out of wood, Ted. This is a toy made with a 3-D printer by your rival, Shaw. I believe he was practising making bomb components out of polymer resin. Of course, they don't approach your artistry. But we found residue on the scene of two bombings in the last two months."

"What did he attack?"

The air was heavy. They were moving to an ending, after which they would never see one another again.

"Two narcotics operations. To finance his terrorism plans," Peter lied.

"So he's back in the terrorism business," the Unabomber said flatly.

"Maybe."

Kaczynski sneered, ugly as only a burning-out psychopath could be. He felt superior, Peter could tell. He could read Ted's mind. The last copy of Ronald Devereau's tract was sitting on the nailed-down table, and Devereau would never be able to transform *Fire and Brimstone* into a blueprint for attacking industrial society, nor ever steal Kaczynski's notoriety. Ted smiled, a man with all the time in the world, who could wait for this British policeman and his ilk to complete the final dirty work of catching his rival.

"Tell me who he is," Peter said.

The other man grinned, his eyes crazed. "Will you kill him?"

Peter let one of his final two allotted minutes go by. He leaned in and touched one orange sleeve, a clear violation of the rules.

"Yes."

"His name is Kelso Vyne."

PART 3

VYNE

Every choice is a loss.
The past is not where you left it.
Ruth Padel, "The Cello."

CHAPTER 40

Joan was so eager to land, to spurn synthetic oxygen after fifteen hours of flight and ultimately engage the desert air, that she forgot to look out the window for the Great Salt Lake. All the way she had waited for the mysterious lake to appear. Her miscue dovetailed with a feeling that had nagged her the whole trip from Heathrow: that plans with Peter were already out of whack. The Unabomber meeting had been moved up two weeks to today, and she had no idea how the encounter would affect Peter's mood. Would it be a momentous breakthrough or an anticlimax? Either way, Joan saw trouble ahead, for her husband was never fun to be around when he was closing in on a target. He had pledged to back off once he had the killer's name, to let the new team make the arrest. So why had she left a daughter-in-law back home, hovering over her laptop keyboard like Glenn Gould, waiting for that name to appear on her monitor?

Joan was pretty sure that she would recognize Elder Tynan, but the arrivals area, while it contained many blokes in white shirts and black pants (these were all Mormons?), didn't include him. As her eyes jumped across the crowd, she caught a lanky figure staring at her, a white sling supporting his left arm. She did a double take: this was Henry himself, thinner than ever but smiling genuinely.

Detective Mohlman stood at his side. Henry beckoned to her with his good arm and moved forward to meet her.

"I'd hug you, but it's too painful," Henry said. "You remember Phil, my partner."

"You're always driving me places," she joshed.

But then Phil saw the alarm in Joan's eyes. "No, your husband's fine. We're the welcoming committee, substituting for the substitute."

"Mr. Tynan sends his regrets," Henry added. "He had an urgent meeting and asked me to pick you up. But with my arm and all, I needed Phil to drive . . ."

"Ignore him, Mrs. Cammon. We're just outside."

On this genial basis, they collected Joan's luggage and walked to Phil Mohlman's dusty police sedan. She noticed that Phil still limped in some pain. Henry insisted that she sit in the front of the car so that she could view the desert better, but Joan understood that they didn't want her feel like an arrestee in the back.

The first feature that struck her wasn't the desert but the snow-topped mountains that sheltered the city on the eastern side. Then Phil made a turn that put the mountains at their backs, and soon they were rushing west into what seemed a hazy infinity. She had to ask, "Where is the Great Salt Lake?"

"Off to our right, not very far at all," Henry said.

"You know, I've never been on the lake," Phil said.

"Maybe because it doesn't resemble anything in Boston," Henry kibitzed from the rear seat.

They chatted amiably about civilian topics — the weather in England, and Phil Mohlman's continuing sense of being an out-sider in Utah. Their jocularity faded the moment they turned onto Coppermount and Henry saw the Escalade in his driveway. Joan felt a rising chill. Henry turned to Phil. "Did you know about this?"

"I'm a co-conspirator," Phil declared, drily and without concession.

Henry stormed out of the back of the sedan. He had the grace to open Joan's door for her but then he rushed to the house. Joan took her time there in the driveway; she had travelled for a full day to experience the sun, and she revelled in it.

Inside, she hardly had time to check out the panoramic view from the patio windows before two men on the sofa turned and jumped to their feet. One, she marked, was the peculiar Elder Tynan, but the other was one of the biggest men she had ever met. At first she thought *wrestler*, and then imagined that Peter had arranged a bodyguard for her, pending some assault from the newly monikered Hollis Street beheader.

"What the hell did you do?" Henry said to Tynan.

"Careful, pardner," Phil warned from behind Henry. "Remember, Mormons don't swear."

It was the wrong thing to say to an outraged man, Joan thought, but Phil showed no concern. This was a tough copper, she recorded.

Tynan spoke for the first time. "Henry, have a seat. I invited José over."

"I won't allow this in my own house!" Henry unwisely flung up both arms in anger and grimaced in pain. He stomped across the vestibule and disappeared to his bedroom.

Joan had already perceived that Henry's eruption flowed from a deep loneliness as much as from anything Tynan had done. The house felt hollow despite the stunning view from the back windows; Henry was alienated from his own home. In temperament, Joan was eternally polite with people and she understood that they should stay put and wait him out.

Everyone had noticed the blood oozing through Henry's shoulder bandage. Tynan, though he hadn't said hello yet, gave Joan an intimate glance, the look of one nurse to another.

"I'll be back," Tynan said.

Joan stepped forward. "No, let me do it. Where are his supplies?"

She faced the chagrined looks of the three men. The big bloke had yet to speak. Did he hope she hadn't figured out that he was a drug dealer? All of them were awkward in her presence. She decided to cut through the tension by showing them she was Peter Cammon's wife.

"Supplies? Bandages? Did you think I meant that silver box of cocaine sitting on the bar?"

José, ruddy from a life of exposure to the desert, turned even redder and got up from the sofa. Phil Mohlman beamed. José massively loomed over Joan but he shook her hand in a chivalrous way. "I am José Mariana. *That* will be gone when you return. It is a pleasure to meet the wife of Señor Cammon."

Joan discovered the bandages and disinfectant in an unsanitary mountain in the main bathroom. She carried the stack into Henry's bedroom, where he was struggling out of his blood-ruined shirt. Joan stripped it off, exposing a wide square of gauze on his left shoulder. She removed the compress and observed that though the shoulder scar was clean, the resurgent bleeding had to be dealt with before infection set in. Henry looked embarrassed.

She swabbed the wound. "Was there any tendon damage?"

"Luckily, no. The muscle injury will heal, they tell me."

"If you stop stretching that shoulder. What painkillers have you been taking?"

It was Henry's turn to look shamefaced. "You saw the drugs?"

"I'm pretty sure the silver box will be gone when you go back out there."

"I was hoping to give you a proper welcome. That didn't include the Mexican."

"Scary fellow."

"Sorry."

Joan was not only scrupulously polite with strangers, she knew how to forge intimacy. "Listen, Henry. Peter and I have been married forty-six years. He tries to shield me from the worst of his mayhem, but I've learned to handle the bizarre bits . . . which always seem to come up."

"I'm sorry."

"Stop saying you're sorry. Let me tell you something. This is a typical Peter Cammon case. Peter becomes relentless when he gets close to solving a crime, and as a consequence things can get weird. To his credit — I think — he ignores the small stuff that could distract him from the big picture. I'm guessing that he'll see José and his white powder as a minor distraction."

It was a sign of how much she missed Peter that she rambled on about him. *I may be light-headed from the flight and the sun, but now I understand why I'm here. Peter's welcoming me into a strange world, where he may be its strangest inhabitant. That's his idea of a compliment.* His assertion that he was flying to America to deal with an evil man had niggled at her from the moment he said it. When he invited her over, she reasoned that he wanted comfort and, possibly, her insight. Now she began to think the reverse: *My bigger job will be to constantly explain my quirky husband to these people.*

"So you've figured out what's going on here?" Henry asked.

"Let's see. The Mexican — Peter told me about him — came to see you after the Denver incident. He was grateful to you. You saved his life."

"I wouldn't say that."

"Peter did. Señor Mariana thought it would be a nice gesture to supply you with some cocaine for your aches and pains. Mr. Tynan wanted to cut off that supply chain, so he asked you to pick me up at the airport while he met with the Mexican gentleman. Oh, to be a fly on the wall for that conversation. Unfortunately, he was still here when we arrived. That wasn't in the plan."

"Exactly right. I expect that José resisted being told what to do, but Tynan's a very persuasive guy."

Joan found a fresh shirt in the closet and helped Henry put it on. "One thing I can't figure out, Henry, is why Detective Mohlman wasn't distressed when he encountered Señor Mariana a few minutes ago. But I suppose the Mexican is just another criminal to him."

"It's a little more complicated than that. Where do you think Tynan got José's phone number? Phil's a good guy, but he keeps some distance from our pursuit of Devereau. He hopes to get back to being a street detective, so he's careful about our obsession. But you can be sure he'll do his best to help us. Devereau wounded him, too."

Joan faced him. "Henry, the cocaine is gone for good. You and I will make sure it doesn't get in your way again. Can we agree on that?"

He murmured, "Yup."

Her next words sounded more portentous than she wanted. "Peter's endgame requires that you be there for him."

They returned together to the living area to find that Mohlman and the Mexican had both departed. Although Peter was absent, she was starting to situate him in this extreme world of hunters, hunted, and wounded. She understood that, to varying extents, these men took their cues from Peter; he was their leader. By association, she would take on a role, too. She had meant what she said to Henry: Peter would need him clean and sober — no more white powder or green elixir. She would be his monitor, his scold, and the peculiar Mr. Tynan would back her up. She had landed in a house of damaged men: she had never seen so many scars.

The afternoon was ebbing and Joan wasn't up for more long conversations. She unpacked in the room Peter was using and hung her outfits next to the garish Hawaiian shirt she had forced him to bring. It made her smile. She sniffed it: he had worn it at least once. She was eager to greet the John Ford landscapes of the West, though she wondered if any part of the next few weeks would feel anything like a vacation.

She was considering a call to Leeds when the telephone in the outer room rang. She heard Henry talking, and a minute later he came to fetch her.

"Hello, dear," came Peter's calm voice. "You arrived okay?"

The rush of her own emotion surprised her. "Are you safe, Peter?"

"Safe? No place safer than the ADX Florence."

"You got the name?" she said.

"Yes. I gave it to Henry. I'll tell you everything when I get there, which should be tomorrow afternoon, early after lunch. I have to

320

touch base with the Hollis Street task force and a fellow called Rogers at the Drug Enforcement Administration in Salt Lake."

Joan was pleased at his openness and the intimation that he was indeed handing off the search to the authorities.

"Have you had a chance to see any of the Utah desert, dear?"

"No, but I've met a drug dealer, two injured detectives, and the very odd Elder Tynan."

She rang off cheerily. Henry announced that he was off to pick up dinner. He grinned at her for the first time. She pledged to eat whatever he bought and warned him in a motherly tone to drive carefully.

With the house suddenly quiet, Joan looked around the place, easily identifying the touches that were Theresa's. Henry hadn't turned it into a shrine, but on the other hand he had done little to clean up the rooms. It remained a sad house.

She opened the glass doors and walked out onto the sand. The immense distances at every compass point, so unlike well-groomed England, resounded with both possibility and loneliness. The beauty, especially the light, won her over to America, at least this portion of it. Quicker than most visitors, she grasped the paradox of the West. It was a place that encouraged contemplation, but while you communed with nature you might easily lose yourself in solitude.

Henry returned with too much Tex-Mex takeout. They sat at the dining room table, and he delighted in identifying the dishes: enchiladas, *tacos de lengua*, bean dip, *albondigas* soup, *arroz con pollo*. He talked openly of Theresa, and Joan was content to listen to his how-we-met stories. Without her prompting, he again swore off cocaine and absinthe. She wanted to believe him, and so she grinned back at him.

At 8:30, jet-lagged, she went off to sleep in the guest room. She left a note by the front door just in case Peter returned that night, telling him to wake her.

Three hours later, in the heaviness of complete darkness, she drifted out of sleep. Her eyes adjusted to the high window, and she was able to grope to the door. She missed Jasper. The glow from the under-counter lights in the kitchen directed her along the hushed corridor. A hundred wild species lurked out there, most of them benign, and she wished her biologist daughter were there to name them. The thought of intrepid Sarah made her bold. She flipped the switch on the patio flood and opened the heavy door, leaving the screen shut while she tested the nighttime desert. Silence reigned. She opened the screen and stepped onto the patio and waited. Red eyes looked back at her from twenty feet or so beyond the rim of the light. Sarah would know who was watching her.

Joan noticed for the first time how the dryness made the air tolerable, pleasant, but she didn't dare walk farther out into the unfamiliar badlands. She returned to the kitchen and took a bottle of water from the fridge. Closing the door, she saw the bird standing in the living room. He was over two feet in length, with a long, straight tail. She knew he was a roadrunner. *Sarah will be proud of me.* She had her mobile and might have snapped a picture and sent it to Joe in England, but she didn't want to alarm the bird. The roadrunner flapped onto the big table and nibbled at a few dinner crumbs. His brown-and-white speckling provided excellent camouflage, she thought; traces of blue feathering marked his breast and belly. With a *coo* and a clatter of its long beak, the creature hopped down and raced out the door.

She was in the mood for omens and signs, even if she had to look them up. A well-thumbed *Peterson Field Guide to Birds of Western North America* sat on the shelf next to the computer stand. She had been visited by the state bird of New Mexico, she discovered. In Hopi Indian culture, the roadrunner protected the tribe against evil spirits: he was good luck. She turned on Henry's computer, went right to her email, and relayed this information to Sarah and Maddy in short messages. In a breathtaking two minutes, the insomniacal Maddy fired back: "What are you doing up at this hour?" In six more minutes, Sarah wrote, "Congratulations. You had an encounter with a sacred bird. *Geococcyx californianus*. Go with it!"

Joan strolled outside to the far rim of the light pool. Not that she was following the roadrunner, but its spirit drew her to the sand.

When Peter had emailed her about arrangements for her journey, he suggested she read *The Teachings of Don Juan* on the plane. "Carlos Castaneda is an old fraud, but you might enjoy it." The tome, she knew, was about solitude, contemplation, and self-realization. Did Peter know how much he was like the ancient Don Juan?

CHAPTER 41

On the way home from Denver, Peter reported the name Kelso Vyne to Furst and Ordway, who currently operated out of the Utah Bureau of Investigation offices in SLC, and to Rogers at the DEA branch. The dyspeptic drug investigator, though he still resented being snubbed by Avelino González at the bizarre Wendover session, was probably best positioned to monitor narcotics-linked incidents across Western jurisdictions.

Ordway called the Coppermount house the next morning to report that their suspect was born in Monroe, Kansas. He had no criminal record under Kelso Vyne, but Peter was pleased that the authorities could now focus on one name linked to a birthplace. This somehow crystallized the manhunt for them. Now if only they could obtain a verifiable photo of their ghost.

On the fifth day after Peter's return from the Florence Supermax, New Mexico State Police came close to nabbing Vyne in Albuquerque when he and three armed men held up a small-time meth distributor and relieved him of his roll of cash and a stash of meth. The NMSP's Clandestine Lab Team, working out of Santa Fe, had been watching the dealer in the hope that he would lead them to his factory source, and were infuriated when Vyne spoiled their surveillance. Furst and Ordway drove down and briefed the New Mexicans about Vyne.

For Joan Cammon, the next fortnight floated past with surprisingly little tension. Each day was full. She and Peter and Henry established a compact under which the men vowed to share everything that had happened in Colorado. In daily sessions at the dining room table, documents spread on chairs and all about the floor, the three of them revisited the facts, theories, and rumours that swirled around Kelso Vyne. They all became experts on the Watson murders. It was the best they could make of the waiting game.

Joan and Peter took their vacation in the form of day trips from Coppermount Drive to the national parks to the south; three times, Henry came along, and they stayed overnight in motels. They toured the Arches, Canyonlands, Zion, and Monument Valley. Joan enjoyed every minute. She had needed this trip, for Peter's full retirement had left her at sixes and sevens, although the arrival of Joe had filled her heart and kept her busy. She hoped to reset the marriage, knowing that this could be Peter's last case and, if he still believed what he had told her that day at the cottage, his last chance to do battle with evil before lapsing (his word) into retirement. A summons from the centre of the United States was a funny kind of courtship, she had to admit, but he had seduced her.

Joan became Henry's nurse and confidante. She changed his bandages daily and accompanied him to physio sessions in Salt Lake. By the middle of the second week, Henry could comfortably flex his left shoulder. He remained underweight but ongoing heartache partly explained that, and she didn't fret. More worrisome were the nights she found him weeping on the patio. With her help, the desert became a therapy pool for him. They walked along the dunes, or sometimes up and down the roughed-in streets of the housing development. As she talked him through the stages of grief, she grew to love the desert. She didn't see the roadrunner again.

As Joan took over these ministrations, Tynan visited less often, but

325

Joan and Peter often saw him, a mere dot on the horizon, searching for Lord knew what in the Utah barrens.

"Would you call him a mystic?" she asked.

"I suppose, if you mean a Mormon mystic with a hammer," Peter suggested.

Joan wasn't ready to label Tynan a hermit. He wasn't terribly reclusive, however quirky his roaming ways. He had an ascetic streak, for sure, but also loved his truck and his tractor and had been labouring well before Henry and Theresa had moved into the big house up the street.

Without Tynan or José around, the Coppermount household became a tad dull. Peter and Joan's sleeping patterns began to clash. She liked to stay up late to watch the sunset, while he was usually awake to mark the dawn. One evening, Joan caught sight of Tynan strolling way out towards the vanishing point, and she walked out to waylay him. She halted and breathed deeply; to her, recently of the damp Cotswolds, the air was a potion.

"I know what you're thinking, Mrs. Cammon," Tynan said.

"'Joan' is better. But I don't know your first name."

"It's Thomas Abraham."

"And what am I thinking?"

"You're wondering how you ended up in the company of all these wounded men."

He had it right.

"I focus on my husband. He's not nursing any wounds and he knows what he's doing. You're correct, though, about the others, that's what I thought the first day. Now what I think is this: All these men are survivors, and Peter relies on them just as they follow him. Therefore, they have earned my loyalty. I place my trust in Henry and Phil. I even trust José."

"True of all of them. I trust your husband most. I also worry about him most."

Not a mystic, perhaps, but definitely a philosopher. And he's a wounded man, too, even as he conceals the reason. "What does that mean?"

326

"Peter understands better than the others what a police detective must do. He's ready to make the tough decisions. Mohlman's like that too. I have no doubt Peter will be present at the finale with Devereau. He's driving towards the climax of this case, and even the Fates won't deny him his destiny. Imagine trying to find a killer who leaves no fingerprints and no photographs. I hear that the name Kelso Vyne hasn't turned up much. Even so, Peter will find him. That's what I'm waiting for."

"Even before he came over here, Peter told me that he was coming to deal with evil. Do you think Vyne qualifies as evil?"

Tynan nodded. "But Peter wants the evil of this man to be pure, unadulterated, easy to condemn."

"He never was quick to forgive where murderers were concerned," she mused.

"But tell me if I'm wrong, Joan. As he grinds away at a case, he learns from the things he discovers along the way, the mitigating and aggravating factors, the human dimension. It's not that he's particularly warm and fuzzy, it's that the humanizing of the criminal helps him make the arrest. That's what makes him a great policeman. But what happens to Peter's method when he starts by announcing that his man is evil? Maybe Peter is afraid that humanizing Devereau at this point will dilute his resolution."

She wasn't sure what to say. "He's restless, that's for sure."

The amazing spectrum created by the setting sun, red and gold and indigo, had made them contemplative.

"Of course, Vyne is a psychopath," Tynan said.

"I shouldn't disclose this, but Peter has started a biography of Kelso Vyne."

But Tynan appeared to be stuck in his own train of thought. "Psychopathy isn't considered a medical category in the *Diagnostic and Statistical Manual*."

She shrugged. "That suits Peter fine. Mental illness won't save him from Peter or Henry or Phil. Peter hasn't much use for the psychiatric profession in any case. He's thinking in terms of evil."

"In Mormon theology, the most significant moral principle is Agency, based on the idea that human beings will inevitably encounter good and evil in their lives and will have to choose between them. Before humanity was created, good and evil were at war in Heaven, in a battle between Satan and God. Humans will be called upon to involve themselves in a mortal and a *divine* struggle."

"Does that authorize the pursuit of revenge?"

"Mormonism is like any other faith. It doesn't countenance revenge or vigilantism."

The air remained steamy; there was no breeze. Joan noted again that Tynan's forehead remained dry, while hers was beaded with sweat. She wondered about the rest of him: under that swathing, did he perspire? In the twilight, his face remained pale, and Joan concluded that Tynan suffered from some form of skin disease. But she couldn't place it. Erysipelas? Melanoma?

"Forgive my asking, Thomas, but are you well?"

There they stood in the empty plain, like two hermits debating doom and divine judgement. Tynan swung about and looked at her. A tear formed and ran down his otherwise dry face.

"I have an ailment called Ross syndrome. It's a disease of the autonomic nervous system, characterized by anhydrosis."

"The inability to sweat."

"Yes, but with Ross, it affects only certain areas of the body — in my case, everything above the neck. To compensate, the rest of me perspires twice as much as normal."

"Can they treat it?"

"Not really. There are medications, but I rarely take them. You see, I abused narcotics in my youth, and that contributed to my . . . problem."

He almost said "curse," Joan detected.

With his sweat glands out of balance, the sun threatened heat stroke. Joan couldn't imagine that the LDS church had shown much sympathy for his addiction. His expiation was to walk the wilderness and endure the furnace heat.

"Is it safe for you out here?"

"I mostly walk at night. Too hot in the day."

His answer evaded her point. "Peter and Henry see you in the day," she replied.

"Only when the need for atonement seizes me."

CHAPTER 42

It was Joan who insisted on the Great Salt Lake when no one else wanted to go. "It's an icon, they named the city after it. We should go."

There were never two men less in the mood for iconic time wasters. Henry, who hadn't sailed the lake since his teenage years, declared that "it stinks." Peter saw no need to play tourist again. Joan argued that she had had her fill of rock formations, "and the lake will be different."

She made an expedition of it, inviting Tynan and Phil Mohlman along; the detective demurred, saying that his leg was distressing him, but the Mormon Elder accepted. Joan fixed the outing for the next Monday and reserved two motorboats from a marina on Antelope Island. That morning, she and Henry packed the F-150 for an 11 a.m. departure, but Peter, who had left the house in Henry's Subaru before she got up, did not return until quarter to noon.

Peter had failed to inform Joan that he was dropping by Hollis Street, because he couldn't have justified his impulse. The night before the trip to the Salt Lake, he had hauled out Henry's first-round interview notes in the hope of discovering something new. Their notice in the

Deseret Star had produced no response, and Furst and Ordway ("Futile Headway," Mohlman now called them) hadn't nabbed their quarry. He remained convinced that the key to the massacre lay hidden inside the Hollis Street community. Hollis was the street where nobody knew anything — from Maude Hampson at one end to the Wazinskis at the bottom of the cul-de-sac. They had sunk back into complacency, creepier now that fire had hollowed out one property and two others were being referred to by real estate brokers as haunted houses.

What was the absolute, basic reality of the street? Jerry Proffet's chart was a treasure map, an archaeologist's schema, a brainteaser. Peter stared at it for ten minutes, and then saw it: the essence of the Hollis layout was its sightlines. Every resident could spy on every other. Ronald Devereau entered the houses at 3 and 5 in full view of every inhabitant, if only they had been looking. He carried Gabriella's body across no man's land and loaded Tom Watson's corpse into his truck there in the driveway. So who was in the best position to observe not only the murders that night but the grow operation over the preceding year? Peter ruled out Maude Hampson, who confused real life with her soap operas. Stan Chambers had been re-interviewed but had added nothing useful.

But there at Number 10 lived Carleton Davis, almost the closest neighbour.

He dug out Henry's notes from the day after the murders. His questioning of Davis had been astute. The one-eyed Vietnam vet had resisted, expressing little sympathy for Gabriella Watson and denying that he had observed any untoward activity. This was interesting: Davis guessed that the killer had beheaded her — Henry had commented, "I never had a witness guess a decapitation" — and went on to speculate that the murder houses contained "buckets of blood." Perhaps sensing that he was sounding too insightful about the crime scene, Davis changed the subject: he mused at length on Tom Watson's grow op, calling it "small-scale competition" for the big drug dealers. Here was a man who knew an awful lot about his neighbour's cottage business.

331

Peter had no intention of accusing Carleton Davis of conspiring with Kelso Vyne to eliminate the grow operation, but maybe a forced tour of the Second House would shake up his memory. Peter wondered if Carleton and Vyne were keeping in touch.

The visit proved uneventful. Davis masked his surprise at Peter's foray with a curmudgeonly denunciation of the police. He declined Peter's invitation to a private tour of Number 5, flattering as it might be. "I don't want *my* privacy invaded; why would I abuse the Watsons' privacy?" Peter departed convinced that Carleton Davis hadn't conspired with the killer.

But one small thing stuck in Peter's detective brain. Phil Mohlman had furnished the combination for the lock box at Number 5, but when Peter climbed the stairs at the Second House to check it out, he found a notice declaring, "The West Valley Narcotics Unit controls access to this site." He was left to consider why DeKlerk rather than Homicide had continued in this custodial role.

Joan made him change into his Hawaiian shirt. The foursome drove north from Salt Lake City and followed the signs to the shore of the massive lake, crossing into the state park as the sun was reaching its zenith.

The Great Salt Lake, which in 1847 caused Brigham Young to halt his wagons and declare that here he would build a great temple and a city to go with it, may have persuaded Young's road-weary acolytes but was a hard sell to modern tourists. Once they got over their amusement at being able to float on its saline waters, visitors found little to do except rinse themselves off and gaze at the 1,500-square-mile expanse of brine and dull shoreline. There were no fish. Bird watchers fared better, charting pelicans by the hundreds, cormorants, gulls, and herons, all feasting on the endless supply of saltwater shrimp.

The setting was peaceful, and Joan intrepidly led them out into the channel by Antelope Island, she and Peter in one small boat and Henry and Tynan putt-putting behind in the other. She made sure that Tynan wore a floppy straw hat with his white shirt and black pants, thereby shaping the group to resemble a Renoir boating party by way of Whistler and Don Ho. Peter and Henry sat immobile and bored in the forward seats. Joan was the only one to read the plaque on the dock listing all the flora and fauna inhabiting the island, and consequently she was not surprised to see a shaggy, full-grown American bison walking the shoreline of the park.

They floated alone on the inland sea. The fact that the Great Salt Lake had no outlet made it feel frozen in time. One section of the coast was as bleak as another; white salt deposits coated the shore, recalling rime on the parched mouth of a castaway, or — Joan hoped Henry's thoughts didn't drift this way — cocaine around the nostrils of an addict. But she began to appreciate the subtle variations in the Dead Sea of the West. In many spots, the still water formed dense wetlands that provided havens for flocks of birds. She turned off the motor and watched a turkey buzzard ride a high thermal on the windward side of a set of burnt hills. She would look up the Latin names when she got back and email them to Sarah.

Joan had been monitoring Peter closely over the last two weeks and had begun to worry that he was retreating into himself. "Where did you go this morning?" she asked, non-confrontationally.

Peter's smile was conciliatory. "Over to Hollis Street. I should have told you I was going. I needed to get back in touch with the crime that started it all. I guess I can't believe that Vyne lost it like that after ten years of living quietly in the suburbs."

"Psychopaths don't mend, you've said it yourself. Did you visit the grow house?"

"Briefly. Mainly I went to talk to Carleton Davis."

"At Number 10?"

"Right. Maybe it didn't matter who I reconnected with, but Davis was one of the more straightforward residents, it seemed to me. He lived nearby and served on the executive committee. I thought I might prompt memories."

"Did Davis recall anything?"

Peter shrugged, causing the boat to wobble. "He did admit that he had heard Tom Watson arguing with someone in the middle of the night, about three weeks before the murders."

"What was Davis doing up in the middle of the night?"

"He was an MP in Danang during Vietnam and often worked the night shift. Old habits. I wonder what was so urgent that Watson had to be confronted at that time of night."

"Does Davis think Watson and Vyne were partnering?"

"He never went that far. Perhaps Davis was a poor choice, but I wanted to get the neighbours talking again. I'm sure they were watching."

Joan saw that Tynan had turned off his motor but slyly stayed in earshot. "I know you want to keep up your momentum, Peter, but it's time to let the police agencies handle this."

He gave her a harsh look, but she didn't back down.

"I've got half the country searching," he said.

"Peter, don't you see? I read *Fire and Brimstone*. You're dealing with a lonely, repressed misfit. You and Henry tried to track him down. Well, now is different. No more cowboy rigmarole. You have Henry and Mohlman and Brockhurst and Maddy to consider."

"I agree."

"You know what else, Peter? This is about you and your brother and your father. You say you discovered that they both had a Good War. They were part of big, historical efforts where they made themselves indispensable. Well, dear, you need to absorb the fact that you had a Good War for forty-five years. Bartleben, Tommy, the whole Yard relied on you for the collective good. Don't go off on your own tack."

Embarrassed, Peter smiled and said, "You sound almost Churchillian."

Joan awkwardly came forward and kissed him.

Both boats had drifted to the centre of the bay, far from the marina. Henry's shout crossed the water. "Hey there!"

Joan and Peter turned to see Henry standing in the small boat. He pulled off his shirt. Joan expected him to vault into the water, where the brine would certainly excoriate his almost healed wounds. Henry ripped off his shoulder bandage and tossed it over the bow, but didn't jump. Tynan, Joan perceived, was about to call out to him, but then the Mormon Elder stood up in the stern, putting both men in peril. He stripped off his own shirt, leaving the two men like hapless sailors in a tub.

Tynan displayed the most epic body tattoo Joan and Peter, both familiar with mortuary slabs, had ever seen. Even at this remove, Joan could see that his skin, neck to waist and probably lower, told the Mormon saga in full. Wagon trains rolled, cathedrals reached to the clouds, and choirs gathered. Even Lucifer was represented, crouching on Tynan's left shoulder. Bared to the sun, his body cascaded sweat. Only Joan understood how difficult this revelation was for him. Tattooing, in LDS teachings, was considered a desecration of the body, like graffiti defacing the human temple. She now understood something more about his neurological affliction: it had probably been caused by the ink.

On a sand dune on the Antelope Island shore, a narrow-faced figure watched the boats through a pair of powerful military binoculars. He didn't know or care about the tattooed man. The tall, half-naked cop and the short man in the flowered shirt were more interesting. He had seen them eye-to-eye in Denver, and the latter was the one Carleton Davis had called him about.

CHAPTER 43

Joan immediately, giddily pronounced the expedition a success, though it ended with Tynan and Henry, in sun-stricken euphoria, comparing battle scars while standing stripped to the waist in their small boat.

In her enthusiasm, she declared that they should organize a Western barbecue on Henry's patio and invite everyone Henry knew. He and Peter exchanged looks: neither could imagine Boog DeKlerk, Chief Grady, and Furst and Ordway rubbing shoulders without gunplay breaking out. Joan, a little sun-addled, was ready for their skepticism. "You two have been anti-social for too long. No shoptalk will be allowed. A real dinner party, then?"

Tynan jumped in. "I volunteer my place."

Peter nearly crashed the truck. No one but Henry had ever visited Tynan's work-in-progress, and he had seen only the outside, reporting to Joan and Peter that the house seemed a bit eccentric. (There had been a hint that Theresa had been in Tynan's house a few times.)

Tynan pressed Joan's case. "This is a great idea. Invite Detective Mohlman, and how about that Officer Jackson?"

"I didn't know you'd ever met Jackson," Henry said.

"That's the point, Henry." Joan said. "We want to meet new people."

In the end, the guest list narrowed to Phil Mohlman and Officer Jackson and his wife. Phil said he wouldn't attend if Boog DeKlerk did. Peter was glad not to have Furst and Ordway coming, suspecting that the state detectives would be uncomfortable as long as Vyne remained at large. Officer Jackson accepted the invitation immediately and said that he would bring along his wife, thereby adding some balance (civilian, gender) to the guest list.

On the day of the barbecue, Joan and Peter left Coppermount in the F-150 to shop for supplies. As they turned onto Highway 15, Peter said, "Why do you think Tynan volunteered his house?"

Joan gave him her you're-the-bleedin'-detective stare. "Tynan is learning to relax with us, I'd say. He's decided to be sociable. He bought a giant grill to cook whatever wildlife Henry is out roping. Whatever the house is like, say you *love* it."

"Understood."

Tynan had become the shepherd of Coppermount Drive. Sometimes his flock consisted of Henry alone but, as Joan and Peter agreed, his optimism probably kept the thinly populated neighbourhood alive. Whatever monastic compulsion set him walking in the desert, his mission evidently was to monitor and protect the inchoate community.

The slow pace of their lives in Utah occasionally made Joan forget the unresolved horror of Hollis Street. It rushed back now. She turned to her husband. "Do you still intend to kill him?"

Had Sir Stephen Bartleben or another colleague at the Yard asked this question, Peter would have replied, "I don't expect to get the chance." Even a year ago, he would have said the same to Joan. But not now. They shared a feeling that they had been in the West too long without results. They had a precise purpose in America, or at least Peter did. This gathering at Tynan's house was important to both Peter and Joan as a celebration of friendship, but at the table would be most of the officers who had been drawn to Hollis Street that fateful day when Officer Jackson found the poodle soaked in blood. The manhunt would hover above them all until resolved. The chief inspector owed these people an honest answer, starting with Joan.

"He has to be eliminated."

Joan wouldn't let it go. "I find it odd that you've been preparing to kill a man you've never met."

Peter could only nod in reply. "Not only a ghost, but a ghost from two decades ago." This answer was evasive, and he gave himself a minute to consider his bottom line. "Henry needs closure, and perhaps I do too. You should know — and the same goes for Phil and Henry — I'm ready to kill the bastard on sight."

It was the evening of the dinner, and Joan was chopping salad "fixins" in Henry's kitchen. Henry himself was off in his Subaru, shopping for steaks and whatever else Tynan's new barbecue could hold. Joan remained heightened to the haunting forces in play at this dinner, including the spirits of Theresa, the victims from Hollis Street, and Avelino González. The detectives at the party carried the scars of Hollis each in his own way, and each had agreed not to talk business tonight (and by "business" they meant death). For Joan, a positive mood was irresistible. Everything was so *American*. Every setting in Utah sprawled generously in a way that it never did in Britain and this dinner ranged with distinctly American energy from Henry's house down to Tynan's. Life seemed benignly peaceful on the desert's edge. The sand threatened to erode the existing houses and the paced-out lots, but no one worried, for tomorrow the wind would carry the sand tidally away.

The wastelands no longer intimidated her. She might even take a torch out into the dunes tonight.

Peter had asked Phil Mohlman to bring the most exotic Belgian beer he could find in Salt Lake City, but the Bostonian hadn't arrived, and Peter was getting thirsty. The doorbell rang. Joan put her knife on the counter and went to the door. Officer Jackson, in civilian clothes, came in with his wife, a thin woman in a white sundress, beautiful and beaming, whom he introduced as Wanda. Peter and

Joan had the same thought: how nice it was to have spirited, and unscarred, youth in the house.

Henry followed a minute later. "I dropped the steaks and some booze down at Tynan's. Along with my Subaru, since our drive is filling up."

"Then why didn't you stay down there?" Peter said — a rational question, but the words came out wrong.

The women laughed, and so did Henry.

"Yeah, Henry," Joan said, "what are you doing hanging around your own house?"

Henry pulled the collar of his shirt to one side. "I opened something lifting the box of liquor and supplies. We have to re-bandage."

"I'll do it," Wanda said. "I'm a nurse."

"So am I," Joan said, "but it will go faster with two of us."

There followed a bizarre re-draping of Henry's left shoulder by the two women right there in the kitchen, while Officer Jackson and Peter stared. Topless, Henry sat on a chair to be ministered to by a team of women in white. They might have been fabricating a plaster of Paris Adonis, or wrapping Henry for mailing.

Peter wasn't entirely at ease as temporary maître d' in Henry's home. He apologized for not having any beer to offer Jackson, and Henry apologized for the absence of hard stuff, which was down at Tynan's. Jackson said he was content with soda water. Finishing with Henry, even buttoning his shirt for him, Joan gathered up the flowers the Jacksons had brought and assigned everyone a load for the safari to Tynan's folly.

"I'll wait for Phil here, and we'll walk down with the beer," Peter said. Joan looked for signs that their conversation in the truck had upset him, and he in turn signalled that this would be a carefree evening without, as Joan had stated in adopted Americanese, "shoptalk."

But, perhaps from a lack of beer in his bloodstream, Peter started up as soon as Phil entered Henry's house. "It bothers me that Boog still controls access to the grow house on Hollis."

"The lock box? I think it's innocent. The Drug Squad has the superior claim to supervise the grow op house at Number 5. After all, it's an active crime site as long as the case remains unsolved. Besides, Boog stepped up to the plate. He's rousted every drug dealer in Salt Lake City to identify Tom Watson's network."

"I'm speculating," Peter conceded.

Phil gave Peter a harsh, dismissive look. He'd really wanted to avoid theorizing tonight. His leg ached. He took out two of the Belgian brews and cracked them open. "You don't mind warm beer, do you?" he said, taking a swig. "Let's talk turkey, Cammon. What you're suggesting is that Boog knew Devereau was the killer of the Watsons."

"I didn't go that far," Peter fired back.

"Well, the answer is no. Yeah, he probably did know about the grow house. He monitors every ounce of Mary Jane traded in West Valley. But how could he admit that to Grady? Watson couldn't have been smaller potatoes, so Boog ignored him. Those plastic bags of grass the killer left behind? Boog concluded that was all Watson had produced that week."

With this standoff, neither man ready to rehash the whole case, they picked up the beer cartons and headed down the slope. Phil turned to Peter. "I want you to know, Peter, I've decided to stay in Utah. I'm not going back to Boston." Peter muttered in acknowledgement of his peace gesture.

When they reached Tynan's place, the women were gushing over the brilliance of his design. It turned out that Tynan possessed taste and his emerging creation was shaping up to be a showpiece. The rooms displayed the best of Western and Native sensibility, with exquisite weavings, Zuni pottery, and deep-carved furniture suited to a Mexican grandee. The sun at dusk deepened the apricot and pumpkin colours of the walls.

Peter was given no time to admire the décor before he was pushed outside for the much-anticipated exterior tour. The plans of the house had forced some compliance with the other homes in the stalled development, but Tynan, with no fear of county assessors coming by, had made the changes he wanted. Each modification was an improvement on the standard blueprints.

Tynan had enlarged the standard patio windows beyond what Henry enjoyed in his house, so that a guest sitting in the living room felt little difference between indoors and the outside. Oddly, there was no piazza like Henry's, merely a small wooden platform holding a barbecue, and beyond that sand and cactus. Peter supposed that Tynan, taking off on his nighttime strolls, preferred to step directly into the wilds, without transition.

The biggest surprise was the widow's walk the Mormon had added. It wasn't quite the captain's walk that Phil Mohlman recalled from New England coastal houses, since it clung to the back slope of the roof rather than the peak, but it allowed the observer on the platform to scan miles across the arid ocean. Inside, the guests climbed an iron spiral staircase — taking turns, since the quad at the top was only ten feet square — to admire the panorama.

"I was in touch with the developers this week," Tynan said to Henry and Peter as they descended from the platform. "They sent a man out at my invitation, and he liked what he saw of our row, with your place looking good, Henry, and mine nearing completion. He says the company will finish the two units between our houses this year and, with luck, move on to the other blocks. The recession in our community may actually be behind us."

This might be Tynan's folly, Peter concluded, but the Mormon was admirably committed to the neighbourhood.

At the long dinner table, Wanda and Joan each found a tissue-wrapped package on her placemat. Wanda's was a small coyote fashioned in coral.

"It's a Zuni fetish object," Tynan said. "The coyote represents laughter and mischief."

Wanda smiled and saluted Tynan with her glass of wine. Tynan and Henry weren't drinking, and Mohlman stayed with beer. No one drank hard stuff.

Joan opened her package to reveal a hummingbird carved in jasper. Peter had a start as he thought of the broken-winged polymer drone left behind by Ronald Devereau.

"The hummingbird is for peace. Also, he can stop time," Tynan said, and Joan smiled. Tynan declared, "I'm sorry, no roadrunner. It's not a traditional fetish animal." Joan flashed Peter a how-did-he-know-about-that look.

Phil reached over and picked up the young policeman's name card. "It says 'Officer Jackson.' That confirms it: Jackson has no first name."

"It's George Theodore," Jackson said. "All my names are presidents."

"My middle name is Abraham," Tynan added. "Another president."

Peter chimed in. "My father was named George Frederick, after Handel. He despised Handel's music and didn't like Germans much."

"Hallelujah," Jackson said, getting a laugh from Joan and Henry.

Wanda Jackson leaned forward and spoke with mock solemnity. "I have you all beat. My middle name is Nevada."

"Not Utah?" Phil said.

"No. My father and mother were watching a movie called *Wanda Nevada* the night I was . . . conceived. Wanda was played by Brooke Shields. Do I look like Brooke Shields?"

The mood remained jocular, muted a notch, in Peter's view, by the fact that the four policemen had Kelso Vyne on their minds. Tynan flirted with the two women. Henry remained quiet, content to watch. The Jacksons held hands. Peter sat back, the sun almost extinguished now, and mused on the confluence of fate. Henry had lost his wife, but now friends from the far-flung world had mobilized around him, not least of all Joan, who had broken through Henry's grief with a natural ease that Peter could not match. Peter and Joan had somehow been destined for this place, and he was happy. He didn't mind that they represented a fading generation, while Jackson and his wife were the future (both were Utah-born, young, and black). Perhaps there was too much baggage, too much old news haunting the Pastern house up the road, but Peter knew that friendship, two generations of it here tonight, was the key to Henry's renewal. Tynan, in whose house they were communally gathered, looked over at Peter. He knew these truths, too.

But Peter was bothered by another thought. If Peter's summing-up was correct, where did Henry Pastern himself fit in this cosmos?

CHAPTER 44

Joan announced that she had forgotten the whipped cream for the dessert, and Wanda agreed to accompany her to Henry's house to get it.

With the women gone, the four cops and Elder Tynan couldn't help drifting to the object of the manhunt. As detective emeritus at the table, Peter might have presided over the conversation, but he consciously held back. He was restive, uncertain about something he couldn't quite pin down. For, two nights ago, Peter had seen José Mariana's big black Escalade slowly cruising the neighbourhood around Coppermount; it hadn't stopped, nor had the driver seemed to spy Peter. Was it possible that the Mexican bodyguard was still supplying Henry with cocaine, Peter had wondered? He doubted it, nor could he believe that José was in league with Kelso Vyne in any way. Peter was a good judge of hard men, and José was a benign force when it came to Henry and Peter. Once a bodyguard, always a bodyguard?

But Peter saw no way of introducing this variable without spoiling the camaraderie around the table. Now Mohlman filled the void.

"What do we think about the trail of robberies that Vyne has launched since Denver? We've all been beating the bushes. Furst and Ordway are watching Utah, Arizona, and Colorado, and all of

ViCAP. Rogers at DEA is taking care of the feds. We've got all levels covered, seems to me, but how are we going to catch him?"

Jackson showed that he had been paying attention. "There was a drug heist last week in Tempe that Ordway thinks resembles Vyne's MO."

Peter broke in. "Brockhurst at the Kansas Highway Patrol has been monitoring everything in his jurisdiction, given the Crispin Breach and Wichita incidents. Vyne seems to like Kansas."

Henry had been listening with equanimity. "Peter, we talked the other day about whether Devereau is panicking. He can't be reaping much profit from raids on these cheapjack drug operations. Is it worth the risk to him? Does everyone think he's lost it?"

Phil, somewhat irritably, Peter thought, summed up the consensus. "Henry, it's not that he's panicking. Vyne's still the same vicious bastard he was before. The thing is, he's moving fast, and we have to keep up the pressure. Maybe we should put Homeland Security in charge. They can spread a bigger net."

Jackson glanced at Henry. "I don't want to speak out of turn. I don't know, gentlemen, but I was there in Number 3 with Henry and Phil . . ."

Mohlman, who had taken a liking to Jackson, said, "You were the first on the crime scene."

Jackson proceeded: "We all hold the picture in our minds of the head in the trash in the Second House. It was the handiwork of a madman. But Number 3 was worse in some ways. It was a *home*, furnished, decorated, lived in. The man who slaughtered Gabriella Watson was way out of control. He couldn't stop himself. He was intent on punishment and desecration from the moment he knocked on that aluminum door. Detective Mohlman is right. Why would he change?"

"The motive for what he did has always evaded me," Phil commented shaking his head.

"He's psycho. I think he's capable of anything," Jackson added, thinking of the pools of blood in both houses.

Peter, having had several bottles of beer, unwisely said to Jackson,

"Did you know that DeKlerk continues to control the lock box at Number 5?"

Phil glared at him. "Yes. Furst and Ordway have enlisted me to check on the Watson residence from time to time. Number 5 remains part of the active Drug Squad investigation under DeKlerk's old group. I hope you're not suggesting again that Boog knew the killer's identity all along."

"No," Peter said. He knew that he was off base continuing to provoke Mohlman on the lock box details, but more and more he found himself thinking of Boog DeKlerk. He backed off for the moment. "You're right, Phil, DeKlerk is merely fighting to save his career. If he knew anything about Vyne's whereabouts, why wouldn't he turn him in and score points?" He paused and added, "I still think one or more residents knew about the drug operation on their street and may have suspected Vyne of killing the Watsons . . ."

"We interviewed them multiple times," Phil responded. Peter had gone too far in implicitly criticizing West Valley Homicide's work. Mohlman stood up. "I'm going for a walk." He strode out to the darkness of Coppermount Drive.

Tynan, who had kept silent for a long time, said, "I'm surprised Joan and Wanda aren't back." He began to clear the table.

Less than two minutes after Phil's departure, a shotgun blast opened up the desert silence. Peter and the other men turned to the source of the shooting.

The back of Henry's house.

Peter instantly knew that it was Kelso Vyne. He further grasped that Vyne had seen the ad in the *Deseret Star*. Peter's stratagem had driven him over the edge. Peter, Henry, and Jackson made eye contact, with the same thought.

Guns.

Jackson rushed to the front door, then halted. "I don't have a sidearm with me. My vehicle is parked in your drive, Henry."

Henry, right behind him, said, "Mine's right outside, but there's no weapon in it. There's a .45 in my bedroom."

"My service pistol is in the trunk," Jackson said. "If we can get to it."

"Then that's the call," Henry said, and moved closer to the door.

Jackson raised a finger in caution. "It has to be me. It's fingerprint activated."

Henry looked back at Peter, who shook his head to show that he had no weapon either. Desperation electrified the air. Peter forced the decision, commanding, "Go, Jackson. The explosion was at the back. But your car is in Henry's driveway, so work on getting in the front. Mohlman and I left the door unlocked, but Joan may have secured it. If it's Vyne we're dealing with, his men will have machine pistols, so seek cover every step of the way. Watch for Phil. Henry and I will come in from the desert side."

Peter understood that Jackson might jettison caution and speed to his wife. A frontal assault would make him extremely vulnerable unless Phil was there to back him up; Peter counted on the veteran detective making the right tactical decision. In any case, it would be essential to launch a simultaneous, offsetting attack at the rear to relieve the pressure at the front.

Jackson disappeared out the door.

Peter was their natural leader, the one among them who knew most about killing. But a counter-assault would be futile without guns. Peter ran through shock tactics they might employ. He considered the pros and cons of hitting the panic button on someone's car keys but — there was often a note of farce in a gunfight — realized that the keys to the F-150 were back at Henry's. Mohlman and Jackson were already working their way up the street. Where did that leave a B team consisting of two unarmed cops?

Tynan seemed to have fallen silent, but when Peter turned he wasn't in the room. "Tynan?"

The Mormon Elder returned cradling two shotguns on his forearms and gripping a box of shells in each hand. "What, you didn't take the tour of the gun room in the basement?"

Peter stared at the weapons, momentarily confused. *Why did I think Tynan was a pacifist?* It appeared that neither gun had ever been used, yet both were expensive, top-of-the-line. Peter took the heavy, matte-finish Remington Versa Max and quickly racked the 3.5-inch shells that matched it. When it came to shotguns, Peter was inclined to maximum bang and shock-wave destruction. Henry adopted the lighter 12-gauge Ithaca pump.

"Henry, you ready to go?"

No answer was expected, none offered. Henry was out the back door. "Stay here, Thomas," Peter said.

"No, Chief Inspector. I know the terrain better than any of you."

"You're unarmed."

"It's a big gun room."

Peter's mobile chirped at the same instant that another shotgun blast resonated from the rear of Henry's house, and weirdly through the phone line as well.

Henry leaned back into the doorway. "I'm going ahead."

"Joan?"

She whispered, "Peter, they're trying to get in the back. The glass is down. There's blood spattered everywhere around the door."

"Get out the front."

'No. Someone's trying to break in there too."

Peter stayed calm, estimating the best line of retreat for the women.

"Wanda?"

"We're together. We're okay."

"The front door's not locked."

"We locked it."

"Go to Henry's bedroom."

Peter worked through the only possible last-stand scenario. The women had maybe five minutes before Phil and Officer Jackson — *What's his name? George?* — made it to the front, and another couple of minutes for Henry to reach the patio. "Go to the bedroom! There's a Colt .45 pistol under the bed. There's a safety, a small lever on the side of the gun. Switch it to off. Now, when you shoot, keep shooting. Use the whole clip if you need to. It'll kick and it will be loud. Don't shoot me, Jackson, Phil, or Henry, Joan. We're coming. You can be sure we'll announce ourselves and the shooters won't. Shoot any triggerman who turns the corner."

"Gotta go, Peter."

"Is Wanda beside you?"

"Yes. We're peachy."

Just before Joan killed the connection the next shot came, the noise weirdly reverberating in Peter's ear.

Peter learned about the plight of the women from Joan after it was all over. They had strolled up the road in the dark, Wanda's bright white dress and Joan's white blouse allowing them to find each other in the near-pitch darkness; a glow from the kitchen in Henry's ranch house provided a pinprick beacon. They hardly spoke, taking in the perfect summer air. Dodging around the three dusty vehicles in the laneway, they went in by the unlocked entrance.

Joan proceeded to the kitchen and took a carton of whipping cream and a glass bowl from the fridge. She set up the mixer. Wanda knew all about Theresa Pastern's illness and death, and there was a note of sadness and respect between the women as they acknowledged that they were working with things Theresa had once valued. Wanda took a chilled bottle of Chardonnay from the fridge rack. Joan later surmised that the noise of the mixer might have masked the intruders' approach to the patio. She heard something in the background, she later said, or maybe she was alert to omens, for she glanced over to the patio door and spied a gloved hand slowly reaching towards the latch.

She didn't know whether Henry had locked the glass door.

He had.

The hand withdrew. She hissed at Wanda, "Get down on the floor over here." Both hunkered down, the bar shielding them from the patio entry. A roaring blast assaulted Joan's eardrums, and a cracking of glass seams recalled to her the groaning of a ship. She peered around the bar to see what hell was coming after them. The shotgun charge had crinkled the panel but not quite blown it open. The glass had held, but the pane certainly wasn't shatterproof. She peeked around the bar once more but couldn't see beyond the starred window. A small hole had opened near the top of the frame. The next shot would bring it all down.

"Out the front!" Wanda breathed. She still held the wine bottle.

"Careful," Joan, in front of her, answered. "They must be there, too." She scrambled towards the vestibule, trying to remember how thick the oak entry door was. She grasped the phone and fumblingly called Peter's cell; meanwhile, Wanda ran past her and turned the door lock. The women pivoted from the door to keep a line of sight on the patio, waiting for the crescendo that they knew was coming.

"Joan?" Peter said.

Just as Peter finished his instructions, the second blast came, incredibly loud. Joan was mesmerized as red liquid spattered the entire pebbled sheet: a gout of blood and tissue expectorated through the hole at the top of the patio-door panel.

After a phony-war pause of no more than fifteen silent seconds, the glass crumpled like a discarded garment. Joan clutched the phone set in her hand. Beyond the patio threshold, a man lay motionless, dead, what remained of his head pointing towards her like a spilled amphora. The world beyond his corpse was stygian black.

Following Peter's orders — it was reassuring just to hear his calm voice — Joan put the phone on its cradle and the women ran beyond the bar and through the kitchen into Henry's room. Joan fished under the bed for the clunky pistol and began to search for the safety catch. To her amazement, Wanda gently eased the Colt from her hand, flipped off the safety, checked the chamber, and positioned herself prone in a firing position on the rug, pointing the muzzle at the bedroom door. She righted the wine bottle.

"George and I do everything together."

Phil Mohlman went everywhere armed, a sweltering night at a barbecue no exception. He bore no grudge against Cammon and, as his harsh-tongued Boston mother would say, his stamping out of the house was only "physical anger." He had calmed down, but his leg ached constantly; the healing had been slow, and being Irish, he was inclined to letting the pain darken his moods. It was also his nature not to complain to anyone about his pain. He wasn't a cynic, despite his reputation, and he liked Pastern, Cammon, and young Jackson, so he prepared to return to Tynan's in a chastened mood. He wouldn't have admitted that he wore the ankle gun because it added just the right weight to his leg, suppressing his limp.

From experience he located the gunshot precisely. Like Cammon, he instantly understood that Vyne had come for Henry and Peter, although it would be a paranoid bridge too far to think that Phil himself, or Officer Jackson, was on his hit list. *There* was an error, he judged: Vyne should have backed off when he saw the parked vehicles, one of them obviously a police-issue sedan. Vyne's poor judgement told him two things: this monster was committed to revenge, and he had brought enough help to overcome more than two cops. All of this he was certain of from the single shotgun blast.

Should he approach from the front or the back? He guessed that the women were still inside, retreating from both the front entry and the rear patio doors. They would flee to the kitchen, with the wet bar providing something of a barrier. They would hole up in the bathroom for their last stand. This undoubtedly was a two-pronged attack, and Phil paused to assess the risk to himself on each side of the house. Threading his way past the three cars in the driveway exposed him to ambush, and it was probably safer for Phil to go around the near end to the back and do what he could with his .38.

But a hunch drove him to the front.

Maybe Wanda and Joan would have time to reach the entry; in that case, they should be running out the door within seconds, and he would cover their flight. He crouched beside Jackson's sedan just as the second shotgun explosion rolled through the house. Nothing;

the women did not emerge. He heard someone cough on the other side of the drive and risked a peek across the hoods of the cars. A figure holding a MAC-10 was retreating from the door, preparing to fire into the lock. Phil wondered whether the oak slab would hold against the peppering to come.

Leaning across the hood, Phil Mohlman steadied his two-hand grip and shot the gunman twice.

This was a reckless move, for there had to be more of Vyne's men in the shadows. His senses were so heightened that he could almost feel the guns turning his way, probing for him. Let them come; he was ready. He could see nothing beyond the driveway. Coppermount disappeared up the hill, and only a distant blue halogen porch light allowed him to place the house at the top of the slope. He heard footfalls behind him, turned, and almost shot Jackson.

"The women?" Jackson said.

"Probably inside. Door locked, I'm pretty sure."

MAC-10 bullets pocked the side of Peter Cammon's truck. A second burst arced over the vehicle roofs. Phil loosed a shot into the dark.

Jackson stepped back, stood up boldly and opened the trunk of his car. Police officers in Utah were permitted to carry their own sidearms, within limits, but Phil watched Jackson bring out a strange aluminum case from which he slipped a .45 like Phil had never seen. The young officer removed a RoboCop lens and fixed it to the gun. Phil couldn't believe this thing met standard specs. Jackson must be a happy hunter, he thought, with all that firepower just asking to be used. *If I had a gun like that, I'd look for occasions to use it, too.*

They became a team. Jackson lay down on the asphalt and waited, watching around the truck wheels. Phil's task was to defend the doorway; let Jackson light up the dark spaces with that thing. Phil chanced a look over the hood of Jackson's sedan and was startled when a skulking form obscured the blue halogen up the hill.

"Twelve o'clock."

Jackson had already found the assailant through his scope attachment. His shot brought the man to the ground, holding his ankle, his other hand still gripping his machine pistol. Jackson stood and calmly fired into the hapless shooter's heart. His aim was precise, with the night lens homing him in, although Phil also suspected a lot of time logged on to *Call of Duty*.

Peter joined Henry in the dunes and led the trek from Tynan's house, Henry and the Mormon cleric in tow, but when Peter turned, Tynan had disappeared. There was no time to worry about him. The sound of the MAC-10 and Jackson's two booming shots, as well as Phil's .38, reached them just at the moment they gained the semicircle of dim light at the patio.

"Henry, I'm worried about Phil and Jackson. Circle to the front with that shotgun and reinforce whatever firepower they've marshalled."

"That leaves you alone."

"Just go."

Henry instantly obeyed.

Unclear though the scale of the opposition was at the front, Peter was certain that Vyne's men were well armed. The MAC-10s worried him most. The popular machine pistol was loud and scary, and it didn't buck like the AK-47. Jackson and Mohlman had only their pistols. Henry's shotgun could be the equalizer.

He halted at the fringe of the patio. The glass in the doors had fallen, and now interior and exterior battlegrounds merged. A headless man lay across the opening. *Who shot him?*

Peter had yet to use the Remington, but as another dark form crept to the door, he raised it; the gun held only three large shells, yet he knew that just one would obliterate the attacker. Before he could fire, a shotgun load erupted from the darkness and caught the black figure in the neck. He fell across the threshold, his dying body painting the floor with blood, the rest of its fluids soaking the patio stones.

Peter didn't dare approach the doorway until he sorted out the gunmen in the dark. He had identified the origin of the lethal flash, but he hesitated to fire back. Was the phantom shotgun shooter somehow on his side? Was it Tynan? There could be a gunman, even two, in the house already. Taking a huge risk, Peter stepped into the light, close enough to see that no blood spoiled the floor farther inside; the battle had stopped short of the bedrooms. The phone, from which his wife had called him, lay on its cradle.

A pistol shot from the shadows nicked Peter's left ear, drawing a spray of blood but causing no deeper damage. That qualified as a miss, he thought, but it drove him back from the doorway into the darkness. His ears rang, and blood dripped onto his trigger hand. A second shot from the same .45 produced a mortal groan off to Peter's right. Who was *this* victim? Were the attackers shooting each other? This time, Peter noted the precise source of the gunfire. With neither the two women nor Henry in his line of sight, he was free to let loose with the powerful shotgun into the void.

His Remington boomed.

No human cry; no ballistic rejoinder.

Peter had to get inside, but moving into the light would expose him, and so he did the unexpected: he charged into the blackness. He fired again, but only sand and chaparral revealed themselves in the flare. He tripped over a body. Crouching on the ground, still holding the shotgun, he leaned close and saw that the second round from the .45 had churned up the man's stomach. José Mariana lay face up, eyes closed in his surrender to death.

Peter wasn't entirely surprised; he had seen the Escalade driving through the neighbourhood. He figured that the big Mexican had been keeping watch over the house for days, perhaps weeks, hoping to trap the killer of his boss, perhaps even maintaining a vigil from the desert wastes, like Tynan.

Much later Peter cobbled together the sequence of events. The night of the party, the Mexican had observed Vyne's six-man team approaching. He knew he had to act and readied himself with his shotgun. But then he had seen the two women in white come into

Vyne's range. Staying calm, he had positioned himself at the back and watched as the point man tried the latch on the patio door — Henry had locked it — and let loose a load. José waited only to verify how the gunman followed up. The second he moved forward, José splattered the man's innards across the back panel. But Vyne's second henchman caught José Mariana as he retreated from the living room glow, and just as Peter reached the edge of the patio. A .45 round opened up the big man's stomach and ribcage, leaving him no chance of shooting back, even reflexively.

Peter remained by the corpse an extra ten dangerous seconds, his hand on the Mexican's torn chest. It was all the tribute that men in the killing profession owed one another. He reloaded.

The next explosion from the .45 in the dark, which zinged above Peter's head, was the prelude to a coordinated move by Vyne and his gunsel. The latter provided cover while, in the lead, Vyne ran forward in a halfback's erratic pattern, bent over, one hand tucked in as if gripping a football. His backup moved into the darkness flanking the window. He fired two poorly aimed shots outward, though they came uncomfortably close to Peter's position.

Peter ducked, losing his chance to fire at Vyne at the doorway. Peter rolled to one side and let loose three deafening shots with the Remington, imagining the holes he was punching in the back of Henry's house. He reloaded with his last shells, waited for the pistol's retort, which again missed, and fired twice at the flash.

One more dead shooter and one shell left.

At the front door, Henry and Phil were struggling with the lock. Henry had no key in his pocket, and he fumbled under the body of the man on the steps, the one Jackson had blown away, for the spare that should have been there. Jackson himself had disappeared into the yard next door in risky pursuit of a third gunman. ("I went after this guy who was wearing some kind of ninja shit. He was no match," Jackson later recorded. His special scope lit up everything

— Henry and Phil couldn't resist playing with it later, before the cruisers arrived and confiscated all the weapons — and the ninja warrior became an easy takedown, so easy that Phil was tempted later to question why Jackson blew his head off.)

In Henry's bedroom, Wanda had tired of holding the .45 in position, yet she refused to move, staying in her zone and resting the gun butt on the rug, still pointed at the doorway. Joan observed Wanda's determined gaze. She instinctively became the younger woman's spotter, and Wanda instinctively let her.

The shooting outside puzzled them. "That's a pistol shot, but it's at the front . . . A machine gun . . . A different pistol now," Joan whispered.

Wanda grunted. "I think that one was that fancy-pantsy .45 Jackson bought last year . . . And that one, too."

"I don't hear the door splintering," Joan breathed. "The gunmen aren't trying to blow through the front."

"Thank God we locked the door."

Joan wished that she could tell which shots were Peter's — maybe none of them — yet she felt her confidence rising. She guessed that he would come in from the desert side, relentless and with a big gun blazing. Anytime now. The thought gave her strength. She wasn't looking for omens — no roadrunners on the patio now — but she glanced over at Henry's bedside table and caught sight of three rolls of gauze bandages. *How many bleeding men are lying around this building*, she thought mordantly.

Joan had seen the panel fall. The subsequent pistol and shotgun detonations at the back of the house were menacing, but she now guessed that Peter was responsible for some of them. He was on the scene, getting closer, and she tried to think of a way to buy her husband a bit more time. She hissed, "One way or another, that window is going to help us. We need to listen for the crunch of shoes on glass."

When Vyne came, Joan and Wanda heard his slow steps. The attacker paused in the outer room, and the crackle of glass stopped.

"Calm before the storm," Wanda voiced. "Do you think your husband is close?"

Joan was gratified that Wanda seemed to understand that Peter was near. "He'll announce himself. The bad guys won't. Shoot whatever appears in that doorway."

Wanda adjusted her bead on the door. "Motherfucker."

Shards of glass tinkled, scuffed by clumsy feet. The aggressor paused. Wanda seemed to expect this, and exhaled as Vyne turned the corner.

The killer knew his business. His machine pistol worked best when held at the hip and by someone who understood how effective short bursts could be against any defender. What he didn't count on was the avenging woman in white lying on the carpet. Too late: he fired high. Wanda's first shot took him in the collarbone at an upward angle, spinning him back and left; a fragment of bone whirled up into his throat. Her second shot penetrated his stomach and doubled him forward — causing him to grimace, despite the fact that he was dead.

Peter followed. He shouted "Joan!" to warn them, and reached down for the machine pistol, which Vyne clutched in his stiffening grip. There was no time to look at the man he'd been chasing since he arrived in America. No one knew how many attackers remained, front or back, but Peter felt a subsidence in the tension. He swivelled towards the patio and raised the Versa Max to guard the glass-strewn space, just as Henry and Jackson entered through the front. He turned to offer assurance and saw that they were in control. Pivoting back, he almost shot Tynan, who was unarmed, coming in from the desert. Peter noticed for the first time the polished wood box resting on the bed of glass outside Henry's bedroom. Tynan rushed past Peter, grasped the container in both hands, and pelted back out the doorway.

Peter deposited his weapon on the floor and ran in pursuit. He was only seconds behind, but Tynan knew the desert better than anyone, and Peter foundered in the dark. He turned and gauged that he was at least 150 yards from the house, which glowed as a tiny square in the desert night.

The explosion happened another three hundred yards farther out.

"Tynan must have flown to get that far," Phil Mohlman said later.

"Flown to his fate," Henry replied, though under the words there was gratitude and respect.

"No," Joan said. "He stayed earthbound. But fast as a roadrunner."

PART 4

KILLER

Wealth dies,
Kinsmen die,
A man himself must likewise die;
But one thing I know
That never dies —
The verdict on each man dead.

Hávamál *(Words of the High One)*,
Viking poem.

CHAPTER 45

The Cammons left for England three weeks later, after furnishing sworn statements to the Utah State Bureau of Investigation. These, and their testimony by Skype a month later, with supporting declarations, satisfied the demands of the many agencies that aspired to a role in the investigation of the Coppermount rampage. Peter volunteered to return to Salt Lake City, but that proved unnecessary.

The shootout was wrapped up quickly and began its slow fade into the graininess of myth. Just like the Denver raid, it prompted mixed reactions. West Valley colleagues congratulated Henry, Phil, and young Jackson on the takedown of the resurgent terrorist but looked askance at the death toll. When asked why he hadn't called 9-1-1 that night for backup, Phil Mohlman replied, "You mean, other than the four cops already on the spot?"

Chief Grady was grateful that the Hollis Street case hadn't duplicated the Susan Powell tragedy, and he rewarded Officer Jackson with a promotion, while welcoming Phil back to the West Valley force on full operational duty.

Henry Pastern pursued new directions. Like Peter, he recognized that the victims of Hollis Street deserved a much better explanation of Kelso Vyne's bizarre hermit life. Taking over the project started by Peter, he gave it a new title:

Kelso Vyne
A Biographical Essay
by Henry Pastern
with input from Chief Inspector Peter Cammon
and Maddy R. Cammon

Henry decided to approach this criminal profile less as a police affidavit and more as a literary product. He wasn't about to romanticize his subject, but from the outset he grasped that, at his core, Vyne had been a compulsive wanderer, rootless and possibly friendless all his life. The essay would chart his nomadic life and eventual descent into uncontrolled anger and bitterness. Two months after the shootout, Henry embarked on this new form of manhunt.

In this effort Maddy proved invaluable. From Leeds, and sometimes Peter's cottage shed, she engrossed herself in internet research in support of Henry's fact-finding trips. She hovered benignly over his Subaru as he drove the Western states, town to town. Each night he emailed her with his map coordinates and a list of secrets he hoped to disinter up ahead. She worked magic for him, accessing primary-school records from Texas and Kansas, military service files from Colorado, Vyne's incomplete transcript from the University of Michigan, tax records for 13 Hollis, and so on.

Henry fixed on a theme: Vyne's uncanny ability to vanish, his will-o'-the-wisp persona. With every revealed fact, the young detective hoped, his quarry would gain focus.

Kelso Vyne was the unwanted son of an unsuccessful cowboy and an alcoholic mother. He was born in a shack in the Texas Panhandle but moved with his rambling father and camp-following mother to Kansas when he was two. Had this uprooting marked the beginning of his identity problem, Henry wondered? Had his "Western" bona fides quickly worn thin as he admitted to the Kansas farm boys in the schoolyard that he had lived in the Lone Star State only two years? Henry decided that early on the boy had developed uncanny instincts for reinvention and self-preservation. How else to explain his ability to disappear with minimal marks on, and from, his surroundings?

Henry was attuned to coincidences between the lives of Kelso Vyne and Theodore Kaczynski, for they might help to explain Kelso's radicalization. Maddy exhumed an application to the political science program at Berkeley by young Vyne in the early seventies, and in a eureka moment Henry concluded that the two must have crossed paths there. But the dates did not coincide: by the time of Kelso's application, Kaczynski had already quit his teaching position and retreated to a factory job in Chicago. Henry and Maddy pursued them to Michigan and soon discovered an incomplete transcript for a "K. Vine" in the undergraduate philosophy program at Ann Arbor. They concluded that the two nascent revolutionaries might have met in the Buckeye State. Henry drove to Ann Arbor but was unable to discover the reason for Kelso's abrupt departure, although it didn't appear that the university had expelled him.

The trail thinned out for a few weeks, and part of the reason was Vyne's proclivity for aliases. He left no criminal record under Vyne or Devereau and, according to Maddy, never registered at any university west of the Mississippi, and certainly not under his birth name. As Henry criss-crossed the states, he began to understand Kelso Vyne's spectral anonymity. Here was an aspiring revolutionary on the make in the pre-9/11 era of the eighties and early nineties, who somehow ingratiated himself with Ted Kaczynski and Timothy McVeigh while gaining the loyalty of the evanescent Jim Riotte. This should have been a period of action and reputation-making. Yet, Henry saw, Vyne came to value his namelessness above all. It was the key to his interaction with the militia groups that sought to advance the varied demented objectives that were lumped together by the FBI as "domestic terror."

Was Kelso ever fully committed to terrorism?

Since the Twin Towers, the spread of Facebook and Twitter, and, at the government level, the advent of data mining and National Security Agency worldwide information gathering, Americans had had a hard time believing that anyone could remain anonymous — or would want to. Vyne made anonymity his first principle.

Vyne had to consider where he fit into the universe of domestic revolutionaries. He would have known Mao's cliché about the guerilla having to move silently among the people as a fish swims in the sea, and he may have embraced Abbie Hoffman's principle that the first task of a revolutionary is to get away with it. Somehow, self-preservation became paramount. Perhaps one day he stood back and realized that no one had his fingerprints on file anywhere. He was well positioned to become the hidden theoretician of the anti-government movement, an intellectual in the mould of Trotsky or Frantz Fanon, working from the unphotographed background.

Henry and Peter discussed Vyne's dilemma: What real impact could an abstract theorist like him achieve if he couldn't infiltrate the paranoid right? Both detectives cashed in favours with former colleagues at the FBI to obtain militia membership rolls from 1980 to 2001, along with lists in the Extremist Crime Database, which covered the modern era of domestic terrorism. No names set off bells. Henry gave it up, not because he lacked a name to bounce off the crazies who populated the militant groups but because he grew to understand that Kelso hadn't ever officially joined them. He was a mystery man to the radicals themselves.

Henry could feel Vyne hovering in the shadows. Even as Vyne tried to influence radical conspiracies, he had kept a certain arrogant distance. These cultish groups were too narrowly focused to suit his grandiose vision. He had become a snob. It was hard to imagine him adapting his theory of revolution to the animal rights movement or the anti-Semitic agenda of the Aryan Republican Army. Henry reread *Fire and Brimstone*, and it wasn't there — no reaching out for coordination and no plea for a consensus on a new government.

Kelso learned the drug business — or, more precisely, the drug rip-off business. Many small-time dealers dealt under the radar of the cartels, and Vyne and Jim Riotte were fast and decisive when they swept up the cash-and-stash assets of these amateurs, selling off the drugs within twenty-four hours. Avelino González lived a long way off, and there was little he could do; cost-benefit analysis led him to write off the losses.

Vyne was so good at this that Henry, Peter, and Maddy rarely discerned his footprints in drug raids from that time, let alone his fingerprints.

That was another thing: he channelled his ill-gotten cash to *individuals* rather than the amorphous, shifting groups themselves. He saw that their leaders were too corrupt, greedy with funds, and resentful of competing revolutionaries. Better to find men of action with concrete plans who would serve as proxies for his own revolutionary ambitions.

Henry revisited the Vyne-Kaczynski connection, hoping that the Unabomber might offer the key to Vyne's actions and perhaps his demise. Another visit to the Colorado Supermax was out of the question, so Henry worked with what he knew. Kaczynski dispatched his first homemade bomb in 1978. No one was impressed by this revolutionary strike, least of all the Postal Service, which only twigged to his pattern after the third or fourth device. But, Henry concluded, Kelso Vyne discovered Ted Kaczynski early in his bombing career and recognized a potential ally.

Had Vyne been involved from the beginning of Ted's rampage?

Henry scrutinized the list of bombings until the overlaps began to glow. The first four Unabomber devices ended up in Illinois or Michigan, which Vyne and the bomber had in common. Kaczynski's grandest assault in this first phase was the American Airlines flight in 1979, his third overall. It interested Henry for several reasons. Did Vyne, with little risk to himself, press Ted to attempt something big, like blowing up an airliner? He might have shaped Ted as the point man for anarchistic destruction of the established order. But even more interesting was the fact that Ted gave up on this kind of thing after one try and began to launch only perverse, individualized attacks. It seemed that the split between Ted and Kelso opened early. Ted's stubborn streak of independence must have alienated Kelso.

The two had their final falling-out in 1987. This was Ted's twelfth effort, which Alma May Reeve witnessed. Henry thought it significant that the seventh through twelfth incidents occurred in Western states, with the exception of another mailing to Ann Arbor, Michigan. Peter had been right. The Unabomber had shifted his efforts westward onto Kelso's home ground.

Vyne had always despised Kaczynski, but when did jealousy set in? Vyne must have been astonished when the Unabomber achieved fame across the nation with his crude attacks on civilians. At the Spector Diner in 1987, he presented Ted with his spare copy of his anti-government screed, with "Fire and Brimstone" handwritten on the cover. He thought he had scooped his rival. Then Ted announced that he had started his own *Manifesto*. Vyne was so angry that he rushed out to plant Ted's explosive device, meantime forgetting both copies of *Fire and Brimstone*. Only later did he realize the danger of giving the text to the demented bomber. Vyne would have turned him in, but Ted hunkered down alone in the Montana woods for the next seven years while he wrote his own magnum opus. It was another lesson to Kelso Vyne in the art of anonymity. The two never met again.

Up until the moment Vyne disappeared, he yearned for the big score. He had made dashing raids on drug operations, but the militias hadn't noticed his élan or his grand design for revolution. His discovery of Timothy McVeigh revived his ambitions. McVeigh was a solo revolutionary with a plan of action, so extreme that the ultra-right militias in Michigan, Kansas, and Arizona were wary of him. He promised spectacular results through indiscriminate violence. Henry never figured out how the two met, but the files noted that Jim Riotte was convicted of buying large amounts of fertilizer in 1994. That September, McVeigh himself bought hundreds of pounds of fertilizer, along with incriminating quantities of ammonium nitrate and nitromethane. Henry presumed a Vyne-McVeigh hookup occurred at this time.

Ted Kaczynski was obsessed with technological oppression by corporate America and the U.S. government, and McVeigh remained a white supremacist to the end. Vyne must have had to swallow hard to ally himself with these losers, Henry thought.

Vyne's disenchantment with Kaczynski and McVeigh mirrored his disillusion with himself. He had proven that he was capable of action, even killing five men in a drug raid — all Mexicans, it turned out, including Avelino González's brother — and didn't these high-risk high-noon skirmishes show that he qualified as a bold revolutionary?

But the militias rejected him, while his two proxies spun out of control. The bombing on April 19, 1995, in Oklahoma City killed Kelso's dreams of leading the revolution. Maddy put together the picture of his mindscape that spring: "The Oklahoma City attack was breathtakingly vicious, and Vyne realized that he had never possessed the guts for true anarchy. While Kaczynski and McVeigh hurtled towards exposure and self-destruction, Kelso retrenched and soon trapped himself in a new idealistic dream of middle-class life. Vyne would no longer work from the shadows; rather, he decided to merge with the background."

Vyne and Jim Riotte vanished two months after Oklahoma City. Henry and Maddy were unable to track their wanderings between 1995 and 2003, when Kelso purchased the two-storey on Hollis Street. With his love for aliases, he likely ran through several false names and kept moving across the states, perhaps back to Texas. Vyne and Jim Riotte kept in touch. Henry doubted that Vyne's stockpiled cash sustained him over those eight years, and he must have resorted to ripping off drug houses again with Riotte. When Maddy offered to crunch the numbers on all drug investigations — this time, a full study of huge data sets from 1995 all the way to 2013 would have required sophisticated regression analysis — Henry told her not to bother.

After Oklahoma City, Vyne turned his cunning mind to self-preservation. Henry read and reread the data on Kelso Vyne. *Did he see the irony of embracing the lifestyle that McVeigh rejected and the Unabomber so heartily despised in his* Manifesto? No matter; Vyne sat back in his new house and watched as Ted was sent to prison for life and Tim McVeigh shambled in chains to his execution.

He cultivated a fresh start in what he saw as a permanent sanctuary. He put cash into a down payment and signed "Ronald Devereau" on the mortgage papers. He embraced HASA, the street association, and though Jerry Proffet was a loudmouth, Kelso found common ground with him in setting and enforcing property standards along the quiet street. Early on, he served as president for a term before realizing that such a profile risked giving himself away. From then on, as was his style, he influenced the street committee from behind the scenes. In that respect, it resembled his old low-profile existence.

Henry and Maddy could only speculate on Vyne's residual links to terrorism. The polymer drone in his freezer might have indicated a continuing interest in bomb making, but Peter suggested that this had the quality of a hobby pursued to counter boredom. Even if Vyne was refreshing his skills, that was a far cry from planting bombs around the country.

"He watched the evolution of society with rising anger," Maddy suggested. It was hard for him to admit that the playground for terrorists had changed at the millennium. In the year after Oklahoma City, he had smugly watched the Unabomber's arrest; the pitiful sight of the Thoreau cabin stiffened his resolve to settle into his suburban refuge. The 2001 destruction of the Twin Towers drove him even further underground. By 2003, he was ensconced in Number 13 and well pleased with his domain. But then Homeland Security began its empire-building, bolstered by the *Patriot Act*. Iraq. Afghanistan. Drone surveillance. Drone attacks. All these were so much worse than the old days.

Henry and Peter debated Vyne's hopes of re-entering the world of domestic terror. Peter saw little evidence that the hermit of Number 13 kept up contact with the militias.

"He didn't have trouble recruiting militia types for Wichita,

Denver, or Coppermount, did he?" Henry argued. Peter reminded
him that Vyne had recruited the dregs of the militias, whose understanding of the Constitution stopped at the Second Amendment.

When Tom Watson established his grow house, Kelso Vyne recognized it right away and was outraged.

Maddy provided the psychoanalysis. "Tom Watson's grow op was
nothing less than a betrayal of Ronald Devereau personally and an invasion of his sanctum sanctorum. From the first he considered burning
out the Second House. It was up to him to cleanse by fire and bloodletting. It is amazing how fast his rage drove him to that scenario."

"Yes, fire and brimstone," Peter added.

The viciousness of the attack on the Watsons showed how easily
his fury took over. Henry recalled the frequent question posed by
investigators in the days after the slaughter: Did he carefully plan to
behead Gabriella, move the body and the head next door, wait there
in the dark, and then eviscerate Tom Watson in front of his wife's
disconnected corpse?

"What's the difference?" Maddy maintained. "It's his limitless
capacity for violence we're discussing here. One way or another . . ."

But it was Peter who saw that more than indignation drove
Devereau to kill the Watsons that night. His greater fear was exposure. For a decade he had committed to playing by the bourgeois
rules of the smug and high-handed HASA executive. Bureaucrats
deal with problems in measured stages, and Jerry Proffet was a particularly fussy president. Devereau watched him dance around the
grow op threat, and finally began himself to lobby his neighbours to
clean up Number 5.

"At what point did he mention marijuana to Carleton Davis?"
Henry asked on one of their Salt Lake–U.K. calls. "And when did
Davis consent to be his spotter on Hollis Street?"

"Davis is lucky Vyne left him alive," Peter responded.

Again Maddy honed the scenario. "I think Vyne gave Tom Watson
one last chance to repent, to be reasonable. He threatened to turn
Tom in to the police . . ."

Echoes bounced through the telephone links from Coppermount Drive to Leeds and the Cammon cottage. The policemen knew the truth.

"No, it was the other way, dear," Peter said quietly. "Tom Watson had figured out who Devereau really was, or at least part of his history . . ."

"Devereau betrayed too much familiarity with the drug trade," Henry said.

"Watson made the mistake of blackmailing Devereau," Peter added.

Ronald Devereau knew that his idyll on Hollis Street couldn't last, but he held on to a final hope. The small pipe bomb was designed to eliminate evidence in the Second House without burning the place down. The house could be rebuilt and maybe his own suburban idyll sustained.

When Vyne screwed up the timer on the box bomb, he made it almost inevitable that the police would trace the device to him. Desperation grew. He read about Whitey Bulger's sudden discovery after several complacent decades in hiding and imagined his own vulnerability.

And Jerry Proffet could stay that dumb only so long.

It was time to leave.

Henry, Maddy, and Peter agreed that Jim Riotte was doomed from that moment. While no one knew where he had holed up for two decades, and none of the Hollisites had seen him visit Number 13, he must have stayed in touch.

"You keep secrets that haunt you and have only one person you talk to about them, you either get unnaturally close or you grow to despise your Siamese twin," Maddy posited.

"I'd say both," Peter suggested. "Psychos don't make close friends."

The friendship ultimately was one of convenience, the freezer probably invoked the day after Riotte picked up Devereau at the roadhouse lay-by up in the Wasatch. If Riotte had closely thought about the corpse and the blood-soaked electrical cable in the back of the van, might he have avoided the cooler?

Henry refused to psychoanalyze Vyne any further, but he unreservedly passed harsh judgement on his record as a terrorist. Kelso had been outshone by Kaczynski and McVeigh, two tougher men. His plans were spectacularly overtaken by the 9/11 hijackers. He was yesterday's terrorist. As to whether Kelso Vyne was purely evil, Henry was no longer willing to say.

Henry and Maddy had bonded so well that when Peter invited him to visit England, it seemed perfectly appropriate. They settled on a July date.

It never happened.

On a sunny, innocent afternoon, ten days before Henry was scheduled to fly to Heathrow, Chief Grady died in a rollover on the I-80 outside Salt Lake City. The funeral occurred three days later.

CHAPTER 46

And on *that* day, it was discovered that Carleton Davis had vanished from his home at Number 10 Hollis.

Henry had already called Peter to postpone his visit. He missed his friend and the disappearance of Davis provided an excuse for calling Leicestershire again. He expected indifference — Davis had been as reluctant to cooperate in the manhunt as any of the residents — but Peter immediately responded with a Sherlockian flourish. "The disappearance of Carleton Davis happened *before* Grady's crash, am I right?"

"Yup. How'd you know?"

"Davis was a semi-recluse. If he disappeared it would take a while for anyone to go looking for him. Daughter or son?"

"Niece. Dropped by. She'd tried to reach him on the phone. She had a key. It appeared he'd left several days before, without packing."

"I'll be there by week's end," Peter said.

Henry, in his refurbished living room on Coppermount Drive, stammered and said, "What do you see that I don't see, Peter?"

"I'll email my ticket times. Find out all you can about Boog DeKlerk's movements. Under the radar."

Henry hung up. An ominous chill moved up his spine. The house was silent. He was wearing his suit from Grady's funeral, and now, as he caught his reflection in the new patio door panels, old feelings returned. It was the first time he had sported a tie since Theresa's memorial service and just for the whiff of a moment, he was drawn back into the church's embrace.

Henry took a walk through the dunes — reflexively, he looked for Tynan out there — and when he re-entered the house, the computer was beeping. Peter would arrive in two days.

The phone rang; it was Phil Mohlman. Henry, who always appreciated Phil's advice, noted the coincidence in timing, but then realized there was no coincidence: Phil had seen precisely what Peter had, that Grady's death and Davis's vanishing were connected.

"Henry, Boog DeKlerk wasn't at the funeral today."

Evil was blossoming again in its shape-shifting way, Henry thought. It begged to be finally crushed.

"Come on over," Henry said.

Phil brought pizza and they ate it on the patio. The older detective didn't acknowledge the bullet marks in the back wall.

"Maybe it was instinct that made me call DeKlerk yesterday to see if he was attending. We hadn't talked in three weeks. Grady never quite fired Boog, you know."

Pushback from the union had caused the chief to content himself with indefinite suspension. Furst and Ordway were still working on their wrap-up report, which would touch on DeKlerk's role in the Hollis Street investigation, so Grady had had an excuse for inaction.

"He swore he would definitely attend the funeral. Attendance was compulsory, wouldn't you agree, Henry? You know what got me thinking? Boog's *voice*. He was full of the old, old bluster, cocky, ripping everyone else, Grady included. Like he had received good news and didn't care about the chief. He was never that cocky during the Watson investigation."

"I don't know," Henry said. "He tore into us those times at Rocco's."

"Mostly he tore into you. With me, he was conciliatory, more restrained about what he tried to control. Did you notice, bottom line, that he wasn't ever really helpful to either of us? For example, he let us lead the charge on the grow house but did nothing to help us with the forensics report on the bags of grass and the drug residue in the house."

"You're right. He did argue that the cartels took out the Watsons, but he never came up with anyone who ever did business with Tom Watson. But why did he agree to the meeting in Wendover? Holy shit!"

"Don't curse, Henry; you're a Mormon. Yes, he said he reluctantly agreed to González's request. Think about the timing of that. Weeks had gone by without our getting anywhere. Grady was considering shifting the case over to the Narcotics Unit, something DeKlerk didn't want, since there was a flurry of talk around the precinct that Boog was on the take with the cartels. González must have flabbergasted poor Boog when he called him, but here's the thing: it was Boog who suggested the meeting in Wendover, not the other way around."

Henry nodded vigorously. "Boog made sure to get Rogers onto the two-man team, and not himself. I was the patsy representing the West Valley force. I didn't know a lot about the drug networks, and Rogers was a volatile character. DeKlerk hoped for a shootout in which the Mexican would perish."

"Not to mention you," Phil continued. "Which is also the story of the Denver raid. Think of it this way, Henry. Boog tried twice to get you killed. He isn't stupid, and he's got an uncanny talent for self-preservation."

"Almost as intense as Devereau's," exclaimed Henry.

"Consider how perverse Boog has been. If he figured out that Carleton Davis was in touch with Kelso Vyne, it would have been a simple matter to track down Vyne and arrest or kill him. Instead, he manipulated *Davis*, learning from him that the Denver raid was in the works. It was another chance to bump off González. The Mexican was always Boog's target."

"And it worked. The question now is, what are we going to do?"

"Okay," Phil said. "We wait till Cammon gets here in two days but I'm not willing to delay much longer."

For Peter, it was the lock box that led him to the same stream of deductions. The Narcotics Squad's extended control over access to Number 5 Hollis told him that DeKlerk feared further scrutiny of the crime scene by Phil and Henry and the West Valley forensics team. Peter never learned what the incriminating item inside was. He didn't understand why the Narcotics Squad had missed this crudely concealed grow operation. Was it possible that Tom Watson had been paying off Boog all along?

Peter agreed that Boog had engineered the Wendover and Denver confrontations to get rid of González; the elimination of Henry and Peter along the way would have been a bonus. Boog must have been in steady contact with Vyne, perhaps through Davis, to set up these sucker plays. Peter himself had stimulated the assault on Coppermount Drive by manipulating Davis. His re-interview led directly to the Vietnam vet alerting Vyne. Or did DeKlerk himself contact the killer?

Peter had a hard time explaining to Joan why he was flying back to Salt Lake City in such a rush. Just as he had established a new protocol of honesty and openness (at least in his own thinking), he found himself lying to her. He was going over for a final review and sign-off of Henry's biographical sketch, he said.

How could he confirm that he had found an unequivocally evil enemy?

Joan saw the lie right away, though she didn't yet grasp his intent. "Are you helping Henry with the investigation into Chief Grady's death? Is that it?"

"Yes, right. Henry thinks he was murdered. No one else thinks so. I'm not sure, but Henry can only cruise on his six-gun reputation for so long. If he stirs this up without evidence, he'll squander all his goodwill."

"What caused the car wreck?" Joan asked mildly. She knew when Peter was dissembling.

"Fell asleep at the wheel."

The gun battle in Henry's house had changed Joan. Another

time, she would have gone on asking how the chief's death might be connected to Kelso Vyne — for she guessed that much — but Coppermount imprinted on her the importance of completion. Police work offers catharsis — an arrest, a conviction, a punishment — but what makes a detective a good detective is the awareness that closure is not easily achieved. Joan knew that truth, even as Wanda was blowing away Kelso Vyne with Henry's pistol. Peter was going to finish this. She stared at him.

"Go. Come back alive. And when you return, tell me everything, Peter."

He hadn't succeeded in his prevaricating, but there was one thing he did avoid explaining: Henry and Phil were the wrong men for this job. Utah-born, Henry had wandered from his church and his home state. The search for Vyne's history had had an unexpected impact on Henry; he had rejoined the canyons and the deserts and the Great Salt Lake. For his part, Phil had declared his decision to stay in the West.

They were no longer outsiders.

Peter was the only one rugged enough for what had to come. The only outsider left.

Peter fell silent beside Henry in the new truck he had borrowed from Randy's Rides. He had a moment of mild regret that he had given up his trusty F-150 — he had returned the rental riddled with bullet holes. But now he was content and grew calmer by the mile. The blasting sun welcomed him back to Utah. He had missed the heat and sand and cactus.

On the back patio they had argued, the three of them, Peter and Henry and Phil, grimly and loudly but without recrimination. Their shouting disturbed no one, but they were sharply cognizant of Thomas Abraham Tynan's ghost listening.

At first Henry insisted that it be him with the gun, since he had arguably suffered most from the machinations of DeKlerk. Mohlman

pointed to his leg and countered with a claim that his betrayal by
DeKlerk was worse, and this was all about professional perfidy. Peter
could hardly claim that he deserved to exact revenge more than they
did but he argued that Henry and Phil wanted to stay on the West
Valley force, and another shootout would ruin their careers.

Peter eventually wore them down. He maintained that he had
killed seven men and knew what had to be done this time. (All of the
detectives accepted that this had to be a gunfight, not an ambush,
an arrest, or a coerced confession.) Henry and Phil pointed out that
they too had shot opponents recently, and were ready to do it again,
but perhaps what persuaded them to Peter's view was the cold look
of determination in his eye.

They toasted Elder Tynan; Henry drank orange juice. They fell
quiet, three bruised detectives who had agreed on what had to be
finished.

They drove the straight highway to Wendover. Henry turned to
his passenger. "You know, Peter, this reminds me of our first car ride
together, back in D.C., when we drove to the Quantico morgue that
morning."

Peter saw no need to reply. As they passed the Bonneville Salt
Flats, he said, "If he walks out that door, let the Mexicans finish
him."

That silenced Henry.

They pulled into the parking area more than a half hour early,
but five Mexicans were already there, heavily armed, ignoring the
heat. Where had they stowed their vehicle, Peter wondered? Henry
and Peter sensed that they were safe with the Mexicans. They recognized two of González's brothers in the group — all the siblings had
the same features — and went over to talk to them. This was about
respect. It wasn't that the gringos needed to explain the arrangement,
not at this point, but Henry wanted the brothers to know about the
Wendover discussion he had had with Avelino. Peter told them about
his time with the drug boss at the Denver stakeout.

Peter saw that they had a few minutes. He entered the Quonset hut through the small door and noted, as Henry had, the pinging of the arched corrugated roof in the sun. The strung bulbs provided a sepulchral light. Peter assumed that the big garage doors at the far end were effectively sealed, leaving the single exit. He began to walk the length of the interior as he considered where to position himself. The table and the two wooden chairs stood where Avelino González had left them weeks ago. He strode to the end of the building. The logical positioning would be to stand by the table and wait for DeKlerk to enter through the small door and come to him.

Peter walked back along the crumbling cement floor but halted before reaching the egress. The hard pad had disintegrated twenty yards from the door, and someone had compensated by infilling with a mixture of sand and oil-soaked sawdust that not only stank but also left a choppy, caked surface that dragged on his shoes.

He exited and squinted against the sun. One of González's brothers handed him a .45 pistol, and Peter thanked him, though it was an old weapon. He turned to Henry and said, "Give me your .45 but empty the chambers."

Peter carried the loaded pistol in his right hand and shoved the empty one in his belt. He noticed one of the Mexican soldiers with a piece that intrigued him: the same calibre as the other two, but with a longer barrel.

"*Preciso?*"

"*Izquierda. Poquito.*" A bit biased to the left.

"Can I borrow this, señor?"

Peter carried a gun in each hand back into the hut; the third, Henry's empty pistol, stayed in his belt. His only concession to Henry's quizzical look was a peremptory nod.

Inside, Peter walked the length of the hut again, extracted Henry's empty .45 and placed it on the table. He stood back and evaluated the impression left by it. He concluded that his plan would work or it wouldn't; so be it. He was in a very fatalistic mood, borne of his cold serenity before a gunfight. Had Henry and Phil been there to see his expression any doubts they might have had about his doing this alone would have evaporated. He placed the Mexican's ancient .45 on the table corner, as far as possible from Henry's.

This left him with the other Mexican's long-barrelled gun in his belt.

Peter carried both chairs back to the small door, where he positioned them fifteen feet apart. By now, his heavy brogues were coated with the oily-sawdust-and-sand mix. He leaned down and buried the long pistol in the dirt, hoping he would remember where it lay.

He waited uncomfortably by the door, mightily tempted to step outside for a last view of the salty wasteland and the haunted mountains to the west. He recalled his wanderings with Joan through Canyonlands and the Arches and wondered if Kelso Vyne had spent those lost years between 1995 and 2002 in a hideaway in such hills, just as Butch Cassidy was said to have done.

Peter's arrangements dictated how this fight would play out, but he went down his list of preparatory decisions once again. If Henry's reputation was to survive today, he could not be seen to pull a trigger. The same went for Phil Mohlman. Thus, Peter and DeKlerk had to meet out of sight, and if that made it a faceoff indoors at high noon, let the gunplay happen and the legend take its own course without the contributions of eyewitnesses.

As he waited, Peter realized that it had to be like this, because the traditions of the West demanded a clear contest.

"Let the myth-makers take it from here," he declared to the emptiness.

Peter's arrangements depended on Mohlman's persuasive powers in the face of DeKlerk's innate paranoia. Phil had assured him that he could pull it off, which he did simply: after a fifteen-minute wait, the door opened and Boog DeKlerk stumbled inside with Phil Mohlman behind him, holding a pistol to the South African's back.

Peter gestured to one of the chairs as he verified that DeKlerk was unarmed. Phil left through the small door.

DeKlerk was thinking along the same lines. "You're not armed?"

Instead of waiting for an answer DeKlerk checked out his

surroundings. Peter looked way down to the table and confirmed that his opponent saw both guns sitting on it.

"You won't get away with it, Cammon." DeKlerk sat down and crossed his legs.

"I have one question . . ."

"Really, Cammon. I'd have thought you'd have a million of 'em. We can talk all day, if you like."

"Just one. When did you know Devereau was the killer?"

"I recognized the bomb design as something I'd come across in a couple of drug takedowns in Moab and just up the road in Ogden. I figured Davis for it, given his anti-social attitude, but then he outed Devereau and I took it from there."

"You could have stopped this before the Proffets and Theresa got killed."

Boog got up and paced near the entry door. He seemed to understand that he was a dead man if he stepped outside unarmed. "Surely you want to know other things."

"Well, I'd like to know where you left Carleton Davis's corpse."

DeKlerk smiled. "Carleton Davis will become the new Susan Powell."

The South African had gained a few pounds even in the short time since Peter had last seen him, and his pot belly put him over 250, but he bolted like a wild animal, in a few yards gaining traction on the concrete pad. He ran for the table at the far end of the hut.

The drug detective had a long lead. Peter took two unrushed steps in the direction of the table, then crouched to root in the dirt. Boog's triumphant smirk shifted to puzzlement as he grasped Henry's pistol, finding it too light. *If this is a duel, why is one of the duelling pistols empty?* He dropped Henry's empty .45 and picked up the other one. The delay gave Peter the extra seconds he needed.

DeKlerk turned just as Peter rose to his feet with the sawdust-coated long-barrel pistol in his hand. He took two seconds to blow the dirt away, but he wasn't about to be any more sporting than that with his adversary. He aimed, compensating a couple of degrees to his right, as the Mexican soldier had recommended. In fact, DeKlerk got off the first round (although there was no one to record this fact and Peter never revealed it; let the legend evolve.) The South African's effort went wide. Peter's shot — he was aided by the long barrel — took DeKlerk in the throat. His blood flooded into the cracks in the broken concrete floor.

Peter let the ringing fade. The detectives outside had strict orders not to enter. He ached all over, and the oil and cordite smells sickened him as he turned to the door. How would he explain this to Joan?

As he passed through the narrow door, from a dark world to a bright one, three Mexicans stepped forward with shovels.

At ECW Press, we want you to enjoy this book in whatever format you like, whenever you like. Leave your print book at home and take the eBook to go! Purchase the print edition and receive the eBook free. Just send an email to ebook@ecwpress.com and include:

- the book title
- the name of the store where you purchased it
- your receipt number
- your preference of file type: PDF or ePub?

Get the eBook free!*
*proof of purchase required

A real person will respond to your email with your eBook attached. And thanks for supporting an independently owned Canadian publisher with your purchase!